Dedicated to my father Albert, son of Jeannot

"May I only live to make you as proud of me as I am of you."

Acknowledgments

John MacKenzie, author of the quite brilliant website "Britishbattles.com," for allowing me to use his magnificent maps of the battlefields

David Sacks, Johannesburg, for unearthing certain letters and articles that proved so very useful

Jeff Shaara, renowned US writer of historical fiction works, for encouraging me to begin this project in the first place

Nick Cowley, for his tireless efforts in validating the historical correctness of the book, and for his superb editing skills

Albert Weinberg, my late father, for retaining in such superb condition the letters and memorabilia from his father Jeannot's life, and to whom this book is dedicated

David Weinberg, my son, for whom this book was written

Ellyn Sisser, my wife, for her endless patience, support, and encouragement that enabled me to achieve what I have

And of course, to my Grandfather, **Jeannot Weinberg**, without whose exploits none of this would have been possible

Contents

Introduction

Author's Note

Thank you for joining me on this exciting peregrination through the war exploits of my late grandfather, Jeannot Weinberg, who fought on the side of the Boers during the Anglo-Boer War (1899-1902).

My sources for this novel, for it is indeed a novel, not a history, have been many and varied. The most significant sources have been a collection of letters written by my grandfather from the battlefield and from the prison camps, and a set of memoirs written by my great-aunt Bertha, Jeannot's sister, who features prominently in the book. I have also referenced many scholarly works written on the subject, which I have acknowledged at the end of the book.

This work is not, as I have said, intended to be a history, but a novel woven around historical events. I have tried, wherever possible, to be as accurate historically as I am able. Still, it stands to reason that I have used my imagination to replicate conversations between the characters. There are very few records of these, but I have done my best to maintain them in historical context. Many of the characters are real, and many are fictitious. The reader will be introduced to various members of my family at the time, as well as the military commanders and politicians who were real people. Again, I have endeavored to make their actions and dialog as authentic as I could.

One character is totally fictitious - Elise, the young Boer girl who lodges with my family and ends up in a concentration camp. I have included her in the novel because I did not wish to miss the opportunity of underlining the conditions in these camps and the inhumane attitude of the British towards the women and children incarcerated in them. The letters between her and Bertha are fictitious but are used to portray the experiences of a young girl in these horrific circumstances. Readers will observe that the language used in these letters is likely to be beyond the ability of the two young girls. This has been done on purpose since it is believed that it might be difficult for the reader to understand were I to use the vernacular of the time. The letters from my grandfather recreated in the book are all genuine and are in my possession. They provide a fascinating insight into the mind of an eighteen-year-old caught up in the events of a war the Boers were destined never to win. Many of the letters were in German, but have been rendered in English translation.

I hope you enjoy the book. It is written as much for you, the reader, as for my son, David Weinberg (whose middle name is Jeannot in memory of his great-grandfather), to encapsulate the history of our family for him and his children to be.

Peter Weinberg
Chicago 2019

Historical Context

[Note to the reader. The novel does not begin until page 47. The introduction section is aimed at informing the reader of both the historical context in which the novel takes place, as well as some insight into how so small a nation could keep so powerful an empire at bay for so long. While I believe it would benefit the reader to become familiar with this, it is intended as background only. If you would like to skip to page 41 and start the novel, please feel free to do so.]

I am aware that many of the readers may not be familiar with South Africa, nor with any of its history. In order to provide a brief perspective of the historical timeline leading up to the events in this book, I offer the reader this very broad overview of the history of the founding of the country we now know as South Africa. This is a 30,000-foot view - no attempt has been made to provide an academic history - it is simply a timeline to assist the reader in placing the novel in its historical context.[1] This overview reflects the history of European settlement in South Africa and does not suggest that the country was uninhabited at the time.

In 1453, the Ottoman Turks captured Constantinople, effectively ending 1,100 years of the Byzantine Empire. Historians have devoted much attention to the social, political and religious ramifications of this event, but have perhaps not spent enough time examining the economic aspect.

Constantinople was the bridge across which the very important and extremely lucrative spice trade crossed from east to west. With this bridge now in Muslim hands, the potential to strangle the western world of its highly valued spices was not lost on the Ottoman rulers. The west was forced to explore new ways in which to conduct the spice trade, and focus was given to the possibility of a trade route to the Indies around Africa. Preliminary work had been done in Portugal by Prince Henry the Navigator, who sent sorties down the west coast of Africa. The first real breakthrough came in 1488 when Portuguese explorer Bartholomew Diaz became the first European to round the Cape of Good Hope. He was followed by another Portuguese explorer, Vasco da Gama, who, in 1497, succeeded in reaching India. In the interim, of course, in 1492, Christopher Columbus, also seeking a route to the Indies, had discovered America, but that is another story.

Trade around the Cape increased considerably during the next 150 years, with the French, English and Dutch leveraging this lucrative trade route. One of the most critical hardships that faced sailors in those days was scurvy, a disease caused mainly by the lack of fresh fruit and vegetables. It was for this reason that the Dutch East India Company ("VOC") decided to create a refreshment station at the Cape of Good Hope in order to provide sailors on both legs of the voyage with the opportunity to stop and revictual. This was in 1652 and was effectively the start of what was to become South Africa. It was never the intention of the VOC to create a colony in Cape Town, but as time progressed, this became an inevitability. The other European country to settle in future South Africa was Britain, which created a colony in Durban, Natal, on the east coast of Africa (incidentally the author's home town), much later in 1842.

Nothing of global significance happened for another 150 years. The population of the Cape grew considerably, boosted by the arrival of Huguenots from France trying to escape religious intolerance (and who were responsible for the start of the wine industry in the Cape), but the majority of the immigrants were from Holland – the Cape was firmly established as a Dutch colony. Then came the Napoleonic Wars. Holland, then known as The Batavian Republic, sided with the French as a client state. The British saw the existence of a Dutch colony at the Cape as a threat to their shipping lanes to

India, so, in 1806, they captured the colony from the Dutch and transformed it into a British colony. This angered the predominantly Dutch locals who, after repeated attempts to accustom themselves to British rule, decided in 1836 to leave the Cape and seek other living space in the interior. This was The Great Trek, in which the Dutch inhabitants of the Cape trekked north in their Conestoga-style wagons, and eventually created two republics in the north of what is now South Africa – the Transvaal and the Orange Free State. The settlers of Dutch origin had primarily been farmers - 'Boers' in their language – so these republics were known as The Boer Republics. The British had, in the meantime, expanded their control in the area of Durban, and now controlled an area along the east coast known as Natal.

By 1880, South Africa consisted of 2 British colonies – the Cape and Natal – and 2 Boer Republics – the Orange Free State ("OFS") and the Transvaal. There was some acrimony between the two sides, culminating in what is often called the first Anglo-Boer War in 1881, but this was a relatively minor conflict, and history has not paid that much attention to it.

This is a map of Southern Africa at the time, showing the 2 British colonies and the two Boer Republics, along with other territories in the immediate vicinity. It also includes some of the major towns that are referred to in this book.

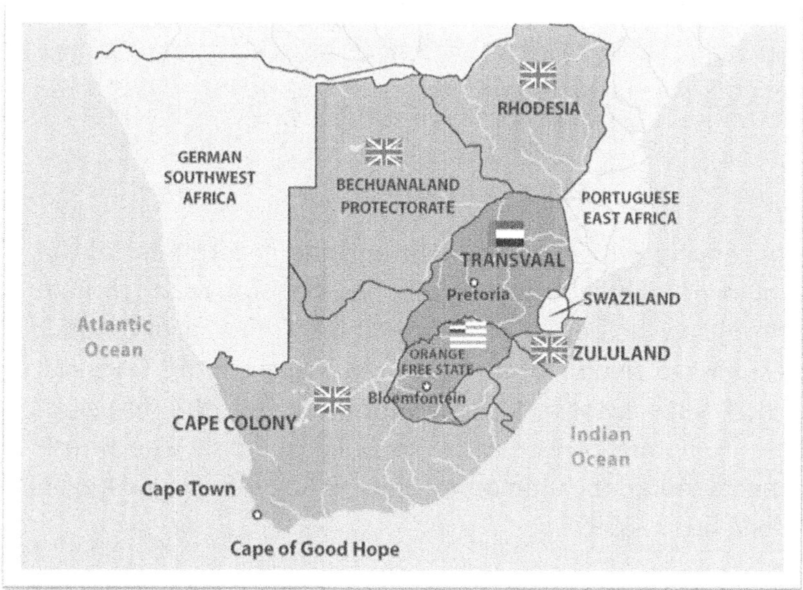

(*Author's Note.* The territory southwest of Zululand on the map was the British colony of Natal, which grew from the port town of Durban – the author's home town – as described above.)

This was all about to change in 1886. In that year, a prospector called George Harrison found, on a farm in the Transvaal called Langlaagte, what turned out to be the richest gold deposit on the planet. This find was quickly followed up by more rich finds, and before the 1880s ended, a major gold rush was on, attracting prospectors from all over the world. Among these pioneers were the author's family, who originated in Latvia, and who arrived in South Africa in 1893.

The immense economic potential of the Transvaal goldfields was not lost on the British Empire, whose desire it was to remove control of the gold from the Boer Republics and vest it in the hands of the Empire. After staging a 'raid' in the Transvaal – the Jameson Raid – there ensued a series of negotiations, demands, ultimatums, etc. between the British government and the government of the Transvaal over rights of sovereignty in the Transvaal[2]. Britain moved troops to the border of Natal and the Transvaal in October 1899, resulting in an ultimatum from Pres. Kruger of the Transvaal stating that, unless these troops were removed, the Transvaal would be in a state of war with the British Empire. The British government ignored the ultimatum, and the Anglo-Boer War began on October 11th, 1899.

If the reader wishes to study the history of South Africa in more detail, there are a number of historical reference works available:

A Short History of South Africa by Gail Nattrass
A Short Guide to the History of South Africa by Damian O'Connor

There is also an excellent book, "The Covenant" written by James A Michener, which provides an extremely readable and informative history of the country in the form of a novel. This book does not attempt to plumb the depths of the political struggle between Britain and the Transvaal. The novel is primarily about the outcome of this political struggle, namely The Anglo-Boer War.

Military Context

At the time of the start of the Anglo-Boer War, the Transvaal had a total white population of around 240,000 (120,000 of Boer origin; 120,000 of foreign origin) and the Orange Free State around 100,000. The population of Great Britain at the time was 40 million, and the British Empire 436 million. What has fascinated students of the Boer War is how two small Boer Republics could compete militarily against the overwhelmingly superior numbers of Britain and its Empire. The short story is that they could not - the war was ultimately won by Britain by sheer weight of numbers and resources. However, it is worth examining how the Boer Republics managed to win a number of critical battles early in the war and to keep the British at bay for nearly three years, despite their numerical inferiority. The answer lies in the military strategies and tactics adopted by the combatants, and this is the topic for discussion here. The reader is encouraged to study this section before starting the book and to go back and reread it before the section on Magersfontein, where the impact of the differences in strategy and tactics is most evident.

Once again, I should alert the reader than this is not intended to be an in-depth analysis of the different military capabilities of the two sides. It is simply intended to highlight in brief some of the factors that make the early Boer victories explicable. There are many excellent works on the Boer War for those who want to study the question in more detail.

We shall examine the topic in these main sections:

— Military Organization
— Strategy and tactics
— The caliber of military leaders
— The caliber of fighting men

— Equipment
— Terrain and weather
— Motivation

Military Organization

The difference in military organizations between the Boers and the British can be summarized in one word - rigidity. The British Army was a very formal structure, with predetermined organization structure, channels of command, and manuals that dictated the way in which battle should be approached. The Boer organization was almost the diametric opposite - loosely knit commando units, with leaders elected by the men, who were equally comfortable fighting in isolation or in consort with other commandos.

The advantage of this organization structure was speed and flexibility. In a war where changes in tactics could occur very rapidly, frequently in the middle of a battle, the nimbleness of the Boer commandos to adapt to changing circumstances was in stark contrast to the rather slow and ponderous response of the British Army. The analogy of the oil tanker is perhaps relevant here - turn the wheel of an oil tanker, and 10 minutes later, the bow starts to come around. It was similar to the British Army - it took a long time and a series of convoluted orders and counter-orders to react to the needs of a fluid military situation. As a result, by the time the British had refocused their forces, the Boers had already left. This frequently happened in both the Western Cape and Natal and was a source of frustration to the British military commanders.

The question of mobility was even more significant in the second phase of the war after the British had occupied the two Boer Republics. This was the guerilla phase, with Boer commandos making 'hit and run' raids on British supply lines and engaging in acts of sabotage on rail lines, storage depots, and supply convoys. Here the emphasis was even more on strike and disappeared, and this exposed the ponderous nature of the British military organization. The British were eventually forced to use vast sweeping maneuvers over broad swathes of terrain to try and smoke out the Boers. This again worked by sheer weight of numbers, but it demonstrated clearly, as it had done in the American War of Independence (1775-1783), that the British military was ill-equipped to deal with a guerilla war.

Strategy and Tactics

The wars fought by the British prior to the Boer War were fought using the traditional approach that had persisted since the time of the Napoleonic Wars at the start of the century. This involved two massed armies advancing towards each other in close formation, firing in a controlled and coordinated manner until one or the other side felt it was impossible to continue and was forced to surrender. The strategy and tactics were fairly straight forward - get as much lead in the air as you can at any one time, and keep this up until the enemy surrendered. Flanking attacks were not uncommon, with the cavalry generally playing an important role, but this was really used as an attempt to shepherd the majority of the enemy forces into the killing ground. Artillery was used, but not in support of infantry movement. It was used to endeavor to eliminate the enemy artillery and force the enemy to keep their heads down while your troops advanced up the field. A classic example of these tactics is seen during Pickett's Charge at the Battle of Gettysburg (1863) during the American Civil War (1861-1865). The emphasis of the British way of fighting was very much a 'close order' approach; this started to change under Gen. Sir Redvers Buller during the last few battles to relieve Ladysmith in 1900 when the advantage of spreading out the troops or 'open order' was realized and successfully attempted. So the characteristics of the British systems of battle were 'standing up' and in 'close order,' frequently in mathematically straight lines.

To the modern student of warfare, this must seem absurd, but it should be remembered that this tactic was developed before the invention of the rifle. The primary infantry weapon was the musket, a front-loaded weapon that was slow to reload, inaccurate, and only lethal at about 100 yards. With weapons like this, the tactic was sound - get as much lead in the air as you can and slowly move towards the enemy. The advent of the rifle – breech-loaded with rapid reloading (sometimes supplemented by magazines) and accurate at distances above 1000 yards - made this kind of tactic suicidal. Unfortunately for the British, they were very much anchored to training manuals that had not kept pace with the technological development and were still using the same assault methods as they had used at Waterloo in 1815. The consequences of not modernizing their approach will be clearly seen later in this book. One should not be altogether critical of the British, specifically during the Boer War for this. Even in the First World War, a variation of this tactic was used with catastrophic consequences at battles like the Battle of the Somme in 1916.

The tactics of the Boers are in stark contrast. The characteristics of their approach were 'entrenchment' and 'dispersed ranks'. No Boer would ever contemplate facing an enemy standing out in the open. The Boer strategy was defensive, rather than offensive. It was rooted in enticing the enemy into the range of their rifles, then laying down withering fire into the enemy ranks. The Boers believed in concealment, surprise, cover, camouflage and trenches - in other words, remain as invisible to the enemy as was possible and give them very small targets to aim at. This was a necessary strategy, given the extent to which the Boers were outnumbered by the British. The Boer positions consisted of an array of trenches carefully positioned to ensure maximum potential killing ground and, wherever possible, to create opportunities to catch the enemy in a cross-fire. Their trenches were about 4-foot-deep, with sandbags or stones piled up in front (sangars), with gaps for rifles to be aimed at the enemy. The Boers also used barbed wire in front of the trenches, so that if the enemy came too close to the trench, their progress would be slowed by having to negotiate the barbed wire. The use of camouflage enabled the Boers to avoid being easily seen by British scouts and ensured that they were not seen by an advancing phalanx of British infantry until it was too late for the attackers to withdraw.

Boer artillery was frequently used in flanking positions, to the left and right of the trenches. In these positions, their guns performed two important functions. The first was by causing serious damage firing into closely packed troop formations (whereas the British artillery was firing on dispersed troops) and by herding the enemy flanks into the primary kill zone. The Boer guns were few but were used to good effect. The other use of the artillery was counter bombardment, attempting to neutralize the enemy artillery before it could do any substantial damage.

There was another technological reason that reinforced the Boer tactics - the use of smokeless powder. We shall see when we discuss the equipment of the two sides that the rifles used by the British did not fire smokeless powder, so it was easy to see the position from which the round had been fired - a characteristic greatly appreciated by the Boer snipers! On the other hand, the smokeless powder used by the Boers further added to their concealment strategy. Frequently a volley of rifle fire would tear into the British lines from a concealed position that could not be identified even after the volley had finished. In many cases, the British must have felt that they were fighting blind.

The caliber of military leaders

The leadership capabilities of the different commanders on both sides are frequently as much a function of circumstance as they are of ability. The circumstances in which many of the British commanders found themselves were occasioned by the strategy and tactics discussed above. If an army fights according to the manual rather than the conditions in which it finds itself, then even the best leader is going to struggle. And this was the problem with Gen. Sir Redvers Buller in his campaigns in Natal. Although a fine soldier (he won the Victoria Cross) and an excellent military commander against armies other than the Boers (in the Ashanti and Zulu Wars), he nevertheless felt duty-bound to fight wars in the way that the manuals laid out - standing upright and in close order. It is a great pity he was not able to read the later works of Albert Einstein, who said: "Lunacy is doing the same thing time after time and expecting different results." If ever an aphorism applied to anyone, it did to poor Gen. Buller. From being the man tipped to replace Lord Garnet Wolseley as commander-in-chief of the British Army, he ended up being dismissed in disgrace for poor performance in the Boer War.

A similar example is Gen. Methuen, who suffered so badly in the western theater of operations. He too was very much a 'by the book' general, and in the battles where he led the cost in human lives and suffering was far greater than it would have been experienced had he listened to some of his more junior generals like Gen. John French. It was French who, at the second foray against Magersfontein, suggested a wide flanking maneuver with cavalry to bypass the Boers at Magersfontein and go directly to Kimberley.

The other attribute which the early British commanders seemed to lack was the killer instinct. War was to them rather like a game of cricket. If the other side did well, then good for them, and they deserved to be applauded. This attitude was no longer viable, especially against a foe dug in and ready to defend its homeland to the last man. It was only when more focused leaders like Lord Roberts and Lord Kitchener entered the war that the gentlemanly attitude faded and was replaced by a serious will to win.

An element not to be forgotten is the fact that the British Army was, in many ways, a microcosm of Victorian society. The class distinction that permeated non-military society was replicated in the army. The officer corps was almost exclusively selected from the aristocracy and upper classes, and the soldiers represented the lower classes, and, to an extent, the non-commissioned officers resembled the tradesmen class who deal with those above and below them, but could not or would not become a member of either. The class divide between officers and men was as wide as it was in regular society, with neither side having any idea about the wants and aspirations of the others. So if an officer gave an order, the soldier would tug on his imaginary forelock and say, "Yes, My Lord." It is fair to say that there was no camaraderie among the different elements of the army - each kept to themselves and were concerned only with their own conditions.

This situation was not present among the Boers. There were few ranks in the Boer army, the most notable being General (who led an army), Commandant (who led a commando), Field-cornet (similar to Lieutenant, who led the equivalent of a platoon) and corporal (who led the equivalent of a section). There was no class distinction between the men who filled these ranks - in fact, other than in the case of generals who were appointed by the politicians; the other ranks were filled by the votes of the men whom they were to lead. Selecting your own leaders creates a far greater bond of loyalty than having your leader foisted upon you by higher authority. As a result, the relationship between the soldiers and their officers was much closer and more intimate than in the British army. Frequently they all came from the same location, were related by blood or marriage, and had known each other prior to the war. This was an army of cooperation rather than a chain of command.

But were the generals themselves any better or worse than the British? The answer is yes, and no. In many cases, the older generals still tended to follow the old maxim of 'if it ain't broke, don't fix it' - typical of this attitude were Gens. Cronje and Prinsloo. The tactics of the past had worked well for them (the great victory at Majuba during the First Boer War was often quoted), and they saw no reason to make any change. On the other hand, many of the younger generals, most notably Christiaan de Wet, Louis Botha and Koos de la Rey, did not feel themselves bound by older strategies and tactics, preferring to approach every battle on its merits and devising a strategy best suited to the set of circumstances being faced. An excellent example of this will be seen in the heated exchanges between Cronje and De la Rey on the best strategy to employ at Magersfontein.

The one advantage that the Boer generals had over their British counterparts was the fact that they had been fighting these sorts of wars for 50 years. The skirmishes with the local black tribes over land and grazing rights were frequently fought at commando level, rather than by two great armies lined up on either side of a selected location. Hence the fluidity of combat, and the use of cover and camouflage, came far more naturally to the Boer generals than it did to the British, who were more comfortable with banners held high and the sound of bagpipes rather than trying to root out an elusive enemy on his own terrain.

To summarize then, there were good generals and bad generals on both sides. The Boers perhaps had the advantage of greater flexibility - their junior generals were heeded more frequently than their British equivalents - and this may have given them a strategic advantage. Both sides had some good strategic ideas that changed the course of battles, and it is fair to say, as painful as it may seem, that Roberts' and Kitchener's strategy of scorched earth was probably the deciding factor in ending the war.

The caliber of fighting men

The British Army had two main categories of fighting men - regular army and volunteers.

In the case of the regular army, the quality of the men was on the whole good, and the esprit de corps of the regiments very high. But the training of both officers and men was antiquated. The low pay, the irksome restraints of the soldier's life, the harsh punishments inflicted for trivial offenses, the long period for which the intending soldier had to pledge himself, were serious deterrents to intending recruits, and it was becoming increasingly difficult to keep the Army up to its establishment.

As regards the volunteers, the great defect of the system lay in its complete disregard of the elementary conditions of voluntary service. The term of service had been fixed by purely actuarial calculations and with absolutely no regard for the personal "special" interests of the soldier. It provided no career for the private soldier, while it kept him in the Army till he was too old, as a rule, to begin life again with success. All the unnecessary rigidity of the system as to terms of service, all the petty restrictions and stoppages which still survived from the traditions of the eighteenth century were retained. Again, the old pay of a shilling a day meant much more to the recruit when it implied permanent employment and a pension to follow than the same sum given for seven years only.

In addition to the difficulty in recruiting decent and capable men, the training was a serious issue for the British Army. A considerable amount of time was devoted to instruction in drill, which undoubtedly has its value in the first stages of a soldier's training, though much of it was of a ceremonial character and of little military use. Three weeks in the year were devoted to field training, i.e., actual training for military operations, and a score of days to route-marching, while the all-important item of shooting was satisfied by the firing of about two hundred rounds per soldier at a fixed target. This meant they were indifferent shots, careless of cover, slow to comprehend what was taking place, or to grasp the whereabouts of the enemy, always getting surprised or lost, helpless without their officers. In a word, the British soldier was well-disciplined but ill-trained— one might almost say untrained.

The Boer Army, on the other hand, was not a mere collection of patriotic civilians. The fact is that the Boers were not a people of civilians at all, as the ordinary populations of European countries, but a fighting race with a fighting history, as described above. The conditions of the life of the Boers provide insight into the origins of all the more distinguishing features of the Boer fighting system. The Boer farmer, living miles from his fellow men, always had to be prepared for single-handed encounters on the veld, or for the defense of his homestead against marauding bands. He naturally developed a mode of fighting, which gave the greatest power and freedom of action to the individual.

The Boer farmer, as with the medieval knight, depended on his personal skill and the training of his horse. If he was a careful scout and an unerring shot; if he could trust his pony to stand steady till the last moment at which it was safe to stay on it firing, then he could afford to despise almost any numerical odds against him. As in the Middle Ages, the prime military unit was the single horseman. And the Boer was a fine horseman and an unerring shot - it was not uncommon to see a Boer ride at full gallop, drop the reins and shoot a buck from the saddle. The Boer did not need to be trained - he grew up with a rifle in his hand and knew how to use it. There was no question with him about using his fire as a means to cover his attack. His fire was his attack, and his one concern was to develop to the utmost the efficiency of that fire. The absolute undivided supremacy of the firearm was, from the first, the foundation of the whole Boer system.

No less important element of fire discipline is the power of holding back fire so as to entice an enemy within a range from which he cannot escape without heaviest loss. This power of self-restraint is one of the most difficult to ensure in troops. The Boers, artillery as well as riflemen, possessed it, not through discipline, but by virtue of the instinct acquired by generations of stalking wild animals and of economizing ammunition. Another characteristic of Boer fire methods was the preference for flanking fire. Whether in attack or defense, the picked marksmen would always take up positions unobserved in front of the flanks of their line. When the enemy concentrated all his attention upon the main line and chose his cover to meet their fire, the flankers could pick his men off at leisure.

Equipment

There are two main areas of discussion when it comes to equipment:

- The nature and type of the equipment itself
- The quantity of equipment

One of the serious mistakes that the British Army made was the belief that the Boers would be armed with obsolete and outdated weapons, and that they would be outgunned in every situation. The opposite could not have been truer. The rich tax revenues derived by the Transvaal government from the gold mining industry had gone to good use - to ensure that a potential Boer army was provided with the most up-to-date rifles available and that it had more than adequate ammunition.

There is always speculation on the quality and effectiveness of different pieces of military hardware, but the general consensus at the time was that the German Mauser 93 and 95 were the premier rifles of the era. Relatively light, magazine-fed (5 rounds), accurate at over a thousand yards, the rifle fired a high-velocity shell capable of killing two soldiers with a single round. In addition, it used smokeless powder, the advantage of which has been described above. It should be remembered that the Boer soldier was fundamentally a rifleman. He had no interest in hand-to-hand combat if it could be avoided - his path to victory was rapid, accurate fire that would prevent the enemy from getting too close. The long range of the rifle also spelled the end of mounted scouting parties by the enemy. With accuracy up to 1000 meters (some Boers claimed 1200 meters), the opportunity to do any close-range scouting was no longer available. So, the British, on many occasions, approached skirmishes with the Boers without the intelligence necessary to determine the most appropriate strategy.

The basic British weapon was the Lee-Metford rifle. Although breech-loaded, it was a one- round-at-a-time rifle, with no magazine. It was not until after the Boer War that all British rifles were reconfigured to accept magazines. The Lee-Metford did not have the range, accuracy, or muzzle velocity of the Mauser, and, in addition, it did not use smokeless powder. Every time a round was fired, the soldier would have to deal with the resultant smoke that eventually became a pall. For the Boers, this smoke on firing provided an excellent target at which to aim. The British soldier did not seem to regard the rifle as the main assault weapon, but rather as a means to get the individual close enough to make a bayonet charge. As a result, there was little focus on pinpoint accuracy or firing only at discernible targets. The old philosophy of 'getting lead into the air' seemed to pervade tactics even to this time. The Boers, on the other hand, would never have considered using the bayonet. They were riflemen, not hand-to-hand combatants.

The fact that the Boer rifle used a 5 round clip, whereas the British rifle was a single-shot weapon, greatly improved the rate of fire of the Boers. This was one of the ways in which the Boers were able to compensate for their smaller numbers - a higher rate of fire will increase the firepower of a smaller group of soldiers. The fact that the Boers were crack shots also impacted the killing range. Since the British rifle did not have the same accuracy distance as the Mauser, and since the British soldiers were not trained to be accomplished marksmen, the Boers were often able to engage the British long before the British could effectively retaliate. This had the effect of keeping the infantry at bay and forced the British to rely on artillery to bring fire down upon the Boers.

In the area of artillery, the British had the upper hand in terms of numbers and probably quality. The difference came in the strategic use of that artillery. The Boer artilleryman worked his gun on exactly the same tactical principles as the ordinary Boer worked his rifle. He made every use of cover, natural or artificial, changing his position whenever he found that the enemy had located it. He held back his fire if he hoped to lure his enemy into an ambush, though otherwise, he preferred to keep him at arm's length, making the fullest use of any superiority he possessed in range over the opposing artillery. Escort in the field was unnecessary, for he always hitched up his team and trekked out of range if there was any danger of the enemy getting too near. The British artillery, like the infantry, was not at all concerned about cover or camouflage but tended to employ their guns in places easily visible to the enemy. It is hardly surprising, then, that their gun crews were continually being picked off by Boer snipers and their guns falling prey to enemy counter bombardment. The role of the artillery was also relatively undefined, especially its role vis-a-vis the infantry. Whereas the two main purposes of artillery should be covering fire for the infantry, and counter bombardment against enemy guns, the British artillery of the time often saw themselves as an extension of the infantry, positioning themselves alongside the infantry (and in one classic case in Natal, in front of the infantry) and using their guns as a type of battering ram, not really ideal against well dug in and camouflaged troops.

The quantity of equipment was also an issue with which the British had to deal. The British Army was not one that 'traveled light.' The amount of equipment and stores required to maintain the British army in the field was considerable and required an extensive system of baggage convoys following each battalion. Not only was this a logistical nightmare for the British, it was also a very attractive target for Boer foragers and skirmishers, particularly during the guerilla phase of the war.

Prior to Lord Roberts' arrival, each battalion was in charge of its own baggage convoy. Roberts felt that this was unwieldy and utilized too many transport resources. He, therefore, decided that the decentralized approach should give way to a more centralized supply system at the army level. Each battalion would then be responsible for requisitioning such equipment and stores as required. The method worked in the early days but became somewhat unwieldy as the number of British troops increased.

The Boers relied mainly on the ability of each individual soldier to look after himself, and on the power of commandeering. At the outbreak of war, the more prosperous soldiers came into the field provided not only with the obligatory pony and ten days' rations, but with innumerable ox wagons, mule wagons, and Cape carts, containing abundant provisions for weeks of campaigning, with spare ponies, and with black servants to look after all these. The transport and ponies which the veldkornets commandeered were simply supplementary and for the use of those soldiers who had none of their own. When the Boer was in a fixed camp like those around the besieged towns of Ladysmith or Mafeking, his family might trek over from the farm, bringing a wagon-full of good things: cakes and Boer rusks (dried biscuits), meat-filled oilcakes and biltong (jerky-like dried meat), warm clothes and new boots.

The greater part of war is based on questions of transport and supply. The Boer was a born transport rider. Whether with ox-wagons, mule-wagons, or Cape carts, the Boer could go twice as far in a day as the British transport officer. There was some truth in the joking exaggeration that, given two- or three-hours' start, Boer oxen could always get away from British cavalry. The Boer lived frugally in times of peace. Hunting or traveling, he was accustomed to taking several days' provision of food, sometimes even of water, with him and to make that provision last. A small bag of Boer rusks, a pocketful of biltong and a little coffee tied up in a bit of cloth, would keep him for a week. For a campaign, he thus started with enormous advantages over the British soldier.

Terrain and Weather

Home field advantage is always a factor in war, but it was especially relevant in the Boer War. The areas in which the majority of the war took place are hard and hostile regions, with little rain and proliferation of rocks, thorn trees, low bushes, and hard ground - a far cry from 'England's green and pleasant land.' Added to this was the intense heat, particularly in the areas around Kimberley and Bloemfontein, something that plagued the British soldier throughout the various battles with the Boers. Then there were the insects that left their marks all too frequently on the exposed skins of the British. It is a hostile country, less so than Sudan, but definitely a landscape with which the British were unfamiliar.

On the other hand, these were the areas in which the Boers had grown up, and they were very much at home in the conditions. They knew the lay of the land, had a scant need for maps, and were able to handle the extremes of heat and cold much better than their enemies. They were also more skilled at fieldcraft, a skill almost completely lacking in the British soldier. They could live off the land, could locate water and game, and frequently did not need to rely on supply columns to provide food - they shot for the pot.
Another advantage was the way in which the Boers used the terrain. Getting within rifle range of the enemy unobserved and

protected from his fire was the keynote of the Boer method, and that could only be achieved by making use of every unevenness of the ground, of every stone, every bush or tuft of grass. In European tactics, the value of ground from the rifleman's point of view is obscured by the traditions of older methods of warfare. The rigid formations necessary for an effective charge, whether on horse or on foot, are incompatible with skillful use of ground by the individual. There is a tendency to regard all the unevenness of the ground as mere incidental obstacles, useful for defense rather than attack. To the Boer, looking at things only from the rifleman's point of view, the formation of the ground was the one important thing, the alpha, and the omega of tactics. The order of the men, the arrangement of the attack or defense, and the positioning of the trenches were all subordinate to it. The ground played a part in Boer warfare that wind, waves, and tide played in the naval warfare of the eighteenth century.

Skill in the use of terrain was as essential to the Boer as seamanship was essential to the admirals and captains of that day. And the Boer, accustomed to spending his life in the open, was superior in his eye for the ground to the British officer and soldier fresh from the barracks and the parade ground. The ideal country for rifle tactics is one where cover is abundant for those who have the skill to use it, while the unskillful is ever left in the open. The South African veld with its clear atmosphere, with its lack of trees and hedges, but with its rock-littered kopjes (hillocks), deep cut dongas (ditches or dry watercourses), and gentle folds of ground, is such an ideal country.

Where the ground did not afford sufficient natural cover, the Boers spared no labor or thought in providing artificial entrenchments - cover either in the form of schanzes or sangars (small shelters of piled stones) or in the form of trenches. They proved themselves masters in trench work. They showed that, if a trench is made deep enough and narrow enough, it will offer almost perfect protection from shrapnel fire. Their trenches and shelters were always made with the same instinctive skill at concealment and use of such natural cover as the ground afforded. The trenches were not field earthworks with great mounds of fresh earth in front to serve as range finders, but holes discreetly concealed with grass and twigs, and invisible even within deadly rifle range. To protect themselves against flanking fire, they would make these trenches discontinuous, and full of sharp curves. Each trench usually had its covered approach from some donga or fold in the ground, which offered facilities for reinforcement or escape.

Motivation

The difference in motivation was also in stark contrast. The British soldier was thousands of miles from home, facing a shrewd and well-armed enemy in terrain to which he was unaccustomed, all for one shilling a day. There must have been times when they wondered what, in fact, they were doing in this war. There was almost no chance for promotion, little chance for glory, and a regimen that required all commands of superiors to be obeyed without question. And frequently these commands emanated from men to whom they could not relate socially, and would never be likely to meet in civilian society, unless as a servant or retainer. The impact of all this on the motivation of the British troops must have been significant. Loyalty and pride in country and empire would have played a significant part in countering this, but was it enough to overcome the uncomfortable landscape, the intense heat, and the attacks of thousands of unfamiliar insects?

The Boers, on the other hand, were fighting for the survival of their homeland, their culture, and their way of life. This was land they had fought for, had seen their forefathers battle to tame, where they had grown accustomed to a way of life in harmony with nature. This was something that would not be relinquished easily, would encourage men to give their lives to protect. And even when things looked dark, and defeat loomed, there was still a group, known as the "Bitter Enders", who were prepared to sacrifice their lives to protect it, even though the prospect of victory was long since gone.

History of the Boer Republics

The Great Trek

The Great Trek began in 1836, and continued into the 1840s, although the majority of Dutch settlers left the Cape Colony between 1836 and 1838. Historians have identified multiple factors that contributed to the Great Trek in varying degrees, although the primary motivation was disillusionment with British colonial rule, taxation, and punishments for non-compliance with new laws.

These included:

— Anglicization policies (especially in official circles, at the expense of the 'taal' (mother tongue).
— Restrictive laws on slavery and its eventual abolition
— Arrangements to compensate former slave owners (which were considered inadequate during harvest season.)
— Land was becoming scarce and expensive owing to the high rate of natural increase in the Dutch-speaking population and the introduction of new British colonists
— Droughts
— Perceived antagonism from British missionaries.
— The official recognition of the equality between settlers and native inhabitants.
— British restrictions on trade conducted with African tribes beyond the Cape Colony's frontiers.

This emigration of some 12,000 to 14,000 Boers is regarded by Afrikaners as the central event of their 19th-century history and the origin of their nationhood. It enabled them to outflank the Xhosa peoples who were blocking their eastward expansion, to penetrate into Natal and the Highveld (which had been opened up by the tribal wars of the previous decade), and to carry white settlement north to the Limpopo River.

The migrating Boers, called Voortrekkers (Afrikaans: "Early Migrants"), left in a series of parties of kinfolk and neighbors, with an almost equal number of mixed-race dependents, under prominent leaders. Though they all crossed the Orange River, they were soon divided as to their ultimate destination—some wanted an outlet to the sea in Natal, and others wished to remain on the Highveld. In both areas, after initial setbacks, they were able to defeat powerful African military kingdoms through the skilled use of horses, guns, and defensive laagers (encampments within circled wagons), though, in later years, they were to find the problems of maintaining control over Africans and establishing stable politics more intractable.

In Natal, the Voortrekkers established a short-lived republic, but, after its annexation by the British in 1843, most rejoined their compatriots across the Drakensberg, where, except for a short period, the British government was reluctant to pursue them. In 1852 and 1854, the British granted independence to the trekkers in the Transvaal and Transorangia (later the Orange Free State) regions, respectively. All was relatively quiet until the outbreak of the First Anglo-Boer War in 1880.

The First Anglo-Boer War

Causes of the War

The First Anglo-Boer is also known as the First Transvaal War of Independence because the conflict arose between the British colonizers and the Boers from the Transvaal Republic or Zuid-Afrikaansche Republiek (ZAR, South African Republic). The Boers had some help from their neighbors in the Orange Free State.

— There were several causes of the First Anglo-Boer War
— The expansion of the British Empire.
— Problems within the Transvaal government.
— The British annexation of the Transvaal.
— The Boer opposition to British rule in the Transvaal.

The expansion of the British Empire

The 4th Earl of Carnarvon was the British Secretary of State for the Colonies under Prime Minister Benjamin Disraeli, who was premier from 1874 to 1880. At the time, the British government wanted to expand the British Empire. Carnarvon wanted to form a confederation under British control of all the British colonies, independent Boer republics, and independent African groups in South Africa. By 1876 he realized that he would not be able to achieve his goal peacefully. He told Disraeli: "By acting at once, we may ... acquire ... the whole Transvaal Republic, after which the Orange Free State will follow." He was prepared to use force to make the confederation a reality, a fact that was proved by the Anglo-Zulu War in 1879.

Problems within the Transvaal Government

T. F. Burgers was the president of the Transvaal Republic from 1872 until its annexation in 1877 by Britain. The Republic was in serious financial trouble, especially as the war had just started between the Boers and the Pedi under their leader, Sekhukhune, in the North-Eastern Transvaal, and also because the Boer people were reluctant to pay their taxes. The Transvaal public was disappointed with their leadership and, although Sekhukhune agreed to peace in February 1877 and was willing to pay a fine to the Republic, it was too late. Carnarvon sent Sir Theophilus Shepstone, the former Secretary for Native Affairs in Natal, to the Transvaal as a special commissioner.

Shepstone arrived in the Transvaal on 22 January 1877, with 25 men as support. Initially, he was vague about his real purpose. He used the weakness in the Transvaal government to make the Boers aware of the dangers of a bankrupt state and focused on the government's lack of control over black people like the Pedi and the Zulu. This demoralized the Boers. Burgers did very little to stop Britain from taking over the Transvaal. Shepstone had told Burgers what his intentions were by the end of January 1877, and Burgers tried to convince the Transvaal government to take the situation seriously, but they refused to see the urgency of the matter.

The British annexation of the Transvaal

Carnarvon thought that annexing the Transvaal would be the first step to confederation. English-speaking people in the republic were positive towards the idea, and the Boers were disappointed in their own government, which the British thought would make it easier to convince them that they could not avoid annexation. Shepstone said that he had more than 3 000 signatures from people who wanted to be part of the British Empire. What he did not tell Carnarvon was that these were many more - the Boer population - who were against the idea and wanted to retain their independence. On 12 April 1877, a proclamation of annexation was read out in Church Square in Pretoria, the capital of the Transvaal Republic. There was no resistance, and the Union Jack replaced the Vierkleur, the republic's four-colored flag. The Transvaal Republic or Zuid-Afrikaansche Republiek (ZAR) did not exist anymore but was now the British Colony of the Transvaal.

The Boer opposition to British rule in the Transvaal

Former President T. F. Burgers and other people loyal to the former Transvaal Republic objected to the annexation, and Paul Kruger and E. J. P. Jorissen went to London in 1877 to present their case to Carnarvon. They failed, and in 1878 they took a petition with more than 6 500 signatures from Boers to London, but the British government insisted that the Transvaal remain a British possession.

Sir Theophilus Shepstone was now the administrator of the Transvaal Colony, and he realized that running it was going to be much more difficult than annexing it. The British government had made promises to the Boers to allow them some self-government, but Shepstone was slow to initiate this process. The colony remained nearly bankrupt, and British plans to build a railroad to Delagoa Bay had to be put on hold.

Shepstone became increasingly unpopular with the Colonial Office in London. British Native Commissioners were trying to control the black people in the area, but they could not get Sekhukhune and the Pedi to pay the fine he owed to the Transvaal Republic because they did not have enough soldiers to force him to do so. Shepstone also failed to control the Zulus on the southeastern border of the colony, and many farmers had to leave their farms. Sir Owen Lanyon replaced Shepstone as an administrator in 1879. In September of the same year, Sir Garnet Wolseley was appointed High Commissioner for southeast Africa and governor of Natal and Transvaal.

The Anglo-Zulu War in 1879 was supposed to increase British standing in South Africa but had the opposite effect. The Zulu and Pedi were both defeated by the British in 1879, but non-violent Boer opposition had grown. The Boers had hoped that the election of the Liberal Party in Britain in April 1880 would mean restored independence for the Transvaal, but the new Prime Minister, W. E. Gladstone, insisted on maintaining British control in Pretoria. The Volksraad (Parliament) of the Orange Free State, south of the Vaal River, backed the Transvaal Boers in their call for the independence of the Transvaal in May 1879. Even Boers in the Cape Colony gave moral support to their comrades in the north. In October 1880, a newspaper from Paarl in the Cape Colony took the view that:

"Passive resistance is now becoming futile."

The War

The first open conflict between the British and Boers began in November 1880 in Potchefstroom. A burgher, P. L. Bezuidenhout, refused to pay extra fees on his wagon, saying he had already paid his taxes. The British authorities then confiscated the wagon. On 11 November 1880, a commando of 100 men under P. A. Cronje took back the wagon from the British bailiff and returned it to Bezuidenhout.

Following this, between 8 000 and 10,000 Boers gathered at Paardekraal, near Krugersdorp, on 8 December 1880. At this gathering, a triumvirate of leaders, Paul Kruger, Piet Joubert, and M. W. Pretorius, were appointed. On 13 December 1880, the leaders proclaimed the restoration of the Transvaal Republic and three days later raised their Vierkleur flag at Heidelberg, thus rejecting British authority. The events of December 1880, thus in effect started the war and ended passive resistance.

[Author's note. The battles of the war are not as important to this book as the causes and political consequences. Hence, they have been largely omitted. The most significant battle was a decisive victory for the Boers at Majuba Hill, which eventually ended the war.]

The aftermath of the War

In the aftermath of the war, the South African Republic (Transvaal) regained its independence. The Pretoria Convention (1881) and the London Convention (1884) laid down the terms of the peace agreement.

President Brand of the Orange Free State had been trying to get both the Transvaal Boers and the British to the negotiation table from the beginning of the conflict. Several peace offers had been made from both sides, with the most important one being in January 1881, when Paul Kruger offered peace on the condition that the Transvaal's independence was guaranteed. Another was made on 21 February 1881, when the British government offered peace if the Boers laid down their weapons. Major-General Sir George Pomeroy Colley didn't forward the message from the British government fast enough, and because Paul Kruger was not in Natal, the battle of Majuba took place on the Transvaal-Natal border before peace negotiations could begin. On 5 March 1881, Sir Evelyn Wood and Gen. Piet Joubert agreed on an armistice in order to start peace negotiations at O'Neill's cottage, which lay between the British and Boer lines. Negotiations were successful, and the war ended on 23 March 1881.

The Pretoria Convention and the Independence of the Transvaal

After peace had been negotiated, a British royal commission was appointed to draw up the Transvaal's status and new borders. These decisions were confirmed and formalized at the Pretoria Convention that took place on 3 August 1881.

The new republic was named the Transvaal and was to be an independent Republic, but it still had to have its foreign relations and policies regarding black people approved by the British government. The new state was also not allowed to expand towards the West. Along with these conditions, it was stipulated that the Transvaal was still under British *suzerainty* or influence. The Boer Triumvirate was worried about some of the requirements, but they took over the rule of the Transvaal on 10 August.

The conditions put forward by the British government were

unacceptable from the Transvaalers' point of view, and in 1883 a delegation, including Paul Kruger, the new President of the Transvaal, left for London to review the agreement.

The London Convention

In 1884 the London Convention was signed. The Transvaal was given a new Western border and adopted the name of the South African Republic (ZAR or in English, SAR). Although the word suzerainty did not appear in the London Convention, the SAR still had to get permission from the British government for any treaty entered into with any other country other than the Orange Free State. The Boers saw this as a way for the British government to interfere in Transvaal affairs, and this led to tension between Britain and the SAR. This increased steadily until the outbreak of the Second Anglo-Boer War in 1899.

This section includes extracts from an article on the First Anglo-Boer War reproduced with the kind permission of South Africa History Online - www.sahistory.org.za

Maps and Flags

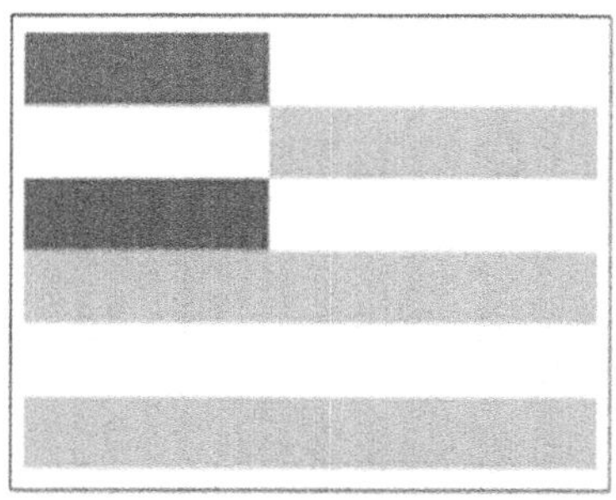

Orange Free State

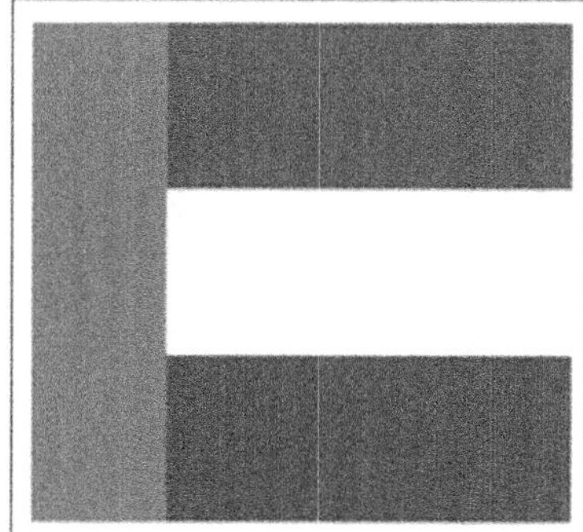

South African Republic (Transvaal)

Great Britain

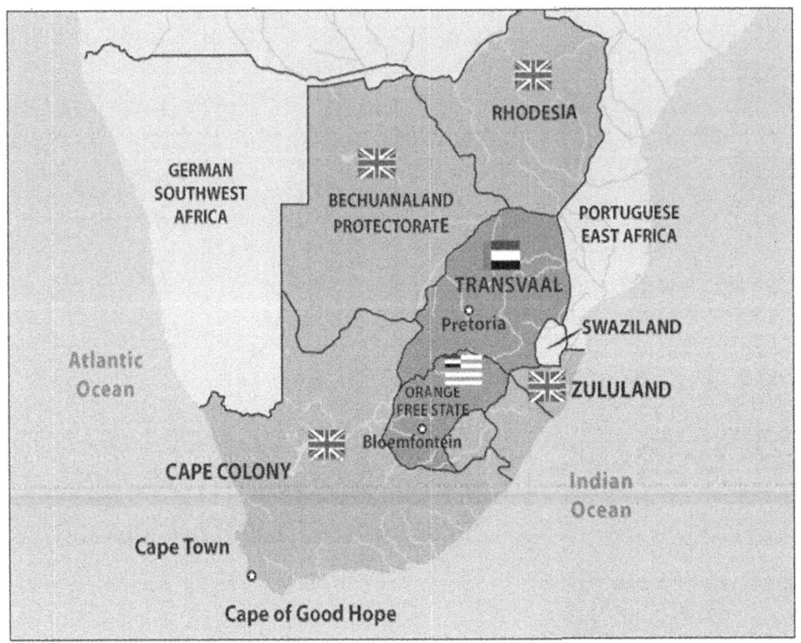

South Africa at the time of the Boer War (the area under the westernmost Union Jack is blown up on the ensuing map)

(Author's Note. The territory southwest of Zululand on this map was the British colony of Natal, which grew from the port town of Durban – the author's home town – as described above.)

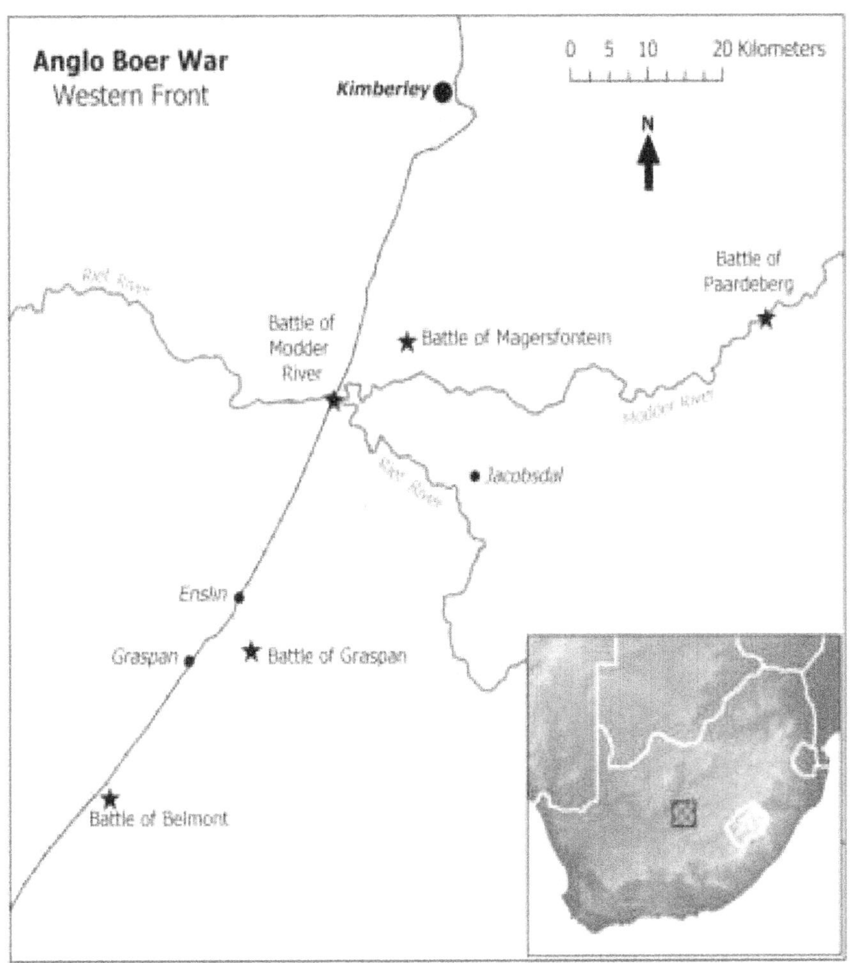

This is the area in which the battles described in this book occurred.

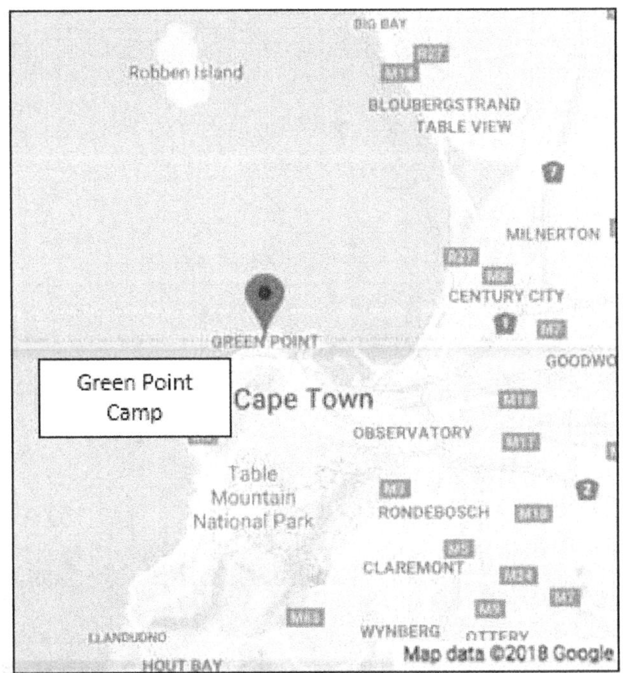

Location of Green Point Prisoner of War Camp

Ceylon (now Sri Lanka)

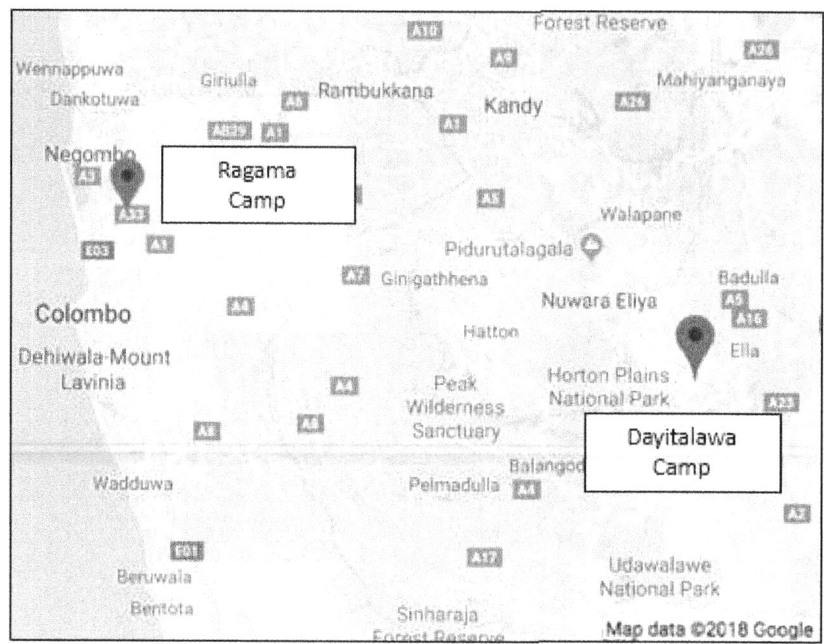

Location of Prisoner of War Camps, Ceylon

Part 1 - Europe

Chapter 1 – Latvia

Riga - July 18, 1881 – Edward

Edward Weinberg did not know how many times he had walked up and down the corridor on the second floor of Riga's 1. Slimnica, the hospital in which his wife Fanni was in labor with their first child. Nor did he know how many cigarettes he had smoked since they had arrived at the hospital on Bruninieku Street two hours ago when Fanni had displayed all the symptoms of being about to give birth. They had registered at the front desk, and they were taken to the second floor by a nurse in a white headscarf with a white apron pinned on her gray uniform. She had directed Edward into a small waiting room at the end of the corridor, then whisked Fanni away, turning her head back to him, saying, "We will call you when it is time."

"Call me when it is time," he muttered. "What kind of comfort is that? Will it be one hour, two, a day? They don't tell you enough in these places. Don't they realize the anxiety of being a father for the first time?" He returned to the waiting room and sat down. The room had light gray walls and a gray linoleum floor on which someone had placed a rug of multiple colors. There were a number of chairs around the perimeter, and a table with magazines that must have come from the previous decade. Edward was in no mood to read, no mood to even page through the magazines, and look at the photos. He was focused on his wife, her safety, and that of the child. Infant mortality was high in Latvia, and there was always a risk that something could go wrong with either mother or baby. While not a particularly religious man, he did offer up a prayer to the Almighty to watch over his wife and unborn child. "He's probably busy with something else." he mused. "But there is no harm in trying."

Edward Weinberg was a tall, well-built man with dark brown hair, a full mustache, and a warm and engaging personality. Always immaculately turned out in a three-piece suit, wing collar shirt, and necktie, he was the kind of person one noticed when entering a room. He made friends and acquaintances easily, always feeling at home in whatever social milieu he found himself. He was a man who placed honesty and integrity above all other attributes, with the possible exception of the love he bore for his wife and family. Edward was an extroverted soul, one who was more at home in an atmosphere of bon vivant, but, at times like this, the cheerful exterior gave way to inner pensiveness and reflection.

Edward and his family had moved to Latvia in the 1850s from Russia when hostility towards the Jews was becoming intolerable. Edward's father Benjamin and his wife Base moved to a rural part of the country in the province of Courland, but in 1873 they moved to Riga. Edward had been just 14 when the move was made. The family was large, with five boys (of whom Edward was the youngest) and one daughter. In 1879, Edward met Fanni, a country girl whose parents farmed on land they rented from the local aristocrat. Fanni had been visiting Riga to meet with some friends, and Edward met her at a dinner given by one of them. The couple dated for nearly a year then decided to get married.

Fanni was a perfect foil for Edward. Slim, of average height, with light brown hair, she was a quiet, gentle person who went about her life with a calmness and dignity that made her a soothing influence on all who met her. She was intelligent, resourceful, and analytical, and was not prone to the quick decision-making that was Edward's hallmark. Together they made a formidable team, with Fanni providing the restraining influence to counter Edward's adventurous nature.

Edward could remember the marriage day vividly. The ceremony was held at the Great Choral Synagogue on Gogol Street, a synagogue noted for the quality of its cantor and choir. But the most memorable part was the fact that the marriage ceremony was conducted by Edward's uncle, a great and scholarly rabbi known as The Tukumer Rebbe - to have such a famous and saintly man conduct the service was sure to bring God's blessing to the couple. The reception was a big affair at a local hotel - the fact that Edward's father had six siblings meant that the place was filled with uncles, aunts, cousins, and many friends.

Edward was a merchant by trade and a member of the Riga Second Guild. He traded in agricultural products, furs, tobacco, and various alcoholic beverages. The couple moved to a comfortable home on Kaleju Street and got down to the business of raising a family. Life was good, but while the attitude of most Latvians towards the Jews was favorable, there was always the possibility that things might change for the worse.

"Mr. Weinberg!" The voice shocked Edward out of his reminiscences. "You can come and see your wife now."
"Has the baby been born yet?" he demanded.
"Yes," replied the nurse.
"Well," said Edward "What is it? Are they both alright? Did everything go according to plan?"
The nurse smiled. "Everything went just fine. You are the proud father of a seven-pound baby boy!"

Edward clasped his hands in a gesture of prayer, lifted his eyes upwards, and silently gave thanks to the Almighty. A boy! What could be better? Someone to carry the family name! He hurried behind the nurse to a room where Fanni lay on a bed with white covers - her face was so pale she almost disappeared into the sheets, but she smiled faintly when Edward came in. "How are you?" he demanded, "Was it bad? Was there much pain? Are you in pain now?" She smiled again and said, "It is not for nothing we are reminded of The Garden of Eden at times like this. God punished Eve for her deceit by making childbirth a painful experience. And believe me, it was! But I am fine now, and we have a wonderful baby boy." "Where is he?" asked Edward. In his haste to see Fanni, he had not noticed a tiny bassinet on the far side of the bed. He moved quickly around the bed and saw the tiny face sticking out above the blanket in which the baby was wrapped, his brown eyes looking up at Edward. His father stared for a long while, tears welling up in his eyes. He murmured, "My son! My son! The greatest gift a man can get is the blessing of a son. My son! My son!" He bent and placed his lips gently on the tiny brow, then turned to his wife. "Have you thought about what we should name him?" Fanni replied, "I would like him to have two names, one for your family and one for mine. For my side, I would choose Isay after my late uncle." Edward thought for a while. "I would offer the name Jeannot. My late grandfather's best friend was Jeannot, who saved his life during a pogrom. I would like to cherish that memory."

And so the baby was named Isay Jeannot Weinberg, although he was always known as ....Jeannot. *[Author's note – The name "Jeannot" is pronounced "djah-no" with the emphasis on the first syllable.]*

Chapter 2 - Emigration

Brussels - 1893 – Edward

Edward's office in Brussels was on the third floor of an old building at the corner of Rue de la Regence and Grand Sablon. From his window, he could see children playing in the Square du Petit Sablon, as well as outside the Great Brussels Synagogue. The family had been in Brussels since 1890. Edward ran a store in a nearby arcade, where he sold furs in winter and lace in summer. He had been moderately successful, but the store was never likely to provide him with the level of income he would need for his increasing family. When he left Latvia for Moscow in 1887, his family had grown to three sons - Jeannot, born in 1881, Bernard, born in 1882, and Max, born in 1883. Bertha, the only daughter, had been born in Moscow in 1888, and Albert had been born in Brussels the year they arrived.

Edward reflected on the circumstances that had occasioned his moving the family from Latvia to Russia to Belgium in the space of 4 years. Life was becoming more and more unpredictable for Jews in Europe at the time, and it was becoming difficult to determine which country would offer a safe haven. Latvia had been quite reasonable in this regard. There was a Russian element that was always going to be hostile to the Jews, but the Latvian people as a whole were tolerant. It was indeed a pity that the business in Riga did not prove as successful as Edward had hoped, and when an offer came to acquire a share in a paint factory in Moscow, he took the opportunity and moved the family to Russia. It was in Moscow that Bertha was born - a tiny baby who Fanni said was the same size as a tablespoon! The boys were particularly fascinated by the new addition, having never had a baby sister before. They did not quite perceive how delicate Bertha was, and sometimes treated her as if she was yet another boy. But she thrived and was soon playing with her brothers.

It was another piece of legislation that caused Edward to leave Moscow. An ordinance was passed forbidding Jews with incomes below a certain level from living in major cities. This piece of undisguised anti-Semitism was a crude form of ethnic cleansing, to ensure the great cities like Moscow and St. Petersburg did not have to deal with 'the lower classes' of Jews. So, Edward was forced to sell his share in the paint factory and remove the family from Russia. It had always been well known that The Low Countries were more welcoming of Jews that many parts of Europe, so this is where Edward decided to move the family.

Brussels had a thriving Jewish community. Following Belgian independence in 1830, Judaism was given the status of an officially recognized religion (besides Roman Catholicism, the majority faith of the country, and Protestantism). On 17 March 1832, the Central Jewish Consistory of Belgium was founded as the official representative of the Jewish religion to the Belgian authorities. The Great Synagogue of Brussels was built in 1876-1877. There was a migration of many Brussels Jews to Antwerp when it took over from Amsterdam as the center of the diamond industry, but Brussels still contained sizeable numbers of Jewish merchants, professionals, and tradesmen. There was an active school attached to the Great Synagogue, and the children all received religious instruction there. There was religious and commercial freedom in Belgium, and the Jewish communities were able to prosper.

But not all did. Edward realized that it was fast reaching the time when he would have to make another decision about where to move the family. He considered England but was not sure what line of work he would pursue there. Italy was another possibility, but the Italian economy was unstable. America? Always a possibility. Then the family received an unexpected visitor. Henry Orkin, a cousin of Fanni, was leaving Russia for the strange new land of

South Africa to join his brother Joseph in a place called Phillipolis in the Orange Free State. He was passing through Brussels to take a ship from England. Edward had heard of South Africa, particularly with regard to diamond and gold mining, but had never heard of the Orange Free State, let alone Phillipolis! And why had Joseph selected South Africa as a destination? It was, said Henry, a land flowing with milk and honey, and where the pigeons flew around already roasted with a knife and fork stuck in their backs! The family laughed at this exaggeration, but Henry was determined that this was a country that would soon provide good positions and businesses to people who were prepared to work hard. The industries that grew up around the gold and diamond fields were always looking for capable people who were well educated and had useful skills. Edward wanted to hear more. How does one get to move there, he inquired? That, Henry informed him, was the reason he was in Brussels. There was a South African delegation from the Transvaal in Brussels, and they were issuing permits for people wishing to immigrate to South Africa. The following day, Edward accompanied Henry to the delegation and was able to inquire about opportunities for immigration. It was clear to the Transvaal authorities that a solid individual like Edward was precisely the type of settler they were looking for, so, after explaining the procedures for applying for immigration status, they invited Edward to bring the family to the offices the following day for documentation and medical examination. Edward graciously accepted their offer but asked for more time to research and reflect on the possibilities. He would, he told them, return within two weeks.

On his return, Fanni was curious to know what he had discovered. He told her that Henry had been correct and that it was a land of rapid growth and plenty of opportunities. He had also received some pamphlets and documents on South Africa, its history, geography, and demographics, and the two adults studied these with interest. Edward also went to the local library to do further research and made an appointment to see the rabbi at the Great Synagogue to determine whether it was a place that welcomed the Jews. The rabbi confirmed that many Jews had settled in South Africa and that some of the most prominent businessmen in the mining sector were of Jewish origin. There was not, he felt, any danger of finding the sort of religious intolerance the family had found in Russia, and seemed to believe that it was a good place for a larger family to enjoy a good and comfortable lifestyle.

Moving to a new continent was not a small decision, especially to a country where they did not speak the language, and where the majority of the population was not white. It was not the 'Goldene Medina' that was America, but by all accounts, it was a place where opportunities existed, and there seemed to be relative peace in most parts. They found a fairly detailed map, and became familiar with the geography - two British colonies, the Cape and Natal, and two Boer republics, the Transvaal and the Orange Free State - they even found Phillipolis, nestled south of Bloemfontein, the capital of the Orange Free State. Names that they had never heard before now became familiar - Cape Town, Port Elizabeth, Durban, Johannesburg, and they were intrigued by the names of the black tribes - Zulu, Xhosa, Shangaan, Sotho, Tswana - names they could read, but not yet pronounce. They also learned of the animosity that had existed and continued to exist between the English and the Boers that had led to the Boer migration north in the 1830s - The Great Trek. The main languages spoken by the white people were English and Dutch, although it was apparent that while the Dutch spoken in South Africa was a language similar to that spoken in Holland, it had a distinctly local flavor. The family had acquired some knowledge of Flemish while in Belgium, which gave them some confidence that they would find the local Dutch dialect easy to grasp.

After much deliberation, Edward and Fanni decided to tell the children what they were contemplating. They wanted the older boys to go and research the country, and to see how they felt about moving there. Bertha and Albert were still too young, but Jeannot, Bernard, and Max camped out in the library for days trying to find out as much as they could about South Africa. They returned each evening in great excitement, especially about the animals - lions, leopards, hippos, rhinoceroses, buck of tens of species, beautiful birds. Jeannot was fascinated by the wide variety of birds, both of the eating and viewing type, for pheasant and guinea fowl were considered delicacies in Europe. None of the children had spent much time at the seaside, and the long stretches of white sandy beaches were very appealing. All things considered, the verdict from the boys was very positive, and Edward and Fanni were glad they had engendered this interest in the children. It was always easier to sell a new place to people who seemed bent on telling you how great it looked.

And so it was that the Weinberg family reported to the Transvaal delegation offices to prepare for the process of registration and visas. They were told that the process would take a month to be completed, during which time both Edward and Fanni would need to be interviewed by officials in Brussels. It would not, however, be necessary for authorization to be received from South Africa since the delegation was entrusted with the granting of permissions and visas. Edward was told to start inquiring about a passage to South Africa. The most frequent line to South Africa was the Castle Shipping Line that sailed out of Southampton on the south coast of England. Passage to England was by ferry, leaving Dunkirk in northern France and arriving in Dover. Fortunately, there was a Castle Line office in Brussels, and Edward was able to secure passage on the Garth Castle, leaving Southampton on October 29th, 1893, and arriving in Cape Town on November 24th, 1893.

And so it was that a European Jewish family of seven left the shores of England on a journey they could not conceptualize, to a country they did not know, to a future they could not predict, and to a lifestyle they could not imagine.

Chapter 3 - The Journey

Garth Castle - October 1893 - Jeannot

The Garth Castle was built in 1881. It was 365 ft. long, 43 ft. wide and drew 31 ft. in depth. It weighed 3,700 tons. It had a single stack and two tall masts that dwarfed the stack. It had originally been designed to carry 372 passengers, but this was reduced to 98 in 1893 to allow for more cargo space. It was an iron screw steamer, driven by coal-fired boilers, and was capable of a speed of 13 knots in favorable seas. The reduction in the number of passengers was primarily achieved by removing the 3rd class cabins, so the Weinberg family traveled in 2nd class, something of an improvement on what might have been the previous year.

The family had two cabins, one occupied by Edward, Fanni, and Bertha, the other by the four boys. The accommodation was cramped, and while each cabin had a porthole, it was ineffective. When open, it soaked the inhabitants of the cabin with water sloshing in from the sea; when closed, there was very little air, and the cabins were very stuffy. The food was not a great feature of the Garth Castle, especially not in the second-class dining room, but in the early days, this did not matter since everyone except Jeannot and Max was seasick, and food was not high on the priority list. There was a toilet and a bathroom on the second-class level, to be shared among eight cabins. Once up on deck, matters improved. There was plenty of bracing fresh air to be enjoyed if the sea was not too rough, and there were deck games of various types, including cricket. This was a game unfamiliar to the boys, but they soon joined in and learned the rudiments of the game. Jeannot seemed to have particularly good hand-eye coordination and soon became quite proficient at batting. In the evenings, there were plays and concerts arranged for the passengers, and for these, the first- and second-class passengers got to sit in the same area. There was also a library, with books in many languages. Jeannot found a book written by Olive Schreiner called "Story of an African Farm," which was the first novel to come out of South Africa, and was scattered with local terminology. Not only did this book give Jeannot great insight into the country he was about to live in, but it also gave him a sampling of some of the words in commonplace usage.

The book taught Jeannot the difficulties that are encountered when European traditions and cultures are overlaid on a society that has a different heritage. Although only twelve, Jeannot understood that the situation described by the author would apply to him and his family. It would be more difficult for Father and Mama since they were older and had lived in Europe for many years. In the case of the younger children, Bertha and Albert, they were young enough not to have formed any concrete ideas on what it meant to be European. But the three elder boys, aged 12, 11 and 10, were clearly Europeans and were going to be faced with the type of cultural adjustment discussed in the book. If Jeannot knew anything about cultural dislocation, it was this: people in strange countries do not do things in a different way from you simply to be different - they do it because time and experience have taught them that this is the best way to do things in the circumstances in which they find themselves. This can be a difficult adjustment for any child who is strong-willed and believes fiercely in what is right or wrong. In "Story of an African Farm," Jeannot noted the example of Waldo, whose father is deeply religious and imbues him with a sense of right and wrong derived from the Bible, rather than from everyday experience. Jeannot could see how reconciling an ancient book like the Bible with modern society can create issues, and he resolved always to try and see every perspective on an issue. The reading of the book had a profound effect on Jeannot and provided him with a maturity beyond his years. Others may have read the book as a story; Jeannot read it as a guidebook to what he might encounter in his new home.

One afternoon, about three days after the ship passed the equator, Jeannot was walking on the deck when he came across Edward leaning on the deck rail smoking a cigar. Jeannot joined him, and together they stared out at the Atlantic Ocean, in silent wonder at its vastness and seeming endless horizon. Jeannot turned to Edward and started a conversation more serious and insightful than had ever passed between the two of them.

"Father," he said. "I know we are all excited about the prospect of going to a new country, but I know that there are many difficulties we will have to face before we are accepted by the local people and before we become accustomed to their ways. What are your thoughts and concerns about what might happen to us?"

Edward was surprised that a boy of only twelve would be asking such a question. He thought for a minute, then responded. "This is a good question, Jeannot, and one that Mama and I have discussed at length. The first thing that I wonder about is whether I will be able to find a position that will provide me with enough money to be able to provide the family with security and a good and comfortable life. As you know, there have been issues with some of the business ventures I have attempted in the past. I can only hope that I will find something that will enable us to live the kind of life Mama and I have hoped to provide for you and the children. If reports are to be believed, there is plenty of opportunity in this land, and it is my duty to take full advantage of whatever is on offer." Jeannot nodded - clearly, this was the first priority, the essence of success and failure in a new land. "Also, we are concerned about your education. I know the continual moving from place to place has disrupted your school life, and we are determined to achieve the stability that will enable all of you to obtain a good education. I am also concerned about the quality of schooling that will be provided. The schools you attended in Europe were all of a high quality, and, although there were disruptions, we were comfortable that the level of education was more than satisfactory. I do not, however, know whether the schools in South Africa will provide the same educational standards that you enjoyed in Europe, and we can only hope that there are good schools that will help you all to develop a good understanding of the basics you need to venture out into the world." Again, Jeannot nodded his agreement.

"Furthermore, we are going into a strange country, populated by people who are foreign to us, both in language and in culture, and the fact that the white people are so outnumbered by the black folk is a situation we have never encountered before. We will have to learn the ways of all these people and to understand that the way things are done in South Africa is likely to be very different than what we are used to. But I believe there are a few simple rules to follow in order to ensure we get along with everyone. Firstly, we need to be seen as honest and reliable people, people who keep their word and can be trusted to deal fairly with all we meet. Second, we need to remember that people have acquired different customs for a good reason - they clearly work in their circumstances. So we need to respect everyone and learn to understand the differences, rather than simply to reject them because they are strange and different. Thirdly, and perhaps most importantly, we need to remember that everyone on this earth has a place in life that is worthy of our respect, and if men treat you kindly and honestly, it does not matter what their skin color is or what language they speak or what religion they practice, we must show respect to them. Then we have the best chance of them treating us with respect. Remember, every man has his story to tell, and it is very important that we try to listen and understand rather than isolate ourselves. Only in this way will we gain acceptance in this new land."

This insight moved Jeannot deeply. It was a simple lesson that people will treat you as you treat them, and this was a life lesson that Jeannot took to heart. "And remember, too, that we are a family. There is nothing more important than your family. These are the people who will love you and support you in everything you do, and we need to make sure that we never forget who we are and what family we belong to. Your Mama and I will not be around forever, and we need to make sure that we provide the family with unity and a solid foundation with which to face the future. As you know, I am not very religious in the traditional sense, but I do believe that there is a higher force that impacts our lives, and we need to recognize this fact and act accordingly. I don't know if you are familiar with the Greek term 'hubris.' It means the belief that you are superior to the gods and therefore need to rely only on yourself in all you do. Remember that everything in the universe is linked to everything else in the universe. There was an English poet named John Donne who wrote in one of his poems, 'No man is an island, entire of itself; every man is a piece of the continent, a part of the main.' What he was saying was that we all depend on each other, and we need to live in peace and harmony with all our fellow men. Does this make sense to you?" "Yes, it does," said Jeannot. "This is great advice, Father. I am so glad we were able to have this talk." "As am I." replied Edward. "I was hoping to have an opportunity to have a conversation like this with you, because, as the oldest, you will be called on to take on more responsibility than you might have been required to shoulder had we remained in Europe. I have every confidence in you, in your intelligence, in your integrity, and in the way to respond to your family and to others. I am very proud of you, and I see a great future for you in South Africa." Jeannot was moved by this, hugged his father, and as the two men stood on the deck with their arms around each other, both felt a closeness and a bond that would stand them in good stead in their new adventure.

Jeannot would never forget this afternoon, would never forget the wise words of his Father, knew that he would do his best to live up to his father's expectations. He was an independent soul, but this talk always resonated with him when difficulties and crises faced him and the family in the future.

Part 2 – South Africa

Chapter 4 - Early Days

Cape Town - November 20th, 1893 - Bertha

Bertha knew that the long voyage would eventually end and, with it, the sea-sickness, poor food, and cramped lodgings. She had been told by a fellow passenger that the first and most majestic sight on arriving at Cape Town was the incomparable Table Mountain, a large mesa formation about 2 miles wide and 3,500 feet high. He told Bertha that Table Mountain was so iconic that, in the days of the early explorers, the ship captain would give a silver dollar to the first sailor to spy Table Mountain on entering Table Bay. This made a deep impression on the five-year-old, who immediately went to Edward and demanded that the same rule should apply to the family. Edward protested that the ship's captain was unlikely to go along with this, but Bertha was not to be put off. "Then you offer the silver dollar, Father!" she insisted. Edward smiled and agreed, and Bertha went off to tell her brothers of the new opportunity.

It was Bernard who won the silver dollar. Table Mountain was as beautiful as described, and on the day they landed, the wind turned, and the remarkable cloud formation covered the mountain top - the so-called 'table cloth.' Cape Town was not their final destination, but the family was to spend a few days there before reboarding the ship to take them to Port Elizabeth. When the ship pulled up alongside the landing stage, Max jumped off so as to be the first member of the family to set foot on their new homeland. It also happened to be his birthday, so Edward had to shell out another silver dollar to the first person to touch ground in Africa!

Cape Town was a new experience for the family. Never before had they seen such diversity of people and language: white people speaking English or Afrikaans, Coloreds speaking their version of Afrikaans, members of various black tribes speaking their own languages and dialects. It was a regular potpourri of sights, smells, and sounds that fascinated the young travelers from Europe. Horse-drawn tramcars crisscrossed the city street; hawkers sold vegetables and fish, as well as skins and beadwork. Unfamiliar cooking smells emanated from vendor carts and restaurants. Bright colors were everywhere since it was summer, and the sun was shining. And how different the clothing was from Europe, especially that worn by the black peoples. It was almost too much to take in, and the family resolved to spend a vacation in Cape Town as soon as possible.

The ship departed after three days in Cape Town, setting sail for Port Elizabeth, a thriving port about two days' journey east. The ship passed Cape Agulhas, the southernmost point in Africa, reputed for its unpredictable weather, and the passengers were relieved when the ship eventually arrived at their destination.

It was Edward's intention to try and find a business in Port Elizabeth, so the family moved into a furnished house until one was found. It was an awful place, with no water laid on, just a well at the back of the house, reached by a set of rickety stairs that eventually collapsed. The boys rigged up a pulley system to get water to the house, and this made things a bit easier. Fanni had a terrible time of it - strange country, unfamiliar language, and, most important, very indifferent domestic help. She simply could not make herself understood to the black maid, and this caused endless frustration for her. And the mosquitos, oh the mosquitos, an infestation that ate the family alive! It was with great relief that a letter arrived from Orkin in Phillipolis telling Edward of a business opportunity there.

Phillipolis – 1894 – Edward

Phillipolis was a delightful town if something of a sleepy hollow. It was the center of a large and prosperous farming community and was the cradle of some of the Orange Free State's most famous men, including Martinus Steyn, who would eventually become President of the Free State. The village consisted of about four main streets with several side streets leading off. At the top of Main Street was an impressive church, and both sides of the street were lined with beautiful tall shady trees. A furrow of crystal-clear water ran under the street, serving the houses on each side. Every household was allowed an hour a day to irrigate their garden. The houses were built right on the pavement, but all had beautiful gardens at the back that stretched to the next street. The family moved to a house with several acres of land, with dozens of fruit trees - apples, pears, peaches, and three varieties of fig; there was also a quince hedge. The house had its own well for domestic water, and there was a small dam that was used to water the garden and the trees.

Edward's business consisted of a grocery store, a butchery, and a bakery. There was a big brick Dutch oven for baking, and the smells of freshly baked bread permeated the surrounding area. When the bread was out, in went the sheep's head. Those who have never eaten this delicacy cannot begin to imagine how delicious it was.

The people were very agreeable and friendly, and when Fanni gave birth to her first African born child, Leo, the family was inundated with gifts of broth, puddings, stews, and vegetables. They were a sociable group, too, with lots of dances and parties being arranged. At one fancy dress party, Fanni went as a Russian peasant and won first prize. She went to a great deal of trouble to make the dress authentic in every detail, and it was accompanied by a wonderful headdress encrusted with pearls.

There were two schools, and the children attended one of them. It was a large hall in which all the classes were accommodated, all taught by a single teacher with only one assistant. There were also music lessons in the afternoons. The children did not have many toys, and as all country children tend to do, they improvised with what was available - sticks, stones, cotton reels, and the bleached bones of sheep and oxen.

Life was good in Phillipolis, but after two years, it became evident to Edward and Fanni that the education in Phillipolis was not going to be adequate to prepare the children for later life. The decision was made in late 1895 to leave Phillipolis and move to Bloemfontein, where there were better schools and business opportunities.

Bloemfontein - 1895- Edward

Edward had tried many different trades and businesses and was an intelligent and resourceful man. Of his own accord, after doing some research, he discovered a way to distill brandy from mielies (corn, also called maize). Since there was a considerable demand for brandy in the Bloemfontein area, and since the transport costs of bringing spirits from Cape Town were very high, the business was immediately viable. He acquired two partners, Mr. Blum, who was in the distribution business, and Mr. Kruger, who owned a farm in Kaalspruit about 10 miles from Bloemfontein. It was on the farm that Edward created the distillery, and the output was distributed through Blum's network.

The family settled in a good house in Elizabeth Street. The boys attended Grey College, the best boys' school in Bloemfontein, and Bertha attended St. Michael's House, a girls' school opposite to their home.

It had been a long road from Riga, but it seemed that Edward and his family had finally found a place when they could settle down and put behind them the life of peregrination that had been the story of the previous ten years. So Bloemfontein would be their home, and here they would stay.

Chapter 5 – Bloemfontein

Bloemfontein - 1897 - Edward

Edward had made a satisfactory living from the brandy distillery, but when the government raised the excise taxes, it became less profitable, and he had to seek another source of income. His opportunity came from an unusual quarter. In the 1890s, rinderpest had become a serious issue, reaching a head in the Orange Free State in 1896. Rinderpest was a virus affecting domestic and wild animals, especially cattle, which, in the most virulent form, had a 100 percent mortality rate. Rinderpest was an age-old disease in Europe and Asia, and its contagious nature and key symptoms were well understood. The virus in Africa had an incubation period of three to five days in cattle, followed by a rapid rise in temperature, severe mouth lesions during a mucosal phase, depression and anorexia, and severe bloody diarrhea, killing the animal from dehydration. Since cattle farming was one of the principal occupations of many Freestaters, an outbreak of rinderpest was an extremely serious threat to their livelihood.

The resourcefulness of country-folk won out in the end. Farmers in the Free State used folk remedies against the disease that seemed effective, such as soaking wool in bile from infected cattle and inserting it under the skin or in the tail of the animal. Edward had become friendly with a doctor in Bloemfontein, Willy Krause, who was helping the farmers in the district to administer this early form of a vaccine. Due to the heavy demand for inoculation, Willy found himself overworked and asked Edward if he would assist him in administering the vaccine. Edward agreed and soon became extremely proficient at the task, so proficient, in fact, that he discovered an additive to the traditional remedy that considerably cut the rate of mortality. News spread fast, and Edward was in demand from farmers as far afield as Graaff Reinet and Pearson in the Cape Colony. Some farmers were able to pay cash, others, not as fortunate, would offer Edward payment in kind, which he graciously accepted. He built a considerable reputation among the farming community, one that would stand him in good stead in the future. Unfortunately, creating a means of arresting an outbreak of plague is a self-fulfilling prophecy, and once the rinderpest epidemic was under control, Edward needed to look for a new venture.

In the same year as the rinderpest epidemic, a man named Barnard had built a hotel called The Royal on Bloemfontein's Maitland Street. Although not a hotelier himself, Barnard had built the hotel with the intention of leasing it to someone who knew the business. Edward had no hotel experience, but in keeping with his entrepreneurial spirit and his history of entering business areas of which he had no previous understanding, he decided that this would be an ideal opportunity to start a venture that appeared to have the potential for longevity missing in his previous attempts. The brandy business had seriously eaten into his capital, and he was reliant on the money he had earned from the rinderpest inoculation to provide him with working capital. So, purchasing the hotel was not an option, but a lease gave him the financial flexibility he sought.

The hotel was a typical Victorian structure, two stories with a flat roof, and beautiful wrought iron work around the corners of the balconies that ran the length of the building on the upper and lower floors. It was gray in color, with white balconies and white sash windows surrounded by white friezes. The contrast between the gray and white gave it an imposing look. It had 15 rooms, ten on the upper floor, and three on the lower, with a bathroom for every three rooms. The bedrooms were tastefully decorated with two beds and nightstands, oak armoire and chest of drawers, oak desk and chair, and a wrought iron washstand with a white ceramic basin. The walls had wallpaper of the period, and these blended with the bed linens and the floor coverings. Each room had a stone fireplace. Mama had a flair for decorating, and the rooms were warm, comfortable, and inviting. It was her great joy to ensure that any room that was occupied had fresh flowers on the desk every day.

The public areas consisted of a reception area with an oak desk and a rack of pigeon holes that housed the keys, a bar, a parlor, and a dining room. The bar had a long oak counter with stools and a brass rail on which customers could rest their feet. Beer on tap was available, as well as fine wines and spirits. The bar was a very popular meeting place for burghers after the working day, and it proved to be one of the most profitable parts of the hotel. Because it was still unusual for women to drink in the bar, there was an adjoining parlor, tastefully decorated with flock wallpaper and comfortable chairs, where women could gather and enjoy a drink brought to them by a waiter.

But it was the dining room that was Edward's delight. Being something of a gourmet, he personally supervised every menu and planned every event. The Free State was blessed with outstanding meats, both domestic and wild, and Edward made sure that there was always beef, mutton, and venison on every menu. Produce was also fresh and plentiful, and this complemented the steaming meat dishes prepared by the chef. The chef had once worked in a patisserie, so desserts were a fine end to every meal. The dining room had an outstanding reputation, and people came from many miles to enjoy Edward's table. In fact, Edward could only remember one complaint about the food. An elderly farmer from a district not far from Bloemfontein had spent the night at the hotel while in town to buy goods for the farm. As he was checking out, Edward, as was his wont with all guests, asked him if everything was alright during his stay. The man nodded but looked unconvinced. "Do you have any complaints?" asked Edward. "Only one," replied the man. "The breakfast." "The breakfast!" exclaimed Edward. Breakfast was one of the hotel's best meals - a variety of fruits and fruit juices, porridges, eggs, various breakfast meats, scones, toast, coffee, and many more dishes. "What is wrong with the breakfast?" "Man," said the farmer, "I really could not eat as much as you offered!" The poor fellow thought he was required to eat every dish on the menu! Edward assured him that this was not the case, and the man left satisfied.

The clientele came mostly from the surrounding areas, but some came from further afield. Edward's work assisting farmers with the rinderpest had made him well known in a wide area, and when these folks found out about the hotel, they made a point of staying at the Royal in appreciation of all that Edward had done to help them.

The management of the hotel was divided between Edward, Fanni, and a manager by the name of Carel van der Horst. It was Fanni who saw to the housekeeping, ensuring the rooms were clean, beds made, sheets changed for new guests, and similar tasks. Edward, being hearty, friendly, and congenial, was responsible for guest relations, ensuring those who stayed at the hotel were happy with their accommodation, and those who ate and drank there were provided with a good table and efficient and prompt service. He would spend much of his time talking with guests, advising them on things to do in Bloemfontein, and generally making them feel welcome. All the rest was left to Van der Horst.

Carel van der Horst was a Hollander who had come to South Africa ten years earlier after his wife died. With no children to support, and nearing the age of fifty, he decided that Holland no longer offered him any prospects, so he decided to see if he could build a new home and career in South Africa. He was a thick-set man with an erect bearing and a solemn face. He had one peculiar physical characteristic that fascinated everyone who met him, especially the younger children. His hair was snow-white, but his prodigious mustache was jet black. When asked how this came to be, van der Horst, not known for his humor, would smile and say. "My hair is white, and my mustache is black because my hair is 20 years older than my mustache!" He would then give a little chuckle and return to what he was doing. He was a strict Calvinist, and every Sunday would be seen in his Sunday best attending the Tweetoring Kerk, the Dutch Reformed Church on St. George Street in his best black suit. Always immaculately attired in a three-piece suit and wing collar, even on those days when Bloemfontein sweltered in the summer heat, he was scrupulously honest and diligent to the point of seeming almost fussy. Edward relied on him very heavily to organize things like purchasing, inventory, bookkeeping, wages, and general staff management. Every evening he would produce a report for the day, showing revenues received from accommodations, restaurant, and bar, and costs both expended and to be expended on future orders, as well as the bank and savings balance. Never was a penny missing, never did a ledger not balance. Van der Horst was extremely proficient in what he did and was generously rewarded by Edward for his efforts.

The business did well. Edward understood the needs of his clientele, as well as those of his employees. He believed that everyone should be remunerated fairly, even somewhat generously, since he set great store by loyalty and happiness among his staff. The result was that once people came to work at the Royal Hotel, few left unless circumstances required. Edward could not remember when he had last been forced to dismiss an employee or to give a serious reprimand. The level of order and discipline maintained by van der Horst prevented the majority of issues from percolating up to Edward, so he was left free to be his congenial self and mix with his guests.

The family did not live in the hotel but in an annex built in the hotel grounds, intended as a residence for the manager. It had four bedrooms and two bathrooms, a sitting room and a tiny kitchen to prepare snacks and drinks. The family always took their meals in the hotel dining room. The master bedroom was occupied by Edward and Fanni. Jeannot and Bernard shared one bedroom, with Max, Albert, and Leo sharing the other. Bertha, as the only daughter, had her own room. When Louis was born in July of 1899, he slept in the bedroom with his parents.

The boys attended Grey College, and Bertha was a student at Greenhill Convent after St Michael's House. The boys excelled in most sports but were particularly fond of cricket and rugby. All were intelligent and proved to be more than capable scholars. Bertha shared her father's love for music, and, quite fortuitously, a Hollander by the name of Uitenbroek was a permanent resident at the hotel. He had been the bandmaster in the Regiment Infanterie Oranje Gelderland and was an accomplished violinist. It was he that taught Bertha to play the violin, a skill at which she became sufficiently proficient to play at local concerts.

Life was comfortable for the family during this period. The business was doing well, the children were receiving a good education, and the town of Bloemfontein was prospering. It was the calm before the storm.

Chapter 6 - Johannesburg

Bloemfontein - December 18, 1897 - Jeannot

The school term had ended at Grey College, and Jeannot had graduated from high school with honors. There now lay ahead of him the balmy days of the Free State summer, days of sunshine and little rain, but with plenty to keep a young man of 16 occupied. But Jeannot had other ideas. One afternoon as the sun was starting to sink, he approached Edward and requested a private discussion with his father in the office. Edward was perplexed. This was not something he had been expecting. But Jeannot was insistent, and the two men repaired to Edward's office with glasses of cool lemonade that the barman excelled at. When they had sat and exchanged some small talk, Jeannot began.

"Father, now that I have finished high school, I am curious to know what you have in mind for me from a career point of view." Edward thought for a moment, then replied. "Jeannot, you are a capable and educated man, and I thought it would be appropriate for you to enroll at the university in Cape Town and further your studies. Do you have something else in mind?" Jeannot shifted restlessly in his chair and stared at the floor. "Well, son, out with it." demanded his father. "Father, I think it is an excellent idea to continue my studies, but before I do this, I would like to have a year of 'adventuring.'" "Adventuring? Tell me more." "Well," continued Jeannot "I have often wanted to go and see Johannesburg, and to find out first-hand what the city is like and how it operates. Bloemfontein is a pretty *dorp* (town), but it is a bit of a sleepy hollow, and I really want to experience the hustle and bustle that I believe I will find in Johannesburg." "And where would you live? And how would you earn a living?" his father demanded. "I thought that perhaps I could live with Uncle Henry and Aunt Sarah, and perhaps get a job in Uncle Henry's store." Edward raised an eyebrow. This was clearly not something that Jeannot had come up with on the spur of the moment. "And have you been in communication with Uncle Henry without my knowledge?" Jeannot nodded slowly, aware that his actions may have been inappropriate. "Actually, I have been writing to him for the past few months, and he and Aunt Sarah are very supportive of the idea." Edward whistled through his teeth. "You little scoundrel! So, you have been going behind my back and making arrangements about which I have no idea, and for which you did not ask my permission?" Jeannot nodded again, his eyes seemingly fixed on a small knot on the wooden floor. Edward sat back in his chair and folded his hands across his waistcoat. "Hah," he said. "So, you have gone ahead and set this up in the hope you could persuade me to agree?" "Yes, father," said Jeannot, his voice barely audible.

Edward looked at the ceiling and pondered the situation. While he was not too happy with the way Jeannot had gone about it, he secretly applauded the boy for his audacity. And besides, the boy was only sixteen, probably too young to be going to university, and a stint in Johannesburg would probably give him a more worldly experience than he could hope to achieve here in Bloemfontein. He allowed Jeannot to stew for a while in his anxiety, and then he looked at him, a broad smile on his face. "You young *skelm* (scoundrel)," he said. "You have given me a difficult decision, but to be fair, I think a year in Johannesburg might do you some good." Jeannot relaxed visibly, his shoulders returning to their usual position. "But we will obviously have to ask Mama's opinion. I am open to the suggestion, but if she says no, then it is no." "Can we ask her quickly?" demanded Jeannot. "Slow down, young man. I will talk to her after dinner this evening, and I will let you know our decision later tonight. You are sure that Henry and Sarah are agreeable to this harebrained scheme of yours?" "Absolutely certain, Father. I can show you the letters if you like." "Not necessary," retorted Edward. "I trust you. Come and see me here in the office at 8.30 tonight, and I will tell you what we have decided."

The following three hours were as slow as Jeannot could ever remember time passing. He tried to decipher his father's mood during dinner, would not, of course, dare to raise the subject. At last, the appointed time came, and Jeannot joined his father in the office. "So you want to go to Johannesburg and become a city boy?" he inquired. "Yes, Father," he replied. "Well, Mama and I are very concerned for your safety. Johannesburg is not a particularly safe place for a young man on his own. There are plenty of undesirable types there, and we would not want you to get hurt or mixed up in anything you cannot handle." Jeannot looked crestfallen. "However." his father continued. "If you promise not to court any sort of trouble, and if you follow the advice and guidance of Henry and Sarah, and if you comport yourself as the gentleman we have tried to teach you to be, then we will allow you to go on this 'adventure' of yours." Jeannot leaped from his chair and gave his father a hug. "Thank you, Father. Thank you. This is too wonderful of you both." Edward smiled and said, "Now, just you be careful to downplay this with the younger children, or the next thing we will find is an exodus from Bloemfontein of another little band of adventure seekers!" "You have my word, Father. I cannot thank you and Mama enough." "We would like you to remain with us for Christmas and New Year so the family can be together, and then you can make plans to travel to Johannesburg in mid-January." Jeannot nodded, almost unable to retain his composure. This was something he had dreamed about, and now it had become a reality. "That sounds fair," he said. "It will give me time to get my things together and also give Uncle Henry and Aunt Sarah time to prepare for my arrival. Will you be writing to them to let them know?" "I will write to Henry first thing in the morning. Now off you go and say your thank you to Mama."

Johannesburg - 1897 - Henry Orkin

Henry and Sarah Orkin lived in the burgeoning suburb of Doornfontein just northeast of the city center. It was an up and coming area, with a population from many countries, but it was usually thought of as being a Jewish neighborhood. The presence of several synagogues, Jewish religious schools, and kosher restaurants underlined this thinking. The inhabitants were mostly middle class, although some of the more affluent Johannesburgers were starting to build homes there. The shops and restaurants were crowded and busy, and it was said that, if you really wanted to know where the major business deals were done in the Jewish community, you should make a note of who ate lunch together at Wachenheimer's Kosher Delicatessen on a Friday!

The Orkin home stood on the corner of Beit and Sherwell Streets. It was a one-story house with a corrugated roof, yellow brick walls, and a small garden out front where Sarah had planted flowers and shrubs. It had three bedrooms, a bathroom, a kitchen, and a living room/dining room. The front garden had a low white picket fence, and there was a front *stoep* (porch) where one could sit and watch the passersby. It was modestly but comfortably furnished, and Jeannot was given his own bedroom, an exciting prospect since it was the first time since he was about three years old that he had not had to share with one of his brothers. His aunt and uncle were very warm and welcoming, and Jeannot felt very much at home with them. Henry was a cousin of Fanni, and he and Sarah had come to South Africa about the same time as Edward and the family. Unlike the other Orkins who had settled in Phillipolis, Henry and Sarah had come directly to Johannesburg. Henry had some savings that he had invested in both the house and his business. He made a comfortable living, and both were respected members of the Doornfontein community.

Henry ran a dry goods store on Bree Street in the downtown area.

In the days before refrigeration, dry goods stores carried a range of merchandise that did not need to be frozen or refrigerated. These included such foodstuffs as dried beans, flour, mielie meal (corn flour), other dried grains, and vegetables, to mention but a few. He also stocked household items like soap, cleaners, brooms, mops, and some linens, as well as a range of tobacco products. His clientele was varied, from miners to bankers, and he made a point of knowing his good customers by name. The economy of Johannesburg was thriving, and Henry's small business was carried along on this wave.

This was the environment in which Jeannot began his first adult job. His role was to maintain the cleanliness and orderliness of the store, arrange the merchandise on the shelves and keep a set of records that showed when inventory was getting low and would need to be replenished. When the store was busy, he would help Henry dealing with customers, a task he both liked and at which he excelled. Jeannot was an extroverted young man, eager to talk to whoever would give him an ear, and with a thirst to know and understand what was going on around him. The cosmopolitan nature of Johannesburg made it an ideal venue for him since he was able to meet and converse with people from many parts of the world, and many differing statuses in life. It was the kind of education one cannot obtain at a school or university; it was an education in life, and it was to stand Jeannot in excellent stead when he encountered difficulties in his future life.

Weekends were also exciting. There was a sports stadium, The Wanderers, near the downtown station, where cricket was played in summer and rugby in winter. Both were passions for Jeannot, and, although he was a bit young to participate, he was an enthusiastic spectator, aficionado, and critic. There were also many parts of Johannesburg to be explored, and it was not uncommon for Jeannot to borrow Henry's bicycle and to ride to many different parts of the city to explore and understand. He was particularly fascinated by the concept of deep-level mining. The majority of other gold rushes throughout the world were either alluvial fields or fields in which the gold was found quite near to the surface. In South Africa, however, the seam of gold was encased in hard rock beneath the surface and had to be removed by deep-level mining techniques. Literally, tons of gold-bearing rock was excavated, hauled to the surface, ground up, and passed through a chemical process to extract the gold. The remainder of the rock that was no longer required was piled up in enormous artificial hills called mine dumps. These dumps, each of which looked like a miniature version of Table Mountain, soon became a regular feature of the Johannesburg landscape, as did the mining headgear equipment with its enormous steel wheel and engine that lowered steel cages full of miners from the surface to the mining face, and then brought them aloft at the end of their shift. Jeannot found this intriguing. There were two main types of miners - black and white. The black miners tended to do the more physical work - hacking away the gold-bearing rock from the face and loading it into small underground rail cars for eventual transportation to the surface. All the tribes in South Africa were represented in the mines - Zulu, Xhosa, Sotho, Shangaan, and many others, as well as from beyond the northern border like Shona and Matabele. Many spoke different languages, but a patois soon developed that enabled miners to communicate among themselves as well as with the white miners. White miners occupied skilled professions like engineering, surveying, and geology, but also developed into an overseer class, ensuring that the black miners performed their work in an efficient and orderly fashion.

White miners and other residents who were not from the Transvaal Republic or any other state or colony in Southern Africa were known as *Uitlanders* or 'outlanders.' They consisted mainly of British, but there was a healthy contingent of Germans, French, Americans, Australians, and other countries around the world. And they came in such numbers that there was a fear among the

Transvaal government that they would quickly outnumber the Transvaal burghers. Had the Uitlanders been given equal political rights, it could have caused a shift in the political status quo with the burghers losing their hold on the governing of the Transvaal. This was anathema to the President, Paul Kruger, who sought to protect the culture and lifestyle of the Boer Republic and did not want to see it turned over to a group of people with political views incompatible with his own. Since the Uitlanders came from countries where their democratic rights were protected, it was unsurprising that they began to chafe under this restrictive regime. The future seemed inevitable. Unless the Uitlanders were given adequate representation, the Transvaal would quickly become a powder keg where a small spark cast into the combustible fuel of discontent could have disastrous consequences.

Johannesburg - May 16, 1898 – Jeannot

It was 5 o'clock, and Henry locked the doors of the store. "Are you coming, Jeannot?" he inquired. "No, Uncle Henry. I think I am going to stay downtown and have a drink and something to eat. Please tell Aunt Sarah I won't be home for dinner. See you in the morning."

Jeannot walked from the store on Bree Street to a well-patronized beer garden on Harrison Street called The Phoenix, where massive German wurst and beer by the liter were served on simple wooden tables. The waiter was a stout old German man who appeared to know no English but was perpetually in a bad mood. His trademark was his thumb - this was used to ensure that the complementary slices of rye bread did not slip off the plate. Every guest also got a complimentary bowl of potato soup when ordering a meal - this, too, was steadied by the waiter's ubiquitous thumb.

The place was humming when Jeannot arrived at 5.30 pm. It was filled with an eclectic mix of customers: miners, artisans, bankers, professionals, virtually all of them men, nearly all of them sipping on great steins of lager. Jeannot went to the bar to get a beer. As he turned from the bar, beer in hand, he was jostled by another guest, and his drink spilled to the floor. The man was of medium height, slightly built with brown curly hair and spectacles. "I say, old chap. I am most frightfully sorry. My fault entirely. Come, let me replace your drink." He stuck out his right hand and said, "Tony Roberts. London." Jeannot transferred the now empty beer glass to his left hand and shook the stranger's hand. "Jeannot Weinberg. Bloemfontein." "I am here with a group of disreputables whom you might like to meet. Will you join us at our table?" asked Roberts. Jeannot said he would be delighted, and followed his new friend to a dark wooden table with benches at which sat five other men, all who seemed, like Roberts, to be in their thirties.

Roberts announced, "Gentlemen, I have captured a native! Say hello to Jeannot Weinberg from Bloemfontein." A sunburned man with a slightly hooked nose and straight brown hair was the first to offer his hand. "John Jones. London." They all followed his example - Jeremy Levison from London, Richard Davis from Andover, Massachusetts, Heinrich Penzhorn from Stuttgart, and Eddie Rouillard from Mauritius. Jeannot was impressed with the cosmopolitan nature of the group. "So, you are all *uitlanders*," he said. They nodded. "And what brings you to Johannesburg, young Mr. Weinberg?" asked Jones. "Well," said Jeannot "I finished high school last December and felt like having an adventure, so I persuaded my parents to allow me to come to Johannesburg to work with my uncle Henry Orkin who runs the dry goods store on Bree Street, "Orkin's" by name," Penzhorn spoke for the first time. "I know it well. I shop there sometimes." Jeannot switched to German. "And I recognize you, Herr Penzhorn. You smoke a beautifully carved Meerschaum pipe and visit us every Friday for 6 oz. of our Latakia mix and a box of matches. Am I correct?" "Himmel," answered Penzhorn. "You are absolutely correct. But your German, it is perfect. How can this be?" Jeannot laughed. "I was born and raised in Riga in Latvia. We spoke Russian and

German in that country, but my tongue at home and school was German." "Interesting," remarked Levison, "But you speak a pretty decent rendition of the Queen's if you don't mind me saying. Where did you learn English?" "Four years of high school at an English medium school, I suppose. My accent is far from perfect, but I feel confident in speaking it."

"And what school did you attend?" asked Roberts. "Grey College in Bloemfontein," replied Jeannot. "Fine school," said Levison. "Roberts here was at Mill Hill, Jones at St. Paul's, and I was at Charterhouse," Davis spoke for the first time. "Why is it that you English always set so much store by the high school someone attended. Isn't university the more important criterion?" "Spoken like a true American," said Roberts. "No, my good fellow, high school is where your value system is developed. And your intellect, sure, but it is the training of the moral fiber that is done at school. So just by asking someone which school he went to will allow you to know instantly whether he is a jolly good chap or a frightful scoundrel!". Davis just stared at him and raised his forefinger to his head, simulating blowing out his brains. "You English are really special, aren't you," he said. "Damn right," replied Roberts. "If you chaps hadn't gone bonkers in the 1770s and kicked us out of your part of North America because you wanted to be a republic or something silly like that, you might have had the potential to become a meaningful country someday," Davis repeated his brain-blowing gesture, and everyone laughed.

"I say," said Jones, turning to Jeannot. "Play any cricket at Grey College?" "Yes, indeed," replied Jeannot enthusiastically. "Opening bowler for the First XI and a reasonable number 7 batsman, although I did tend to chase balls outside the off stump." "Splendid!" said Jones "We are all cricketers here, most of us with a great future behind us. I mean the English only, of course. The Germans and the French don't have the patience for the game, and the Americans don't have the intelligence to understand it. Roberts and I played against each other when we were at school. He was a wicketkeeper, and his nickname was 'The Ancient Mariner.'" Jeannot knew the poem by Samuel Taylor Coleridge, but could not make the connection. He looked quizzically at Jones. "Don't you remember the famous line 'he stoppeth one of three'? Well, that about sums up Roberts's wicketkeeping prowess." All laughed. Roberts retorted, "Only a churl would say something so beastly about one's embarrassing past. The remark of a churl, but with a modicum of truth, I'm afraid." Davis leaned back in his chair and said, "Churl....churl....wonderful word, that. Not much used where I come from. Must remember to use it sometime. Churl, a boorish and uncouth individual. And 'boorish' is spelt 'b-o-o-r-i-s-h' rather than 'b-o-e-r-i-s-h'. No offense meant." "None taken," said Jeannot.

Levison now entered the fray. "Ah, yes, America. Wonderful country if it weren't populated by Americans. I'm afraid I'm on the side of Oscar Wilde when he said that America was the only country to go from barbarism to decadence without a period of civilization in between." Everyone laughed again, and Jones slapped Davis on the back. "Present company excluded, of course, old chap." Davis raised an eyebrow. It was clear to Jeannot that these men were very comfortable with one another, knew each other well, and were unfazed by the ribbing and laughter. He wanted to know more.

"It seems that you are all good friends here," he said. "Have you known each other long?" Rouillard spoke for the first time, in a softly accented English distinguishable as being of French origin, but not of a resident of France. "Most of us work for the same company, Consolidated Goldfields. Davis is a mining engineer, Levison, a lawyer, Penzhorn, an electrical engineer, I am a chemical engineer, and the Almighty alone knows what Jones does, yet he still seems to get paid! Something about provisioning or such like. Roberts is the only one who doesn't work with us. He is a journalist who sells his stories to various English newspapers. We have all been here for about five years and have become close friends, both at work and socially." Jeannot was captivated by the fact that these men from different backgrounds and skills could come together in the melting pot called Johannesburg, and meld together into a robust and coherent unit. Gold, he supposed, had that effect on people.

At this stage, the waiter wandered over. Nobody knew his name; in fact, there was some doubt he had one. "Any food?" Conversation was not his long suit. "What's good tonight?" asked Penzhorn. "Nothing," grumbled the man. "No change." "Shall we say bratwurst and potatoes for everyone and another round of beer. Is that acceptable?" All nodded, and the waiter wandered away, mumbling to himself. Jeannot said, "It is very kind of you to include me in your party. I am a lot younger than all of you, and I am keen to hear about your experiences." "Nonsense, young Weinberg. We are intrigued by you and the decision of your family to move here. By the way, does the name 'Weinberg' indicate a member of the tribe of Abraham?" Jeannot nodded. "Splendid!" said Levison. "Me too. Good to find a *landsman* in a far-off land." Jeannot smiled and said, "Mr. Jones, you said you were from London but isn't Jones a Welsh name? Does your family originally come from Wales?" "Interesting conjecture, young Weinberg," replied Jones. "But incorrect. My family is, in fact, originally from Holland. We moved to England in the late eighteenth century. The name was Jonas then, but when all the shenanigans with Napoleon and his gang started up, and when Holland threw in their lot with the damned French (he glanced at Rouillard and winked), the old man decided Jonas probably didn't give off the correct odor, so he changed it to Jones. So no, my new friend, I am not Welsh, nor can I sing!"

"Another thing," observed Jeannot. "Even though you are good friends, you call each other by the surname rather than the first name. Why is that?" "Ah," said Roberts "It's a peculiarly English thing and comes from the public school system. When you first meet a chap, you call him by his surname. When you get to know him a little better, you start calling him by his first name. Then when he becomes a real chum of yours, you go back to using the surname. Strange, I suppose, but seems to work for us." Davis again made the shooting gesture with his finger. Jeannot was intrigued. "So you are calling me Weinberg because we are sort of at stage one of the process. Then you will progress to calling me Jeannot, and when you go back to calling me Weinberg, I will know I have been accepted as your friend. Fascinating!"

The waiter returned with their food and drinks, and they began to eat. Jeannot asked, "You fellows have been here for five years now. What are your thoughts about Johannesburg and the Transvaal?" Jones almost choked on his wurst. "Do you want the party line, or do you really want to know how we feel?" "The latter, I think," said Jeannot. "Well," Jones continued, "There are so many things that are wrong here that it would take all night to tell you about it. Take taxes, for example. We are taxed far more heavily than the Transvaal citizens - at some income levels, almost 90% goes to the government. And we get very little to show for our contributions to the Transvaal Treasury. From what we are given to understand, The Turgid Transvaal Toad spends most of it on armaments!" "By Turgid Toad, I am assuming you are referring to President Paul Kruger," Jeannot said. "Exactly," said Jones. "Have you taken a look around at the shithole we live in. No water pipes, no proper drains, diseases not known to Western medicine. Don't you think we deserve better than this when we are responsible for over 80% of all taxes collected by The Toad." "Adding to that" interjected Levison, "We do not have any right to vote, nor do we have any representation in the Volksraad, which is full of The Toad's buddies who think just like him." "So we are talking about taxation without representation, I guess," observed Jeannot. "Precisely, my young Boer friend. Precisely." At this point, Davis leaned forward. "So what I am hearing here is a bunch of Brits complaining about taxation without representation, no? That's pretty rich, considering you had no compunction about doing the same thing to the Americans in the last century. Smacks of a bit of hypocrisy, I would suggest." "All I can say to that," said Roberts, "is that we now know how you buggers must have felt, and, believe me, it isn't pretty."

Penzhorn joined the discussion. "I am married, and I have three children of school-going age. But the government here allocates virtually no funding to provide schools for *uitlander* children, especially when compared with what they provide for Boer children. There is just no fairness in the whole thing. Why take out your dislike of *uitlanders* on innocent children - they've done nothing to Kruger and his henchmen?" "Well said, Heinie," said Jones. "I have two children, and I feel exactly the same way." "But aren't there municipal authorities here in Johannesburg you could appeal to?" Rouillard chuckled. "The most corrupt bunch of thieves I have ever seen. *Merde* (shit)[2], if I were to shake hands with one of them, I would count my fingers afterwards. They have an interest in one thing and one thing only – *balle* (money). If you are prepared to come with a bribe, then perhaps you might have a chance to get something done. Without it, you are *baisée* (screwed)." "And the law doesn't offer any protection?" asked Jeannot. "Oh sure, if you are a Boer. Only they can sit on juries; only they can pass legislation in the Volksraad, only they get to have a say in what is legal and what is not. Some of the judges are not too bad, but what chance do you think an Uitlander stands in front of a jury of Boers?" Roberts added, "Another thing that gets up my nose is the ridiculous tariffs and restrictions the government puts on things like dynamite and liquor - it's outrageous! Isn't it enough they fleece us with taxes - now they get us on purchases of essentials? It is hardly surprising that their revenues have gone from about 150,000 pounds in 1886 to 4 million last year!" "But, can't you take any action to redress this, and what about the press?" asked Jeannot. "The current government in the Transvaal is about as democratic as Attila the Hun. No way will we get anywhere with that kind of approach," said Davis. "And our situation was not improved by Jameson and his friends - The Toad is now completely anti-Uitlander, and there seems nothing we can do to stop him. We even tried some very mildly worded petitions, but those got scant notice - wonder if he even read them!"

Jeannot was nonplussed by the conversation he had just heard. He had been aware that there had been friction between Kruger and the Uitlanders, and he knew that the Boers thought them to be a bunch of ingrates who never stopped whining about how badly they were being treated, but this gave him a new perspective on the issues. If this was allowed to continue, and if Oom Paul (Uncle Paul, as President Kruger was often called) didn't try to meet these people halfway, who knew what the consequences might be? And it was not as if these men he had just met were a group of lowlifes and ne'er-do-wells. These were educated, respectable men who had come to South Africa to make a career for themselves, and, in doing so, would undoubtedly benefit the country as a whole and the Transvaal in particular. He resolved to discuss it with Uncle Henry as soon as the opportunity arose. It was now 10 pm, and Jeannot decided it was time to go home. He thanked the men for their kindness, said how much he had enjoyed their company, and hoped they would all have an opportunity to meet up again in the near future. With that, he set out to walk back to Doornfontein and Henry and Sarah's house.

When Jeannot arrived home, it was 11 pm. Uncle Henry had not gone to bed but was sitting in the living reading a book, smoking a cigar, and enjoying a glass of brandy. When Jeannot came in, he beckoned to him to sit, fetched a brandy for Jeannot, and gave him a cigar. Jeannot told him about his evening, how he had met up with the group of Uitlanders, and the discussions that they'd had. Henry listened intently, and when Jeannot had finished, he sat back in his chair, took a long draw on the brandy, and spoke. "It sounds like you have had a most interesting and illuminating evening. And I can see from your demeanor and your tale that you are not entirely comfortable with the situation. Let me give you my take on it. Firstly, I think you were very fortunate to meet such a good group of men. These are clearly men of caliber and education, and I am glad you became somewhat friendly with them. But you must not lose sight of the fact that the vast majority of the Uitlanders are not quality individuals like these fellows. Many of them are dishonest and tricky, and this is not the first place in which these men have plied their trade. Many are from the criminal underbelly of Europe who have come here to see what new victims they can dupe and rob. So while I am sympathetic with your friends, I do not have the same feelings towards those who have come here for less than honest reasons." He drew on his cigar and continued.

"You must also remember that there are now as many, if not more, of them than the Transvaal burghers. And Oom Paul - by the way, I love their nickname for him; he really does look like a giant toad! - is all too aware that enfranchising these people is going to result in him and the burghers losing control of the Volksraad. Once this happens, it is the end for them - the Uitlanders will rule the country in a way that ensures that they and they alone become wealthy off the Transvaal's gold reserves. Now Oom Paul has offered them enfranchisement after five or seven years - I can't remember off the top of my head - but this is not acceptable to these people. They are used to living in a democratic society in their home countries, and they are chafing under the restrictions placed on them. And I have some sympathy for their plight. But you need to also look at it from the burghers' point of view. These are the descendants of the Voortrekkers; actually, some are not descendants but were trekkers themselves, Oom Paul among them. These people left the Cape because they wanted to rule themselves according to a set of laws that they were familiar with, and which suited their lifestyle and beliefs. They trekked north to get away from British law and British justice, and they will do everything in their power not to return to the hegemony of England. The trek was monumental in their history - they were citizens who had settled lives and livelihoods, but were prepared to give all of that up to trek to an inhospitable hinterland, just to be able to rule themselves. People like that do not give up these rights easily. They are a proud and stubborn people, quite like the Jews in many ways, and they simply will not be told what to do by people who do not think and act as they do," He took another sip of brandy and continued.

"The big danger is the fact that so many of the Uitlanders - I would estimate at least 75% - are English. And we know that the English and their little puppet Rhodes are itching to get control of the goldfields. They tried to tempt Kruger into a war by sending that idiot Jameson on that pathetically unsuccessful raid a few years ago, and I believe that Rhodes, Milner, and Chamberlain are, as we speak, conspiring as to the best way to get Kruger to declare war on them. And I believe that they will leverage the *uitlander* question to make this a reality. Britain has long felt the need to come to the assistance of its citizens who are unfairly treated in other countries - why, I don't know - surely, and this is the logic that Oom Paul uses, if they come to a foreign country, they must expect to live under the laws and regulations of that country. If you are not prepared to do this, then you should go back to your own country. So you can see that the situation is very delicately poised at present. Kruger doesn't want a war, even though he has been buying arms like there was no tomorrow. He knows that the Boer Republics cannot withstand the military might of the entire British Empire - my goodness, they could mobilize ten times the number of troops than we have men, women, children, and oxen in the Transvaal and Free State. We might win a few skirmishes as we did during the war in 1880 and 1881, but in the long run, if the British put their mind to it, there is very little Kruger can do to stop them. We Jews are sort of in the middle. We do not owe allegiance to any of the European powers anymore, so our only choices are to remain neutral or to throw in our lot with the Boers. I don't think the former will sit well with the Boers - even if the war is lost, they will still have a place here, and they have a long memory for those who did not come to their aid. But to fight for them against an enemy we don't really have any animosity towards also seems like a difficult choice. Fortunately, my boy, I am too old to have to worry about that, but for you, it is going to present a major decision. I only hope you do the right thing in terms of your own soul. And now this old man is going to bed - I will see you at breakfast tomorrow."

Jeannot lay awake for a long time, perplexed by the arguments and counter-arguments that had flooded his mind in the past seven hours. He knew that he would need to come down on one side or the other, knew his life and future could depend on how he chose, but what was the right course of action? He resolved to discuss it with Father at the next opportunity. Finally, he fell asleep, his mind still spinning with all the new challenges.

Chapter 7 – Swaziland

The Transvaal Republic was not the only place in the area to be suffering from political upheavals. In the late 1890s, the Transvaal's northeastern neighbor, Swaziland, was also in the grips of a political crisis, and ironically provided Jeannot with his first taste of what was to come.

Ngwane V (also known as Bhunu) ascended to the throne of Swaziland in 1895 when he was only sixteen years old after a short regency of Queen Mother Tibati Nkambule. Bhunu became the king after the Swaziland Convention of 1894, which had led to the classification of Swaziland as a protected state of the South African Republic, then led by President Paul Kruger.

Bhunu's rule was very short, but dramatic. The Swaziland Convention of 1894 had ensured that some institutions in Swaziland were reserved particularly for European interests, such as the concessionaires and other white settlers. The concessions were strictly enforced, and Bhunu and Queen Mother were paid a stipend or proceeds from administrative revenues such as postal service, taxes, and concession agreements. These taxes were collected from Swazi residents, which meant that many had to seek employment in the tin and gold mines within the Kingdom or in the numerous mines of the South African Republic. The Transvaal authority in Swaziland was never fully implemented, and Swazis continued to be directly ruled by traditional methods.

In 1897 Bhunu allegedly ordered the killing of the royal governor and his collaborators. "Killing off" was a way of removing potential competitors for the throne, and was much used in Africa to cement the authority of the ruler. This arbitrary demonstration of total judicial power was unacceptable to the Transvaal authorities, and so, as a result, Bhunu was prosecuted. He first fled to Zululand, which was under British Natal administration at the time. His return occurred after guarantees for his safety, after which he was to be tried in court in Bremersdorp, the seat of Transvaal authority in Swaziland. Bhunu brought with him to court a sizeable Swazi army, and this was of concern to the authorities in the Transvaal, who were worried about possible violence at the trial. To combat this risk, a commando was created to go to Bremersdorp and counterbalance the threat of the Swazi army.

Johannesburg - June 1, 1897 – Jeannot

Jeannot was serving behind the counter one afternoon in early summer when a young man came bursting in the door of the shop. It was Jannie Retief, an Afrikaner lad Jeannot had gotten to know from watching rugby at the Wanderers. He was a few years older than Jeannot and spoke little English.

"Jeannot," he exclaimed in Afrikaans. "Did you hear the news from Swaziland?"

Jeannot shook his head. "No. What's going on?"

"They are putting the king on trial for murder, and the belief is that he will arrive at the trial with his army," said Jannie.

"Not a bad way of ensuring that justice is done, except if you are the accused!" quipped Jeannot.

Retief continued. "So now Kruger is putting together a commando to send to Swaziland to counterbalance this Swazi army and make sure old Bhunu doesn't get up to any mischief." "And," he said breathlessly. "I am going to join up. The commando is gathering in Pretoria during the week and will leave for Swaziland soon after that."

Jeannot looked at Henry, who shook his head. The last thing he needed in his life was to explain to Edward how he had allowed Jeannot, who had been placed in his care, to go gallivanting off on some wild, harebrained, and likely very dangerous adventure. This was frankly not going to happen.

"Jeannot," he said, "I cannot and will not allow you to even think about joining this commando. It is dangerous; you will be in a strange country with people you don't know or trust, and in situations not suitable for someone of your age and experience. How do you think I would describe it to your father? Oh, your hot-headed son up and went to join some lame commando going to Swaziland to fight the Swazi king's army. Are you out of your mind?"

Jeannot nodded his head slowly. "I guess you are correct, uncle. It does not seem to be a good choice for me. Although I think it could be a great adventure."

"Adventure!" shouted Henry. "Adventure! You could get your arse shot off, then what do I tell your mother? Sorry, Fanni. Your 'adventure-seeking' son went to Swaziland and now has a rifle wound in his tuchas (backside). Now see your friend to the door, and let's hear no more of this."

Jeannot walked Jannie to the door, shook his hand, and wished him good luck. Before the boy left, Jeannot made sure his uncle couldn't see him and gave Jannie a huge wink.

Johannesburg - June 2, 1897 – Henry

It was 7.30 in the morning, and Henry had heard nothing stirring in Jeannot's room. He stuck his head in the door and was about to rouse him when he saw that the bed had been neatly made, and the closet seemed empty. "Oh Jesus," he muttered to himself.

"What has he done now?" He went outside to where the bike was kept, to find that it was no longer there. He called Sarah and told her what he thought had happened. She went white when he related the conversation with the Retief boy yesterday and the commando he was off to join. "Jeannot could not have done something so irresponsible," said Sarah. "Maybe he just went to the store early this morning." "And taken all his clothes with him. I don't think so. I think the young idiot has gone to Pretoria to join the commando. Oh God, what do I tell his parents?"

Sarah thought for a minute, then said. "Let's wait until this evening and see if he has come to his senses and returned home. If not, I guess we need to write to Edward and Fanni."

They waited until 8 pm. Jeannot was clearly not coming home. Wearily Henry sat at his desk and proceeded to compose the most challenging letter of his life

.

Pretoria - June 13th, 1898 – Jeannot

Letter from Jeannot Weinberg to Edward Weinberg

Pretoria
June 13, 1898

Dear Father

I must let you know that I am leaving for Swaziland today in order to take part in the war. Please do not let this frighten you or anything, because I shall be in Swaziland before you can stop me. There are many young people who are also going there as volunteers, and they have advised me to go too. If I am lucky enough to return alive, then a lifelong position will be assured to me. We are leaving here soon, but will not be at the scene for 6 or 7 days. Perhaps there will be no fighting because war has not yet been declared in earnest.

Yesterday I received my uniform, with blankets, rifle, water bottle, bandolier, etc. I am also writing to Mother about this. So please don't excite yourself or send me telegrams etc. because I have prepared myself to go, and I will go, and if anyone tries to stop me, I'll know what to do.

Meanwhile, I remain your loving son

Jeannot

I have no money to be photographed in my uniform but hope to send you a photo of the whole corps. I will write regularly from camp. Only don't get worried. A person only lives once, so I don't see the difference whether he dies of old age or from a bullet.

Welgelegen - June 16th, 1898 - Jeannot

Letter from Jeannot Weinberg to Edward and Fanni Weinberg

Welgelegen
June 16, 1898

Dear Parents,

We arrived here last night after heavy going, as it uphill country. This morning we had maneuvers. Many of the recruits do not know how to hold a gun, and so we had a lot of fun. We are camping with 13 others in a large tent. Our sergeant and corporal are good fellows, and we are all chaps who know each other well.

Altogether we are about 1,000 men at this Camp. One thousand are still coming, and 1,000 are already in Swaziland. If these 3,000 with about 20 machine guns are not enough, then the burghers will be called up.

Within two days, we will be at the border, then we'll at last have something to shoot at. A telegram has just arrived that King of Swaziland awaits us at the border. We are all very pleased to hear that. At 4 o'clock a company of artillery will arrive with eight canon, and then we will march away at 2 o'clock tomorrow morning. In all, we have 16 ox-wagons and four ambulances for the wounded. I belong to the 7th Section, Infantry Division, under Captain de Korte of the Pretoria Volunteers Corps. The food here is not too good, but that which we have, we eat with a good appetite.

Honestly, I have never felt as well as now, because I have a lot of work to do. One lot of my things I left with Polevnick at Joffe's in Pretoria. When I come back, I will fetch it, but if I don't come back, you can have it sent to you by Joffe. I have with me much underwear, a civilian suit, a brush and comb set, two blankets, and a whole lot of other things.

The lieutenant has just called us all to shooting practice. So, adieu: don't worry to write because I'll not get the letters anyway. Rather wait until I write to you from a town because at present I am on a farm.

Regards to all friends and the children,

Your loving son,
Jeannot

Fort de Korte - Bremersdorp, August 9th, 1898 - Jeannot

Letter from Jeannot Weinberg to Fanni Weinberg

Bremersdorp
August 9, 1898

Dear Mother

I have not written lately because I knew you were away. I received your and Father's letters. I hope Father has found a business that will be profitable because I think it is time you had something steady and settled once and for all in a good place. How are Joseph and Leopold? Lately, I have heard nothing from them.

Some are saying that we may be leaving here in a few days, but I don't believe any of that nonsense because when we are to go, we will probably be notified at least a week before in order to get ourselves ready. In the fort, things are lively. We have formed an orchestra and have promenade concerts every evening.

It is less cold here because I have read that it snowed in Bloemfontein. We had a layer of ice as thick as your finger on the water one morning. We have also had rain, together with a storm.

I have written to Heyman asking for the GBP1.10 and for German newspapers because I have neither here, but he did not even respond to me. But Max said he would send me the GBP2.10 he owes me at the beginning of this month, but I have not received it yet. Perhaps I will get lucky with the post this afternoon. In any case, I don't need it so badly because if I receive it, I will simply spend it here, and when I get to Pretoria, I will also need money.

Then I will have to ask Father.

For the time being, don't worry about me. The Government's silence story fell through because nothing came of the shooting we expected.

Greetings to all friends, the children, and Father.

Your loving son
Jeannot

The Swaziland Rebellion, as it came to be called, was something of a 'much ado about nothing.' No fighting took place, the King and his army left for the capital, and the commando was left cooling its heels with never a shot fired in anger. And so ended Jeannot's Swazi adventure. His letters showed an independent spirit that displayed little or no fear of battle or hardship - confusing and frightening attributes to be heard by a mother who loved her son and wished only for his safety.

His bravado was typical of the boy, thought his father. He just doesn't know when to be cautious and have a different perspective. Perhaps he will mature with age. He is a hot-head, a firebrand, quite unlike his mother and me. Wonder where it comes from? Probably from my grandfather, who earned his spurs running from Cossacks! Well, we'll get him home immediately. This Johannesburg thing has gone on long enough, and I want him back under my protection. Not that I hold Henry and Sarah responsible in any way. This young fellow is so strong-willed; they never had a hope of keeping him from doing this. What worries me is that he seems to have a sense of hubris that is very dangerous in times like these. There is a fair chance we will be at war with Britain in the next few years, and, having been on this commando to Swaziland, there will be no restraining him from going to war again. He needs to get a better sense of his own mortality and to give some thought to the responsibility he owes to himself and his family. But I know this will all fall on deaf ears. He is who he is, and no-one will tame that fiercely independent spirit. I just hope it doesn't get him into real trouble in the future.

Chapter 8 – Elise

Royal Hotel Bloemfontein - January 3rd, 1899 – Bertha

Bertha sat in a rocking chair on the hotel verandah reading a book. The evening sun cast shadows from the beautiful wrought iron latticework that decorated the front of the hotel, making an intricate design on the floor of the verandah. Spotty, the dog, lay at her feet doing what he seemed to do best - sleeping. It had been a warm January day, and Bertha was making the most of her last few days of holiday before starting the new school year. She was going to be ten this year and was looking forward to going into Sister Ignatius's class.

This scene of ennui was disturbed by the arrival of a cart drawn by two uninterested looking donkeys that stopped outside the front door of the hotel. There were two people in the cart, a man of about forty and a child who appeared to be eleven or twelve. The man had the appearance of a farmer - broad of shoulder, with a spade beard and a soft felt hat pulled down on the crown of his head. He was dressed in an open-neck khaki shirt, loose-fitting moleskin trousers, and boots that had become dusty from the road. The girl was small and thin, with dark hair and inquiring brown eyes. She wore a printed cotton smock, leather sandals, and a bonnet on her head, tied beneath her chin.

Bertha did not take too much notice of the pair - probably just a father and daughter checking in to the hotel. But she perked up when her father came out of the hotel and greeted the man warmly. "Erik, how are you? It is wonderful to see you again, man. And this young lady must be Elise." "Ja, Edward." said the man. "I have brought her to you as we discussed." Now Bertha was interested. What did this mean? Had this man brought his daughter to his father? What was he planning to do with her? Then Edward, seeing Bertha on the verandah, called to her. "Bertha, my dear, come and say hello to Mr. Schoeman and his daughter Elise." Bertha approached apprehensively, still not knowing what to make of this. She held out her hand to the man who shook it with deference and then to the daughter, who returned the grip with a weakly nervous press.

"Well, Bertha," said Edward. "Mr. Schoeman is an old friend of mine. He owns a farm about ten miles from Ladybrand, growing the best mielies in the district. Did you ever wonder why the mielies we serve at the hotel are so delicious? They all come from Mr. Schoeman's farm. I have been buying from him ever since the hotel opened?" "That's nice, Father." she replied, "But why is his daughter here?"

Schoeman laughed and took up the story. "Well, you see, young lady, my Elise, who is eleven, has been schooled in the Ladybrand area until now. The school is a good one, and the children are well taught, but I wanted something better for Elise. She seems to be quite clever and works very hard at her lessons. So, I wrote to your father and asked him whether he could help us to get Elise admitted to the Greenhill Convent that you attend. And he did, and so Elise is going to be starting at Greenhill this year in the same class as you."

"But where will she live?" inquired Bertha. Edward took over. "Mr. Schoeman has asked Mama and me if she could possibly board at the hotel with us during the term time, and, of course, we agreed. She is going to be sharing your room. I expect you will become firm friends." Bertha's heart leapt. As the only girl in a family of five brothers, she was starved of the company of girls of her age. This was a dream come true, almost as good as getting a new sister! She walked over to Elise and threw her arms around her in a hug. "A sister of my very own," she exclaimed. "I have always wanted a sister. And my sister you shall be." Elise looked relieved and a bit overwhelmed by the whole scene, but she managed a wan smile. "She doesn't speak much English yet, Bertha, but I am sure the nuns at Greenhill will remedy that. And I am hoping that living with you and your family will also improve her language," said Mr. Schoeman. "Not a problem," said Edward. "We all speak Afrikaans, and I am sure she will feel at home." At this point, Fanni, hearing the commotion outside, came out to greet them. She quickly whisked Elise away, carrying her suitcase to get her settled in. Bertha followed in a state of great excitement.

"Edward, I don't know how to thank you enough. Gertruida and I really do want what's best for Elise, and I believe she now has the opportunity to really advance her education. And living in the town with all of you will hopefully knock some of the farm out of her, and make her more of a little lady." Erik grinned and shook Edward's hand. "It is only a pleasure to help you, my friend. And it is a real Godsend for Bertha. She has a bit of a testing time having five brothers, and while the boys mean well, she doesn't have much female support to fend off their frequent teasing."

Bloemfontein - 1899 – Bertha

It did not take Bertha long to find out all about Elise and her family. She had two brothers, Stephanus, who was ten and Rudolf, 8, and a sister Marie, 6. Their family had originally come north with Andries Pretorius in 1836 during the Great Trek, but, as a result of illness, they did not make it to the Transvaal, preferring to settle in the Ladybrand area of the eastern Free State, not far from the Basutoland border. Their farm was called Schoonspruit, because of the beautiful stream that ran near the house. Her father was born on Schoonspruit, and when his father died in 1887, he took over the running of their farm. The main crop was mielies - the soil was perfect for the cultivation of this crop - but her mother Gertruida also tended a vegetable garden. There were chickens and ducks and two milk cows.

Elise seemed quiet at first, but Bertha assumed this was because she was shy in her new surroundings. She was also conscious of the fact that she spoke little English, and that made her reluctant to join in the conversation at mealtimes. She was slightly built, but despite this, her upbringing on a farm and the various chores it brought with it had made her quite strong and wiry. She had a particular love for animals, and she and Spotty became firm friends.

When the term began at Greenhill, there were plenty of new experiences for Elise. She had never worn a school uniform before, and Fanni took her to Van Jaarsveld's, the clothing store that carried Greenhill uniforms, to kit her out. The uniform was a white shirt and green pinafore, khaki socks and brown shoes, and a khaki felt hat with the school badge on the front. Elise spent an hour parading in front of the mirror when she got home, proud of her new appearance. The school was within walking distance from the hotel, and every weekday at 7.45 am, the two girls would leave the hotel and make their way to school. Such a regular sight did this become that the neighbors used to watch for them each day and say, "Here come the Greenhill girls!" The first few weeks were difficult for Elise. Except for Bertha, she knew none of the girls at the school and had never experienced the kind of routine and discipline that the school demanded. The nuns were a source of great fascination to her, particularly their unusual attire. The nuns were from the Dominican order and wore all white robes, a white wimple, and black headgear. To Elise, they appeared like great white angels who seemingly floated on air. She was enthralled by them, until she learned that, angels or not, they were particularly adept with a ruler on the knuckles when a student failed to answer a question correctly. Anyone who has attended a Catholic school understands that the teaching method is a balanced combination of encouragement and chastisement, with the balance being determined by the behavior of the student!

As the term progressed, and her English began to improve, Elise began to feel more at home at Greenhill and found that the other students readily accepted her. She made a few friends, but her great affection was for Bertha. Bertha had assumed the role of a guardian angel, even though she was a year younger than Elise. If ever Elise needed assistance or advice, Bertha was there at her side. The bond between the two girls grew stronger as the term continued, and by the end of the term, they were firmly 'best friends.'

Elise also became more comfortable with the routine at the hotel. She had never been in a hotel before, and the concept of ordering from a menu was foreign to her. A meal was what Moeder put on the table - choice was not a factor. You ate what you were given, and that was the end of it. But in her new home, she was captivated by the fact that, even at breakfast, she had the choice of how she wanted her eggs prepared, and which kind of porridge she preferred. And having a waiter in a smart white coat and black trousers bring you your meal was a marvel to her. Personal hygiene was also different. Here she bathed every day, cleaned her teeth twice a day, and made sure she wore clean clothes to go to school - none of these had been enforced on the farm, where there was no bathroom, and the toilet was in an outhouse fifty yards from the main building. Flushing toilets and taps that produced water when turned on were also new to her, and she was secretly quite glad not to have to go to the well many times a day to fetch water for Moeder. But she quickly adjusted and knew she would find it difficult to readjust herself to farm living when she went home to visit the family during the Easter vacation.

She was totally devoted to Bertha. She had a sister, Marie, but she was too young to really count as a friend - she was just '*klein sussie*' (little sister). But Bertha was something entirely different. She was worldly, well-traveled, had lived in Europe, and made a grand sea voyage all in her ten years. This was in stark contrast to Elise, who had lived all her life on the farm, leaving it only to attend the local village school, to go to church on Sundays, and to visit with other farm families, especially for *nachmaal.*[1] So her exposure to the culture, music, literature, and cuisine that had now become a part of her life had been very restricted when growing up. She saw Bertha as her guide through these new and fascinating experiences, knowing that she could learn a great deal from this very warm and high-spirited young woman. She was also very fond of Edward and Fanni. Edward was a perfect gentleman, never being too busy to ask her how her schooling was going, or to take her to various parts of the hotel to show her where the wine was stored or where the cheese was left to mature. Fanni could never replace Moeder, but she was gentle and kind and did her best to anticipate the areas in which Elise might feel uncomfortable or out of place. The boys were a different matter. They were boys and paid as little attention to Elise as they paid to Bertha. They were not unkind, just indifferent, in the way that young boys can be. They would always help her if she was in need, but she and Bertha were generally regarded as 'other members of the family who made up the numbers at dinner.' Jeannot, being much older, was a bit remote, but Elise admired him for his strength of character and his sense of adventure and hoped she would get to know him better in the future.

It was on the weekends that the girls got to spend time together and explore the area. Sunday morning was reserved for Elise to go to church and Bertha to go to Hebrew School, but the rest of the time was free to wander. They loved to have the hotel make a packed lunch for them, and then take their bicycles down to the lake and lie on the grass talking and laughing, pausing only to cool off with a swim in the lake. Elise was a strong swimmer, and she helped Bertha improve her techniques in the water. They talked about everything young girls of that age speculate on: career, marriage, their families, school, and the nuns (always a favorite topic). They would often meet school friends on their adventures, and Elise got to learn more about town life and the things people do.

By the time Easter arrived, and Erik came to pick up Elise to take her home for a few weeks, the two girls were as close as if they had been blood siblings. No secrets existed between them, and, to quote Fanni, they were 'as thick as thieves.' Bertha could not wait for the holidays to be over and to have her 'sussie' back.

The next term at school went by quickly, as did the third term, but when Elise left for the Michaelmas break in late September, the talk was all about the possibility of war and impact that it might have on the lives of people in the Free State and Transvaal. Bertha hoped against hope that nothing would come between her and Elise and that she would be back as usual in a fortnight, ready for the new term.

Few could have anticipated what would eventually happen.

In the Dutch Reformed Church, the sacrament of the Eucharist or the communion service usually occurs four times a year. When this service is held, families from outlying farms will try to attend, and there is often a large gathering with a festive meal. It is a particularly meaningful way of keeping the community in touch with one another, and also for discussing essential subjects like possible marriage suitors for the children.

Chapter 9 - The Eve of War

Pretoria - May 1899 – Paul Kruger

Suzerainty! There was that *verdomde* (damned) word again. It had seemed to slip innocuously into the preamble to the Pretoria Convention of 1881, yet had caused Kruger more than his share of headaches since that time. He went back and reread the passage for the thousandth time:

"*Her Majesty's Commissioners for the settlement of the Transvaal territory, duly appointed as such by a Commission passed under the Royal Sign Manual and Signet, bearing date the 5th of April 1881, do hereby undertake and guarantee, on behalf of Her Majesty, that from and after the 8th day of August 1881, complete self-government, subject to the* ***suzerainty*** *of Her Majesty, her heirs, and successors, will be accorded to the inhabitants of the Transvaal territory, upon the following terms and conditions, and subject to the following reservations and limitations.......*"

Herein lay the problem. There was no formal definition in either British or Roman-Dutch Law of the term 'suzerainty'. People knew what it meant in general terms, but when looking at the hidden crevices and interstices of the law, there was no precedent or guidance. And this issue was going to involve all the hidden crevices and interstices the law had to offer. It could be further argued that the term had not been repeated in the London Convention of 1884 that to all intents and purposes superseded the Pretoria Convention. However, somehow that irritating term 'suzerainty' still seemed to be hanging around - especially when it suited the British. Kruger had consulted his legal advisors, in particular his State Attorney, Willem Leyds, a man known for his ability to find a legal loophole when none seemingly existed. Still, even he could shed no light on it from a legal or jurisprudential viewpoint.

Kruger pondered the renewed interest in this concept of suzerainty. While the Transvaal had been a sleepy agricultural state, poor and struggling, there was no interest from the British in exercising any kind of control over their affairs. But then came Mr. Harrison and Langlaagte, and an event so monumental in the change it wrought and so far-reaching in its impact that the rest of the world all of a sudden sat up and started to take notice of this small, isolated backwater of a country. Gold. The magic metal. The substance that fired men's greed and caused them to commit all manner of abomination to secure it. Gold. The precious one. The one of legends. And we have it. In quantities never dreamed of before. And now they want it. Seems simple enough. But we have it. And they need to try and take it from us. And they will use whatever means at their disposal. Including suzerainty. Rhodes and his lackey Beit (or was it the other way round?) would never rest until they had gotten their grubby capitalist hands all over our wealth. They know the power it brings, and the wealth and those are their two guiding angels.

Paul Kruger was a larger than life character, a man of imposing size and unforgettable ugliness. He stood six-foot, four inches tall, but his stooped shoulders belied his true height. He was heavyset, his clothing stretching across his considerable belly. But it was his countenance that was most striking. He had a rectangular face, ending in a large white beard, but he did not have a mustache. His nose was large and bulbous, and, along with his eyes, dominated his face. The eyes were like two slits in the face, framed by large bags beneath, and heavy lids above. His skin was dotted with moles, and his white hair was almost always concealed below his tall top hat that seemed to be a permanent fixture. All in all, not a particularly pretty sight. But his ungainly and unattractive body was contradicted by a razor-sharp mind, a geniality and kindness towards his fellow man, and his deep religious fervor. His people unconditionally loved him, and he was never too busy to listen to their issues and stories.

But they must not underestimate me, thought Kruger. I did not trek up from the Cape in 1836 to settle in this part of the country because it offered me a better standard of living or a more comfortable environment. Certainly not. I did it for freedom, freedom to live under our own rule, freedom to worship as we wish, freedom to make our own laws and regulations, freedom to nurture our culture, and our heritage. And I am not going to let them take this from me just because they want our gold. We Afrikaners are more complex than they think. We are not slow-witted or stupid, just because we do not share their level of book learning. We have grown up with centuries of struggling to keep ourselves alive in the face of droughts, floods, wars, and conflict. Don't they realize that this has given us an astuteness and a survival instinct they cannot hope to match? Their rhetoric sounds impressive, just like the call of a heraldic trumpet, but both have one thing in common at the end of the day - hot air. Do they think they can fool an old campaigner like me with their blustering? I have one thing they do not have. Patience. I have lived here for a long time, have seen changes come and go, and I know this land and these people. We are not about to panic, nor do we scare easily. Hell, it took us 30 years of British rule in the Cape before we decided we could stand it no longer - not exactly a decision made on the spur of the moment. So let them come. Let's see what they have to offer. We shall take our time, think it through and do what is best for land and volk (people).

So how were the British seeking to control us in terms of this vague concept of suzerainty? There was clearly no mention of it in the London Convention, but the British still seemed to believe that it carried over from the old convention. And now they were using it against the Transvaal to protect their citizens who had come to work in the mines, and who were called "uitlanders." They claimed that their right of suzerainty extended protection to the Uitlanders and that any efforts to ill-treat the Uitlanders were a threat to British suzerainty. Whatever the legal niceties of the situation, Kruger was aware of the two main reasons for the increased desire of the British to get their hands on the Transvaal - and both came from that unholy alliance of the jackals Rhodes and Milner - were the expansion of the British Empire and control of the goldfields. The discontent of the Uitlanders was a pawn in a much larger game of chess, but at the moment it had been maneuvered into a position to threaten Kruger's king.

Kruger reflected on the history of the Uitlander question. There had been discontent fomenting as early as 1890, and this had gained continual momentum during the ensuing six years. The most significant of their many grievances centered around enfranchisement. Most of the Uitlanders came from democracies where the ballot box was used to address the majority of contentious issues. Without representation, the Uitlanders could not hope to redress any of their other grievances. They had begun to create political movements to challenge Kruger, and he was all too aware of the potential impact of the Political Reform Association, established in 1892 and aimed at "extension of the franchise, railway communication, and education, limitation of taxation, opposition to monopolies and concessions." This was followed by the formation of the Transvaal National Union, whose objects were the maintenance of the independence of the South African Republic, obtaining by all constitutional means equal rights for all citizens of the Republic and the redress of all grievances. The Uitlander issue came to a head in December of 1895, when, at the supposed request of the Uitlanders to support their rebellion, a force of some 600 men under the command of Leander Starr Jameson invaded the Transvaal. This force had been secretly put together by Rhodes, who was seeking to draw Kruger out into the open and provide a pretext for a war with the Transvaal. But Kruger outsmarted him. He knew of the raid, known hereafter in history as 'The Jameson Raid,' intercepted and defeated the raiders and hauled their leaders off the jail in Pretoria.

Kruger's advisors recommended that Jameson and his colleagues be tried in a Transvaal court, but the wily old man was too smart for this. No, he said, let's send them to England and place the onus on the British justice system. A trial held in out-of-the-way Pretoria will never get the kind of publicity that a trial will get in the Old Bailey, and it is publicity we need now to cement our relationships with the Germans, the French and the Dutch. Let the English try their own naughty boys; I'll have none of it. And with this, he bundled up the raiders and handed them over to the British High Commissioner in January 1896.

The trial in England exceeded all of Kruger's expectations. In addition to finding all parties guilty, it also declared Rhodes to have primary responsibility for engineering the raid, and he was severely censured. Joseph Chamberlain, the British Secretary for the Colonies, was also found to have his fingerprints all over the incident, even though he had denied so in public. So it was Round One to Kruger and his team.

The rebellion among the uitlanders had not eventuated, as Kruger had predicted. Too many of the uitlanders were not British subjects but were men from elsewhere in the world, including the other South African territories. These men were more interested in making a living than playing politics, and Kruger knew and understood this.

One afternoon in May, Oom Paul was sitting in his office in Pretoria, an unusual place for him as he usually entertained visitors on his stoep, but the chills of May had forced the old man to seek the warmth of the interior of the house. There was an apprehensive knock on the door. Piet Joubert, the Deputy President, opened the door. Kruger could see from the unconcealed concern on the man's face that something was amiss. "Well." he asked, "What is going on?" "Oom, Paul," replied Joubert. "I have just received a telegram stating that the Uitlanders have created a petition to send to the Queen in London. It was apparently signed by 21,000 Uitlanders" "Do we know what it contains?" inquired Kruger. "Not yet," replied Joubert. "But I have sent a man to the British Commissioner here in Pretoria to get a copy. He should be back shortly."

Kruger stared ahead of him. What were they up to now? Why didn't they just come and talk to him? He might be conservative, but he was not totally unsympathetic to their issues. What would this mean for the future of the Transvaal?

His thoughts were disturbed by another knock on the door. Joubert went to the door and returned with an envelope which he opened. He scanned it quickly then handed it over to Kruger. "More of the same," he observed. "Franchise, education, taxes, you name it. Nothing we haven't heard before." "That may be," remarked Kruger. "But sending it directly to the Queen suggests that these people are nearing the end of their rope. We need to do something that will calm the waters a bit." He reflected for a minute, then asked Joubert to leave. He picked up his pen, thought for a moment, then began to compose a letter. It was to President Steyn, the leader of the Free State.

Cape Town - May 1899 – Milner

Milner had not wanted to come to South Africa. If it hadn't been for that infernal Jameson, he would be sitting in an office in Somerset House in London as the Chairman of Inland Revenue, rather than High Commissioner for South Africa and Lieutenant-Governor of the Cape Colony. It was clear that Chamberlain and Whitehall had had quite enough of the group that had so badly bungled things in the Transvaal these past few years - Rhodes, Jameson, Beit, to name just a few. A safe pair of hands was needed to clean up the mess of the Jameson Raid, and Milner was that selected pair.

Milner had been born in 1854 in the town of Giessen in the Duchy of Hesse in Germany. He was educated at Tubingen and at King's College School, before attending Balliol College at Oxford University. He graduated in 1877 with a degree in classics. He joined the Pall Mall Gazette as a journalist in 1881, eventually becoming the assistant editor. He went into politics after his stint in journalism, standing as a candidate for the Liberal Party in the Harrow division of Middlesex, but lost in the general election. He broke with the Gladstonian wing of the Liberal Party over the issue of home rule for Ireland. He served as private secretary to George Goshen, a former Liberal who became Chancellor of the Exchequer in 1887 under Lord Salisbury and the Conservative Party, and who used his influence to get Milner appointed as under-secretary of finance in Egypt, then a colony of Britain. Milner served in this post for four years and returned to England in 1892. Now a senior civil servant, he was appointed as chairman of the Board of Inland Revenue, where he remained until being sent on this mission to South Africa.

He was an extremely competent and capable man, highly regarded as an outstanding intellect and a diligent civil administrator. He was considered one of the clearest-headed and most diplomatic officials in the British service, and his position as a man of moderate Liberal views marked him as one in whom all parties might have confidence. The moment for testing his capacity in the highest degree had now come. One part of his character was seen as problematic, particularly in Pretoria. He was a self-confessed Anglophile, believing the British to be a superior race, and this made him hold the Boers in very low regard. He was also an imperialist who wanted to ensure that every available, desirable land and resource was claimed for the Empire. Yet another reason why he was not a popular figure in the minds of Kruger and his supporters.

Milner was distressed by the Jameson Raid, not so much for its intention (any action likely to advance the Empire seemed justifiable), but for the clumsy and inept way in which it had been planned and executed. He quickly realized the value of the Uitlanders and their grievances in promoting conflict with the Transvaal, but Rhodes and Jameson had set the cause back by several years. He was also somewhat leery of Rhodes, not because of his part in the Raid, but because of the man's apparent tendency to commit only to things that he knew would advance his own power, reputation, and wealth. Not really a team player was our Mr. Rhodes, but one out to further his personal aggrandizement. The same could never be said about Milner. He remained true to his firmly held, if somewhat misguided belief, that all things British were in and of themselves superior to anything else, and that the Empire must be put first in all matters of state and economics.

He had a vision. He could see a united South Africa, the Cape, Natal, Orange Free State, and the Transvaal, all united as a colony of the Empire. Self-governing for sure - the people had demonstrated their ability to conduct legislative, administrative, and judicial functions in an adequate manner - but subject to the Privy Council and under the ultimate authority of the Queen. It would be the first stage of a much grander plan that involved a federation of much of sub-equatorial Africa under the British banner - South Africa, Rhodesia, Kenya, Tanganyika, Uganda, Nyasaland, all British colonies, all ruled by a federal assembly of Southern African states, all under Queen and Empire. But first things first. He needed to attend to matters in the Transvaal and at least create a foothold in what had become one of the wealthiest countries in the world.

Milner had carefully studied all the events that followed the first Boer War, the various conventions, the creation of the Uitlander population, the apparent unfairness in the treatment of all who were not burghers of the Transvaal. But most of all, he had studied

Kruger. Although he had never met the man, he had become sufficiently familiar with his views and methods to have acquired marked respect for his ability - even though his significant attributes seemed to be cunning and deception. This was not some bumbling backwater despot. This was a shrewd and calculating individual who knew what he wanted and was prepared to use all available means to get it. Kruger was a master at the game of brinkmanship - leading his angry opponents on, then appeasing them at the last minute - a technique he had used in the past, and would surely use again. With him, it was never over until it was over. One never knew when the old fox would find one last bend in the road and disappear from sight. Milner knew not to treat him lightly, a mistake he believed most of his predecessors had been guilty of.

Milner was not by nature a patient man. He was a man of action, eager to take the fight to the enemy. But Chamberlain had warned him, nay instructed him, to exercise restraint and proceed cautiously. Kruger, he advised, was better at defense than attack. He was the master of ambush, goading his opponents into a trap and then finishing them off. Such a man had to be treated with extreme caution. The tortoise was not an animal that stuck out its neck without good reason - Kruger was just such a politician. Milner's job was to wait until that neck left the shell and then pounce.

There was another political nuance that needed exploring. Not all Boers had gone north with the Great Trek - many had remained in the Cape and had not only prospered but had built a substantial power base. If there was to be a conflict with the Boer republics, Milner wanted to avoid a situation where the strong Afrikaner faction in the Cape rose up and supported their northern brethren against the Crown. There was clearly a need to drive a wedge between the two Afrikaner groups, and Milner set out to create this. He used as his platform a speech made in Graaff Reinet, about

600 km. from Cape Town, at the opening of a new railway line in March 1898. Knowing that the majority of his audience would be Afrikaners, he set out his stall very clearly - you are either with us or you are against us. You either continue to take advantages of all the benefits of British rule - peace, prosperity, freedom, justice, equality, and self-government - most of which were somewhat lacking in the two Boer republics - or you throw your lot in with your people, the majority of whom do not seem to be benefiting from the newly acquired wealth up north. In many respects, the arguments were the same as those in the 1830s before the Great Trek, but Milner knew that 60 years on, the Cape Afrikaners had more to lose now. He was not under any illusion that he would convert every Afrikaner - there were too many emotional and familial ties to expect this - but he wanted to present an unburnished picture of what the alternatives looked like. At a minimum, he was hoping for some pressure to be put by the Cape Afrikaner intellectuals on Pretoria not to risk a war with the Empire.

During the two years after he arrived in the Cape, Milner was in constant communication with Chamberlain regarding strategy and policy on the situation in the Transvaal. It became clear to both men that the seething cauldron that was the Uitlanders would eventually become the tipping point in the current political stand-off. The shooting of the uitlander Tom Edgar by Kruger's police was a catalyst that stirred the Uitlander community to send a petition to Milner in March 1899 demanding imperial intervention. This could have been the break Milner was waiting for, but again Kruger pulled an ace out of the hole with the offer of a Great Deal to address some of the grievances in the petition. There were to be some concessions made to the mining houses, some reduction in taxation, but, most importantly, an offer of enfranchisement to any Uitlander after five years of acquiring Transvaal citizenship. Whether or not the offer was genuine was hotly debated in Milner's team. Most believed it was merely a stalling tactic, aimed at getting Milner to show his hand; others felt that there was a chink in Kruger's armor and that he was being compelled to reach across the table with something to appease the Uitlanders. The debate continued - how should Milner and the British government react to this? How to avoid pouring cold water over the uitlanders who clearly were not satisfied with the terms of the Deal?

Then, in late May, a telegram from Pres. Steyn of the Orange Free State. Would Lord Milner please attend a conference in Bloemfontein on May 30th, 1899, at which the current situation in the Transvaal would be discussed with Pres. Kruger? The conference would be mediated by Pres. Steyn.

The world was about to stop rotating. Southern Africa held its breath.

Bloemfontein - May 31st, 1899 – Steyn

The conference began with the usual pleasantries. Milner was all good humor and manners. Kruger played the fool and dug Milner in the ribs, playing up to his British newspaper image of an elderly buffoon. But it became apparent to Steyn after a very short time that a meeting of the minds would be highly unlikely. Despite Milner's protestations that Britain had no designs on annexing the Transvaal, Oom Paul was not impressed. Indeed. Kruger had confided in his colleagues the day before that he would give everything away for peace except if the sovereignty of the Transvaal was in jeopardy.

To these two men - Milner with his unwavering desire to extend the hegemony of the Empire to the whole of Southern Africa; Kruger with his iron resolve never to give up his country's independence and right to self-determination - the other issues were really a sideshow. The grievances of the Uitlanders were discussed at length, and some give and take occurred, but it appeared very early to Steyn that these would never supersede the real issue. Milner wanted the land, Rhodes wanted the gold, Kruger wanted both.

Kruger had not come to the talks in the capital of the Orange Free State with high expectations, but he did observe the rules of the game. Concessions and compromises. On the third day, he produced a carefully prepared reform bill, like a rabbit out of a hat. Five seats in the Volksraad for the gold-mining districts and voting rights for Uitlanders within variable time frames: within two to seven years, depending on how long they had been in the Transvaal. Milner refused to compromise his original demands. And despite encouragement from British Colonial Secretary Joseph Chamberlain for him to continue the talks, Milner walked out of the conference on June 5; no resolution concerning the fate of the Uitlanders was reached.

The impasse finally resulted in the ending of the conference. Milner had made three demands from Kruger. He demanded an enactment by the Transvaal of a law that would immediately give Uitlanders enfranchisement and the right to vote. He demanded the use of the English language in the Volksraad. And he demanded that all laws of the Volksraad would need to be approved by the British Parliament. Suzerainty was now being given a recognizable face. Kruger would not budge from the contents of his proposed reform bill.

The conference had been a failure. Steyn had genuinely tried to bring the parties together, but it was clear to him that the differences were irreconcilable. A war between the two factions now seemed inevitable, a situation that concerned Steyn deeply. Should the Transvaal go to war with the Empire, the Free State would be bound to enter the war on the side of the Transvaal, in terms of a treaty signed in March 1889 between Kruger and the then President of the Free State, Francis Reitz. The treaty stated, *'The South African Republic and the Orange Free State hereby enter into a mutual alliance and declare themselves willing to assist one another with all force and means, should the independence of either of the two States be threatened or undermined from outside.'*

So, if war came, we are in it up to our necks, thought Steyn. But I cannot see how this could benefit the Free State in any way. It is the Transvaal that has the gold, not us. There is only a downside for the Free State.

Pretoria - June to October 1899 – Kruger

Milner's haste to leave the Bloemfontein talks did not surprise Kruger but alarmed Whitehall. Chamberlain was not ready for war so soon - he had much work to do in mobilizing the army and securing the necessary resources. He needed to play for time - and Milner was going to be the stalking horse.

Ironically it was Kruger who played the first card. In mid-July 1899, Pretoria agreed to more concessions than Kruger had already proposed in Bloemfontein. A new law gave the Uitlanders six seats in the Volksraad and voting rights after seven years, with a retroactive effect. Chamberlain applauded this move - it gave him and Milner a chance to postpone a showdown for even longer. Due care must, of course, be taken to study the implications of this new offer - we will get back to you. Secretly Milner was deeply suspicious that this was yet another of Kruger's wily traps. He was not far from the truth. Kruger also needed time to mobilize his forces if a war was inevitable. The spring rains would not come until September, and Kruger knew that these were required to provide adequate fodder for the horses.

Milner's answer was the creation of a royal commission to investigate the franchise situation in the Transvaal. This was, of course, rejected by Kruger, who saw it as the unwarranted interference by a foreign power in the domestic affairs of a sovereign nation. And he withdrew his concessions of mid-July. Milner took his time in replying.

On September 8th, following a Cabinet Council in Cape Town, a message was sent to Kruger, offering a 'peaceful' settlement - acceptance of a five-year enfranchisement term. But there was a sting in the tail - if the reply of the Transvaal was inconclusive or inadequate, the British government reserved the right to consider all issues *de novo*. And as if to emphasize their serious intentions, troops in Natal were moved to the northern boundary with the Transvaal.

Milner had finally committed his knight, and it was threatening Kruger's king. On October 11th, Kruger issued an ultimatum requiring the troops to be withdrawn, or the two nations would be in a state of war. Milner refused. The Anglo-Boer War was on. The date was October 12th, 1899.

Chapter 10 - The War

Bloemfontein - October 12th, 1899 – Edward

Edward was at the dinner table in the hotel dining room when the newspaper was brought to him. As expected, the front page was full of news on the fact that the Boer Republics and the British Empire were now at war. The family was all at the table and, of course, knew of the situation, but no-one seemed ready to discuss it. It was one of those topics that were surrounded by so many questions and uncertainties that it was hard to come up with the right issue. Jeannot had made it clear to his father that afternoon that he would be joining up - this was no surprise to Edward after his involvement in the Swaziland campaign. But Bernard and Max were different stories. Bernard had turned 17 in June, and Max would not be 16 for another month. Bernard would be hard to keep at home, but he knew Fanni would not want Max to get involved. There was work to be done on Max, and Edward knew it would fall to him to try and talk some sense into the boy. He was aware that commando laws required all able-bodied males from 16 to 60 to be drafted during a mobilization, so he had a month of respite with Max. Perhaps it will all be over before he turns 16, he mused.

After dinner, Edward went into his office to ponder both the war and the family's role. To a European, war was almost a daily occurrence - it seemed that for the last 300 years, at least one European country was at war with another, usually over religion or land. The territorial conflicts were one thing - whether a few square miles of land belonged to one country or another was not too serious a matter (except of course if you lived on that land!). Still, it was the wars with a religious undertone that brought out the most brutality and violence. The conflict between Catholics and Protestants had been particularly violent. The Eighty Years War in the Low Countries and the Thirty Years War in the Holy Roman

Empire had pitted friend against friend and family against family, with bloody and disastrous consequences. Then there were the internal rebellions like that by the Huguenots, who were brutally put to the sword by the Catholic rulers of France. Oddly enough, it was this rebellion that created the South African wine industry, since many Huguenot winemakers sought refuge in the Cape.

But it was the Jews and their future that concerned Edward more. He could not remember instances other than the American War of Independence and the American Civil War, where Jews had fought on opposing sides. And given the fact that there was a sizable Jewish population in both the Free State and the Transvaal, and since it was inevitable that some of the British troops would also be Jewish, this situation was about to occur here in South Africa. He was also aware of the nascent anti-Semitism in England. The fact that a number of the mining millionaires were Jewish did not escape the notice of certain factions in England, and the new wave of Jewish immigrants in the East End of London was being targeted both as the unseen hand behind the war and as a group unlikely to support the British Empire. Edward reflected on the fact that there would need to be affirmative action on the part of these Jews to identify with the British troops to avoid a small pogrom in a land they had come to avoid such bloodshed in Eastern Europe.

But in South Africa, things had been different. While there were Jews among the Uitlanders, this did not concern Edward as much as he feared for the boerejode (Jewish Boers), those Jews who were citizens of the Free State and the Transvaal. These Jews needed to be perceived by the Afrikaners to be loyal and supportive and to take up arms on behalf of the two republics. If they did not, it would be an excuse to identify the Jews as traitors to the cause, and a wave of anti-Semitism could break out. So Edward was in a dilemma. On the one hand, he was reluctant to send his sons into a conflict that might result in their death or serious injury. On the other hand, he did not want the Jewish community to be seen as doing any less than any other group in defending their homelands.

There was one element in favor of the acceptance by the Boers of the Jewish people. The Boers were all Calvinists, mostly members of the Dutch Reformed Church. Although a staunchly Christian religion, the Dutch Reformed Church nevertheless set great store by the word of God as contained in the Old Testament. The Voortrekkers often likened themselves to the early Israelites, leaving a land of oppression for the new Promised Land. Many likened the crossing of the Orange River to the crossing of the Jordan into what was to become Judea. For this reason, there was a sense of identification with these ancient Israelites, and the modern representatives were seen as the inheritors of this great lineage. This respect was to be short-lived, but at the end of the 19th century, it was still a factor in a feeling of mutual respect between the two groups.

Edward suspected, as most people probably did that it was unlikely that the two republics would be able to defeat the might of the British Empire. He also believed that the British would take this war far more seriously than the one in 1880-1881 since there was something significant at stake in the current conflict that the British wanted - the Transvaal goldfields. Britain would not be prepared to step away from the situation as it had in the First Boer War - the stakes were far too high, and the stakeholders more powerful and more insistent. So he believed that, while the Boers might be able to win some battles as they did in the first war, they would eventually crumble under the sheer weight of numbers that the Empire could bring to bear on the situation. For this reason, it appeared likely that the war would be a short one, with some early Boer successes eventually reversed when the British put their full weight behind the conflict. If this were the case, then the exposure of his sons would not be protracted, and this made him feel more comfortable about letting them go to war. Hopefully, they could keep their heads down and not try to do anything too heroic - he felt confident that Bernard and Max could be relied on to follow this advice, but Jeannot was a different issue!

In the end, Edward realized the situation could only be resolved by the boys pledging their loyalty to the Free State and taking up arms to defend it. This would at least ensure that no fingers would be pointed at the Jews for not playing their part. But again, he prayed to the Almighty that He would protect his sons and bring them home safely.

Part 3 - Magersfontein

Chapter 11 - Siege Mentality

Pretoria - October 1899 – Kruger

It was Kruger who decided on the siege strategy. He was aware of how significant the impact of the invention and proliferation of the railroad had been on warfare. No longer were armies dependent on horses to move troops and equipment - these could now be transported more quickly by rail. In addition, the logistics behind rail transport were simpler than horse-drawn wagons - there was no longer a need for forage and water for the horses, to say nothing of the casualties these animals suffered in time of war. The horse was not eliminated from the transportation chain; it was merely supplemented by the quicker, more reliable, and lower maintenance train. The importance of rail transportation had been demonstrated during the American Civil War, and this conflict had underlined the importance of controlling the critical rail junctions as part of both an offensive and defensive strategy. This lesson was not lost on Kruger, and it was unsurprising that the rail junctions formed an important part of his initial approach.

It was clear to Kruger that the British forces would direct their invasion of the two Boer Republics towards the capture of the principal cities, Pretoria and Johannesburg in the Transvaal, and Bloemfontein in the Orange Free State. The invasion of the Orange Free State would be launched from the Cape, leveraging the most important rail junctions at De Aar and Kimberley. The invasion of the Transvaal was more complicated since it could potentially come from two directions: Natal in the southeast via the railhead at Ladysmith, and via the Northern Cape in the west. The latter would require the British forces in the Cape to come close to Bechuanaland, bypassing Kimberley and heading north until they were on the same latitude as Pretoria, at a town called Mafeking. These various invasion options brought three towns crisply into focus: Kimberley, Ladysmith, and Mafeking. All three had British garrisons, and all three posed a threat to the Boer Republics.

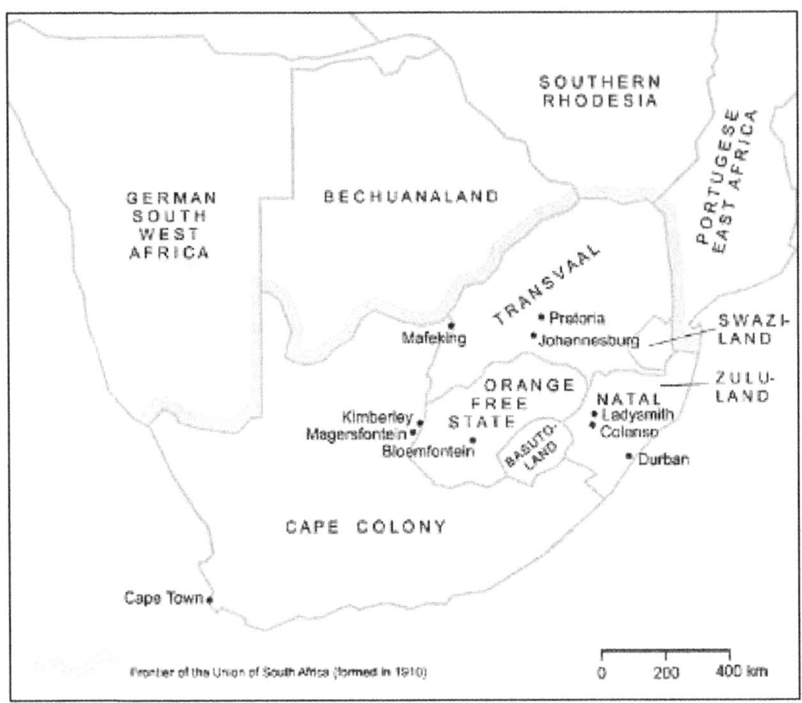

It is not surprising, then, that the first actions taken by the Boer Republics were to lay siege to these three strategic towns. If the British garrisons could be forced to surrender, then the Boers would effectively control the gateways into their territories. The strategy had another advantage. By taking the initiative and laying siege to the three towns, Kruger would force the hand of the British Army to relieve the sieges, and this would enable him to know exactly where they would be deploying their forces. Cut off the British Army from the approaches to these towns, and you effectively cut off their most accessible invasion routes into the Boer Republics.

The siege of Mafeking began on October 13th, 1899, with the

arrival of Boer forces in the area. The British garrison was under the command of Col. (later Lord) Robert Baden-Powell, who commanded a rag-tag assortment of regular army officers, three hundred and forty of the Protectorate Regiment, one hundred and seventy police, and two hundred volunteers, made up of a 'mixture of adventurers, younger sons, broken gentlemen, and irresponsible sportsmen who have always been the Voortrekkers of the British Empire.' The Boers, under Gen. Cronje, numbered about 5000 and, after a bombardment on October 16th, settled into a protracted attempt to starve out the garrison and the civilian population it was protecting.

Ladysmith was the main British garrison town and supply depot in northern Natal. It was well situated in peacetime, where the railroad and main road from Durban to Johannesburg met. However, in wartime, it was very vulnerable. The town itself was built on a plain surrounded by hills that were just too far away to be used by the defenders. To the south, the Tugela River and a series of ridgelines would block any relief effort. The border with the Orange Free State was close to the north-west, and a second railway ran from Ladysmith to Harrismith, just over the border. Natal was the main Boer target. One force, of around 14,000 men under Commandant-General Joubert, crossed the Transvaal border, heading for Dundee and then Ladysmith, while another force of 6,000 men from the Orange Free State, under Marthinus Prinsloo, crossed the Drakensberg heading directly for Ladysmith. This combined force would outnumber the 12,000 British troops in Natal. The siege commenced on November 2nd, 1899.

But it was the siege of Kimberley that was the most significant event in Jeannot's war. Lying in the north-west of Cape Colony on the western border of the Orange Free State, Kimberley was the center of Cecil Rhodes' De Beers diamond mining empire. As war became imminent, the citizens of Kimberley appealed for help, and the commander-in-chief sent Lieutenant Colonel Robert Kekewich with half his battalion of the North Lancashire Regiment to defend the town. A few days later, Rhodes raised the stakes dramatically by himself moving from Cape Town to Kimberley, which would otherwise have been left to the advancing Boers. The insistence of Rhodes that Kimberley should not be permitted to fall into Boer hands dictated the actions of the British in the West, although not to the extent that the need to relieve Ladysmith dictated Buller's strategy in Natal.

A capable and resourceful officer, Kekewich was obliged to create his defensive strategy in line with the requirements of Rhodes. Kimberley was De Beers, with most of its citizenry made up of De Beers employees. The essential resources of the town were controlled by De Beers and, therefore, by Rhodes. Rhodes dictated the course of the defense as much as did Kekewich.

On 14th October 1899, the Boers invaded the northern Cape Colony and surrounded Kimberley, beginning the siege.

Chapter 12 - The March to Magersfontein – Boers

Bloemfontein - October 16th, 1899 – Jeannot

Jeannot was instructed to report to Veldkornet Raaff at Market Square on Monday, 16th October 1899. He was to bring his horse, his personal effects, clothing, and, if possible, a rifle. He was also to provide himself with food for 48 hours - Mama and chef had ensured that this was not a problem. His attire belied the fact that he was a soldier, for he wore no uniform. He was a tall man, standing six feet in his bare feet, and weighing about 170 pounds. He was fit and wiry and had a shock of black, curly hair punctuated by a blond flash or 'bless' above his right eye. He wore an open neck, collarless shirt tucked into sturdy moleskin trousers, held up by a strong leather belt to which was attached a bandolier. He also wore a leather waistcoat and a felt hat with one side pinned up to the main part of the hat. He had a rifle across his back, a saddlebag containing a coat, a change of clothes, and his shaving and cleaning kit. Across the back of the saddle was a rolled groundsheet with blankets inside and a small pillow. There was also a canvas bag with food and two screw-top water bottles attached to the saddle.

Saying goodbye to the family was, of course, difficult. Mama and Bertha both sobbed, and the boys and Edward made a good show of being manly and restrained, but there was a tear in many an eye. Simon, the butler, was also there. "Hamba kahle[1] (go well), Master Jeannot. Go with God," he called after him. Jeannot turned in the saddle, waved to the family, and rode off to join the men in Market Square.

A short fat man called Uys saw Jeannot arrive and beckoned to him. "Name?" enquired the man. "Weinberg, Jeannot." came the reply. "Ah, good. You will report to Veldkornet Raaff, the tall fellow with the big mustache over there." He pointed to a lanky Boer on a black horse at the edge of the square. "My name is Assistant Veldkornet Uys if you need any more information."

After making himself known to Raaff, he tied up his horse and went to talk with some of the other Boers who had gathered near Raaff. There were about 40 men who had reported for duty so far, and it seemed that a further ten were expected shortly. Jeannot learned that their destination would be Twee Riviere, a day and a half's ride from Bloemfontein, and quite near to Kimberley. This was to be their initial staging post for other commandos coming from west of Bloemfontein. After the various commandos had been consolidated, they would then move to a more permanent camp at Jacobsdal, where commandos would join them from the rest of the Orange Free State and possibly some from the western Transvaal. This would form the Boer Western Army under Gen. Piet Cronje. All were aware of the initial Boer strategy to lay siege to three railhead towns, Kimberley and Mafeking in the Cape, and Ladysmith in Natal. It was going to be the responsibility of this army to protect those besieging Kimberley from British troops moving up from Cape Town to relieve the siege. The British were expected to travel by train first to De Aar, then to Hopetown, about 75 miles from Kimberley, and then to move on foot and horse towards the besieged city. Since maps were very scarce and lacked accuracy, the Boers were sure that the British would follow the rail line to stay on course from Hopetown to Kimberley.

The collection of Jeannot's colleagues in arms was the most varied group of men. They ranged from about 17 to 55 in age, with about two-thirds being farmers and the rest from Bloemfontein and surrounding towns. No-one had any form of uniform or distinguishing badge of rank. All were dressed as if they were going on a long hike that might last several days. All had horses and carried a variety of weapons. It was unlikely that any of these weapons would be used when the fighting began since the army would supply the soldiers with a rifle and ammunition. However, experience had shown that having an extra weapon was always a good strategy. There were two men whom Jeannot knew quite well. Lt. Herbert Baumann and his brother Otto were members of one of the prominent Jewish families in Bloemfontein, and their father was a prominent lawyer. Jeannot had been at school with the younger Baumann brother, so it was comforting not only to recognize people he knew but to realize he was not going to be the only *boerejood* (Jew fighting with the Boers) in the commando. The men shared their thoughts and apprehensions, and it was clear to Jeannot that there was an air of optimism in the commando. Memories of the First Boer War were still fresh in the minds of some of the older soldiers, and how the Boers had massacred the British at Majuba was an often-touted example of why the Boers would have the English licked in a short time.

Eventually, Veldkornet Raaff gave the order to mount up, and the commando began to make its way out of the Market Square. The streets leading out of town were filled with burghers, some throwing flowers, all calling words of encouragement, many invoking God's blessing on this brave group of men. Once they left the outskirts of Bloemfontein, a silence came over the commando as individuals pondered the future battles, their role, and their own mortality. The pace was slow, little more than a walk, and the horses were rested regularly. Every man needed to care for his own horse since they were totally reliant on them for transportation. Anyone losing his mount would have little chance of finding a new one unless it was from a fallen or wounded comrade. Raaff rode at the head of the column, Uys at the rear. Lt. Baumann moved up and down the column, encouraging the men and reminding them to take advantage of any water they found and to ensure that their canteens were full. It was a hot day, in the 80s, but being on the plateau, there was little humidity. Nevertheless, the horses quickly became thirsty and frequent stops were made to water them.

There were, as expected, about fifty men in the commando. When they stopped for the evening, they were divided into sections of ten men each, and each section would stand guard for a period while the others slept. The commando was nowhere near any point of action, but it was a good exercise for the men to understand the importance of securing the perimeter at all stages. Even though this was second nature to most of the men, it was useful to keep them on their toes. Jeannot now understood the reason for the 48 hours of rations they were required to bring. There would be no food provided until they reached Twee Riviere the following evening, so each man had to look after himself until then. A fire was lit, and the men sat around exchanging tales and getting to know their comrades, the men with whom they would be risking their lives in the days to come. At about ten o'clock, everyone was ordered back into the saddle, and the night march began. This continued until about 2 in the morning when the column halted to rest. Sleep came easily to Jeannot. He knew the trick of digging a small hole in the shape of his hip and filling it with dried branches and twigs, before placing the bedroll on top. In this way, he was able to ensure a good night's sleep even though the ground was quite hard.

Twee Riviere - October 18th, 1899 – Jeannot

The following day was uneventful, and the commando eventually reached the area of Twee Riviere at dusk. Each section was given a tent to erect, and this would be their home until further notice. The lights of Kimberley were visible from the camp, and regular patrols were sent out to scout the surrounding area and assist the men involved in the siege itself. No opportunity was lost to inflict some kind of harm on the enemy, and acts of sabotage were frequent - rail lines were destroyed, rolling stock blown up, anything that would either hinder the British from reaching Kimberley or prevent the inhabitants of Kimberley from making contact with the outside world. It was a siege in the classic sense of the word, centered around isolating the population and removing their ability to bring food and weapons into the city from the outside. And the Boers were a very patient lot and did their job well. Jeannot was involved in a number of these patrols, both day and night, and he began to get a sense of what soldiering involved. On the evening of October 20th, he arrived back from such a patrol and was able to snatch some time to write to his father before dinner.

Letter from Jeannot Weinberg to Edward Weinberg - October 20th, 1899 - Twee Riviere

Twee Riviere
October 20th, 1899

Dear Father
You must have read in the newspaper that Major Albrecht blew up a train with one or two locomotives and a rail car.

Things are very difficult for us and our horses too, as we ride day and night. From our camp, Kimberley is visible – only last night, 790 men were ten minutes away, and we cut the telegraph wires. The English appear frightened and do not venture outside their territory. Yesterday we caught two spies on bicycles.

We were ordered to the Orange River to cut off a strong force on their way to Kimberley. Rumor has it we will bombard Kimberley one of these days with heavy guns that are due with Cronje from the Transvaal, Mafeking, Newcastle, and Charlestown. It is hard to believe the Boers have occupied these towns.

We scarcely have time to write. Don't forget to send newspapers to J. Weinberg, Bloemfontein Commando.

Regards to Mama and the children.
Your loving son

Jeannot

After about a week in Twee Riviere, the commando moved south to Scholtznek, which they reached on October 29th. This was also a holding area - the men in Jeannot's commando had not yet been called to action.

Letter from Jeannot Weinberg to Edward Weinberg - October 30th, 1899 - Scholtznek

Scholtznek
October 30th, 1899

Dear Father

Your letter and Mama's just received.

We have heard officially about Ladysmith, everybody is very pleased, and all yelled and carried on for 15 minutes. De la Rey is expected to join us with one large and six small guns, and we hope to attack Kimberley together. I hope that God will stand by us as he did for the people at Ladysmith.

This morning I wrote a letter as I did yesterday to go to the mail at Jacobsdal, but all were returned because the river was swollen at Modder River Drift and could not be crossed. A few swam across.

We took an Englishman prisoner who was sent to Jacobsdal under escort with Field-Cornet Raaff and Lt. Baumann. On the way, the Englishman attacked Jasper Kruger with a dagger. We wonder why Raaff did not have him shot. The wounded man is now in the Jacobsdal Hospital. The Englishman was tied to a piece of wood and thrown into the river. Although he tried to dive, two men alongside him lifted his head by grabbing him by the hair. All day we hear gunfire and dynamite explosions; we presume it to be Boshoff's men fighting those who got away from Kimberley. I hope to report the fall of Kimberley shortly or a soon as I can. We expect to march forwards in a few days.

Tell Mama to keep cool, because, as you realize, it is not as dangerous as one imagines.

Greetings
Jeannot

After a little over two weeks in Scholtznek, Jeannot and his colleagues were sent to Jacobsdal, which proved to be the last staging point before he saw action.

Letter from Jeannot Weinberg to Edward Weinberg - November 18th, 1899 – Jacobsdal

Jacobsdal
November 18th, 1899

Dear Father
We arrived here this morning. Jacobsdal is a small town. We traveled through the Modder River, and we took the opportunity to cleanse ourselves thoroughly, not having had a bath for ten days. A small packet is waiting for me, and I shall take delivery in town shortly.

Yesterday many Englishmen waving white flags left Kimberley, and they attacked the men from Jacobsdal, who were camped in Alexanderfontein. Three of the Jacobsdalers were wounded; the English have yet to be counted.

I made an error in a previous letter, having written that there were 4 Maxims – in fact, there were only two, although this should be enough in any case. When I think back to the whistling and shouting, it made me feel uncomfortable.

We shall break camp this evening. Funny, just as I am writing, an order to move did arrive with the information that there are 20,000 English waiting for us at the Orange River. I guess that half that number is nearer to the truth, and I believe there are 10,000 of us to attack them. It came from van Heerden, who is the local magistrate.

I do not understand why the new order is so frantic; it is impossible to stop the Boers under these conditions. We shall have to be very resolute and be on the march for three days.
Do not worry about me. I have smelled the powder, and it does not appear all that threatening. The effect of the English guns at the Orange River is no more dangerous than the climate, and the Redcheeks do not aim well enough!

Greetings to Mama and the children and all friends.
Your loving son
Jeannot.

My address is:
c/o Veld-cornet Raaff, Griqualand West, Orange River

Author's Note: The term 'Redcheeks' is a rendering of Afrikaans 'Rooinekke,' a term commonly used by Boers for the British in reference to the sunburn they tended to suffer in Africa. It actually means 'Rednecks,' but I have avoided a literal translation because of the connotation that this word carries, especially in the USA.
Note to reader: this map is intended to help understand the area of combat at the battles of Belmont, Enslin and Modder River, as well

as the location of Jeannot's camp at Jacobsdal. For the sake of scale, the distance between Belmont and Jacobsdal is about 45 miles.

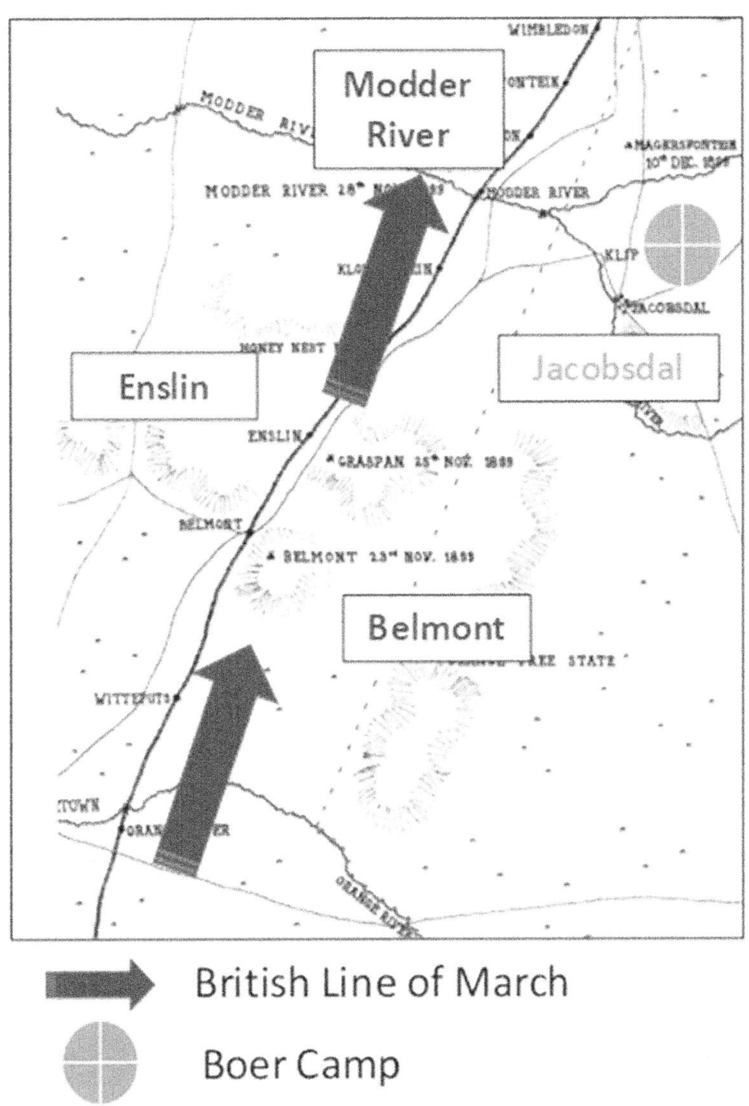

Battle of Belmont - November 23rd, 1899 – Jeannot

While Jeannot was encamped in Jacobsdal, the first real skirmish between the British and Boer forces took place on November 23rd, 1899, near the town of Belmont. Belmont was on the rail line to Kimberley, and this was the first time the Boers attempted to intercept the advance of the British. Although members of the Bloemfontein commando were present at the battle, Jeannot did not participate.

The British forces were under the control of Gen. Methuen, a seasoned fighter, but one of the 'old school.' He believed implicitly in the existing British strategy of 'standing up in close order,' and he was not about to abandon this at Belmont. He had 9,000 troops at his disposal and saw no reason why what he believed to be a much smaller Boer contingent should not be overwhelmed. He was correct about his numerical superiority, wrong about his strategic approach.

The main Boer force at Belmont was composed of around 2,000 men from the Free State under Jacobus Prinsloo (Kroonstad, Fauresmith, Bloemfontein, Brandfort, and Jacobsdaler commandos). Another 800 men from the Transvaal, under de la Rey, arrived in time to cover the Boer retreat at the end of the battle. The Boers used their traditional tactic of occupying the high ground in entrenched formations. There were five principal hills containing Boer trenches, Table Mountain (not the one in Cape Town!) and Gun Hill in the fore, and Mont Blanc, Razor Back, and Sugar Loaf to their east.

Methuen based his plan of attack on a faulty understanding of the nature of the hills. He was not aware that there was a gap between Table Mountain and Mont Blanc, believing there to be more high ground between the two hills. His plan was for the 9th Brigade to attack Table Mountain and the Guard's Brigade to attack Gun Hill.

The Coldstream Guards would then seize the non-existent high ground, while the 9th Brigade would use it to attack the northern flank of the Boer positions on Mont Blanc. They would do this after a night march that would place them at the base of the hills under cover of darkness.

The plan went wrong almost from the start. The British were not accustomed to the terrain, and, at night, their navigation proved a disaster. As a consequence, when daylight fell, none of the units was in their intended positions. This required considerable reorganization, but when this was finally achieved, the British advance did meet with success. The Boers followed a pattern they would repeat on many subsequent occasions. They would fight like demons up to the point where they were in danger of being overwhelmed; then they would steal away like thieves in the night and survive to fight another day. The British were left wondering where the opposition had gone - it was a bit like fighting specters. This is precisely what happened at Belmont. As each hill appeared to be overrun, and when the British were about to annihilate the opposition, they found that the Boers were gone. So history will recall that the British won the Battle of Belmont, but at the cost of 74 dead and 220 wounded, against Boer losses of 12 killed and 40 wounded.

The Boers clearly set out their stall at Belmont, and it was assumed by the British to be the standard way in which the war was to be fought. What Methuen did not realize was that, in many respects, these early encounters had the effect of lulling him into a sense of false security, believing he now had a clear understanding of how the enemy waged war.

The news of the battle was well received at Jacobsdal, even though the battle was a loss for the Boers. Most of the men acquitted themselves well, but some turned and ran.

Letter from Jeannot Weinberg to Edward Weinberg - November 24th, 1899 - Jacobsdal

Jacobsdal
November 24th, 1899
Dear Father

A report just received informs us that 12,000 Englishmen have fought with the Freestaters in the vicinity of Belmont. As I previously wrote to Mama, we have ten dead and 40 wounded. It is said that the Boers did badly; many took off, and there were a number of cowards among the men from Bloemfontein and Jacobsdal.

They left Alberts alone with his cannon and fled. A gunner named Osmond was killed, and van der Merwe was injured in the hand. The spokes of the cannon were shot away. It is said that the British have lots of guns, which make a big show and a lot of noise. There are many Indians among them, and it is said that they attacked the Boers with fierce determination. Another report speaks of 2,000 English casualties.

Two artillerymen watching from a hilltop saw the action take place. Forty lancers approached on a narrow path – 2 Boers killed 35 of them, and the other five fled!

Tonight, we will join with the others as the English have now struck camp. General Cronje is expected to attack from below their position, and we will join forces with those of General de la Rey so as to attack the Redcheeks from 3 sides. The expected date for the attack is tomorrow morning, and may the Almighty help us to get our revenge. I still reckon on us getting beaten even with their 2,000 dead. The Boers will have to retreat from Belmont first before taking back some of the territory from the enemy.

General Prinsloo is distributing the new Mauser rifles, and our Martini Henrys are being returned. I had a good horse and a rifle, and I consider myself lucky, even though some of our men have received even better mounts.

Today we received from the ladies in Bloemfontein a big box of cakes, and I could immediately recognize the one baked by Mama – they were the buns and apple tart that she usually bakes!

Greetings to you all and Abe as well – I have no time to write to him separately.
Your loving son
Jeannot

Battle of Enslin (Graspan) - November 25th, 1899 - Jeannot

Jeannot was correct in his assessment of an attack the following evening. On November 25th, 1899, what came to be known as the Battle of Enslin (or Graspan) took place on a hill called Graspan, near the small town of Enslin.

Methuen continued his march towards Kimberley after his victory at Belmont. It became clear to him that the next town up the line, Enslin, was likely to be the next line of Boer resistance, or at least that was what his patrols and spies had told him. He was correct. At dawn on the morning of 25th November 1899, the 9th Brigade marched out, heading north and approached Graspan (the name refers to the circle of hills that surrounds the area) or Enslin Station, to find a substantial Boer force in position on the hills to the east of the railway line, covering the approach to Enslin Station. The Boers were positioned on a long ridge of low hills rising gradually from the veld, beyond which was a further hill, the top being a precipitous ridge. The Boer force numbered around 3,000 men, equipped with a heavy gun, five field guns, a Maxim 1 pounder 'pom-pom' and a Maxim machine gun, commanded by General de la Rey. On the most northern of these hills was positioned a commando of 300 Transvaalers newly arrived from Kimberley. This was a much different obstacle than what Methuen had faced at Belmont. De La Rey, although a younger general, was a strategic genius, far more so than Prinsloo, who had led the Boers at Belmont. He had learned from the experience at Belmont and was determined not to make the same mistakes. But he still played his cards very close to his chest, not revealing a set of different strategies he was planning for later battles

Methuen, however, stuck to his guns and used a frontal attack as his primary strategy. Again, the Boers held out strongly, helped by the presence of more artillery. However, if Methuen had learned one lesson at Belmont, it was to use his own artillery more liberally to soften up the entrenched Boers. Yet again, the British infantry advanced, yet again the Boers resisted strongly. Attacking uphill is a difficult matter, as the British had learned at Belmont, and the slope of Graspan proved a valuable asset to the Boers who occupied the higher ground. But again, the force of numbers came into play, and the Boers were forced to abandon their positions and retreat. Yet, for the second time in two consecutive battles, Methuen had his opportunity for a decisive victory taken from him by the lack of mounted troops. The path of the Boer retreat lay across the open veld, and Methuen had posted his few mounted troops in a position to intercept them. A sizeable mounted force could have wrought havoc on the retreating Boers. Still, the numbers were just too small, and the horses were already too worn out from a full day of reconnaissance to take advantage of the situation. In fact, Methuen's cavalry was threatened by the retreating Boers and had to be rescued by the mounted infantry. Once again, the Boers fled with light losses. The commando headed north-east, more or less intact, towards Jacobsdal.

Graspan was another victory for the British territorially, but not numerically. The British suffered heavier losses than the Boers, and it was generally believed that the Boers only lost 21 men. It proved another classic example of the Boer 'now you see me, now you don't' strategy, aimed at tiring the British forces and building their frustration levels. Methuen had come so close on two occasions, but had in both instances, failed to force home the desired result. The Boers knew the land and made it their friend.

Modder River - November 27th, 1899 - Jeannot

Around 8 am on November 27th, Field-cornet Raaff ran over to the area where the Bloemfontein Commando was camped. "Quick, manne. Gather round. I have big news." he shouted. The men dropped what they were doing and formed up in front of him with an air of expectancy. He continued. "Tomorrow, we are going to see real action for the first time. The Redcheeks will be moving towards the confluence of the Modder and Riet Rivers, and we are going to meet them there and give them a good licking!" A cheer broke out among the soldiers - the waiting had been both frustrating and nerve-wracking, but now something positive was going to happen. Raaff beckoned them to form a circle around him. He smoothed out a patch of ground, and with a piece of stick, he started to draw a rough map. "So, here is the Modder, and here is the Riet. Here is the little island in the middle, where a hotel is located. We expect the British to attack on two fronts, one to the south of the island and one to the north. The Transvaalers are going to be on the south bank, and we will be on the north. Our positions will be here, here, here and here." He marked out the locations with his stick. "Our job this afternoon is to ride to our muster area, meet with the Commandant who will show us where our trenches are to be, then we will dig ourselves trenches to await the arrival of the enemy. We expect them to attack tomorrow morning, but if we have learned anything from Belmont and Graspan, they will move at night and try to surprise us while we are sleeping. So tonight there will not be a lot of sleep - we will be waiting for them whatever their plan." He stopped and looked out at the men, a combination of grizzled veterans and fresh-faced youths, many of whom were facing angry fire for the first time. "And remember, manne, the better the quality of our trenches, the better we can defend our position. Our strategy is a bit different in this case since there is no hill or high ground, except a small kopje where the artillery will be located. Our trenches will be on the opposite side of the river to the direction of attack so that we can use the river as a natural defense. We need to keep the Redcheeks on their side of the river. Once they start to cross, we need to be sure we bring maximum fire down on them because they will be at their most vulnerable while they are in the water. So be sure when you dig your trenches that you have a direct line of sight to the opposite bank and to the river itself. Alright, manne. Reassemble in 30 minutes and be ready to ride."

The next half hour was a flurry of activity. Men packed their possessions, grabbed something to eat - who knew when they would next be given a meal - checked their rifles and ammunition, and loaded everything onto their waiting horses. Modder River was about 15 miles from Jacobsdal, so it would take them about an hour and a half to get to where they needed to be. Horses were fed and watered, and saddles checked and tightened. The commando was ready to depart.

At 9 am, Raaff blew his whistle, and the commando formed up in front of him on their horses. The other Free State commandos were also ready to depart, each under the watchful eye of their field-cornet. Eventually, a commandant appeared, assembled the veldkornets, gave them last-minute instructions, and the ride began. Raaff rode over to his commando and gave the command. "Follow me. At a canter. Ride!" And the commando was on its way. The route from Jacobsdal to Modder River was north-west and roughly followed the Modder River. Within an hour, the island came into sight, and a half-hour later, they arrived at the mustering point. The ride had been relaxed despite the heat and dust. Those irritations were overtaken by the adrenalin of knowing that they were finally going into battle, and the long wait of idleness was soon to be over. Gen. Koos de la Rey was waiting for the Free State contingent at the muster point in the village of Rosmead. When they had assembled, he addressed his troops. "Manne, we are going to give the enemy the shock of their lives in this place. They have been used to seeing us in trenches at the top of kopjes, and they have been learning how to deal with us in that kind of formation. But here they are going to get a surprise. We are not going to deploy in the high ground - we are going to put our trenches at ground level along the bank of the river. The kopjes have been obvious aiming points for the British artillery, and the trajectory of our fire from the top of the kopjes has meant that we cannot effectively hit them until they are quite close. But we have the Mauser rifle that has a flat trajectory, so if we use them at ground level, we can sweep the veld from a long distance and increase our killing ground. Gen. Cronje has agreed, and this is the strategy we are going to use. And remember, boys, we need to be able to see them, but they must not be able to see us until it is too late for them to escape. So conceal yourselves well and keep silent at all times."

De la Rey gave instructions to the veldkornets as to their required positions and direction of fire. Jeannot's commando was located just below the town of Rosmead in an S-bend in the river. Here they quickly dug four-foot deep trenches and camouflaged them with branches - there was a section of 10 men to a trench, with a five-foot gap between each man. At each firing position, a supply of ammunition was piled up so the rifleman could have access to replacement ammunition without leaving his post. There was also an ammunition carrier assigned to every three trenches to ensure the level of ammunition was maintained. It was up to the individual to decide what he brought into the trench and what he left off the battlefield. Everyone, of course, brought water bottles, food, and groundsheets, but some brought additional clothing in case the weather turned.

The standard weapon was the Mauser 95. It was breech-loaded and clip-fed, each clip containing 5 x 57mm smokeless cartridges. It had two sights, one front one rear, and had an effective killing range in excess of 1,000m. It was an incredible piece of equipment, and the men felt very secure in their ability to bring down the enemy before they were in range to fire back

Battle of Modder River - November 28th, 1899 – Jeannot

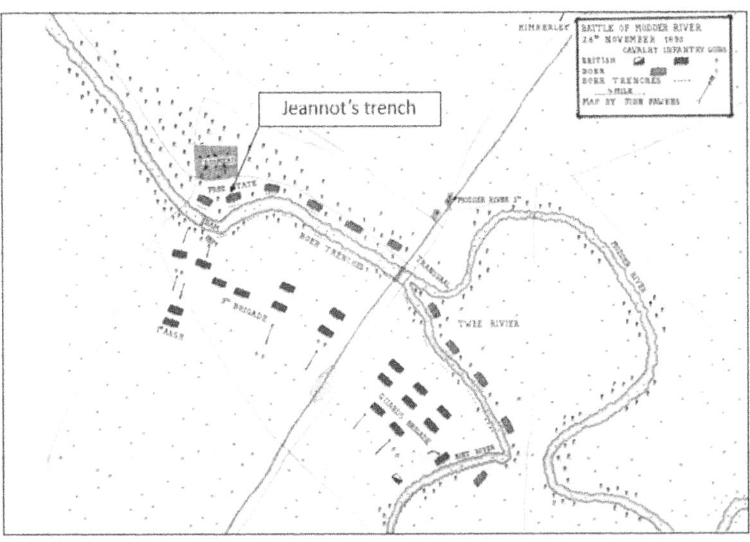

No-one slept that night. They had entered the trenches at 10 pm the previous night and assumed their defensive positions. De la Rey had left the Freestaters under the command of Gen. Prinsloo, a move not entirely popular with the men, given his previous performances at Belmont and Graspan. Jeannot's trench was second from the western end of the line. He was located towards the middle of the trench, with Reg Britz on his left and Barry

Havenga on his right. He had not known these men before the war but had come to know them quite well at Jacobsdal. Britz was 24, a farmer from the Petrusburg area; Havenga was a clerk at a store in Bloemfontein - he was 20. They seemed to be just as nervous as Jeannot, this being the first time they had been in the line of fire. No-one spoke very much, each dealing with his own fears and apprehensions, each thinking of his family and loved ones. The night passed slowly.

At 5.30 am, shots rang out from the left of their trench. They were quite far away, and the shooting did not last long. Jeannot wondered what had happened. Half an hour later, word filtered down the trenches that a British scouting party had been spotted, and sent on its way by Boer rifles. It was not until 7.15 that the men started to see British soldiers appearing on the horizon. Once again, it was going to be a war of numbers, the British having 8,000 men in the field to the Boers' 3,000.

Jeannot felt his stomach tighten as he watched the slow progress of the British troops across the field. He could make out different regiments by the uniforms they wore, although he did not know which regiment was going to be attacking his trench. As it turned out, they were facing Pole-Carew's 9th Battalion and the Scots Guards. The men had been told to hold their fire until ordered. When the British were about 1,000 yards away, the order came, "Prepare to fire!" Everyone cocked their rifles and took their positions at the wall of the trench. Slowly the British advanced. When they were about 900 yards from the trench, the order came "Fire! Fire at will!"

For a moment, all hell broke loose. The ambush quickly drove the advancing infantry to ground. The Scots Guards bore the brunt of this fusillade, with their machine gun section 'swept away' in a hail of bullets and pom-pom fire, but the ambush had been sprung far too early to be really effective. The premature ambush had affected the 9th infantry Brigade even less than it had the Guards. As well as being sprung at long range, the 9th had also been partially shielded from the ambush by a fold in the ground. The commanders realized they were facing Prinsloo's Freestaters whom they had defeated twice in a week - Pole-Carew started pushing his battalions to their left (i.e., west) while keeping in touch with the Guards. They began slowly but steadily working their way to the Boer right.

Jeannot could see the enemy moving closer and closer. They were about 500 yards away now, and although many were dropping from Boer rifle fire, the phalanx just kept advancing on the trenches. "My God!" yelled one man. "How many of them are there?" Jeannot knew he had hit a number of Redcheeks, but did not know whether he had killed or wounded them. He felt sure he must have killed at least one, and the feeling was one he had never experienced before. To take another man's life was something he had been taught never to do. Yet here in the heat of combat, it seemed the most natural thing to do. He knew he was suppressing his emotions, knew that the time would come when he would have to face his own conscience, but now his only thought was the battle and his comrades. He had heard screams from either side of him in the trench, knew that comrades had been hit and lay dying or wounded, but his job was to keep up a rate of fire and try to win the day. Yet on they came, bayonets glinting in the sunlight, volleys of shots thudding into the ground in front of him or whistling over his head. Then he heard the welcome sound of the Boer artillery opening up on the advancing troops. The most effective weapon seemed to be the 'pom-pom' gun, a rapid-firing weapon that discharged one-pound rounds almost at the speed of a machine gun. These cut vast swathes into the advancing men. And still, they came.....

Suddenly a series of loud explosions were heard coming from behind the enemy lines. "Artillery!" shouted someone. "Take cover!" The first salvo fell well short of the Boer trenches, the stones, and earth being thrown into the air as the projectiles exploded. The next salvo landed in the river, not fifty yards from the trenches - the British gunners were getting their range. When the next salvo arrived, it was almost on top of the Boer trenches, and the men flattened themselves on the ground. Jeannot felt his heart pounding - a direct hit on the trench would mean the end of him. The battery lasted about 15 minutes, during which time hundreds of shells landed near the Boer trenches. The noise was deafening - the roar of the explosions and the zing of flying shrapnel. Fortunately for the Boers, the way in which their trenches were arranged, very few casualties were sustained. Jeannot saw a few men being carried back from the front with wounds - some might have been dead - it was impossible to tell. Well, he thought to himself, that was my first experience of an artillery bombardment, and I seemed to have come through it in one piece. Let's see how things go when the infantry gets here.

By this time, the infantry was only 100 yards from the river. And they came in their hundreds. The Boers poured fire on them, but could not stop the advance. Eventually, the command rang out, "Pull back!" The commandos hurriedly abandoned their trenches and moved swiftly back towards Rosmead. Just before the village was a small kopje on which an artillery battery was deployed. The gunners called out to them. "Manne, come and help us. We need covering fire in order to be able to continue firing." Jeannot looked around his and saw several men from the Bloemfontein Commando near him. Without thinking, he shouted. "Bloemfonteiners, follow me." Six men heeded the call, and they quickly climbed the ridge. The artillerymen had a case of rifle ammunition, which the commandos rapidly divided up and sought cover in the rocks of the kopje. For the rest of the day, Jeannot and his six comrades formed a shield for the gunners, allowing them to continue firing into the advancing British. The British artillery had noticed this battery of guns, but, try as they might, they could not land a shell on target. There was plenty of shrapnel in the air, but no direct hits on the battery. Surveying the field and the advance of the British infantry across the river, the gunners decided that the position was hopeless, and signaled the retreat. The seven boys from Bloemfontein followed them to safety, always glancing behind them to see if they were being pursued.

It was not until 6.30 that evening that the exhausted men made it back to the Boer encampment. The day had been another loss for the Boers, but they had given the British a severe bloody nose. And most importantly, de la Rey's strategy of deploying riflemen at ground level had proved itself to be highly effective. Jeannot was so tired and thirsty he could hardly reflect on the day and the impact it would have on him. He knew he had done his duty, especially in the latter part of the day, when he and his colleagues had chosen to stay and defend the gunners rather than withdraw with the rest of the infantry. He felt proud in one sense but realized as well that he had put himself seriously in harm's way, and the outcome need not have turned out as it did.

Later that night, the commando returned to their camp at Jacobsdal. The British had won the day at Modder River, but had taken heavy punishment and would need time to regroup and recover. This was a blessing for the Boers as well, since they also desperately needed some time to marshal their forces for the next battle.

On the following day, Jeannot wrote to his Father.

Letter from Jeannot Weinberg to Edward Weinberg - November 29th, 1899 – Jacobsdal

Jacobsdal
November 29th, 1899

Dear Father
You have probably heard by now of the battle at Modder River and have no doubt been concerned about whether I have been injured. I was a part of the Free State group that defended the north side of the battlefield, and I am happy to tell you that I am unharmed. And please tell Mama not to be concerned - I have tasted battle, and it does not frighten me.

It was a very long and hard day, and our group of men fought very bravely, but eventually, we had to withdraw because the Redcheeks sent more men than our troops could handle. I know my rifle barrel got very hot because I had fired so many bullets. I must have hit many of the enemy, but I don't know whether I killed them or only wounded them. We lost a number of our men, but I think we fared much better than the enemy when it comes to casualties. I think the most nervous I got was when the enemy artillery fired on us because you can never tell where the bombs will land. At least if you are fighting against the infantry, you can look them in the eye!

After we were ordered to retreat, a group of us from the Bloemfontein Commando went to help out a battery of our artillery who needed our covering fire to carry on their bombardments. We got under cover on a small kopje and held off a great number of Redcheeks by sniping at them and forcing them to look for cover. When we got back to Jacobsdal, the officers had got wind of this, and we were hailed as heroes. I doubt if we deserved this notice because, according to my view, that wasn't exactly a heroic deed on our part but rather stupidity, because if a cavalry regiment had suddenly stormed in, they would have taken us prisoner.

We are hearing rumors that the next major battle will be at Magersfontein, but we will have to wait and see what the enemy is up to.

Please thank Mama for the food package that was waiting for me when I got back from the battle. I have been eating a lot of biltong lately, and to get one of her cakes is a wonderful change. Please write to me if you can - my address will be the same because I am still under Veldkornet Raaff.

Regards to all friends and the children, and of course to you and Mama.

Your loving son,
Jeannot

So ended the Modder River experience, and the Boer forces were glad to get a few weeks' respite before the next battle. The British were making steady progress, expensive progress some would say, but progress nevertheless. The Boers were bloodied but unbowed and were beginning to become familiar with the British battle tactics, a lesson that would stand them in good stead as the advance proceeded.

Chapter 13 - The March to Magersfontein - British

Cape Town - October 1899 - Buller

Gen. Sir Redvers Buller was in a quandary. The Boers had besieged three towns, Ladysmith in Natal, Mafeking in the far northern Cape, and Kimberley about 225 miles south of Mafeking. He did not have enough troops to attack all three sets of besiegers. At best, he could attack two until further reinforcements arrived from Britain and the colonies. So, he was forced to decide which town would have to wait until at least one of the other sieges had been lifted. The strategic decision was easy. Kimberley and Ladysmith held the keys to the Orange Free State and the Transvaal. Mafeking would provide a jumping-off point for an invasion of the Transvaal from the west, but it was the furthest town from the areas in which the main British forces were stationed - Cape Town and Durban. So, the brave and resourceful Baden-Powell would just have to wait until either Kimberley or Ladysmith were retaken.

Sir Redvers Henry Buller, the Commander-in-Chief of His Majesty's Forces in South Africa, was born on 7th December 1839 in Downes, near Crediton, Devon, the son of James Wentworth Buller MP, and Charlotte, daughter of Lord Howard. He was educated at Eton, and pursued a military career following his schooling, having been commissioned as an Ensign in the 60th Rifles in 1858. He was believed to be an ideal candidate for the position of Commander-in-Chief in South Africa. He had an illustrious career in many theaters of war but was especially suited for a South African operation, given his extensive experience in the area. He had served in South Africa during the 9th Cape Frontier War in 1878 and the Anglo-Zulu War of 1879. In the Zulu War, he commanded the mounted infantry of the northern British column under Sir Evelyn Wood. He fought at the British defeat at the Battle of Hlobane, where he was awarded the Victoria Cross for bravery under fire. In the First Boer War of 1881, he was Sir Evelyn Wood's chief of staff, and the following year was appointed head of intelligence, this time in the Egypt campaign, and was knighted.

Buller was essentially a 'Renaissance man' - fond of the arts, literature, sport of all kind, and especially fine wine and cuisine. He was a large man with a large, square face punctuated by a large mustache that almost covered his top lip. It was this mustache that often rendered his speech incomprehensible. His answer of "Yes" or "No" frequently sounded like a "Hrmph," making it unclear to his listeners whether he was assenting or dissenting! And the tiny peaked cap he always wore made him a target of many a cartoonist.

Buller was a cautious and patient general, willing to endure setbacks to achieve an eventual victory. Despite the criticism leveled at him for his rather unimaginative strategy, Buller was 'a soldier's soldier' and was beloved by his men. He was conspicuously humane in a generally inhumane profession. He had done much whilst in administration to improve conditions, and on the campaign, he ensured that his men were well equipped. Under him, the army never lacked for anything, nor did they suffer the same hardships or disease which characterized other generals. On the few occasions when his men went short, Buller shared their discomforts, at one time going hungry and sleeping on the ground without a tent in the Drakensberg mountains when his troops had advanced ahead of their supplies.

But now Buller had to decide who should lead the forces to relieve Kimberley and Ladysmith. After much discussion and deliberation, he determined that he would lead the attack on Ladysmith and that Gen. Methuen, on his way from Britain, would have the task of lifting the siege at Kimberley. He would set off for Durban, join the troops stationed there, and begin the journey north to Ladysmith.

Methuen would gather his forces - the British 1st Division - and take the train to Hopetown, after which he would march the hundred or so miles to Kimberley. Even though the rail line went right into Kimberley, Buller was afraid that, if all his troops were transported into enemy territory on a train, this would provide too tempting a target for the Boers. He would run the risk of having the whole force wiped out in one train attack, So he advised Methuen to go only as far as Hopetown by train.

General Paul Methuen, or the Third Baron Methuen to give him his full title, was a public school educated man in his early forties who had served in the British Army since 1867. He saw active duty in the Ashanti campaign of 1873 - 1874 on the staff of Sir Garnet Wolseley and was the commandant of headquarters in Egypt for three months in 1882, being present at the Battle of Tel el-Kebir. He became brevet-colonel in 1881 and served in the expedition of Sir Charles Warren to Bechuanaland in 1884-1885, where he commanded Methuen's Horse, a corps of mounted rifles. He was promoted to substantive colonel in 1888, major-general in May of 1888, and commanded the Home District from 1892-1897. He was promoted to lieutenant-general in 1898. His role as commander of the 1st Division was his first significant field command in his career.

Methuen was fortunate to have as part of his 1st Division a group of talented and experienced regiments and field commanders. These included the First Guard Brigade under Maj-Gen Sir Henry Colville, the 9th Brigade under Maj-Gens. Featherstonehaugh and Pole-Carew, a cavalry unit under Col. Gough and 2 (later 3) batteries of field artillery under Lt.-Col Hall. Methuen could also call on the 3rd (Highland) Brigade under Maj-Gen Andrew Wauchope (diverted from 2nd Division), in reserve at De Aar. In all, the division numbered some 10,000 men.

British Camp on the Orange River - November 1899 – Methuen

The train ride from Cape Town had been uneventful, if uncomfortable. The intense heat of the Karoo turned the interior of the troop train into an oven for both officers and men, and it was a welcome sight when the final destination was at last reached. The troops detrained and set up camp along the banks of the Orange River. Later that week, Methuen called an order group of his senior officers.

Present were Colville, Pole-Carew, Featherstonehaugh, and Gough. They were seated in a semi-circle around a map in Methuen's command tent. The map showed the area between their current position and Kimberley. Accurate maps were a rarity, and this one was, at best, accurate in the location of the major towns and rivers, but was lacking in topographical details so crucial to military strategy.

Methuen began. "Gentlemen, we know our objective, and we know the troops we have been given with which to achieve this objective. We do not, however, have any sufficiently accurate information on the strength and position of the Boer troops." Pole-Carew interrupted. "May we understand why this is proving so difficult, General?" Methuen paused for a moment, then continued, "Two reasons, really. In the first place, the Boers do not wear uniforms, so it is extremely difficult to tell one group from another. Sometimes, if we are fortunate enough to get sight of the general, we can try to identify the group, but this is rare. And they are so mobile that it is impossible to know whether a group of commandos we see in one location is not the same group we saw at another location a few days earlier. So it all becomes a bit confusing." Pole-Carew nodded. "The second reason is even more concerning. The Boer rifles seem to be effective at a range of about 1000 yards. This means that our reconnaissance patrols are never able to get close enough either to see how many troops they have or what they are up to. We have tried patrols on foot and on horseback, and neither has been able to penetrate close enough to their lines to provide us with anything really useful.

Colville coughed. "So what you are telling us is that we are fighting blind." "I am afraid so," said Methuen. "We do know from demographic statistics how many they can theoretically throw against us, and while it is fairly certain that the majority of Transvaal burghers will be fighting in the Ladysmith area, it is difficult, nay impossible to tell whether all available Freestaters are ranged against us here, or whether some of them have gone to help their brothers in Natal." Pole-Carew let out a slow exhalation of breath and shook his head. "So, what is our strategy, General?" Methuen went to his briefcase and pulled out two further maps. "Gentlemen, these are the battle formations at the recently fought battles of Talana and Elandslaagte near Ladysmith. They were sent to me by Gen. Buller."

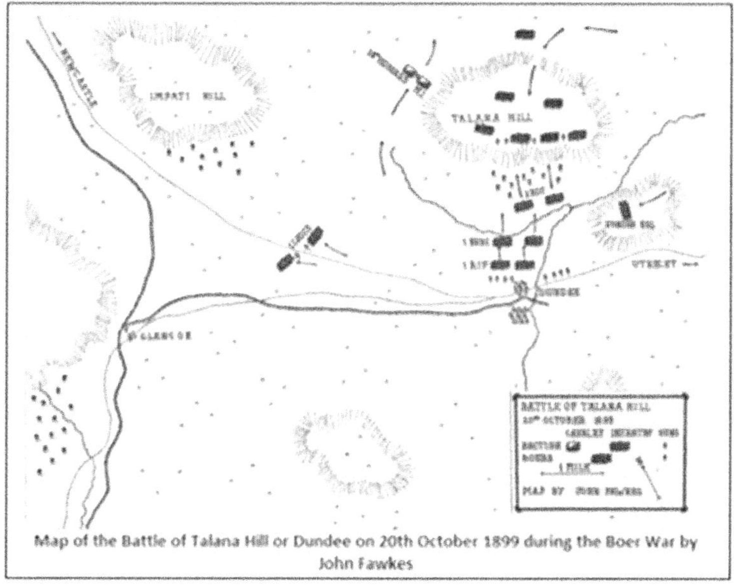

Map of the Battle of Talana Hill or Dundee on 20th October 1899 during the Boer War by John Fawkes

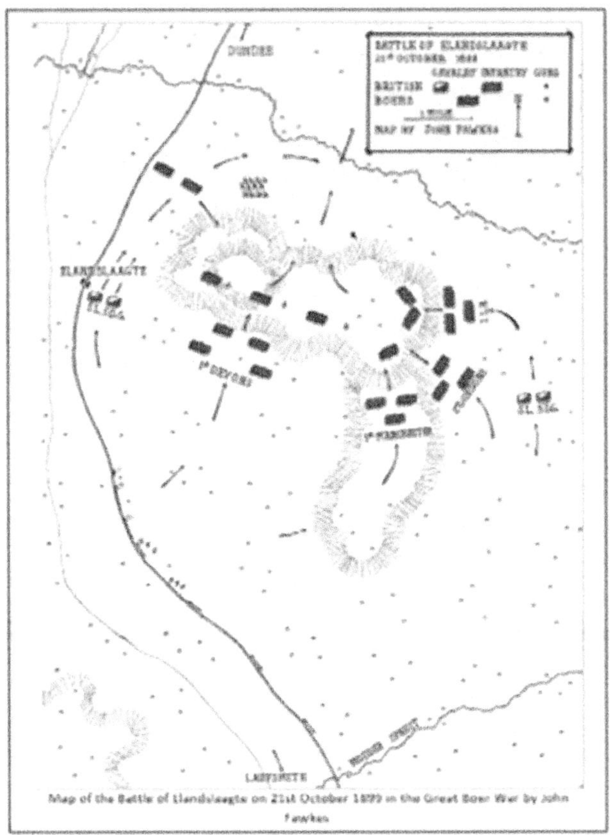

Map of the Battle of Elandslaagte on 21st October 1899 in the Great Boer War by John Fawkes

"You will notice one distinct similarity in both battle maps - the predilection of the Boers to dig in on the leading face of a hill and invite the enemy to come and get them. This is a settled strategy. Belief in controlling the high ground is fundamental to Boer strategic thinking, and we have no reason to believe that this will not be replicated here in the Cape. So your task, gentlemen, is to formulate the most effective way to dislodge the Boers from their positions and drive them back in the direction of Kimberley. If we look at the terrain between Kimberley and us, we will notice several points that have high ground and seem the most likely places to encounter Boer resistance."

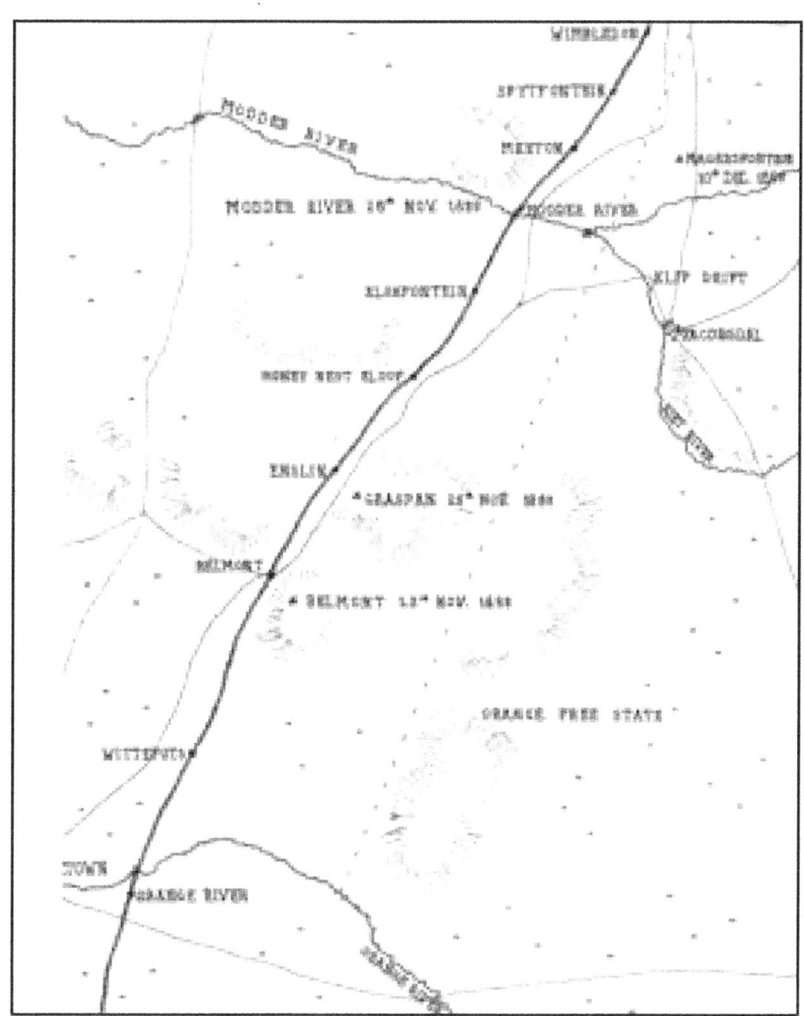

The men arose and gathered around the map. Methuen used a wooden stick to indicate places and positions. "We are following the line of the railway to Kimberley. This is no secret - the Boers well know we would never risk it in the open veld, and we can expect them to try to oppose us at points they feel they can defend well. So, if we bear in mind the fact that they will be seeking high ground from which to find, it seems logical.." and here he tapped the map in various places with the stick "that they will oppose us here at Belmont, here at Graspan, possibly at Monty Kent Kloof, definitely at Modder River and possibly at Magersfontein. So we can expect three or four skirmishes until we break through their defenses and reach Kimberley."

Methuen paused for a moment, then inquired whether anyone had any questions or comments. Featherstonehaugh returned to his seat and asked, " How do you propose to use the artillery and cavalry in these skirmishes? And do you expect the Boers to used mounted riflemen to oppose us?" Again, Methuen thought for a moment before replying. "I do not think the Boers will use mounted infantry. Yes, I know they were in common use in their conflicts with the black tribes, but remember those people had no horses of their own. So, I do not anticipate any traditional cavalry battles - the cavalry will be used to pursue the retreating Boers after they have been routed from their positions by the infantry. One of the things we do know about these people - they are not the sort to hang around until the last man is killed. Once they perceive their position to be untenable, they will cut and run. And that is where we shall use the cavalry to cut them down." Featherstonehaugh nodded his approval. "As regards the artillery, I shall hand the baton to Col. Gough."

Gough rose and addressed the gathering. "The artillery will play a dual role. The first will be counter-bombardment. Word has it that the Boers have some pretty tidy pieces of artillery acquired from Germany - Creusots, and Maxims, to name a few. It will be our job to neutralize the enemy guns to prevent them from being used against our infantry. And secondly, we will provide fire support for our advancing infantry. We need to get Gen. Cronje and his boys to keep their heads down in their trenches long enough to allow our foot soldiers to get in range. Once we get them close enough, this will compensate for the fact that their rifles have a longer range than ours. Any questions?" There were none, and he resumed his seat.

"And our infantry strategy?" inquired Pole-Carew. "That will be business as usual. Close formation by regiment, number of advancing regiments determined by the size of the front, regiments moving off at staged intervals as required by the needs of those ahead of them. Classical approach, classical results, what?" Pole-Carew was not entirely satisfied. "How did this approach work for us at Talana and Elandslaagte?" The question nonplussed Methuen. "It is my understanding that our losses there were more a question of bad luck than bad strategy. I remain confident that our infantry strategy has worked in the past and will continue to work in the future. Gentlemen, are there any further questions before we discuss logistics?" There were none, and the meeting moved on to other topics.

Battles of Belmont and Graspan – November 1899 - Methuen

The encounters at Belmont and Graspan were textbook examples of the approach delineated by Methuen in his briefing on the Orange River. The Boers occupied the high ground, dug in, and invited the British to advance on their positions. Several night marches had not entirely gone according to plan since the men had no maps, and the nights were dark, but everything seemed to work out in the end just as Methuen had predicted. The Boers fought until they felt outnumbered, then melted away into the veld.

There were a few troubling aspects of the first two battles. The first was that the cavalry seemed totally incapable of mopping up the Boer retreat once they had been dislodged from their defensive positions, mainly because there was uncertainty as to which direction the Boers would scatter. They frequently chose multiple directions of retreat, and this made it particularly difficult for the cavalry to focus on the main line of retreat. The other was the unexpectedly high rate of casualties suffered at these two skirmishes. At Belmont, British casualties were 75 officers and soldiers killed and 223 wounded. Boer casualties were said to have been 83 killed, 20 wounded, and 30 captured, including a German artillery commandant and six field cornets. At Graspan, British losses were 20 officers and men killed and 165 wounded. The Royal Naval Brigade suffered 101 casualties from 365 men. Boer losses were estimated at around 220 dead and wounded.

Methuen was deeply concerned about this. Even though the British had ultimately been victorious and driven the Boers out of their entrenched position, the British army was unaccustomed to suffering such heavy losses. Methuen heard that a Boer prisoner, Jan Herold, had been brought to the camp, and he determined to have him interrogated. He summoned one of his intelligence offices, a Captain Bond, and together they went to where the prisoner was being held. Methuen himself was in a Boer hat, a pair of Norwegian slippers, khaki trousers, and short sleeves, an outfit that never failed to amuse the men as typifying the 'eccentric Englishman.'

Herold was a thin, short man dressed in shabby clothes. His left hand was bandaged, and he had a scar across his temple. He sat in an upright chair, his hands and feet bound. He looked like he needed a good meal and a night's sleep. Capt. Bond addressed him.

"Do you speak English?
"A little, sir. Not too good."
"Where were you captured?"
"Graspan, sir."
"Have you been treated well since your capture?"
"Yes, sir. Thank you, sir, I have no complaints."
"Do you want to go home to your family?"
"Yes, sir. Please, sir."
"If you help us, maybe we can help you. Do you understand?"
"Yes, sir."

"Tell me, Herold, do you think the British are good soldiers?
"Oh, yes, sir. Very good, sir."
"But, do you find it easy to shoot us?"
"Yes, sir."
"Why is that?"
"Because we can always see you."
"What do you mean?"
"We can always see the shiny things on your uniforms, so we know where to shoot."

Bond looked at Methuen. He shrugged.

"What kind of shiny things?"
"I don't know, sir. But when your soldiers come towards us, things blink in the sunlight."
"And this gives you something to aim at?"
"Yes, sir."
"And how do you know which ones are the officers?"
"They are not with a rifle, so you know they are a officer."
"Alright, Herold, you can go back to your cell now. We will let you know later if you are to be released."
"Yes, sir, Thank you, sir."

Bond and Methuen went back to Methuen's command tent. "So, it seems," said Methuen, "that we are not doing enough to camouflage ourselves. We have adopted the khaki uniform to make us as inconspicuous as we can, but I'll warrant none of the officers is covering up their rank insignia or buttons. I am sure these are the 'shiny things' that man was referring to." "I would agree, sir," said Bond. "I think we need to issue an order that no soldier is to go into battle with anything that is likely to reflect light, even in darkness." "See that this happens," said Methuen. "And anyone who objects can come and speak to me."

And so it was that officers were required to reduce their profile by dulling their buttons and accoutrements and, where possible, to carry rifles, in line with their soldiers.

Battle of Modder River - November 28th, 1899 - Hamilton

It was 3.30 am, and Sergeant Colin Hamilton of the 1st Argyll and Sutherland Highlanders was furious. His regiment had, the previous day, marched from Enslin to the approaches to Modder River in 110-degree heat, and now they were being told that they were going into battle at dawn without breakfast. Word had come from on high that Gen. Methuen had ordered the cooks not to prepare any food until the river had been reached. Fighting on an empty stomach was one thing. Doing it after an enervating march the day before that had sapped the energy of his platoon was simply unacceptable. He hurried to his platoon commander, Lt. Tony Tatham. Hamilton noticed that the officer's buttons and rank markings had been dulled by applying the solution used to restore the color of puttees.

"Sir, begging a moment of your time, sir.
"Yes, sergeant, what is it?"
"Sir, is there any truth in the rumor that we will not be getting anything to eat before we advance on the Boer positions?
"That is my understanding, sergeant."
"Sir, is command aware of the impact this will have on our troops? Most of them are worn out from yesterday's march, have had very little sleep, and are now being asked to fight on an empty stomach."
"I appreciate your concern, Hamilton, but there is little I can do. The order is from Gen. Methuen himself. The officers aren't getting breakfast either, so we are all in the same boat, old chap."
"I see, sir. This is not good for the morale of the men. They were pretty excited after the victory at Graspan, but I'm afraid the heat and the insects in this God-forsaken place have sucked all the enthusiasm out of them."

"That may well be the case, sergeant, but that's what you and I are here for. To ensure that we continue to keep morale high, and lead the men into battle in an orderly fashion. Anything else, sergeant?"
"No, sir. Thank you, sir."

Hamilton was far from appeased but was powerless to resist. When he returned to the platoon, he was accosted by Corporal McEwan, a short man with blond hair and a wispy blond mustache.

"Any luck, sarge?"
"None whatsoever. They don't seem to care about whether we eat or not. Tatham says the officers aren't going to be fed either, but I'll bet that's a fucking lie. Methuen and his precious brass wouldn't give up a meal if their lives depended on it."
"So, it's up to us to keep a stiff upper lip and soldier on." The remark was more than liberally laced with sarcasm.
"I guess that's right, corporal. The price of leadership, I guess. Alright, pass the word on to the troops and make sure they have their canteens full of water. This is going to be another scorcher, and I don't want anyone to fall over unless it is because of a Boer bullet."

Hamilton returned to his private thoughts. They had received a taste of what it was like to attack Boer positions at Belmont and Graspan, and they had been exposed to fire from the Mausers firing smokeless cartridges. Although both battles had eventually been won, Hamilton was aware of the most dangerous thing about fighting the Boers - you never knew where the buggers were. Not only were they entrenched behind camouflage, but even when they fired, the smokeless cartridges meant that you still could not see where the damn shots were being fired from. Then when you finally made it up the hill where the firing had come from, the buggers had scarpered. So, all you were left with was a set of empty trenches, and the prospect of picking up your dead and caring for your wounded. Not exactly the way we were taught to wage war.

Where were the bayonet charges, the close combat, the 'don't shoot till you see the whites of their eyes!'? Jesus, we haven't even got close enough to see if they have eyes at all! And now I have to lead my platoon down the slope towards the river without knowing either whether they are there or, if they were there, exactly where their strength is concentrated. At least we will be advancing downhill for a change. Slugging up those stony kopjes in 100-degree heat is nobody's idea of fun. It would be bad enough even if no-one was trying to kill you. And the bloody ground! It was so hard that, if shooting started and you had to dive for cover, you knew you would come back with skinned knees and elbows from the stones and soil. That's if you were lucky enough not to jump into a bloody thorn bush, of which there are thousands—and located just where you need to dive for cover, almost as if the Boers put them there to torment us. No, it was not possible to come away from a battle in this country without spilling at least some of your blood. And the heat! Never any cloud cover, just the baking sun, day in and day out, sucking the life out of you. Not at all like I was used to in Darlington! The Boers are supposed to be used to it, but I'm sure even they don't enjoy it.

At 5.15 am, Methuen and Colville moved up to the top of a kopje to survey the terrain sloping down towards the Modder River. The troops had been drawn up into the advance positions and were starting to move tentatively down the slope. As the British troops came within 1,200 yards of the river, Methuen remarked to Colville, "They're not here." Colville replied, "They're sitting uncommonly tight if they are."

At this point, the Boers opened fire. It was an impressive salvo, stretching about 4 miles across, a blaze of fire and dust.

Hamilton yelled, "Face down, laddies. Take cover." But he was too late. Three members of his platoon sank to the ground, one dead, the others severely wounded. The rest had made it to whatever cover was available, and for the next fifteen minutes, they were entertained by the zing and crack of rifle fire in and around their position. There were no further casualties in this first foray. Hamilton's platoon and the rest of the Argyles were positioned on the left flank of the British advance and were due to ford the Riet River just below the town of Rosmead. The rays of the rising sun were now starting to creep over the horizon, and the slope leading down to the confluence of the Riet and Modder Rivers began to become visible. Although the trap had been sprung too early, the platoon was in a difficult situation, unable to withdraw or to advance, mostly in the open without cover. As the morning progressed, the troops were again exposed to the blazing heat of the South African sun. The temperature rose to 110 degrees, and the troops lay in the open, few with any remaining water. The movement and shell explosions disturbed innumerable ants' nests, the ants adding to the discomfort of the soldiers lying among them. It was almost impossible for anyone to raise his head - it was immediately met with the crackle of rifle fire. The Boers had snipers, and they were doing a very effective job of keeping the British troops pinned down. The only way forward in the absence of artillery support was to crawl flat to the ground, and this is what Hamilton and his men were forced to do. Under the terrible heat, and over the stony and thorny ground, they inched their way forward.

At around noon, the 62nd Battery arrived after a twenty-five-mile march in which several horses died of exhaustion. The battery came into action on the left flank at a range of 1,500 yards, but after a few salvos, they moved up to 900 yards and resumed firing. Once the Boer guns were silenced, the battery withdrew out of rifle range, only to be redirected to the British right flank where they were required to repeat the operation, firing six rounds a minute until the Boer guns there were silenced.

As the afternoon wore on, Hamilton and his platoon made progress towards the river. Most of the ground they gained had been under cover of the artillery barrage, and now they found themselves in sight of a farmhouse occupied by the Boers near the bank of the river. Tatham signaled to Hamilton to join him, and the sergeant crawled over. "Sergeant, we are going to storm that farmhouse. I want your platoon to attack the left side of the house; I will lead the other two platoons against the right-hand side. We will have to climb a small gully before we get there, so make sure the men keep low. Once we reach the gully, fix bayonets and await my command to charge. Is that clear?" "Yes, sir," said Hamilton, and he returned to his men.

He beckoned the platoon to crawl within earshot. "Lads, we are going to storm that farmhouse with the rest of the company. Lt. Tatham and the other two platoons will attack the right-hand side and we the left. There are Boers inside, but we do not know whether they have a machine gun. So be careful and stay behind cover wherever possible. In front of us is a small gully. When I have finished this briefing, we will crawl down into the gully, fix bayonets and wait for the lieutenant to give us the order to charge. Everyone clear?" Mutters of assent came from the platoon members. "And no talking or smoking in the gully. Surprise is going to be critical."

The platoon moved cautiously forward and dropped into the gully. The edge of the gully was about four-foot-high, low enough to scramble up, high enough to provide temporary shelter. The men lay on their backs and noiselessly fixed bayonets. When the platoon was ready, Hamilton waved a thumbs up to Tatham, who was down the gully from his position. The men waited in anticipation and fear, knowing what was in store for them when they broke cover.

After 10 minutes, the command came - "Charge!" Hamilton was the first to his feet. "Come on, laddies. For Scotland!" The men followed him, and they were greeted by a hail of fire from the farmhouse. The distance from the gully to the farmhouse was about 50 yards, but it seemed like a mile. Six men dropped during the first salvo, but the rest rushed at the target, yelling at the top of their lungs, bayonets pointed to the front. The air was thick with dust and lead, and Hamilton felt a bullet pass through the fabric of his tunic. He looked down quickly. "No blood, thank God." By this time, about half the platoon had made it to the farmhouse and was about to engage in a bayonet charge when Tatham yelled: "Hold your fire!" They looked to see a group of about ten Boers exiting the house under cover of a white flag. The attack had been a success - a foothold had been acquired, and the Argyles had acquitted themselves admirably.

What happened next was both eerie and unexpected. As the platoon moved past the farmhouse, they got their first sight of the Boer trenches. They were empty! Ghost trenches that offered no clue that, an hour earlier, they had been filled with fierce Boer riflemen intent on annihilating the British advance. They had withdrawn, disappeared, like mist on a summer's morning. No firing, no chatter, just silence. No rifles, no ammunition, no men. Tatham called to Hamilton. "This is just like Belmont. Just when you think you have got them in position to give them a jolly good thrashing, they slip out of your grasp as easily as a scrumhalf leaving a lock for dust. It is like fighting phantoms." Hamilton nodded. "Well, sir." he said, "At least they are not here peppering us with lead. What orders for the platoon, sir?" "Regroup, look to the wounded, count your dead and injured, and report back to me." "Sir," said Hamilton.

Hamilton gathered his men and informed them of what they were to do. The stretcher-bearers were already arriving, and the men helped them to load the wounded onto stretchers. Hamilton had been in the army for a long time, but the sight of the wounded never failed to churn his stomach. The cries of the wounded men were pitiful, exacerbated by the thirst and the continuous stream of insects that populate any area near the water. One man had taken a bullet in the left side of his head, ripping off the ear and shattering a section of the skull. He lay holding a bandage to his head, now soaked with blood, whimpering and calling for water. Another man's leg had been shattered by a bullet, pieces of bone sticking through a raw, bleeding wound. A corporal had been hit in the stomach and was doing his best with the help of one of the men to prevent his guts from spilling out on the ground. The sights and sounds of war thought Hamilton. This is the part the top brass never see, the human misery that results from their high-ranking decisions. At least I am spared to fight another day, he thought, not like some of these poor bastards. And who knows what that day will bring for me?

Suddenly Tatham called Hamilton over. "Sergeant, there is a small battery of Boer artillery on a kopje about half a mile from here that needs to be flushed out. Take the platoon and make it happen." Hamilton rallied the men, and they moved off in the direction of the kopje. They could see the guns on the side of the hill, but as they approached, they were met by a hail of rifle bullets. "Cover!" shouted Hamilton, and the men scampered to find rocks and bushes to hide behind. Two men had been wounded, and lay groaning on the ground, one holding his shoulder, the other his stomach. A corporal tried to go to their aid, but a new hail of bullets sent him flying back into cover. So began an afternoon of stalemate. Every time the British tried to leave their hiding places and advance on the kopje, they were driven back by Boer snipers. Not that they could see the snipers - they assumed the invisibility that seemed to cloak all the Boers. After an hour, Hamilton sent one of the men back for reinforcements, and a second platoon came up from the farmhouse. Together the two platoons tried to charge the kopje, but they were repulsed by a hail of rifle fire that killed four and wounded a further seven. The stalemate continued. Eventually, word got to the British artillery, who brought a barrage to bear on the kopje.

Everything went silent. Hamilton cautiously placed his helmet on the end of his rifle and held it about his head to see if it attracted fire - he had tried this trick once before, and the hole in the helmet was evidence of its lack of success. But this time, nothing. He motioned to his platoon to follow him and cautiously made his way to the kopje. No-one fired from the kopje, so the platoon climbed it quickly, and found - nothing. The Boers had melted away, taking their artillery with them. The kopje was strewn with empty shell casings, but not a Boer was to be seen. The enemy had vanished into thin air.

Chapter 14 - The Strategy

Belmont December 9th, 1899 – French

Gen. Methuen had recovered sufficiently from the wound he had received at Modder River to resume command of the British forces on December 7th, 1899. The leg was still painful and had to be continually rebandaged, and walking was difficult, but he felt able to return to his duties. On December 9th, he convened a strategy order group of his senior officers to discuss the progress. The army had had nearly ten days to recover and recuperate from the taxing skirmish at Modder River. Methuen felt the time was fast approaching when he needed to resume the initiative. Kimberley was continuing to suffer - the telegraph communications indicated food and medical shortages, and, apart from the seemingly excellent morale among the people, there seemed to be little good news. Methuen felt the pressure to relieve the besieged town as soon as he could, but he knew that, before he could do so, he would have to break the back of the Boer resistance that stood between him and the besieged town.

The order group was held in Methuen's command tent and was attended by, among others, Gens. French, Wauchope, Pole-Carew, and Colville. Methuen again produced a map of the terrain between Modder River and Kimberley.

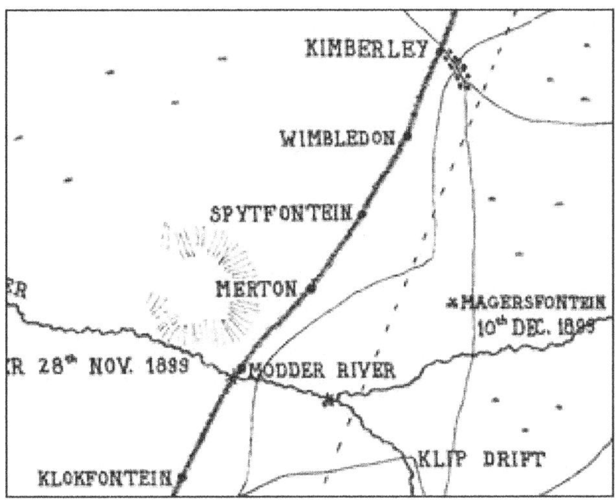

Methuen stood in front of the map, pointing stick in hand. "Gentlemen, our reports indicate considerable Boer activity in the area of the hill called Magersfontein. We have observed the enemy creating entrenchments on the side of the hill, as well as on two or three smaller hills in the vicinity. The distance from where we are at present and Magersfontein is about 10 miles. We believe that Cronje is assembling all his forces at Magersfontein and that this is the place where the next Boer resistance will take place. As you are aware, it is my view that we will not be able to relieve Kimberley until we have broken the back of Cronje's army. Are we all at one in that regard?"

He paused and waited for a reaction. Most nodded, but French raised his hand. "Do you think, sir, that there is any merit in bypassing the Boer army, not engaging them, and going straight for Kimberley?" This was a somewhat radical suggestion: a few of the generals looked amused by the idea, and there were some coughs and stifled laughter. Methuen raised his hand. "Gentlemen, I think it is a bold idea, but not practical in the circumstances. If we were to skirt around the Boer positions - and I've no doubt, given the openness of the terrain that we could do so - we would expose ourselves to an almighty attack from our rear. Unless we cripple Cronje and his army and take them out of the fight, we will forever be looking behind us for their mounted infantry - and we all know how useful they are on horseback." French was not to be dismissed so summarily. "With respect, General. Our experience shows that, while the Boers have been magnificent in defense, they have not been eager to assume an attacking posture. Their philosophy seems to be 'you come to us' rather than 'we will come and get you.' So I have serious doubts whether they would indeed attack us from the rear." Methuen nodded. "Gen. French, your suggestion is noted, but at this stage, I believe the correct strategy is to take on Cronje at Magersfontein." French stared at the ground, clearly uncomfortable at the decision.

Pole-Carew then raised his hand. "Sir, you are aware that I asked this question before Modder River, but I am still concerned about the quality and reliability of our reconnaissance. You indicated that there has been Boer activity on the slopes of Magersfontein and the surrounding hills. How confident are you that this is where they plan to defend? Have we done anything new to improve the standard of our intelligence?" Methuen responded. "The difficulties in acquiring good intelligence continues to plague us. We are still not able to get within a reasonable distance from the Boer positions to determine with any degree of certainty what they are doing. And this terrain is made more difficult by the presence of many crisscross farm fences that hamper the movement of our scouts. However, in the absence of better information, I believe we should act on what we have. Do you have another suggestion, General?" Pole-Carew shook his head. "I do, however, have a serious concern." He moved to the map. "If you look at the terrain between Modder River and Kimberley, you will see that the most direct route would bypass Magersfontein and proceed between Magersfontein in the east, and Merton and Spytfontein in the west. What guarantee do we have that the activity at Magersfontein isn't a feint, to encourage us to advance via the most direct route, bypassing Magersfontein and leading us into a possible ambush from Merton and Spytfontein?

There was renewed interest from the other senior officers - this was clearly a scenario they had not anticipated. Methuen also looked thoughtful, rolled the idea around in his mind. "It is an interesting theory, Reg. But we need to remember a few other factors. We know that Cronje's forces are gathered in the Jacobsdal area to the south of Magersfontein. For them to get into position in Merton and Spytfontein, they would have two options: the first is to cross from Jacobsdal to Merton south of Magersfontein, which means they would in fact be passing right in front of our positions here at Modder River, and their game would be up; the second would be to go north of Magersfontein and use the hill as cover from our recce patrols. This is a possibility, but it is a long way around, particularly for his artillery. No, while I think there is considerable merit in your suggestion, my sense is that Magersfontein is going to be their main defensive strategy." Pole-Carew nodded his agreement, as did the rest of the officers present.

Methuen then turned to the detailed discussion. "Gentlemen, we have seen the strategy employed by Cronje at Belmont, Graspan, and Modder River. He adopted the classic Boer strategy of occupying and fortifying the high ground and inviting us to dislodge them with our artillery and infantry. Does anyone believe that they are likely to try anything different this time?" He looked out at the faces of his senior commanders.

Most seemed satisfied with the view, but there was concern in the faces of French and Pole-Carew. "Reg, John, you seem uncomfortable. Anything you would like to add?"

Pole-Carew was the first to speak. "While I agree with you in general, sir, I think we saw a change in tactics at Modder River. If you will recall, there were indeed Boer entrenchments on the high ground, but there was also an array of trenches on the lower ground at the river. Do we think that this is a new approach the Boers are using or was it simply occasioned by the terrain?" French nodded his agreement.

"Again," said Methuen, "an excellent observation. But I put it to you that there is no way that Cronje would not have used the Modder River as part of his defenses. He certainly was not going to provide us with the luxury of crossing the river unopposed. It is for this reason that I believe we saw Boer trenches along the river - it was aimed at preventing us from crossing the river. Now there is no river near Magersfontein, so my view is that we will see another classical defense strategy from Cronje. Any comments?" The answer he had given seems reasonable, and all nodded their agreement.

"Now, let's get to the details. I believe we can assume that the main Boer force will be dug in on the slopes of Magersfontein hill. There may be other flanking defenses to left and right, but I believe Cronje will have his main forces on the hill. Now let's consider where we went wrong at Modder River. We used the night march, but when the sun rose, we were nearly a thousand yards from the enemy lines. This was simply not good enough. For a night march to create the surprise it is intended to achieve; the troops need to be within one to two hundred yards from the base of the hill when the sun comes up. We can then immediately start our charge up the hill and not allow the Boers to pick us off from long range as they did at Modder River. So, Andrew," he pointed at Gen. Wauchope. "I want you to advance with the Highland Brigade, and various other units I shall describe later, during the night and take up position about 100 yards from the base of the hill. We will aim to get the troops into position by 2.30 am so they can have rest before the sun starts to rise. Then we let them have it with all we have got. Just before sunrise, the artillery will bombard the Boer positions on the hill for 30 minutes before you attack at around 5.15 am. Actually, on the previous evening, we will have an extensive artillery bombardment to try and create as much havoc as we can with their trenches and guns. The morning barrage will be to get them to keep their heads down so you can get momentum for your charge. The advance will be made in three columns. The first column will be the Highland Brigade, the 9th Lancers, the 2nd King's Own Yorkshire Light Infantry, and supporting artillery and engineers sections, as well as a balloon section. This column will march directly on the south-western spur of the kopje, and on arrival, before dawn, the 2nd Black Watch will move east of the kopje, where I believe the Boers will have a strong-point. The 2nd Seaforth Highlanders will advance to the south-eastern point of the hill, and the 1st Argyll and Sutherland Highlanders will extend the line to the left. The 1st Highland Light Infantry will be held in reserve. The second column, on the left under Reg, will comprise a battalion from the 9th Brigade, the Naval Brigade with a 4.7-inch naval gun, and Rimington's Guides (*a mounted infantry unit raised in Cape Town*). The third column, led by Henry, will remain in reserve: the 12th Lancers, the Guards Brigade, and artillery, engineer, and medical support element. All units will advance in a mass of quarter columns, the most compact formation in the drill book: 3,500 men in 30 companies aligned in 90 files, all compressed into a column 45 yards wide and 160 yards long. Any questions, gentlemen?"

There followed a period of discussion among the generals on the merits of the plan. Again, it was French who broke the silence. "General, what are your plans for the rest of the cavalry?" Methuen responded quickly. "Same as before. Mop up the Boers as they retreat from the positions and obliterate them as they retreat. But let's not make the mistake we have made previously. This time, we split our cavalry force into two, with one group moving to the east of the hill and one to the west, so we eventually catch the Boers in a pincer movement from which they cannot escape." French thought for a minute and responded. "Do you think there may be merit in using the cavalry in an offensive mode rather than as a mopping-up force. If we were to send a cavalry unit to the east of Magersfontein and attack the enemy from the east instead of the south, we might be able to turn the enemy's flank, and reduce his ability to hold the hill." Methuen thought for a moment before responding. "Anyone have a view on this?" It was Colville who walked up to the map. "John, I see one problem with your suggestion - which, by the way, I believe, has merit. Magersfontein hill is shaped rather like the prow of a ship, with a south-pointing section here, and east and west slopes on either side. Even if our cavalry were to attack from one of the sides, it is my view that the Boers would ignore it. Horses cannot climb hills, so you could not mount a cavalry charge up the hill. The Boers would most likely place a few snipers in the area and pick off the cavalry like shooting fish in a barrel." Most of his colleagues nodded, and French fell silent. He knew he had not won the day, but remained convinced that Methuen was not making the optimum use of his cavalry resources.

Methuen continued. "If there are no further questions, I believe we have a workable strategy. Please go back to your units and prepare to execute them. Many thanks, gentlemen and I will look forward to receiving your final orders in the morning." They all rose and filtered out of the tent.

When they all had departed, French beckoned to Pole-Carew. "Reg, come and walk with me for a while."
"What's on your mind, John?"

"I am concerned about the point you raised about the positioning of the trenches. We know that Cronje is in charge, but we also know that de la Rey is there as well, and if he has anything to do with it, he will have a surprise up his sleeve. If you are correct, and they do

dig trenches at the base of the hill, then the Highland Brigade will land 100 yards from their trenches and will be obliterated."
"My fear exactly." Pole-Carew shook his head and rolled his eyes. "We don't ever seem to learn from our mistakes. We are using the same bloody tactics as we used at Waterloo. To get this old guard to change its mind is going to take something catastrophic. The same thing is happening in Natal. Buller is getting a bloody nose time after time, and he still uses the same outdated approach. When will they learn?"

It was French's turn to shake his head. "If we are going to win this war, we need to understand both the terrain we are fighting in and the nature of the enemy. This is not a 'one size fits all' solution, but our folks seem hell-bent on proving that the manual is immutable!"
The two talked for a while further, resigned to the fact that they were not going to be listened to. Not now. Possibly not ever.

Scholtznek - December 2nd, 1899 - de la Rey

Koos de la Rey sat outside his tent on a small folding stool, drinking a cup of coffee he was not enjoying. They had not received fresh coffee for a few days now, and it was clear to him that this has been made from grounds that had been used once or maybe twice before. He lit his pipe, sat back in his camp chair, and reflected on the events of the past three weeks.

He was aware that the first two encounters, Belmont and Graspan, were not all-out efforts, but rather a toe in the water to test the enemy and to blood their own troops in battle. The results had been more or less what he had expected, and he was pleased that the casualty count in those skirmishes had been relatively light. He was also pleased to see that Methuen, as expected, had played everything by the book. His strategy, formations, and tactics came straight from the British Army Infantry Manual, a manual that Koos de la Rey had studied extensively. He well understood the maxim 'know your enemy,' and it slightly amused him that the British were so eager to share their military secrets with anyone who was interested. We have no such manual, he thought to himself, and just as well. They had no way of finding out our strategy - they could only base it on what we show them. And they certainly don't know what I have in store for them at Magersfontein! He called his adjutant, Louis Lausberg, over to his position.

"Louis, go over to Oom Piet's tent and find out when he is planning to get us all together to discuss our plan." The young man hurried off and came back in fifteen minutes. "General, it seems that all commanders are going to meet in about two hours, at 6 pm, at the general's tent." "Thank you, Louis. Now please see if you can get me a fresh cup of coffee - I would not even wish this swill on the Redcheeks!" The young man smiled and took off.

After Modder River, the army had withdrawn to Jacobsdal for a few days, then moved north to Scholtznek to the north of Magersfontein by a night march. Some troops had been left in Jacobsdal and were ordered to be very visible in an attempt to encourage the British to believe that the main body of the army was still in Jacobsdal. Clearly, the more confusion could be sown in the minds of the enemy,, the easier it would be to prepare for the upcoming battle.

De la Rey had surveyed the Boer troops at Scholtznek and Spytfonteinand realized the vulnerability of their position to British artillery fire. He was convinced that this was not the correct place to oppose the British advance - the terrain was not suitable for the kind of trap de la Rey was hoping to set for the British. His strategy was to create a set of trenches in a crescent shape to lure the British into so that they could be caught in a murderous cross-fire once they entered the killing ground. The areas of Merton, Spytfontein, and Scholtznek did not allow for this. But Magersfontein did. And de la Rey was determined to convince Cronje to make a stand at

Magersfontein rather than the more obvious Spytfontein.

The meeting was attended by Cronje, de la Rey, Prinsloo, and Maj. Albrecht, the artillery commander. Cronje unrolled a map, laid it on a table, and indicated to the men to come around and view it. "My view is that the British will take the most direct route from Modder River to Kimberley. They will continue to follow the rail line, and this will bring them past Merton, Spytfontein, and Scholtznek. So this is where I propose to meet them and drive them back. Scholtznek is an ideal hill on which to position our troops. It has a steeping slope, and the flat crown of the hill will enable us to keep our reserves and supplies out of sight of the enemy. In addition to putting our main forces there, we should have artillery here and here," he pointed to Merton and Spytfontein. "In that way, we can bring fire on to the infantry and also enable us to silence their artillery. What are your thoughts, men?"

Maj. Albrecht was the first to respond. "Sir," he said, with Teutonic precision." Sir, there is one thing I must bring to your attention. The British have brought up many reinforcements, including much artillery. I am afraid their guns now exceed ours both in terms of number and firepower. If we deploy our guns where you suggest, I am concerned that their guns will be turned on us before an attack and obliterate us. There is just not enough cover there for our guns. Believe me, sir, I have walked those areas for days now, and I can find no way to position them to support our troops without exposing them to the enemy artillery."

He stopped and looked at de la Rey, who took up the argument. "I agree with Maj. Albrecht. While Scholtznek is not a bad place to stop an advance, other factors need to be taken into consideration, an important one being the point just raised by the major. In addition, it is my view that we should try the same strategy as we did at Modder River - locate our troops at ground level and not on the face of a hill. We saw how effective the riflemen were at

Modder River - their range of fire was greatly increased by being at ground level, and the enemy artillery needed almost a direct hit to dislodge anyone from their trench."

Cronje looked solemn and lit his pipe. "So, where do you think we should deploy, Koos?" De la Rey answered immediately. "Magersfontein." "Magersfontein!" exclaimed Cronje. "But it is not on the shortest route to Kimberley. What if the Redcheeks simply go past us and do not engage us at Magersfontein?" De la Rey was ready for this response. "Oom Piet, the British know that they can never relieve Kimberley without first definitively defeating our army. It would be far too dangerous to go marching off to Kimberley, knowing that we could attack them from the rear at any time. Not even Methuen is that *dom* (stupid)*!*"

"Koos, I do not agree. What do you think, Marthinus?" He turned to Prinsloo, who had been inspecting his fingernails. He stiffened as he realized his opinion was being sought. "Oom Piet, I am with you. I think we have moved our troops into the Scholtznek area, and this is where we should make a stand. I understand the arguments of the others, but I believe we need to be conservative in our thinking here." Cronje nodded his approval. "Then we are decided, gentlemen. Maj. Albrecht, will you prepare plans for the deployment of the artillery? Marthinus, you do the same for the infantry. We will reassemble in a few days to review this. In the meantime, Koos, please be sure to set up trenches near Merton to position an advance guard to watch out for any enemy movement in this direction. Dismissed, gentlemen."

De la Rey walked next to Albrecht. "Conservative in our thinking? Conservative? My God, what else have we been but conservative, and we have got our *gatte* (backsides) kicked! This cannot be allowed to happen. I did not come down here to sacrifice this army because a bunch of grayheads won't try anything new! I am going to take some action that may not make me popular but will save plenty of lives. You see if I don't" At which point, he stormed off to his tent and lit a cigar.

Once de la Rey had calmed down, he sat down at his table, took out a pen and a piece of paper, and wrote a telegram. It was to the president of the Orange Free State, Pres. Steyn, telling him that if he did not wish to learn about the massacre of the Boer army in the west, he should come to Scholtznek immediately to resolve the strategic differences between his commanders. He sent the telegram that evening, and the next evening he received a reply. "Understand your concern. Arriving December 4th under the pretext of troop morale. Kruger in agreement. Steyn." De la Rey breathed a sigh of relief - help was on its way. He did not, of course, share with Cronje any of the context - just informed him that Pres. Steyn would be arriving to deliver some guns and troops and to visit the Boer forces to improve morale.

Scholtznek - December 5th, 1899 - de la Rey

Pres. Steyn had arrived the previous day with 1,500 reinforcements and several guns that had been gleaned from the investment at Kimberley. It was thought that these men would be more useful in the upcoming battle than maintaining watch over the besieged city. Cronje was delighted with these additions and was even more enthusiastic when he learned that Gen. de Wet was on his way with further reinforcements. It was now time to finalize the battle plans that had been discussed a few days previously.

The *krijgsraad* (council of war) assembled at 4 pm that afternoon. Present were Gens. Cronje, de la Rey, and Prinsloo, Maj. Albrecht and Pres. Steyn. Cronje displayed the map that had been used at the previous discussion group and summarized the different views of himself and de la Rey for Steyn's benefit. When he had finished, he turned to de la Rey.

"Koos, are you satisfied that I described your strategy correctly?"
"Perfectly, Oom Piet. Thank you."
"Do you have anything to add?"
"Just one point. If we set up our line of resistance at Magersfontein, and we are not successful, then we can always use Scholtznek as a fallback position to provide a further obstacle to prevent the British from reaching Kimberley. In this way, we get two possible shots at the Redcheeks. If we put all our eggs in one basket at Scholtznek and we lose, then the enemy has a straight shot at Kimberley, and we will be helpless to stop them."

At this stage, both men looked to Steyn. The president moved closer to the map, studied it for a few minutes, then addressed the gathering.

"Gentlemen, I think we have two excellent strategies from which to choose. Both have merits and issues, and we need to consider just how critical the next skirmish is going to be, not only for the outcome of the siege of Kimberley but for the entire war itself. I know we have put our men through a number of weeks of hard fighting, and it is to their credit that they have performed as well as they had. I know we have had some deserters, but this is inevitable. And my attitude to them is very much like we read in Shakespeare's Henry V "he which hath no stomach to this fight, let him depart." Sorry to quote an *Engelsman* (Englishman) at this time, but it seems appropriate. Now we have to look to the future. Do we stake the future of Kimberley on one battle at Scholtznek, or do we give ourselves a chance to have two goes at them by making our first stand at Magersfontein? So, I ask you both. Do you think our men still have enough fight left in them to manage two potential battles, or do you think one would be all they can manage?" He looked at Cronje and de la Rey.

Cronje began. "Sir, I believe that these men will continue fighting until hell freezes over. One fight, two fights, a dozen fights, these

men are loyal, battle-hardened, and determined to preserve the freedom of the Boer republics. Yes, of course, they can manage two further battles.
De la Rey nodded his agreement. Steyn continued.

"Well, Piet, if that is the case, I am going to throw my weight behind Koos's suggestion that we make our first stand at Magersfontein, and give us the opportunity to fight another day at Scholtznek if we fail. That is my view, but I am open to suggestions."

Cronje sighed and nodded his head. "Sir, I am fine with selecting Magersfontein as our first option. In many respects, it is a more easily defensible position, given the wide expanse of slopes. These will make excellent ground for us to dig trenches in and command the high ground."

De la Rey looked pleased that the decision had gone in his favor, but he frowned at the latter suggestion.

"Mr. President, Oom Piet, I thank you for agreeing to my suggestion. I think we have a real opportunity to do some damage to the Redcheeks at Magersfontein. However, Oom Piet, I would like to make an observation about the strategy you have just outlined for defending the position. Let's cast our minds back to Belmont and Graspan, where we only occupied the high ground. We were somewhat successful, but we could not press home the advantage of the long range of our Mausers since the slope required us to wait until the enemy were quite close before we opened fire. At Modder River, where our trenches were at ground level, our riflemen were much more effective and were able to bring fire to bear on a much larger part of the advance at a longer range. And we know the damage they did at Modder River." Cronje nodded, and de la Rey continued.

"Now consider one other factor. The ground in front of the hill at

Magersfontein is a maze of old farm fences. I am not sure if the Redcheeks know about them, but they will find out soon enough. They will either be forced to climb over them or stop and cut holes to enable troops to get through. Either way, they will be held up for some time, and this will make them extremely vulnerable to men firing from trenches at ground level. I am not sure, Mr. President if you are familiar with any of the battles in the American Civil War - I am sure Oom Piet has studied them as I have - on the last day of the Battle of Gettysburg, there was a famous attack by the army of Gen. Lee known as Pickett's Charge. One of the reasons for its failure was that nobody knew that, halfway across the battlefield, was a fence that the Confederate troops had to climb over before continuing their charge of the Union lines. This so delayed and disrupted the charge that the day was won by the Union forces. I think there is a similarity here with the fences. I think if our riflemen are deployed at ground level, we will be able to pick off the enemy as they try to negotiate these fences." He paused for a moment and studied the reactions of the others. Prinsloo was not looking impressed, but that was to be expected - he was the most conservative of the generals. Cronje looked interested, and Steyn had an excited gleam in his eye. De la Rey went on.

"I have another suggestion. It is a double bluff. We know the British have studied our strategies, know that we have almost always gone for a defense of the high ground. So we must let them think that this is exactly what we are doing. We must dig dummy trenches on the slope of the hill, not very deep, but deep enough to be seen by the enemy. We must also make a lot of noise in doing this so that their attention is focused on this area, while we secretly dig in at the foot of the hill. We can even haul a few guns up the hill, and fire some rounds to make them think we are setting ourselves up on the high ground. But we dig, and we dig, and we dig, and we camouflage, camouflage, camouflage. Methuen has always used a night march to try and get troops up near to our lines to neutralize the range of our rifles. I see no reason why he will do anything different this time. Only now, he will find himself a few hundred yards away from our men standing in their trenches, ready to rip them apart as soon as they start to move in the daylight." He sat and folded his hands, waiting for the reaction. Steyn was the first to speak.

"Koos, I like this plan. It makes full use of our strengths and uses a bit of Boer cunning to outwit the enemy. I received reports about how effective the trenches were at Modder River. I think the British probably expected us to have trenches there because we would not have left the river undefended. But in this case, we are defending a hill, and I think they will be expecting us to go back to our traditional formations. I think we go with Koos's plan. What do you think, Marthinus?"

Prinsloo sucked on his pipe and thought for a while. "Mr. President, I am by nature, a conservative man, and I am a believer in the tried and trusted ways of battle. This is a new way of doing things, so my instinct is to stay with the tried and trusted method." Steyn looked furious.

"Damn it, man. Can you demonstrate how successful this traditional method has been to date? The British kicked our arses at Belmont and Graspan, but we did much better at Modder River. I think it's time for a change in approach, and I think now is the time to attempt it, especially as we have a second chance at Scholtznek if it does not succeed. Piet?" Cronje looked long and hard at de la Rey, then answered.

"Mr. President, my first instinct is to agree with Marthinus, but I have to admit that I do like the sound of what Koos has described, especially the bit about the fences. I, too, am familiar with Pickett's Charge, and the damage the fence caused. So, I am reluctantly going to agree that we try Koos's plan." De la Rey smiled and held out his hand to Cronje. "Thank you, Oom Piet. I'll not let you down.

Now let's get down to the real planning. "

At this stage, Steyn rose. "Gentlemen, I don't think I am needed for the more detailed planning session, so with your permission, I shall leave and start to make my way back to Bloemfontein. Thank you for giving me the honor of attending this session. I think you have an excellent plan, and I wish you all God's blessing for a successful battle," The men rose and saluted. Just before he left the tent, Steyn turned and said, "Marthinus, can I please have a word with you?" Prinsloo looked anxious as if he knew what was coming. Steyn had already discussed relieving him of his command with Cronje and de la Rey before the meeting, and both generals believed that de Wet would be a better commander for the type of action they were about to undertake.

Chapter 15 - The Night Before

Boer trenches Magersfontein - December 10, 1899 10.15pm – Jeannot

Suddenly Britz said something unexpected. "You know, there are times that I feel really sorry for those Tommies out there."

Havenga looked up, spat next to his boot, and said, "Why? Because tomorrow their chests will house our Mauser rounds?"

Britz chuckled. "I suppose that is true too, but it wasn't what I meant. Think about it, man. Here they are, thousands of miles from their home, in a place they have never heard of, fighting against people they don't know and probably don't hate, in conditions completely unfamiliar to them. For what? For the ambitions of men, they have never met, or are ever likely to meet? And all the thanks they get for their troubles is their weekly pay? "

Havenga thought for a moment. "Ja," he said, "I think there is some truth in what you say. Compare them to us. We indeed have something to fight for - our country, our families, our farms, our cattle. We are defending our existence and our livelihood."

"And our culture and way of life" added Britz "There is no greater motivation for a man than to defend his homeland from someone who is threatening to steal it from him. That is why we will win this war. We have our hearts and hopes in this war; they are simply doing it for their pay. And God is on our side."

Jeannot looked up from the letter he was writing. "And which God might that be, Britz? Your Christian God or my Jewish God? Don't you think the Tommies over there worship the same God as we do? It is nonsense to say God is on our side. God doesn't take sides when it comes to people. He just shuffles the cards, and we all play the hands we are dealt. Make no mistake; I am not saying God doesn't enter into this. I pray every day for God to protect my family and me, and my country, but I don't ask him to take sides. That is all down to the cards."

Britz was about to respond when there were familiar footsteps coming up the trench. The men recognized Gen. de la Rey. Havenga called out to him. "Evening General. Will you join our discussion here? We are discussing the fact that we are more motivated for this fight than the Tommies, because we are fighting for our land and our families, and because God is on our side. Britz says the Tommies are only motivated by money, and our *Joodjie* (little Jew) says God doesn't take sides. What do you think, Commandant?"

De la Rey sat cross-legged on the ground next to the men, his *sjambok* (whip) across his knees, and accepted the small tin cup of coffee offered to him by Britz. He thought for a moment, lit his pipe, and drew deeply on it, causing a warm glow in the otherwise dark surroundings. "You know, *manne* (men). You are all right, and you are all wrong. The Tommies are indeed fighting here because they are professional soldiers or paid recruits, but there is a problem with this. How does Her Majesty know how much to pay each man to ensure that he gives her his best efforts? Who can estimate the value of a man's soul? There are surely men out there who are satisfied with their lot in the British Army. For many, it is an improvement in the lives they led at home in Scotland or Ireland, where there are famine, oppression, and lack of justice. These men will fight well because they want to keep their jobs. Then there are those who are the grumblers - every army has them, boys, even among our troops. The pay is not enough; the food is poor, the conditions are unsatisfactory, the officers are idiots, the list goes on and on. These men will give minimal effort in battle, only enough to give an adequate show to their superiors and avoid being punished. These are the men that, at the first sign of real danger, are the most likely to turn and run."

He stopped, sipped his coffee (where the hell did they get this, he thought, it's better than we get?), and continued, "The British Army has done a good job of providing both of these kinds of soldiers with something to hold on to - tradition. Their regiments are old and historical, and there is honor in serving in the more distinguished ones. We have something similar with our commandos here, but we do not have the proud military history of the great British regiments. You will see this particularly among the Scottish regiments, some of which we will face tomorrow. For goodness sake, these men won't go into battle without having a piper play them onto the battlefield! Can you imagine the Jacobsdal Commando going to battle behind Oom Schalk van Rensburg playing his accordion and singing ' Round the nachmaal campfire'?"

The men laughed. De la Rey went on. "They rely heavily on their tradition to stir up passion among their men. Sometimes this is successful, and I am guessing that this is what makes some regiments more formidable than others. Tomorrow we will be facing one such regiment - The King's Own Yorkshire Light Infantry - the Brits refer to it as KOYLI. This regiment is almost 150 years old and fought against Napoleon at Waterloo. These men are proud soldiers, bearers of an ancient flag, and with a history of honor in combat. These are not men who will turn and run at the first sign of trouble. These are men who will stand and fight for their regiment."

The men nodded their assent. This was something that they had known, but not really considered until now. The strength of the opposition is not only a question of how many, but who they are. De la Rey paused a moment then said, "Remember always. It is not the size of the dog in the fight; it is the size of the fight in the dog." The men grinned. "And this is why we will always go into every battle and every skirmish with the advantage. We have more fight in us than they do. Britz is correct. When you are fighting for hearth and home, the fire in your heart is far greater than if you are fighting for a flag or a payment. We are a proud people. We are an independent people. We are a people who have never taken kindly to being told what to do and how to live our lives. Think of our forefathers, the Voortrekkers, who sacrificed a good and comfortable life in the Cape to move to an unknown, harsh territory that has been our home for the past 50 years. Did they do it because the grazing was better here? Of course not, we all know that. Was it because of the abundance of water and the fertility of the soil? Definitely not. Was it the absence of black tribes with whom to dispute territory and grazing rights? I don't think so. It was because of freedom, the freedom to be governed by our own people, the freedom to develop our own culture and way of life, the freedom to worship as we please, the freedom to live according to laws we make for ourselves, not made by some aristocrat sitting on a velvet chair in London."

De la Rey noticed that while he had been speaking, a small group of men had joined the original three. The commandant was speaking, and his men wanted to hear his words. De la Rey was a true leader of men, understanding when to cajole and when to encourage, when to be rigid and when to relax the yoke. His men loved and respected him as much for his character as a man as for his unquestioned brilliance as a strategist and tactician. When the commandant spoke, you listened.

"And now let's think about whose side God is on. As you know, I am a religious man and have great faith in the Almighty to help us in our endeavors. But I am sure that there are men among the Tommies who are just as religious as I am, and who are relying on God in much the same way. The problem is - it is the same God - except for Joodjie there who worships the Old God while we worship the Old and the New." He smiled towards Jeannot, who smiled back. He was accustomed to this kind of teasing, knew that it was well-intentioned and not meant to offend. Hell, the Long Tom gun they used was known as 'The Jew' because the front part of its barrel had been cut off! "So how can God be on both sides in this war? He can't and he shouldn't. So to that extent, I agree with Jeannot. But there is another thing I would like to say. I don't think God is really interested in countries or armies or regiments. I think He is interested in people, people like you and me, people like the Tommies over there. Good people, devout people, people who care for their families and friends. Those are the people God will protect. It is written in the Old Book 'that you may so revere the Lord your God that you will keep all his statutes and commandments that I am giving you -- you, your children, and your grandchildren -- all your lives, to prolong your days.' God is on the side of the just man, and who among us has enough wisdom to decide who is just? None of us - only the Lord will decide on the justness of man. So stop trying to rely on God just because the predikants tell us He is on our side. Rely on him because you are good men, pure in spirit, and determined to do what is best for volk and family. Then you will surely have God's ear."

There was an uncomfortable shifting of positions after this speech. Most of the men were young and had received an only rudimentary education. Their guidance in life came from their parents and The Good Book - neither was available to be questioned or gainsaid. Philosophy and introspection were uncommon to them - the daily chores of life filled their days, and their nights were spent in family activities. For many, this was the first time they had heard anything that remotely resembled a philosophical interpretation of why they were there and what their responsibilities were. Until now, there had only been the excitement of future danger and glory, the camaraderie of the men they were with, and the unwavering loyalty to their commanders and their land. But de la Rey had introduced a new perspective to them, a perspective that gave them a more intimate and personal insight into why they were doing what they were doing. It was less about the fanfare and glory of battle; it was more a sense of the importance of the individual, and the impact that each man could make on the success of the others. Each man knew only the contents of his own heart, could not hope to understand the trials and rigors of another's, and so must examine the content of his heart and make peace with himself that he was doing what was expected of him, and what he expected of himself.

1st Argyll and Sutherland Camp - November 10, 1899 - Hamilton

Someone was tugging on his leg. He wasn't sure whether it was in his dream or for real. Colin Hamilton slowly opened his eyes and saw the familiar face of Corporal McEwan. "You'll need to wake up, sarge. We are being told to get ready to move." "What time is it, for God's sake?" Hamilton was not happy about being woken up. "11 pm, sarge. We are forming up and are expected to move out around midnight."

A light rain was falling, and the sky was dark with cloud. No moon tonight thought Hamilton. Great time to be doing a night march. We will probably end up getting lost like we did last time. Buggered if I know why they want to get there early! They'll still be there when we arrive, no matter what time it is.

The camp was a buzz of activity, with officers and NCOs marshaling the troops in preparation for the night march. McEwan had assembled the platoon while Hamilton went to the staging area to find out where they should fall in. He came back shortly to join his platoon.

"The first group is going to be the Black Watch, followed by the Seaforths and then us. So, McEwan, go and make contact with the corporal of 3rd platoon Seaforths, and have him alert us when they are about to take up their positions. We'll be right behind them."
Hamilton addressed the men. "Listen up. We are going to be

marching about 4 miles tonight in the dark and the rain. It's not going to be pretty, but I'll not have any of you getting lost or falling over. We need to stick closely together, so pick a mate and see that you stick together at all times. We are going to be issued with ropes to try and help us from getting lost. Make sure you don't drop the fucking thing, or I'll have your guts for garters. If you end up with a Boer bayonet up your arse because you wandered off, dinna come crying to me. Do you read me?" The men muttered their agreement. "And who does not have a full set of canteens? I warned you about this. When you are lying out there in the heat tomorrow with your balls shot off, you'll thank me for making you bring water." No-one raised a hand. "Alright then, we wait for the Seaforths to form up, then we slot in behind them."

March to Magersfontein - December 11th, 1899 – Hamilton

By midnight, the army was ready to march. The rain had increased and was now a steady downpour, turning the ground into a quagmire of mud and slush. The four regiments assembled into tightly packed formations of quarter columns, forming a dense rectangle of 4,000 men in 96 carefully spaced lines. In front was the Black Watch, followed by the Seaforth and Argyll units, with the Highland Light Infantry bringing up the rear. They moved off at a relatively slow pace, feeling their way in the darkness. The leading group had scouted the ground as best they could on the previous days, but could not get sufficiently close to the hill to determine any of the Boer positions. Their first landmark was a farm owned by a Scot named John Bisset. He had agreed to place a lantern at the back of his property out of sight of the hill to guide the troops. But once they had passed the farm, there was no other guidance other than the outline of the hill itself. Fortunately for the troops, there was lightning at times, and this illuminated the drenched veld in front of them.

The going was not easy. Moving 4,000 men in close formation over rocky terrain with thorn bushes would not have been easy on a sunny day, but on a rainy night, it was a real challenge. The muddy ground proved treacherous. Men slid and fell over, rifles disappeared into the mud and had to be dug out, and men were forever falling into thorn bushes. The language that could be heard was not moderated, and the various Scottish accents could be heard cursing a blue streak.

Hamilton turned to his platoon. "Shut the fuck up, you lot. I'll not have any more whining about wet boots and sodden shirts, and thorn bushes and rocks. I've heard all the fuck I want to hear out of you girls tonight, so shut your *geggies* (mouths)!" His remark was met with low muttering from the platoon, but they kept their voices down. A minute later, Hamilton tripped on a rock and plunged headfirst into a thorn bush. "Fucking hell!" he yelled. A voice came from behind him. "Shhhh." He had to smile. He was guilty of precisely what he had told his men not to do.

On and on they tramped, the boots becoming soggier, the clothing clinging more and more to the skin. The Scottish regiments had an extra piece of dress, a khaki apron designed to cover the kilt and sporran, to prevent the regiments from being identified and also maintaining the khaki camouflage. These too became drenched, and the water seeped through into the kilts. What a fucking country, Hamilton thought to himself. One minute you are in stifling heat with insects eating you alive; the next, you are in a storm and wet as a Finnian *haddie* (haddock). As far as I'm concerned, let the Boers keep this fucking place. I'll none of it!

The farmhouse came into view, so the army knew it was on course and making reasonable progress. There was relief when the rain started to abate and eventually stopped. But this was a mixed blessing, as there was no more illuminating lightning. The falling and swearing increased, as the Scottish troops slipped and slid their way towards the hill. Magersfontein was visible against the sky, shaped like a great ocean liner. It was a forbidding sight.

During the previous two days, the British artillery had pounded the forward slope of Magersfontein, the Royal Field Artillery with 15 pounder guns, the Royal Horse Artillery with 12 pounders, and the Royal Garrison Artillery batteries with 5-inch howitzers. The Royal Navy provided heavy field artillery with a number of 4.7-inch naval guns mounted on field carriages and the long 12 pounders. This was done for two main reasons - to create as much damage to fortifications and trenches already constructed by the Boers, and to prevent them from coming onto the hill to create new ones. Little did they realize that the whole exercise was a waste of ammunition - the Boers were not on the slope, but were busily digging in at its base. The Boers were able to watch the shells going over their heads with complete impunity. The artillery was due to lay down a further bombardment just before dawn, to make the non-existent Boer riflemen on the slope keep their heads down while the Highland regiment initiated its charge.

Suddenly the men marching in front of Hamilton stopped dead in their tracks, and Hamilton careened into them, followed by his platoon bumping into him from behind. "What the fuck is going on?" he demanded. A man in front turned to him. "No idea, mate. Everyone in front of me has stopped as well." Word soon came down the line that the march had been held up by a fence that had to be either climbed or broken down - the latter course had been selected, and the engineers were busy. The column set off again, but fifteen minutes later, it came to another halt. Hamilton fumed, "Another wee fence, laddie?" "Buggered if I know." replied the man in front of him. And it was. It was the second of nine fences they were going to have to negotiate that night, and each held up the column for five minutes while the engineers, now leading the column, cut their way through. It was infuriating and did little to calm Hamilton's already irritated disposition.

The dawn was now approaching, and it was suggested that the troops halt and get some rest. Wauchope would have none of it. He wanted to get as close to the hill as he possibly could. When the column finally left the bushes, they were about 700 yards from the base of the hill, but, unbeknown to them, within 400 yards of the Boer trenches! Here the column stopped, rested, and waited for the artillery to begin its bombardment.

"So much for getting a rest!" complained Hamilton. "King, make sure all the men are alright and that everything is shipshape. As soon as the artillery makes those buggers keep their heads down, we are off!"

Chapter 16 - The Battle

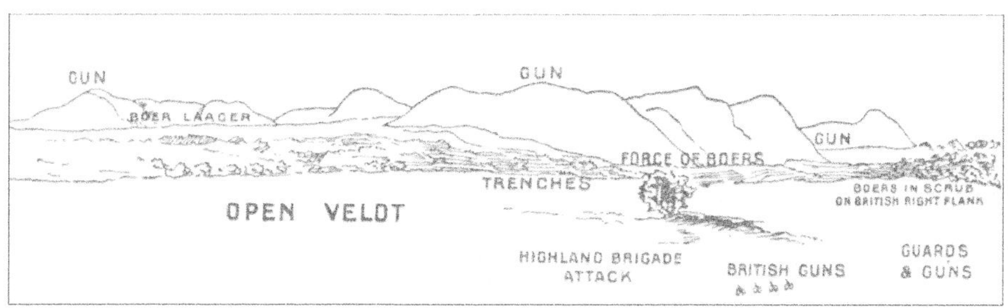

Sketch of the battlefield at Magersfontein

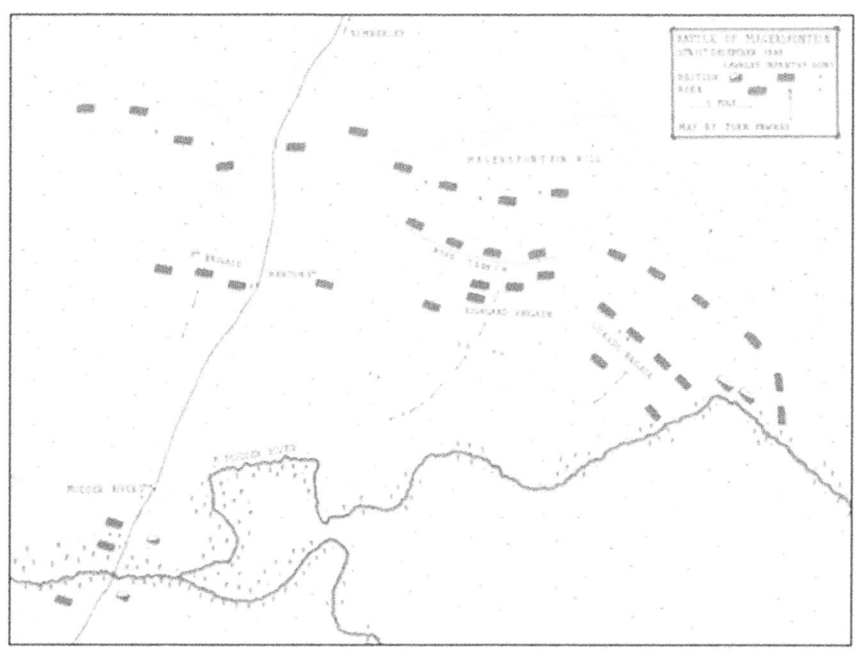

Map of the battlefield at Magersfontein

Magersfontein Trenches - December 11th, 1899 5am – Jeannot

The rain had made the trenches a miserable place to spend the night. Jeannot had tried to cover himself with his groundsheet, but it made little difference. I suppose, he mused to himself, if I'm going to get wet, I'm going to get wet. There was little opportunity to sleep. Guard duty consisted of one hour off, one hour on so that the Boers could not be surprised by a British night attack. Now everyone was awake and manning the trench as the dawn approached.

Suddenly a remarkable sight greeted the Boers. Out of the bushes, about a thousand yards from the trenches marched a column of British soldiers. They were clearly Scottish because the aprons covering the kilts could be seen. They came in droves, all packed tightly together, marching in a column. They came another 500 yards, then suddenly stopped and sat down. The Boers were dumbfounded - they had never seen the likes of this. An order came down the trench - no-one is to fire until the order is given. And silence was the order of the day. It was clear to Jeannot that the British had no idea that they were so close to the Boer lines. They must believe, he thought, that we are up on the hill, and they have done this night march to get as close as they can to the hill to be able to storm our positions. It was almost surreal - the British did not realize that they were walking into a murderous trap. Jeannot inwardly congratulated de la Rey for his strategic genius. By putting the trenches at the foot of the hill and heavily camouflaging them, the British were duped into thinking they now had a clear run at the hill. And, thought Jeannot, they will try to soften us up with an artillery bombardment, then they will charge. We must wait until they are within the crescent of our trench formation, then we will open fire and cut them to pieces.

He turned to Britz. "Man, did you ever see anything so unbelievable. It is going to be like shooting buck in the Wanderers Stadium." "What is the Wanderers Stadium?" asked Britz. "The big rugby stadium in Johannesburg. It is going to be like bringing a herd of eland onto a rugby field with us sitting in the seats. That's how easy it is going to be." Britz shrugged his shoulders. "I am guessing they don't know we are here. And they probably don't know about the machine guns we have at the ends of each trench formation. They are going to get cut to pieces." "Yes, I think you are right," said Jeannot. "And our artillery is going to enjoy themselves as well from Scholtznek and their other positions. The British have nowhere to run to."

No sooner had he finished his sentence than the air filled with the distant rumble of artillery fire and the whistle of shells overhead, each sounding like an express train. The Boers turned and watched them smash harmlessly into the hill as they had done the previous two days and earlier in the morning. This time the British were using lyddite airburst shells, projectiles that burst while still in the air, spraying shrapnel downwards. "It's a good thing we are down here," observed Britz. "That would be pretty nasty if there were anyone in those trenches." Then he smiled and dug Jeannot in the ribs. "But we are here, *Joodjie*, my friend, and we are going to give the Redcheeks a good *dondering* ((hammering) today!" Jeannot smiled back - they could scarcely believe their luck.

The bombardment lasted about fifteen minutes. The dawn was now breaking, and the Boers could see the British troops quite clearly now. A command must have been given because everyone suddenly got to their feet and fixed their bayonets. Slowly the front rank started to move, followed by the ranks behind them. The order came down the trench to hold your fire until commanded. Nearer they came - four hundred and fifty yards, then four hundred, three hundred and fifty, three hundred, two hundred and fifty. Suddenly the command rang out, "*Vuur* (Fire)!"

And a scene from Dante's Inferno played out before their eyes.

Magersfontein - December 11th, 1899 5.35am – Hamilton

They had watched the artillery shells exploding on the hill, and this lifted their spirits. King commented to the man next to him. "If anyone survives that, I'll be a monkey's." "*Haud yer wheesht,* ye *wallaper* (Shut up, you idiot!)" hissed Hamilton. "Ye'll give the fucking game away!" King gave a mock salute to show he understood.

At about 5.40 am, a whispered command came through the ranks - stand up and fix bayonets. Hamilton could see the Black Watch and Seaforths rising to their feet. He signaled to his squad to do likewise, and the men stood up and fixed their bayonets. Then the order came to move forward slowly, retaining formation. Hamilton had a soldier's instinct for observing the surroundings and gaining insight from his observations. He was uncomfortable. There had been no enemy fire at all, no long-range rifle fire to force them to keep their heads down. The area was ominously quiet. But there was nothing to be seen, no trenches, no guns, nothing. Had the brass miscalculated and chosen the wrong place to attack? No, that would be impossible. I know our scouting is poor, but we surely couldn't have got the location wrong.

On and on they moved, walking slowly to avoid making any sound. They were now 600 yards from the base of the hill. And they could see the rock formations on its face. But no sign of the enemy. They moved on a further fifty yards, then the phalanx halted. Someone in the front must have seen something. No, false alarm. The men moved off again. The column reached a point about five hundred yards from the bottom of the hill.

And then it happened!

The ground in front of them lit up as if a thousand dragons were belching fire in their direction. There was an ungodly roar as a

thousand rifles poured lead into the Black Watch, scything through their front ranks, killing and maiming. Men went down like dominoes, their packed ranks preventing them from running. The rest dropped to the ground, desperately seeking shelter. But there was none. And still the rifles sang and stuttered, and the tap-tap-tap of machine-gun fire could be heard in the distance. It was a slaughterhouse. No other word for it. Wounded men screamed, whimpered, begged for assistance. The veld was red with blood.
Hamilton hugged the ground. He did not dare raise his head. He had seen others do this, and their reward was a bullet through the skull. The Boers were no more than two hundred yards away, and at that range, they could decide which eye to shoot you through. Behind him, his platoon lay on their stomachs, white-faced. Men were shivering despite the warm dawn air. Hamilton hissed an instruction to the man behind him. "Find out if any of our lads are killed or wounded." The request was noiselessly circulated among the platoon, and the answer came back - Bullivant, Smith, and Marsay were dead; Glew, Stephens, Wimpey, and Dingle had critical wounds, and about five others had minor scratches. Stephens was in danger of bleeding out - a bullet had pierced his femoral artery, and he was losing blood rapidly. Hamilton felt helpless. No medical staff would risk moving into the area, and the men were not equipped to deal with these kinds of wounds. He punched the ground in frustration. My God, can all we do is lie here and watch our comrades in arms die? Fuck, I feel so Goddamned helpless. I am supposed to be their father in this mess, but if I try to help, I'll get my fucking head shot off. Best to just keep my head down and wait to see how things turn out.

In front of them, the Black Watch was taking heavy casualties. They were so close to the Boer trenches and were so tightly packed together that the Boer riflemen were picking them off at will. Eventually, one of the officers had had enough. The cry rang out, "Black Watch, retreat!" This could be clearly heard above the rifle fire, and what remained of the Black Watch jumped to their feet and fled from the direction of the firing. This caused a mass stampede. The rest of the Highland Brigade followed their example, and the field became a herd of kilted men running for their lives. The Boers took advantage of this, pouring lead into the retreating ranks. Men fell by the dozens and were trampled by their fleeing fellow soldiers. It was a rout.

The Highland Brigade had been decimated. Nearly a thousand men had died or been wounded in the initial attack. When the men got to a relatively safe distance from the trenches, they sank to the ground and kept their heads down. The wounded were left where they lay - it would have been suicide to try to rescue them.

The attack had been a catastrophe. It was definitely the worst defeat the British Army had suffered in this war, possibly the worst day in its entire military history. The dead and the dying bore evidence to the inferiority of British strategy and tactics, and the Boers were left wondering why it was that these seasoned troops had stumbled so gormlessly into their ambush. Only one small piece of resistance was noted. A small group of Scots under Seaforth Lieutenant Robert Wilson had an excellent opportunity to make amends for the early catastrophe. He noticed a gap in the Boer trenches and led several hundred troops through this gap, hoping to surprise the Boers and fire at them from their unguarded rear. If they could only reach the kopje, they could then direct fire on the Boer trenches and catch them in a crossfire. But it was not to be. By a strange quirk of fate, Gen. Cronje, who had spent a miserable night in a rain-sodden trench, was on an inspection patrol with a handful of his officers when they stumbled upon Wilson and his men heading for the kopje. Even though there were only seven of them, they quickly took cover and opened fire, making such a noise that the British imagined that they were being attacked by a much larger force. If Wilson had ordered a charge, he could easily have overwhelmed the small Boer contingent, but instead, they fell flat and started returning fire. This was heard by the Boers in the trenches, who immediately closed the gap to prevent further troops coming through, then went to relieve the general and his men. The British were slaughtered, with only a handful surviving to surrender. This was perhaps the best opportunity the British had on the day, and it proved unsuccessful.

Boer Trenches Magersfontein December 11th, 1899 9.30am – Jeannot

The section in Jeannot's trench could not believe their luck! The British, after lying prone for so long, were now retreating, providing the men with such a target-rich environment that arguments broke out as to who was going to shoot which soldier. *"Hy's myne!" "Nee, hy's myne* (He's mine! No, he's mine!)" could be heard up and down the trench, as the riflemen competed to kill as many of the enemy as they could. The carnage was pitiful. Wounded men could be seen lying in the growing heat, begging for water and help. There was no help to be had, and it was not until later in the day that sympathetic Boers took water to the wounded.

So high was the confidence of Jeannot and his comrades that when they saw a group of about a hundred Highlanders cautiously approaching their trench, they whispered to each other not to shoot. When the group came within a hundred yards, they jumped out of the trench and shouted: "Hands up!" The Scots were so taken by surprise that they immediately threw down their arms and held their hands high in the air. Now it was the turn of the young Boers to be perplexed. They had instructions on what to do regarding shooting the enemy, but no instructions about taking prisoners. They looked at one another for help, but most just shrugged their shoulders. Then Britz came up with a suggestion. "If we take them prisoner, we will have to abandon our trenches and escort them back to camp. I am sure we should not do this. Also, prisoners have to eat, and this would leave less food for us." "So, what is your suggestion?" asked van Jaarsveld. "Well, what if we take away their guns and ammunition and send them back to their lines? We can't shoot them in cold blood - that would not be the honorable thing. I know they will live to fight another day, but I think that is all we can really do here." The men nodded, picked up the rifles and bandoliers, and told the Scots to go back to their units. The Scots, at first, didn't seem to understand. "Do you mean you are setting us free?" asked a big red-headed corporal. Jeannot, who spoke the best English, answered in the affirmative. The Scots looked even more bemused. "Don't you want to take us prisoner?" the big corporal asked. "No.," said Jeannot. "We have no real facilities here for prisoners. We don't want to shoot you, so we thought it best to send you back without your weapons. We are not butchers, you see, and we respect bravery in men. You showed great courage in approaching our trench, and we respect that." The corporal looked around at the men and said, "These young men are setting us free. We owe them our thanks for our lives." At which stage, he yelled. "Attention!" The men all came to attention. Then they all saluted, turned about, and walked back to their comrades.

Later that evening, when the story was recounted to the senior officers, there was initially some concern, but it was agreed that the boys had done the right thing under the circumstances. In any event, they were still laughing about another incident that had happened earlier in the day. It seemed that an old Boer who was a bit short-sighted refused to fire at the Scots because he thought they were a herd of ostriches!

Back in the trench, the men took a well-earned rest. The initial skirmish had succeeded beyond expectation, but the men felt that this would not be the last action of the day. The element of surprise had taken its toll on the British, but they had now learned where the Boers were dug in, and would no doubt plan a fresh attack that factored this in. Veldkornet Raaff moved down the trenches, making sure everyone was unhurt - the Boer casualties during the first assault were negligible, and no-one from Raaff's platoon had been injured. When he came to Jeannot's trench, the men gathered around him. "What do you think the Redcheeks will do next?" asked one man. "Not sure," replied Raaff. "They are regrouping as we speak, and I am sure they are licking their wounds and wondering how they could have been so stupid. Or how we could have been so smart." He grinned, and the men laughed. "But if there is one thing I know about these people, they are not the kind who will give up after only one shot, so expect something big to happen later in the day. Some of the other units still have remnants of the first assault in their sights and are keeping them pinned down, so there will be more casualties for the British before too long. But your sector seems to have cleared out since you forced them to turn tail and run. You men did very well, and Oom Koos will be very proud of what went on here today. Only do not let your guard down. Remain vigilant, and don't get caught by their counterpunch."

The men went back to their positions and assumed the one hour on, one hour off routine. The cries of the wounded were becoming more and more pitiful, and the men were deeply affected by this. After an hour of listening to the moaning, Havenga stood up. "Fuck this, manne. We need to give those poor buggers some water." He fashioned a small white flag on the end of a stick, and, gathering a water bottle from each man, climbed out of the trench and approached the wounded men lying on the ground. He flinched when he saw how badly wounded some of the men were, and how weak they had become. It was a sweltering day, and again the heat and the insects made it living hell for the wounded. When they saw Havenga approaching, they raised supplicating hands towards him. "I not have water, everyone," he said in his broken English. "But take bottle. Give who needs." And he distributed the water bottles among the wounded before returning to the trench. It was a brave and selfless act, and the men felt pride in the fact that they had done something humane in a day of tragedy.

Magersfontein Battlefield – December 11th, 1899 5.00pm – Methuen

Hamilton and his men had made it back to the point from which they had first advanced, about 1,000 yards from the base of the hill. The platoon had been decimated by the events of the morning, and there was a general feeling among the men that they would never go back into that hellhole. A number of Highlanders remained strewn across the battlefield, and some had been lying stationary on the veld for so long they had fallen asleep. Many men seemed to believe that it would be more dangerous to flee than to remain lying flat on the ground and waiting for the cover of darkness to get to safety. The condition of the Highlanders' legs, exposed by the kilts, was terrible. Many of the poor fellows lay in the open for hours—some of them from 4 am to 8 pm—and the backs of their legs were, almost without exception, covered with blisters and extensive burns from the scorching sun.

The remnants of the Highland Brigade, who tried to make it to safety in the rear, were aided by the artillery, which provided cover by bombarding the Boer positions. One of the mysteries of the battle had been the silence of the Boer guns all morning and most of the afternoon. With thousands of men lying out in the hot sun unable to move, a barrage of artillery would almost certainly have created considerable damage. There are many possible reasons for this. The Boer projectiles were high-explosive, which means that they burst on impact with the ground, sending out a flat cone-shaped mass of shrapnel. If soldiers are lying flat on the ground, there is a good chance of them not being hit by this type of explosion. If the Boers had had airburst projectiles like the British, these would have been lethal, detonating in the air and blowing shrapnel down on everything below. Another possibility is that Cronje may not have wanted to create any more carnage than had already been wrought on this day. The humane side of the Boers had been seen in their carrying water to the wounded soldiers, and the possibility exists that Cronje did not call in his artillery for similar humane reasons. The artillery under Maj. Albrecht did start firing late in the afternoon, but it was more to try and silence the British guns that were providing cover for retreating troops.

Colville had been encouraging Methuen to regroup and mount a new attack, but Methuen seemed demoralized by the events of the day. His shoulders were slumped, and his whole demeanor was one of a broken and defeated man. Every time he looked out at the Highlander-strewn battlefield, a shiver of responsibility and self-deprecation ran through his body.

"No," he said, "It is enough slaughter for one day. We need to regroup and evaluate where we stand. Perhaps we will attack again tomorrow if the Boers haven't used their usual tactics of disappearing after a battle. Please send a message to the regimental commanders to provide me with a report on the dead, wounded, and missing as of 6 pm today." His adjutant turned and left. The numbers are not going to be pretty, he thought. This is a catastrophe beyond my wildest expectations. And losing Andrew Wauchope is a disaster! Wauchope had been killed by a Boer bullet when the Highland Brigade made its first charge of the morning. He was buried that day in a small private ceremony at which a lone piper played 'Lochaber No More.'

The humane side of the Boers was also shown by Gen. Cronje, who, at the end of the evening, sent word to Methuen that he would make fifty burghers available to assist the British to bury their dead. This offer was gratefully accepted. This continued into the following day, in spite of a bombardment by British naval guns that momentarily broke Cronje's armistice until the guns were silenced by the British.

Magersfontein Battlefield - December 12th, 1899 9.00am – Methuen

It was Methuen's sincere hope that the morning would dawn to find that the Boers had abandoned their trenches and retired to their camp. This was not to be. The Boers remained firmly entrenched behind their sangars and barbed wire, with seemingly no intention of retreating. This was, after all, a victory for the Boers, and they were not giving up their positions.

Methuen reflected on the statistics of the battle. The British had lost 971 dead, wounded or missing in action, compared with Boer losses of 250, caused mainly by airburst artillery. It would have been easy to look for a scapegoat - Wauchope was the most obvious candidate - but Methuen was a man of honor, and knew that the buck stopped with him. He was the commanding general, he had dictated the strategy (against the wishes of some of his officers), and he would be held accountable for its failure. He knew this was the end of the road for him in South Africa, and it was with little surprise that he later learned Lord Roberts, accompanied by Lord Kitchener, were on their way from Cape Town to replace him. His last duty would be to ensure an orderly retreat from Magersfontein to a safe area near Modder River and to consolidate the troops into a battalion to be handed over to the new commander. It was a bitter pill for him, an unfortunate end to an illustrious military career, for he feared he would be asked to leave the army on his return to Britain.

Magersfontein Battlefield - December 12th, 1899 10.00am – Jeannot

As weary as Jeannot was of being in the trench, he was inwardly delighted that the Boers were holding their ground. This was clear evidence to the men that they had won the day, and that there was to be no sneaking away as had been the case at Modder River. The

British did not show any signs of attacking again - their primary concern was burying their dead and moving their wounded off the field, all made possible by the truce offered by Oom Piet. The men busied themselves, cleaning their rifles and trying to make the trench habitable after the excitement of the previous day.

Later that morning, Cronje visited the trenches to congratulate the men and to thank them for their efforts. When he got to Jeannot's trench, he was greeted by Havenga, who called out to him. "Morning, Oom Piet. We showed those Rednecks a thing or two yesterday, not so?" Cronje smiled. "We certainly did, manne. This is a victory that will go down in our history as one of the greatest battles our people ever fought in. And it was due to brave boys like you that we were able to succeed. The strategy was right, the timing was right, the terrain was right. And we had the right men for the job. You can all be proud to have been here, and it will be something you can tell to your grandchildren." "Oom Piet," said Jeannot, "how long are we going to remain in our trenches? When will we be moving to a new camp?" Cronje was quick to reply. "We are not going anywhere for the time being. We will hold our positions until we are quite sure what the enemy is planning to do. Clearly, Methuen still has Kimberley in his sights. But having got a bloody nose here, it is unlikely he will use the same strategy to break through next time. But if we abandon our position here, we invite him to come and occupy Magersfontein, and that would be bad for our people in Kimberley. So we need to wait a while to see what the British have in store for us. We will not require you to remain cooped up in the trench itself for 24 hours a day. There will be reliefs, and you will have some freedom to move around in the area, but we must consolidate around our trenches and continue to hold this valuable ground."

The men looked at each other. This was not good news. The trench was not the most comfortable place to spend time, and, if the stay extended to a week or more, it would become intolerable. Even being able to move around a bit was not much consolation - the trench was unpleasant, and would remain so.

During his sojourn in the trench, Jeannot wrote to his father.

Letter from Jeannot Weinberg to Edward Weinberg - December 17th, 1899 – Magersfontein

Magersfontein
December 17th, 1899

Dear Father

Yesterday the British attacked our position at Magersfontein with the large force of Scottish soldiers. They did a night march to within 5oo yards of our lines and, because we were dug in at the bottom of the hill and not on the hill as we usually do, they had no idea we were there. So when the daylight eventually broke, they were right in our sights, and they couldn't see us because our trenches were well camouflaged.

I have never seen anything like the first fifteen minutes of the battle, the Redcheeks came marching straight into the barrels of our rifles, and when Raaff give the order to fire, we cut them to pieces. It was a massacre - hundreds of their troops fell dead or dying, the rest ran away or lay flat, so we couldn't shoot them. Those who ran away made easy targets and the men were in competition as to who could pick off the most Tommies. The field was covered in bodies- more than I have ever seen in one place. And the wounded we just left there in the hot sun with the flies. Eventually, one of our boys took pity on them and brought them some water.

On Wednesday and Thursday morning, there were still 116

bodies lying on the field. General Cronje asked the English General if we should bury them or if they would bury them themselves. Only then the ambulances came and covered the corpses with sand because the holes were so shallow that the feet of some stuck out. The stench is terrible, and thousands of vultures are flying about. Even though the fighting was fierce at times, we suffered very few casualties. My section still has not lost a man, and we have been together since Scholtznek. We consider ourselves to be living charmed lives.

It is really terrible how the English military is being treated. The soldiers who are here are now afraid of attacking us, but as soon as there are a few thousand new soldiers who haven't been involved in the fighting yet, they are sent to the front of the battlefield.

We have now been in these blasted trenches for over a week, and it is not pleasant. The stink of the bodies out on the field and the fact that we are all living on top of each other is very unpleasant. I only hope Oom Piet will give us our marching orders soon so we can find a more comfortable spot. But we don't know how long they are going to keep us here.

Please give my love to Mama and the children. And please don't worry about me. I have looked into the jaws of hell and lived to tell the tale.

Your loving son
Jeannot

What Jeannot did not know was that he and his platoon would man the trenches for a further two months, until the middle of February 1900.

Chapter 17 - The Aftermath

Orange River January 1900 - Roberts

Magersfontein was not the only defeat that the British Army suffered at that time. In a disastrous week from 10–17 December 1899, dubbed "Black Week," the British Army suffered three devastating defeats by the Boer Republics at the battles of Stormberg, Magersfontein, and Colenso, with a total of 2,776 men killed, wounded and captured. The events were an eye-opener for the government and troops, who had thought that the war could be won very easily.

Black Week was a low point that the British Army had never anticipated. It brought into crisp focus the fact that the commanders had approached the conflict in South Africa with an outdated strategy and a group of generals too hide-bound in their adherence to mistakes of the past to be able to change to suit the terrain and enemy they faced. Black Week was a triumph of the agile over the ponderous, the concealed over the revealed, and the competent over the under-trained. For the British to recover from this series of defeats, there would need to be an injection of new leadership and a modern battle strategy to bring the British fighting force to a stage where they could compete.

Both elements arrived in the form of Lord Frederick Sleigh Roberts, and his second in command, Lord Herbert Kitchener. From the time they arrived in Cape Town on December 23rd, 1899, it was evident that the army in South Africa was about to experience a major overhaul. In a month, Roberts had assembled 30,000 infantry, 7,500 cavalry, and 3,600 mounted infantry, together with 120 guns, in the area between the Orange and Modder Rivers. The largest British mounted division ever assembled was created under the command of Major-General John French through the amalgamation of virtually all the cavalry in the area. This was the force that Roberts was going to employ to relieve Kimberley.

Roberts came from an English patrician family. Born in 1832, he was educated at Eton, Sandhurst, and Addiscombe Military Seminary before entering the East India Company Army as a second lieutenant with the Bengal Artillery in December 1851. He served with distinction in the Indian Rebellion of 1857. He saw service in Abyssinia, Afghanistan, and Ireland before being appointed to his role as Commander-in-Chief of British forces during the Boer War. Affectionately known as 'Bobs,' he was a kind of 'soldier-hero' so much a part of the Victorian colonial mythology. He was extremely popular with his men since he never adopted the traditional British officer pose of distancing himself from the common soldier. Indeed, he declined, in the field, to wear any rank insignia, preferring plain khaki tunic and khaki trousers to anything more elaborate. He was a highly skilled military strategist and had demonstrated his abilities in many fields of operation. He was clearly 'the man for the job.'

He surrounded himself with a group of senior officers who were forward-thinking and more sensitive to the situation with which they were faced. One such officer was Gen. John French, who had already locked antlers with Methuen over the battle strategies at Modder River and Magersfontein. He was a man who thought like Roberts and understood how the cavalry and artillery should be deployed on the modern battlefield, unlike Buller and Methuen, whose approach was outdated. Roberts knew his talents and was determined to use them to his best advantage. Kitchener was also an excellent officer, battle-hardened, and highly intelligent. He, too, favored a more modern approach to warfare, and, with Roberts, made a formidable team.

Shortly after his arrival at the Orange River, Roberts called a strategy order group of senior officers. Among those present were Lord Kitchener, General French, General Kenny-Kelly, and General Colville. Roberts had set up a large map of the area, attached to the side of the tent. Roberts stood in front of the map and opened the meeting.

"Gentlemen, our remit for this expedition has been to relieve our troops and the civilians besieged by the Boers in Kimberley. To date, we have not succeeded in fulfilling that remit. The series of failures we have experienced is about to end.... now." Several officers shifted uncomfortably in their seats. "Our strategy to date has clearly been defective. We have fought this war as if we were fighting opponents in Abyssinia. We are not. We are fighting a well-armed, strategically intelligent, devoted group of hard men who are prepared to lay down their lives for their freedom. We cannot go marching up to them in close order and expect them to scatter in terror. They will not - we saw that very clearly at Magersfontein. At no stage during this expedition has any attention being paid to outthinking or outmaneuvering our enemy. That is about to end.... now. I am not prepared to lead troops into the kind of slaughter we saw at Magersfontein, a slaughter that showed little strategic thinking except for the night march. And, damn it, since we used a night march on almost every other occasion, it hardly took the Boers by surprise. Gentlemen, Mr. Cronje, is sitting in his laager and laughing at us. And I, for one, gentlemen, am not one who enjoys being laughed at." The officers nodded their assent.

"So, this time, we are going to do two things. One, we are going to relieve Kimberley. And two, we are going to achieve this by treating this like a serious battle that requires careful thought, not a Sunday afternoon cricket match where we send in our team with little concern for the opponents. This time, gentlemen, I intend to outthink Mr. Cronje and not give him the chance to escape. He has used subterfuge; we will use subterfuge. He has used mobility; we will use mobility. He has used his artillery cleverly; we will use our artillery more cleverly. This is a game of chess, gentlemen, not a playground game. We need to be thinking three moves ahead so that if he changes his strategy, we are ready for him. We must examine every possible scenario and have a contingency plan for each. Nothing must be left to chance. We are all professionals here, let's damn well behave as such. Do I make myself clear, gentlemen?" All nodded.

"Then I am going to pass the baton to John French, who will walk you through some preliminary strategies we have been drawing up. These are not a fait accompli - they are open to discussion and modification. Gen. French." John French stood up, walked to the map, and proceeded to lay out the proposed plan for the relief of Kimberley.

Kimberley - February 13th, 1900 – French

Gen. John French was the kind of man who did not want to make the same mistake twice. Unlike some of his fellow generals, he was mindful that the defeat at Magersfontein had been primarily due to a failure of both tactics and strategy. From a strategic viewpoint, the belief that the road to Kimberley must follow the railway line had produced mixed results - success at Belmont and Graspan, a stalemate at Modder River and a crushing defeat at Magersfontein - and this led French to believe that staying close to the railway was not the only way to approach Kimberley. South Africa was, after all, a vast country, and to constrain the advance in a predictable direction seemed absurd. On the question of tactics, he was also not satisfied. All the battles to date had been waged primarily by the infantry, with the artillery providing covering fire, and the cavalry being used to pursue the retreating enemy. French was a cavalryman and knew the impact that cavalry could have in warfare as fluid as the encounters to date with the Boer armies had been. Above all, French knew that Boer strategy was primarily defensive rather than offensive. The Boers were unlikely to leave their trenches and engage in a full-frontal attack in open terrain. He also knew that an entrenched enemy is vulnerable to being flanked, provided it can be distracted into believing a frontal attack is underway. French's plan for the relief of Kimberley was simple. Create a diversionary attack on the Boer trenches at Magersfontein, and simultaneously lead a flanking maneuver to the north of the mountain, out of sight of the laager at Scholtznek, and approach Kimberley from the north-east, rather than the east.

Cronje believed that Roberts would attempt to attack him in a flanking maneuver from the west and that the advance would mainly continue as before along the railway line. With this mind, Roberts ordered Methuen to advance with the 1st Division on 11 February in a feint movement on Magersfontein, while General Sir Hector MacDonald led the Highland Brigade 20 miles west to Koedoesberg, thereby encouraging Cronje's forces to believe that the attack would occur there. However, the bulk of the force initially headed south to Graspan, then east deep into the Orange Free State with the cavalry division guarding the British right flank by securing drifts across the Riet River. On 13 February, Roberts activated the second part of his plan, which involved French's cavalry separating from the slower main force and piercing forward quickly by swinging northwards, just east of Jacobsdal, to cross the Modder River at Klipdrift.

As French's column neared the Modder River on 13 February, a force of about 1,000 Boers made contact with his right flank. French wheeled his right and center brigades towards their enemy, thereby allowing the brigade on the left to hold course for Klipdrift while giving the enemy the false impression that he was not headed for Klipdrift. The whole force then wheeled left at the last minute and charged the Klipdrift crossing at full gallop. The Boers at Klipdrift, who were taken completely by surprise, left their camp and provisions behind, which French's exhausted men and horses were glad to seize. Although speed was critical, the cavalry had to wait for the infantry to catch up to secure the lines of communication before moving forward to relieve Kimberley. The cavalry's route had taken them deep inside the Free State over Cronje's line of communication, thereby cutting off any Boer forces who did not immediately fall back. Meanwhile, Roberts led the main force in an easterly direction to capture the Free State capital of Bloemfontein.

French's flanking maneuver took a very high toll on horses and men in the blazing summer heat, with about 500 horses either dying en route or no longer fit to ride. When Cronje became aware of French's cavalry on his left flank at Klipdrift, he concluded that the British were trying to draw him eastwards away from his prepared defenses. He dispatched 900 men with guns to stop the British push northwards. French's men set out from Klipdrift at 9:30 am on 15 February on the last stage of their journey to Kimberley, and were soon engaged by the Boer force sent to block them. Rifle fire came from the river in the east while artillery shells rained from the hills in the north-west; the route to Kimberley lay straight ahead through the crossfire, so French ordered a bold cavalry charge down the middle. As waves of horses galloped forward, the Boers poured down fire from the two sides. However, the speed of the attack, screened by a massive cloud of dust, proved successful, and the Boer force was defeated. British casualties during this day's fighting were five dead and ten wounded, with approximately 70 horses lost through exhaustion. However, the route to Kimberley was open; by that evening, General French and his men passed through the recently abandoned Boer lines and relieved the town of Kimberley after some initial difficulty in convincing the defenders via heliograph that they weren't Boers. The cavalry had covered 120 miles in four days at the height of summer to reach the town. When French arrived in town, he snubbed Kekewich, the local military authority, by presenting himself to Rhodes instead. Kimberley had been relieved.

Scholtznek - February 17th, 1900 – Cronje

Cronje knew the game was up. The relief of Kimberley meant that the next prize Roberts would seek was the capture and occupation of Bloemfontein. He was aware that Roberts had been massing his troops at the Orange River, waiting for the relief of Kimberley to provide him the opportunity to move on the Free State capital. There had to be a last-ditch effort to protect Bloemfontein, and Cronje had decided where it should be. It was now left to him to marshal his remaining forces from Scholtznek, Magersfontein, and Jacobsdal, and somehow get them to Paardeberg. This would have been a difficult enough task with just fighting men, but he was now hamstrung by the vast laager of people that had encamped at Scholtznek - women, children, servants, cattle, and other hangers-on that had made Scholtznek resemble a small town. So, he summoned his commanders and set out his strategy.

Chapter 18 – Paardeberg

Magersfontein - February 1900 - Jeannot

Jeannot was nonplussed. They had been moving between Magersfontein and Scholtznek for two months, and still no action. There had been some talk about the British attack on February 15th, but the Bloemfontein Commando had not been called up to participate. Then they learned late in the day about Lord Roberts's daring relief of Kimberley and the fact that the marvelous victory at Magersfontein had been in vain. The British were in Kimberley, and the rumor was that Bloemfontein was going to be next. The rest of the day was a day of watching people scurrying around the laager, holding order groups, and probably making plans on how to protect Bloemfontein. It was not until the evening that they were ordered to decamp, saddle up and be ready to ride.

Jeannot's commando went in search of Veldkornet Raaff to see if they could find out more about what was going on. Raaff had been in various order groups and would be likely to have the latest information. He eventually appeared, looking strained but content. It had been a major exercise to control his men and keep them motivated these past weeks, and it was starting to show. He gathered the men and addressed them.

"Manne, we are going to be returning to Jacobsdal for a mustering of all of Gen. Cronje's army. Where we will be going to after that is anybody's guess." He looked out into the crowd and asked whether there were any questions. Gerhard Stander had a question. "Veldkornet, do you believe the next target for the British will be Bloemfontein?" Raaff nodded. "That is exactly what the generals seem to be expecting." "And will any reinforcements be joining the army?" Raff shrugged and replied wearily. "I don't think so. Other than a few stragglers from the Kimberley siege, it is unlikely that there will be any further reinforcements." "So how many men do you think we will end up with?" "I estimate we will be about 7,000 strong. And they have close to 30,000. So it seems like fair odds!" The men smiled and did the calculation - 1 Boer equals 4 British - sounded about right! "So, make ready, manne. We ride in an hour."

The ride to Jacobsdal was uneventful for Jeannot and his comrades. When they arrived, they found commandos arriving from all directions, all looking bored and uncertain—bored because the past two months had involved sitting around and not doing very much; uncertain as they wondered what the next action would involve. They were told not to encamp since there was to be a night march. Rumors went around the army like water in a whirlpool. Some said they would go straight to Bloemfontein and set up defenses there. Others were convinced Cronje would not put all his eggs in one basket but would try to slow up the British by forcing them to fight a series of skirmishes on the way to Bloemfontein. The name 'Paardeberg' was heard frequently, as was Poplar Grove. At any rate, it was reasonably certain their route of march would follow the course of the Modder River.

The army traveled north along the Modder River, the commandos in front, the laager with its ox wagons following behind. On the evening of February 17th, they were in sight of Paardeberg, and the order came for the commandos to begin with entrenchments on the west bank of the Modder. The laager moved past these trenches and established itself about a mile north of the trenches at Vendutie Drift. On the following morning, a contingent of two guns and 600 men under Gen. de Wet arrived from Koffiefontein and was ordered to take up a position on a kopje on the east bank of the river, about 2 miles from the stream (a kopje soon to be known as Kitchener's Kopje). Jeannot's commando was attached to de Wet's group. Unbeknown to de Wet, Gen. Kelly-Kenny had sent a detachment of infantry to occupy the kopje, but, unbeknown this time to Kelly-Kenny, another staff officer had ordered them to withdraw, believing them to be more useful elsewhere. They were replaced by a few mounted men who, while watching the progress of the various other battles taking place that day, were suddenly called on to defend themselves against de Wet and his men. The Boers did not waste any time driving them from the kopje, then proceeded to dig themselves in on the top and prepare to use the two guns to assist Cronje, who was fighting the enemy in a number of skirmishes.

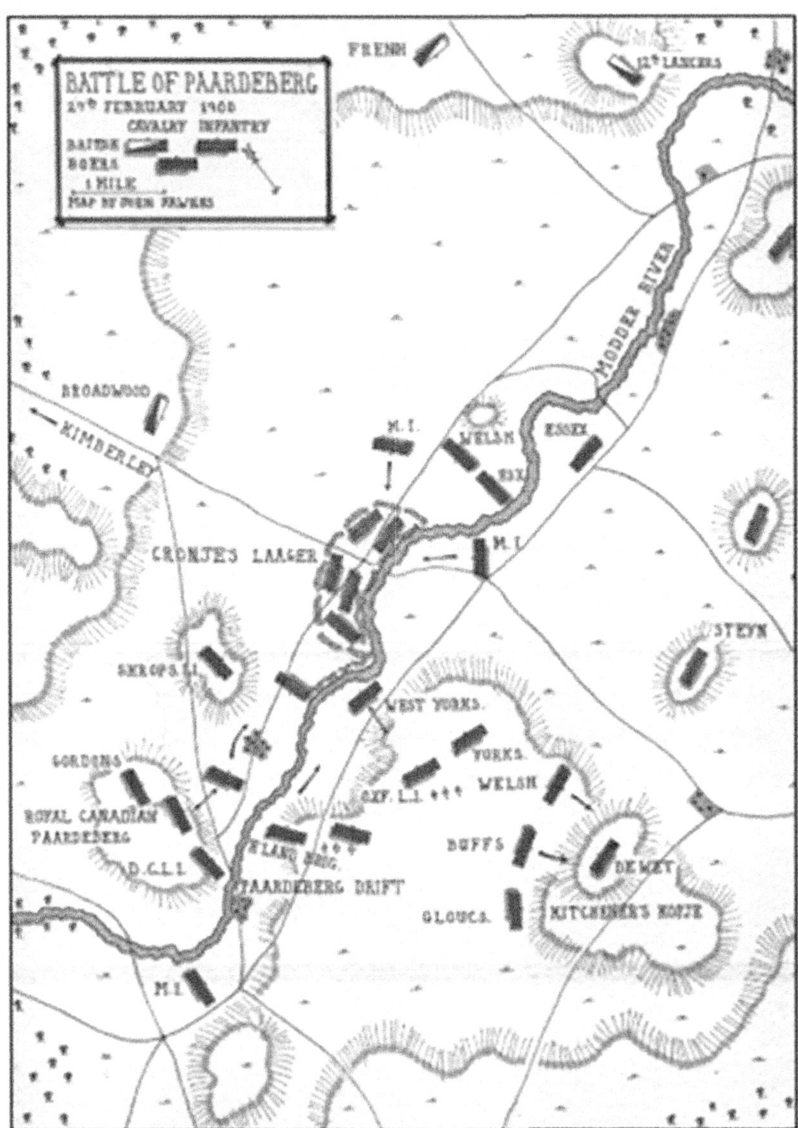

There was speculation as to why Cronje chose Paardeberg to make a stand against the British. Unlike Magersfontein, he did not take advantage of the high ground offered by Paardeberg hill but chose instead to set up his defenses at ground level much in the way he had done at Modder River. Leaving aside the tactical approach, there were some who believed that Paardeberg should have been bypassed and a final stand made outside of Bloemfontein. If this had been done, Cronje would have been able to draw on additional resources from the Bloemfontein area, ensure his supply of food and water, and have a town in his rear, thereby preventing the British from outflanking him and attacking from the rear. But this was not to be, and February 18th saw the start of one of the bloodiest conflicts of the entire war.

It was fortunate for Cronje that, on the day the British commenced their attack, Roberts was not present, having been laid low by illness in Jacobsdal. The attack was planned and coordinated by a committee of generals, including Kitchener, Colville, and Kelly-Kenny. And it was typical of anything designed by a committee! Without the Commander-in-Chief to take his usual firm hand and direct all activities, the generals seemed unable to agree on a universal strategy, and the ensuing battle, which Kelly-Kenny had thought would last only a few hours, stretched out to several days. It was only when Roberts came up from Jacobsdal on the afternoon of February 19th that the strategy came together.

The British forces attacked on a number of different fronts during the first day of Paardeberg but found that the Boers were so cleverly entrenched on the banks of the Modder River that they were unable to break through and surround the laager, as had been their intention. It was, however, the actions of de Wet and his group on the kopje that eventually turned the day's battle in favor of Cronje. At 4.30 p.m., he opened fire on the 6th Division baggage and artillery. This was the first indication to the British high command that they were no longer in control of the kopje since they were focused primarily on Cronje and the laager. It was not like de Wet to pass up this sort of opportunity to catch the British unawares and to pour lead into them from a strategic position. His efforts forced the British commanders to withdraw troops from the front against Cronje and move them to the defense of the areas being bombarded by de Wet. Dealing with this unexpected attack from the rear, the hope of carrying Cronje's position before nightfall was lost.

By the end of the first day of hostilities, the laager was holding out, and the chief result of the day's work was a contraction of the line held by the Boers on the river; an attempt by Kelly-Kenny to recapture Kitchener's Kopje had failed; fully one-quarter of the perimeter commanding Vendutie Drift was in possession of the enemy; the troops were exhausted, and the casualties exceeded 1,200.

When Roberts arrived on February 19th, he did not, as many had anticipated, focus his attack on the laager. Instead, realizing the strategic nature of the kopje occupied by de Wet, he turned his attention to smoking out de Wet and his commandos. The laager was left to starve itself to death, with occasional artillery fire being directed at it to increase the chaos and suffering. Cronje drew strength from the presence of de Wet on the kopje and be believed it was his God-given duty to defend the women and children living in pitiful conditions in the laager. De Wet, it turned out, was not in a hurry to hand over the kopje to Roberts. For three nights and two days, he defied all efforts to dislodge him. On the 19th, a body of cavalry was brought round from the north, but de Wet was able to beat them off. Towards evening an infantry brigade was thrown at the kopje, but after it had obtained some success and had partially entrenched itself on the slopes, it was forced to withdraw to avoid further casualties. No action was taken on the 20th, but on the 21st, a cavalry attack forced de Wet out of his position on the crest of the kopje. Despite being dislodged, the Boers did as they had done in the past - disappeared into thin air!

Kitchener's Kopje – February 21st, 1900 – Jeannot

The men believed that they would go directly to the laager to assist

Cronje, but de Wet had other ideas. Believing Cronje's plight to be hopeless, unless he was able to break out of the laager, de Wet was reluctant to put himself similarly in harm's way. If Cronje could not succeed in breaking out of the laager – and the British noose was tightening by the minute – de Wet could see no alternative for Cronje and his men than a wholesale surrender. And this is what he feared most. Better to die in battle, than to be a *'hensopper'* (one who surrenders). That evening he addressed the men under his command.

"Manne, we have fought bravely, but we are not going to beat the British here. Gen. Cronje has almost been surrounded, and, if we go to his aid, we will be putting ourselves into the same predicament as him. Unless he is able to escape from the British, I am fearful he and his men will be slaughtered to the last man." The men looked at one another in shock. How could it happen that, so soon after the glorious victory at Magersfontein, they would be in a position to be wiped out? De Wet continued. "For my part, I am going to lie low and look for a way to escape to a place somewhere between here and Bloemfontein and to set up a defense there. And I am hoping that you will all accompany me. As the old expression goes – 'He who fights and runs away, lives to fight another day.'

Again, the men looked at one another. After a while, Havenga spoke. "General, sir, we hear what you have told us, and we understand your feelings. We, too, have been having the same thoughts. But, sir, there is one difference. My friends from the Bloemfontein Commando and I are under the direct control of Gen. Cronje. We have been sent here on loan to you for the last skirmish, but our loyalty must lie with Gen. Cronje, who is our commanding officer." The other members of the Bloemfontein Commando, Jeannot included, nodded. "So, while we know that it is hazardous, and while we fear too that our general's position is a difficult one, we feel we must show him our loyalty and stand with him, even if it for the last time."

De Wet's expression was difficult to read – he was in a quandary. He understood well the pull of loyalty – he himself was conscious that his actions might one day be regarded as disloyal. Still, on the other hand, he felt it was foolish to go willingly into an impossible position. And, slightly selfishly, he had been impressed by the boys from Bloemfontein and was reluctant to lose such talented fighters. At last, he clasped his hands behind his back and spoke. "Manne, I just hope you know what you are doing. Going back into the laager is very dangerous, but I know that you know that. I will not do anything to stop you if it is your wish to return to Gen. Cronje. But I recommend you do it immediately while it is still dark. The British have not yet fully surrounded the laager, and you have a good chance of making it back there under cover of night. So, to those of you who wish to go, I say thank you for your service to my men and me, and may the Almighty give you his protection." He held out his hand to Havenga, who shook it vigorously. "Go with God, General. It has been a privilege to serve with you." He was followed by the other men of the Bloemfontein Commando, who solemnly shook the general's hand and took their leave of their other colleagues.

Then they slipped noiselessly into the night.

Cronje's Laager – February 22nd, 1900 – Jeannot

Nothing could mask the stench. Rotting flesh, from both man and beast, filled the air with a nauseating intensity quite unlike anything Jeannot had ever experienced. Several of the men were sick to their stomachs, and the quiet of the night was interrupted by the sound of men heaving. Sleep was impossible in this inferno, and Jeannot lay awake, waiting for morning and the hope of some relief from all this suffering. It was reported that, earlier in the day, Roberts had extended an offer to Cronje to remove the women and children to safety, but this had been firmly rejected by Cronje.

The morning dawned through a hazy mist rising from the Modder River. Jeannot had dozed off a few hours before sunrise but was awakened by the sound of movement in and around the laager. Raising himself from his bedding, he looked around him. The laager was a pitiful sight. Debris from damaged wagons lay among scattered pieces of clothing and cooking utensils. The corpses of dead animals lay everywhere, no-one having the strength to remove them from the area. Outside the perimeter, dozens of shallow graves could be seen, the bodies having been so imperfectly interred that the occasional hand or foot protruded. The inhabitants looked tired, sick, and starving. Children with hollow eyes and bellies distended from hunger were everywhere to be seen. Women with haggard faces and stooped shoulders tried to scrape up enough food to provide some breakfast, but there was not much food in evidence. No supplies had reached the laager since it arrived at Paardeberg, and the rations were practically non-existent. Jeannot was again reminded of the smell. It made him think of what the hell must smell like on a hot day, a chokingly disgusting mixture of rotting flesh and excrement. Nothing he had ever experienced could have prepared him for the sight, sounds, and odors of this place that had clearly been forgotten by God. No hope gleamed from the eyes of the inhabitants, just a dull stare of hopelessness and misery. It was like the pit of hell.

He went off in search of his comrades, and found them outside of the laager, discussing what to do next. It was clear to all of them that Cronje was nearing the end of the road here, and that the laager and its defenses could not hold out much longer now that De Wet had been dislodged from the kopje. It was only a matter of time before the sheer weight of numbers of the British, and the lack of incoming supplies and reinforcements for the Boers would force Cronje to surrender.

Hostilities went on for four more days, the Boers growing ever weaker and, in spite of offering heroic resistance, were sorely short of ammunition and food. It was becoming clear that the situation could not prevail for much longer. On the evening of February 26th, Jeannot was passing Cronje's tent when he heard voices arguing within. He crept closer, making sure he was not seen and listened to the conversation. One voice was Cronje; the other was unfamiliar to Jeannot. Cronje was talking.

"We have a covenant with God for the possession of this land, and in His name, we must hold our position.

"That may well be, Oom Piet, but without supplies and reinforcements, we cannot hold out any longer. We would be sentencing 4,000 of our men and all the women and children to needless slaughter."

"But I have a solemn pledge to the President to hold our ground and never to give it up."

"And where is the President now? What does he know of our plight? Do you not think he would also want to avoid the murder of men, women, and children? "

"Ja, I understand, Danie. But I have a sacred duty to protect our volk and homeland."

"Sacred duty be damned, Oom Piet. You are juggling the lives of human beings here, man. Men, women, and children who will be dead in a few days if you do not act, and soon, they will either die from starvation and sickness or from Tommy bullets."

Now Jeannot could identify the other speaker. It could only be Danie Theron. Theron was the leader of the Boer Intelligence scouts, the *Theron se Verkenningskorps* (TVK) (Theron's Reconnaissance Corps). A fearless fighter who seemed to fear no man or situation, he was a continual thorn in the side of the British. He and his men were masters of deception and quick escape, and his name had become a legend among soldiers on both sides.

Cronje sat back in his chair and tugged his beard. His eyes filled with tears. He understood very well the conflict between his own conscience and the lives placed under his protection. He sighed, shook his head, and wiped his hand across his eyes.

"Danie, I must do my duty."

Theron was quick to respond. "Gen. de Wet is of the view that you should attempt to break out of the laager, surprise the Redcheeks, and come and join him in Poplar Grove, where he is digging in. I agree with him, and my TVK will help you. Remaining here is suicide. He told me to tell you that our fate depended upon the escape of yourself and the thousands with you, and that, if you should fall into the enemy's hands, it would be the death-blow to all our hopes."

Cronje pondered this for a moment. "Danie, that is much easier said than done. If de Wet were on this side of the laager, he would understand how trapped we are and how little chance we have of breaking out. I am not a madman, and I do not want to put the lives of brave men in danger any more than I have to. I have pledged myself to protect these people, and protect them I will. I will not go along with your suggested breakout, help, or no help from the TVK. It is just too risky, could lead to the wholesale slaughter of men, women, and children." He shook his head, sorrowfully. "I just refuse to have their deaths on my conscience. No. Tomorrow I will go to Roberts and offer to lay down our arms if they guarantee safe passage to the women and children. As for the men, I think they would rather become prisoners of war than sacrifice their lives. Hopefully, the British will be humane." He thought a while, then said wistfully, "I will be the first Boer general to go into a POW camp."

Jeannot could not believe what he had heard. Cronje was going to surrender to the Redcheeks in the morning, leaving de Wet to fight another day. He immediately turned over in his mind what this would mean to him. If he stayed around, he would be forced to surrender along with the rest of Cronje's men. He would not be able to join de Wet - he and his commando had only been seconded to them for a short while, and they were again part of Cronje's army. What about escape? Surely every burgher had the right to return home from commando when he felt the need, so there was no regulation to prevent him from going. But what of his moral duty to his comrades and leaders? This weighed heavily on him, but he reasoned that he would be less useful as a POW than as a free burgher who might save the Free State. But how to escape, and where? And should he tell his comrades? To the latter question, his answer was no - telling anyone else would cause the word to spread around the army, and there would be chaos. Better to remain silent and slip out of camp without anyone noticing he was gone. But how to get out? He was vaguely aware of where the British forces were situated, and they basically surrounded the laager. The only place he remembered that was reasonably clear was a kopje to the southeast of the laager, which Commandant Steyn had occupied when he was on the nearby kopje with de Wet. There were no British on this kopje as far as he knew. If he could get there under cover of darkness, he would be able to hide out until he had surveyed the encampments of British troops in the area. He could not take his horse since this would attract too much attention when crossing the Modder River. He would need to steal a horse, or face a walk of about 40 miles to get to Bloemfontein.

He left at 3 am on the morning of February 27th. He had quietly packed his few possessions on the previous evening and had pretended to sleep in an area away from his comrades. He slipped quietly out of the laager and made for the bank of the Modder River. It was too deep to walk across, so, with his pack and rifle on his back, he slipped quietly into the cold water and started to swim for the opposite bank. He used a stroke similar to breaststroke to make the minimum of noise. It took about half an hour to cross, since he moved very slowly, ever aware of the possibility of patrols, and not wanting to attract attention. Once on the other bank, he made quietly for the kopje he had identified as his hiding place. He approached it cautiously - he was, after all, behind enemy lines, and did not know whether the kopje had been occupied by the British. He crept silently towards the kopje, still hidden by the darkness. It would not be dawn for another hour, and he needed to make it to the top before the sun rose. The kopje was about 500 feet high, and not very steep, so it was not too difficult to reach the summit. Fortunately, the kopje was deserted. Jeannot found a place on the summit where he would be hidden from sight and lay down in the sand to get some rest. The past two hours had been exhausting both physically and mentally, and he needed to quiet his mind.

He awoke around 9 am. He looked out towards the laager and saw a sight that brought tears to his eyes. As Cronje had intimated the night before, he was in the process of surrendering his force to Lord Roberts. Boers were in the process of handing over their rifles and being herded into groups by the British soldiers. Women and children were being fed by the British kitchens, and medical staff could be seen moving among the pitiful survivors of the laager. Jeannot realized two things. Firstly, he needed to get away from here as soon as possible, or he would be captured and made a POW along with the others. Second, the attention of the British forces would be on the surrender, and this would be an ideal time to steal a horse. He looked around him and saw that there was a small camp just at the foot of the kopje he had occupied with de Wet a few nights before. There was a small corral of horses some way away from the camp, presumably used to draw supply wagons. The corral seemed undefended, the troops having gone to the laager area to assist with the surrender. The corral was about a mile from his vantage point. He crept slowly down the side of the kopje. The sun was now high in the sky, and there was little cover other than scattered thorn trees. He traversed the distance, moving quickly from tree to tree, dropping to the ground each time he reached one to scout the terrain ahead. So far, so good. There seemed to be no-one about. He was now about a hundred yards from the corral when he saw a section of soldiers approaching the corral. He flattened himself on the ground, praying not to be seen. It appeared that the soldiers were bringing provender to the horses. They were carrying bales of hay, which they distributed among the horses. Jeannot feared they might take the horses down to the river to drink, but fortunately, this was not the case. After about fifteen minutes, the men left, talking, and smoking as they went. Jeannot remained unseen on the ground behind a small thorn bush.

Once they were out of sight, he crawled the remaining distance to the horses, and only rose when he was among them and unable to be easily spotted. There were about fifteen horses in the enclosure. Jeannot selected a chestnut gelding and quietly led him to the entrance to the corral. Once outside, he mounted, spurred on the animal, and galloped away. He had not been gone 30 seconds when he heard a shout go up in the camp, and, looking around, he saw soldiers hurrying to the corral. It was not long before the zing of bullets was heard about him. He laid himself flat on the horse and urged the beast to gallop faster. Still, the shots passed over him. In the distance was a small kopje, and he directed the horse in that direction - this would at least remove him from the line of sight. Once behind the kopje, he rode for all he was worth in the direction of the sun, east, east to where Bloemfontein awaited him.

Part 4 - Bloemfontein

Chapter 19 - Jeannot returns

Bloemfontein - February 27th, 1900 - Jeannot

It was a typical highveld evening. The sun was nearing the horizon, and there was a silence of peace over the town, so typical of an African sunset. The heat of the day had passed, and the slight breeze moved through the trees as a harbinger of the approaching night. Birds could be heard singing their evensong chorus.

A lone horseman, a thin, tall man, rode his horse slowly down Maitland Street. His face was streaked with dirt and blood, and his clothes were little more than rags. His rifle was slung over his back, and his boots bore the red dust of the Free State veld. Yet he rode erect on the unsaddled horse, with the quietude and dignity of a man who has seen great tragedy. He stopped outside the Royal Hotel, dismounted and tied his horse to the verandah rail. He walked in slow steps up the stairs and entered the hotel lobby.

Simon, the butler, was the first to see him, "Master Jeannot!" he cried. "Master Jeannot, you are safe." His voice carried through to the office, and Edward emerged, his arms outstretched. "Jeannot, my son, my son. We had despaired of ever seeing you again. Oh, Jeannot, my son, my son." He embraced Jeannot and hugged him, tears of relief flowing down his face. "Come, we must go and tell Mama and the children." Jeannot stopped him. "Where are Bernard and Max? Are they safe?" "They arrived home two days ago. They are tired and despondent, but, thank God, they are both unharmed". Together they walked to the sitting room in the annex to the hotel where the family lived.

The whole family was in the room. Edward beckoned to Jeannot to wait in the corridor. "I have a joyous surprise for everyone," he said.

"Our beloved Jeannot is home. And unharmed." At this, Jeannot entered the room and was immediately swamped by everyone. Hugs, tears, whoops of delight accompanied his arrival. Mama was quite overcome, a mixture of relief, joy, and excitement. "We had no letter from you after the one you sent just after Magersfontein. We have been so worried. We heard of the relief of Kimberley and the defeat at Paardeberg. We didn't know whether you were dead or wounded or taken prisoner. So many families have had such awful news about their loved ones. We did not know what to think. But now you are here, you are here! Oh, thank God you are here and unharmed." Jeannot smiled and embraced her with a hug that would have done justice to a bear. "Oh Mama, the things I have to tell you, the battles, the marches, the brave men who didn't make it - my friends, my brothers." "Sit down, Jeannot. You look exhausted," said Edward. "No, Papa. There is no way I would spoil Mama's couch in my disgusting and dirty clothes! Let me get cleaned up first." "Are you hungry? You must be," said Mama. "And thirsty, too. Do you want something to eat and drink?" "Mama, I have been dreaming of a cold beer for the whole of the time I have been away. But never as much as I do now!" Max hurried to the bar and returned with a glass of beer, the outside glistening with condensation. Jeannot downed it in one swallow, wiped his mouth, and beamed at the family. "Ah," he said. "Now I feel human again!"

Mama hurried him off to the bathroom, drew a bath, and brought him a robe. Jeannot stripped off his clothes as discreetly as he was able and handed them to Mama. "Burn them, Mama. I am done with them forever. Now give me some time to remove all the veld I have dragged in with me." Mama left, and Jeannot slid into the bath, luxuriating in the warm water, his body unaccustomed to such a treat. He had been able to bathe occasionally during the action, but the cold and muddy water of the Modder River was no match for this. He spent a half-hour scrubbing the grime and dirt from his body, drained the tub, refilled the bath, and lay for another fifteen minutes, just enjoying the feel of the hot water on his skin and tired muscles. He was home.

Dressed, he now returned to the sitting room. Mama had prepared a meal of beef and potatoes with gravy, and Max had brought another cold beer. Jeannot ate with great enthusiasm, pausing only to take a swig from the glass. The family noticed that his clothes were a bit loose on him, not severely, but evidence enough that an irregular diet had taken its toll. When he finished eating, he lit a cigar his father offered, exhaled deeply, and leaned back in his chair. He knew the family was anxious to hear his story but too respectful to push him. He grinned at them. "So, what do you want to know?" He was bombarded by questions, every member of the family wanting to get a hearing. "Stop, stop," he said. "All in good time. What is the last thing you heard?" Mama said, "We got your letter after the action at Magersfontein, but we have heard nothing since then." "So, you haven't received my letter from Jacobsdal last week? I assume it is still in transit. Difficult to see how anything could have got through with the confusion that has been going on recently." Mama shook her head.

"I would love to tell you everything that has happened, how I got to where I am today, but to tell you the truth, I am absolutely exhausted, and I want nothing more than to sleep. Can it wait until morning?" "Of course," exclaimed Mama. "We are just so relieved that you are home and unharmed. Go to bed, Jeannot. Now. We will talk in the morning."

Bloemfontein - February 29th, 1900 – Jeannot

Jeannot had taken a while to fall asleep the previous evening. The soft bed, so unaccustomed after the hard ground of the veld and the events and images that cascaded through his mind, caused him to lie awake, staring at the ceiling, almost not believing he had managed to escape unscathed. How had his comrades fared? Who was still alive? Did de Wet get away? Where was he now? At last, sleep acquired mastery of his imagination, his eyes closed, and he slept like the dead.

He awoke at 5 am, his accustomed rising time when on commando. He tried to rise, but his muscles ached, and the soft comfort of the bed enveloped him. He turned over and slept for three more hours. He was awakened by a soft tapping on the bedroom door, and Sanni, the colored maid, brought in a pot of coffee and some rusks. "Morning, master Jeannot. I hope you slept well." Jeannot looked at her in confusion. Where am I? What room is this? How did I get here? At last, his brain cleared, and the sleepiness left him. He raised his head, looked at Sanni, and grunted. "Thank you, Sanni. You are my savior. I slept better than I can remember. Please tell Mama I will be down for breakfast in half an hour." He lay back on the pillow, his mind recounting the happenings of the previous day - the hot ride from Paardeberg, his arrival at the hotel, his family, and the bath, oh the bath. He felt his strength returning. He washed, shaved, and dressed in the clothes Mama had placed on the wooden rocking chair, presumably left there during the night. He put on a pair of regular shoes and marveled at how comfortable and soft they felt after weeks in those heavy, uncomfortable boots. With a last glance at his tousled bed, the haven that had enveloped him for twelve hours, he closed the door and made his way to the breakfast room. The family was seated at the table especially reserved for the proprietor and his family. As he entered the room, every man, woman, and child stood and cheered their returning hero. It was heartwarming in the extreme, and Jeannot nodded his thanks to them before taking his seat at the left of his father and next to Bernard. The faces were wreathed in smiles, a welcome sight to one who had been deprived of this warmth and intimacy for so many long weeks.

And so, he told his tale............

Poplar Grove - March 7th, 1900 - de Wet

The surrender of Cronje's forces at Paardeberg had not meant the complete collapse of the Boer army. A strong contingent led by de Wet had broken off from Cronje's force shortly after leaving Jacobsdal and had leapfrogged over the main force to set up a rear-guard action nearer to Bloemfontein. The selected site had been Poplar Grove, fifty miles to the north-west of Bloemfontein. Unbeknown to the British, in the party, was Pres. Kruger of the Transvaal who had come to see the situation first hand. He had contingency plans to escape if things turned against the Boers - it would have put a swift end to the war if Kruger were captured. De Wet, mindful of the importance of his guest, made sure he would have an unhindered escape route should things start to go wrong.

The Boers at Poplar Grove were badly outnumbered. After Paardeberg, de Wet had only around 6,000 men left to defend the Orange Free State capital, and the morale of the Boer commandoes was at a very low ebb after Cronje's surrender. The British sent two infantry divisions in an advance straight at the Boer position, while the cavalry made a full flanking move to the south, coming up behind the Boers to prevent their escape. That advance never needed to turn into an attack. The British infantry came into view from the Boer camp at about 8 am and, demoralized by recent events, the burghers simply turned and fled. De Wet blamed the fiasco on Cronje's surrender, only two weeks earlier, although it probably helped save his army. If the Boers had stood and fought at Poplar Grove, then French would have been able to get into place to cut off their retreat, and the entire army might have been lost.

Before the Boer forces scattered to safety, de Wet called them together and addressed them. "Manne, we have lost the battle, but we have not lost the war. Pres. Steyn will not be in Bloemfontein to surrender the city, nor will he participate in the re-establishment of the Orange Free State as a British colony. This will be left to those in opposition to the Free State Volksraad. Just where Steyn is going is something I am not in a position to reveal. But suffice it to say that we are far from done yet in this land of ours. We will probably not be fighting in the same format in the future - we know that the British can defeat us by sheer weight of numbers in a conventional battle. So, we are going to take the fight to them in our own way, using the skills that differentiate us from the British, and causing them as much hardship as we can. We may not win the war, but we will ensure that the Redcheeks have to struggle for every inch of our country if they want to take it over. I am fighting on, so is de la Rey, so are Botha, Smuts, and a whole string of other generals. We have been proud to command you in the past months and will be proud again to lead you in the future. So, I invite any of you who do not feel we should sacrifice this beautiful land of ours without trying everything in our power to join me in the months going forward. For now, I want you to go back to your homes and your farms, see your loved ones and get some rest. If you want to join my colleagues and me going forward, give your name and address to Veldkornet Vermeulen, and we will contact you when the time is right. Those of you who do not want to fight further; I totally understand and will respect your judgment and decision. This is a time when a man must plumb the depths of his soul and do what he believes God has mapped out for him. I thank you for the honor of serving with you, and I salute you as the bravest soldiers I have ever fought with." The group erupted in a volley of cheers for their commander. They shook his hand, thanked him for his leadership, and pledged their support for him and his cause. When they turned to go, and de Wet mounted his horse to retreat, his heart was heavy, and a mist came into his eyes. These brave boys had answered the call and achieved the impossible. He would never forget them.

Bloemfontein - March 13th, 1900 – Bertha

The British victory at Poplar Grove meant that the road to Bloemfontein was now clear for Roberts' advance, and he wasted no time in consolidating his army and marching in that direction. Early on Tuesday the 13th of March, he sent an officer bearing a flag of truce to demand the surrender of the city. The officer was met by a delegation of the citizens who were already en route to meet with the British to formalize the handover. This group included Mr. Fraser, the leader of the opposition in the Free State Volksraad when Brand controlled the assembly, and Dr. Kellner, the mayor of Bloemfontein. Both men were extremely cautious to ensure that nothing was done to disrupt the peace and security of Bloemfontein. They did not want to endure looting or other such unpleasantries that frequently occurred during the occupation of a town. And most importantly, they wanted to ensure that the British army did not requisition all the food and other resources and leave the city to starve. They met Lord Roberts at Spitzkop, five miles from the southern suburbs, and made a formal surrender to him of the Free State capital. At noon Lord Roberts rode into the town at the head of Gen. Kelly-Kenny's division.

Bertha wanted to watch Roberts' arrival, and she persuaded Jeannot to go with her. They stood at the side of the road on Maitland Street, which the crowd said was the one that Roberts would be using. The streets were lined with curious Bloemfonteiners, interested to see the general and his troops. Near to Jeannot and Bertha were two men, a Mr. Ellison and a Mr. Wilson, both of whom Jeannot was familiar with from the hotel. After a while, there was a buzz in the crowd, and a cloud of dust could be seen at the far end of the street. Cries of "They're coming!" spread through the crowd. The sound of a brass band could now be heard, as well as the sound of horses' hoofs. Eventually, the figure of Lord Roberts could be seen riding a magnificent black stallion. He was not dressed in his usual field garb of khaki jacket and khaki pants with no insignia or symbols of rank. Today he was in the full regalia of a British general, red coat, blue trousers, blue hat with a white plume, and ceremonial sword. He looked extremely impressive, done no doubt to remind the inhabitants of whom they were dealing with. Behind him marched his staff, followed by the band and the various regiments, led by their regimental commanders. When Roberts drew alongside Bertha's position, Ellison was heard to say. "What a magnificent horse Lord Roberts is riding." Jeannot could not prevent himself from responding. "Yes, but if he were out on the battlefield, he would not be atop that beast for long!" At this remark, both Ellison and Wilson turned and looked at Jeannot quizzically. Bertha tugged on Jeannot's sleeve. "Don't say things like that, Jeannot. You could get into trouble!"

Roberts rode at the head of the column until they reached the market square, the very place from which Jeannot had left five months earlier. A dais was set up, and his troops did a march past, with Roberts taking the salute. After that, the troops were dismissed, and Roberts began to set up his headquarters in a building that had once housed Pres. Steyn. The troops were surprised at the welcome they received. There were cheering crowds everywhere, and Union Jacks fluttered from many windows. It seemed more like a triumphal entry than an occupation. Roberts was somewhat concerned about the look and demeanor of his troops. They were a ragged looking lot, many with uniforms in tatters, many without boots - not exactly what might be expected of a conquering army. But these men were battle-weary, hot, thirsty, and hungry, and it was all their officers could do to stop them from breaking ranks and going off in search of food and drink. And Roberts was concerned just how long their discipline would hold.

Bertha and Jeannot returned to the hotel after the march, and Bertha hurried into the kitchen to find something to eat and drink.

No sooner had she arrived when she heard a fracas in the yard near to the back door to the kitchen. Outside the door were four or five British soldiers, haggard of face and ragged of dress, arguing with Simon about getting some food. Simon was standing his ground, but it was a losing battle. Eventually, they stormed into the kitchen and started eating whatever they could find, including the raw dough that had been prepared for baking bread for dinner - so acute was their hunger. Bertha fled from the kitchen and ran to fetch Edward, screaming that the Redcheeks had invaded the hotel. Edward grabbed his pistol and raced for the kitchen to witness the pandemonium inside. He quickly fired a shot from his pistol, and the room fell silent. He addressed the four soldiers. "Young men, I sympathize with your plight, and it is clear that you have received no rations for several days. This is, however, something you need to address with your superiors. Your action today in breaking and entering into my establishment and stealing food is a court-martial offense that could have all of you shot. Do you understand me?" The men nodded. "However, I am not the sort of person who would report you, nor would I want you to get into any trouble. I had three boys in the field, and I know how difficult times can be. Now if you will please sit down at that table, I will have Chef make you some sandwiches, and I will bring you some beer from the bar. You are my guests for the next half-hour, and after that, I never want to see you again. Do I make myself clear?" The men nodded again, and one, a corporal, stood up, "Bless you, Sir. You make us ashamed of our conduct here. We are not thieves or robbers, but we last ate three days ago, and my men and I are starving. We apologize, and we thank you for your hospitality." Edward nodded and reminded them, "Even though we are your enemy, we are men too, and expect at all times to be treated as such. Good luck to all of you." He turned and returned to his office, hoping that this would be the end of such behavior.

Chapter 20 - The Arrest

Royal Hotel, Bloemfontein - March 23rd, 1900 8.15 pm - Fanni

They had finished dinner in the dining room and had retired to the sitting room in the private wing of the hotel. It was the Sabbath, and in the corner of the room was a small table with a white tablecloth on which stood two lit candles, a half-eaten Challah, and a silver Kiddush cup. Because the family traditionally took their meals in the hotel dining room, Edward felt that it was inappropriate to perform the Sabbath prayers in public, so they were chanted in the sitting room before the family moved to the dining room for their meal.

Edward sat in a leather armchair to the left of the fireplace, his pipe lit, and a cup of coffee on a small wooden table next to his chair. Fanni was knitting, and Bertha was reading a book. Jeannot was smoking a small cigar and reading De Volkstem, the newspaper printed in the Transvaal, but available in Bloemfontein. Bernard and Max played cards at a table in the corner of the room. The fire was not lit, it being only March and not yet cool enough to require heating.

There was a knock on the door, and Simon, Edward's butler, entered the room. His eyes were downcast, and he had the look of someone reluctant to reveal the purpose of his visit. "Master Edward," he said, "There are soldiers here looking for Master Edward and the boys." "Where are they from?" inquired Edward. "I do not know, Master, but they are surely British. And there is a local policeman with them. Cobus Reinart, Master, knows him, he drinks in the bar at the hotel." Fanni had glanced up from her knitting, a look of concern spreading across her face. "What do they want, Simon?" she asked. "I do not know, Madam. They just asked to see Master Edward and the boys." By this time, everyone had abandoned their activities and focused on the butler. "Ask them to come into the sitting room. And mind they wipe their boots - I'll not have the British Army hauling highveld mud onto my carpet." Simon bowed and disappeared.

They looked at one another. What was this all about? Had not the boys all signed the Act of Obedience and surrendered their weapons after Paardeberg? And Edward? What had he done other than run a hotel and cater to every need and whim of the British officers who frequented it? Edward regarded the anxiety in the faces of his wife and children. Bertha had moved closer to her mother and was holding her hand. The boys looked confused and slightly afraid. "Let me do the talking," he said, "We need to be polite and respectful. Nothing can be gained by rudeness or aggressive behavior."

There was a knock at the door again, and it swung open to reveal four men, three British troops,, and a small, thin man in a brown uniform and a peaked cap. The British were led by a young officer, Lieutenant Andrew Fitzgerald. Fitzgerald removed his hat and bowed towards Fanni and Edward. "I am sorry to disturb your evening, but I have something I have been ordered to deliver to the Weinberg family." Edward looked at Jeannot, who stared back without expression. "It is a warrant for the arrest of the following citizens of the Orange Free State: Edward Weinberg, Jeannot Weinberg, Bernard Weinberg, and Max Weinberg." "On what charges?" demanded Edward. "And by whose authority?" The lieutenant continued, "On the authority of Lord Roberts, Commander-in-Chief of British Forces in Southern Africa, and interim Governor of Bloemfontein. The charges are as follows: in the case of Jeannot Weinberg, the charge is high treason against Her Majesty Queen Victoria and her representatives in Southern Africa; in the case of the other three, for aiding and abetting the treasonous activities of the said Jeannot Weinberg."

The room fell silent. Blood drained from Jeannot's face, and his fists clenched by his side. Edward looked perplexed as did the other two boys. Bertha held her mother's hand tightly and began to sob. It was Fanni who spoke first. "High treason?" she asked, "What has Jeannot done to justify a charge of high treason?" Fitzgerald looked at her contemptuously. "I am not in a position to discuss the matter. The men are to be arrested and taken to the Bloemfontein Jail awaiting arraignment. That is all I am permitted to say." Edward now focused his gaze on Reinart. "Cobus, what is this all about, man? You know us, have known us for years. Do you believe my family and me to be capable of this type of sedition? Speak, man." Edward's tone had become sterner, but there was a trace of panic. The young policeman looked at the floor. He was clearly uncomfortable at having been forced to accompany the enemy to arrest his countrymen whom he knew and respected. "I cannot say, Oom Edward, I was just told I had to be here because you are a non-combatant, and the others are combatants. I am here to arrest you in my civil capacity." "Combatants! Combatants!" yelled Edward, "In what way are they combatants? They all took the Oath of Allegiance, they all surrendered their arms, they returned peacefully to their homes, how can you term them as combatants?" The young policeman looked away, unable to formulate a response. The lieutenant came to his rescue. "They are considered combatants because their actions do not accord with the proclamation of March 14, 1900, issued by Lord Roberts". Edward knew the proclamation only too well. It was a heinous document that provided for punishment to be meted out to virtually any Boer who had ever pointed a Mauser at a British soldier. It was Roberts' way of telling the population of Bloemfontein that the British were now in charge, and they would deal extremely harshly with anyone who questioned their authority.

Jeannot was enflamed. "The proclamation is quite clear, sir. It states that any citizen of the Orange Free State who has not used violence to any British subjects will not be made prisoners of war. In the case of my brother and me, this arrest is understandable. We all fought in the war, and, as such, are possibly not covered by the proclamation, even though we laid down our arms and took the Oath of Allegiance, but how can you arrest our Father? He is a hotelier and has never taken up arms against the British, yet now you are seeking to arrest him. This does not seem to be in accordance with Lord Roberts' proclamation." Fitzgerald was not impressed. "Mr. Weinberg, I have my orders. They are to arrest you, your father and your brothers. You will need to raise this when you are put on trial."

It was Bernard who broke the silence. "Are we entitled to contact our lawyer?" "Yes," said the lieutenant. "But only once you are in custody." Jeannot was not satisfied. "Are you telling me that you are going to arrest me, my father, and my brothers on some vague charge that you refuse to disclose to us without the right to consult our lawyer in advance of being held against our will? Is this the British justice we have heard so much about?" Fitzgerald looked at Jeannot for a moment, then responded. "Sir, I have personal sympathy with your frustration and anger, but I am powerless to do anything other than I have been instructed. If you give me your word that you will not try to escape between here and the Bloemfontein Jail, I will dispense with the need to handcuff you." Edward was angry. "Goddammit, man. What kind of people do you think we are? Common criminals? Of course, we will not try to escape, and I resent your suggestion that we might. We are honest folk and, even though we do not accept the charges brought against us, we will be supportive of seeing justice done. At any rate, that is how justice works in the Orange Free State."

Fitzgerald looked relieved. He had asked for a larger contingent of men but had been given only two. It was not a pleasant prospect to be charged with the arrest and escort of three men who had, until a month ago, faced him down the barrel of a Mauser, and were, in all probability, extremely resentful at having to take the Oath of Allegiance. He replied, "I thank you for your understanding, sir. And I hope you will not take offense when I ask the police officer here to ensure that none of you is carrying any form of weapon or other harmful objects. In this way, we can conclude this business with the minimum of disruption". Edward looked to the boys, who nodded. Reinart came nearer to Edward. "Sorry, Oom Edward. But I have no option but to obey the Englishman." Edward's face relaxed, but his eyes still burned. "It's OK, Cobus. We understand your predicament. Treat someone well, and they will do the same. Come on, let's get on with this."

Once the search had been conducted, they were escorted through the back of the hotel and commenced the short walk to the Bloemfontein Jail. The lieutenant had respected Edward's request that the back entrance be used since he did not want to alarm hotel guests by the sight of the proprietor and his sons being marched out of the front door under armed escort. The night was warm, with a slight breeze that raised eddies of dust on the surface. There were few people about, and, as the streets were poorly lit, no-one recognized any of the prisoners. Men being accompanied by an armed escort had become sufficiently commonplace since the British occupation that the group barely attracted any glances.

After being registered by the duty officer at the jail, and their valuables were taken for safekeeping, the men were taken down to the cells. Edward, Bernard, and Max were placed in a cell for six, containing two other inmates known to them. Jeannot, as the principal perpetrator, was put in solitary confinement in a tiny cell with a small barred window high up on the wall, a straw mat on the floor, and a bucket for ablution in a corner. There was no bedding and no blankets. Jeannot was relieved that the night was warm. Trying to survive in this cell in July would have been a different challenge.

Chapter 21 - The Defense

Bloemfontein Jail - March 24th, 1900 11 am - Fanni

Fanni had hardly slept the previous night. Anxiety for her family after the surreal events of the evening had left her unsettled and unable to sleep. After the men departed, she tried unsuccessfully to calm Bertha, who was now weeping uncontrollably, and was asking a hundred questions on what would happen to them and what would become of the family. Fanni knew she could not answer any of these. She hugged her daughter and told her to have faith in the honor and honesty of her father and brothers. She was sure there had been some terrible mistake, and that all would be resolved in the morning.

Fanni was a woman of calm and serene temperament. As a Jewish wife and mother, she was accustomed to playing a responsible role in the family, and her unflappable demeanor made her an ideal person to rely on in a crisis. The Jewish wife and mother has a primary role, second to none. It is largely – and in many respects exclusively – her great task and privilege to give her home its truly Jewish atmosphere. She is entrusted with and is entirely in charge of the kashrut of the foods and beverages that came into her kitchen and appeared on the dining table. She is given the privilege of ushering in the holy Shabbat by lighting the candles on Friday, in ample time before sunset. Thus, she actually and symbolically brightens up her home with peace and harmony and with the light of Torah and mitzvot. It is largely thanks to her merits that God bestows the blessing of true happiness on her husband and children and the entire family.

Fanni was, therefore, no stranger to assuming responsibility for her actions and understood that, in the absence of Edward, it was her duty to care for the family. But the first order of business was to get the boys released. And quickly. She had lain on her bed, thinking of incidents that might be construed as treasonous behavior. She knew Jeannot was a hothead, was unafraid to speak his mind, and sometimes indiscreet in his selection of audience. She was aware that Jeannot had been invited to take a drink with Gen. French, who frequented the hotel, presumably to gain some insight into the mind of the young Boer soldier. "Oh my God," she thought "what if Jeannot insulted him, or said something disparaging about the British. That would be the end of it for him! But surely, he would not have been so stupid as to tangle with someone in such an elevated position." She felt an iciness in her chest, her breathing coming in short bursts, her heart pounding. Yes, that was it. He had said something to French that had annoyed the general, and he was taking his revenge.

Trying to put this uncomfortable scenario out of her mind, she dressed and prepared to visit the family lawyer. It being Saturday, the lawyer, Mr. Baumann, would undoubtedly be at a service. Since there was no synagogue in Bloemfontein at the time, services were held in private homes. Fanni referred to the services schedule put out by the congregation, and saw that the service that day was at the home of Moritz Leviseur on Louw Wepener Street. On arrival, she asked the maid if she could call Mrs. Leviseur from the service and tell her there was an urgent matter that needed attention. Minutes later, Sophie Leviseur appeared, dressed in her Shabbat gown. "Fanni," she asked, seeing the distress on her face "what is going on?" "They arrested Edward and three of the boys last night. They are in the Bloemfontein Jail as we speak. I want Mr. Baumann to try and get them released." "That is shocking. Just a moment - I will go and get him."

When Baumann arrived, he was not alone. The rest of the congregation, eager to hear what had transpired, gathered around Fanni. She related the events of the previous evening to a silent and shocked audience - this was the first incident of Jewish arrests they had seen in Bloemfontein. Was this a genuine case, or was it the start of anti-Semitic action against the Jews of Bloemfontein? Baumann recommended that he and Fanni leave immediately for the jail to find out the status of the prisoners.

The Provost Marshal at the jail was Major Bennett-Hitchcock, a man who appeared to have outgrown his uniform. His florid jowls hung over his collar, and his belly strained at the fabric of his coat. He was sweating, clearly uncomfortable in the muggy heat, and the too-tight uniform. "Yes?" he said as Fanni and Baumann approached his desk. Baumann took charge. "We have come to inquire about the conditions of the four Weinberg men taken into custody last night. This is Fanni Weinberg, the husband of Edward and mother of the three boys. I am Mr. Baumann, their lawyer." Bennet-Hitchcock moved uncomfortably on his seat. "This is a matter for the British Army and is of no import to civilians."

Baumann was not fazed. "I would remind you, sir, that these men are civilians and citizens of the Orange Free State Republic. Can you please explain why they are now under the command of the British Army?" Bennett-Hitchcock eyed him, clearly expecting this line of approach. "We have reason to believe that these men have committed treason against Her Majesty's government. Since the army is in control of the town, and since martial law has been declared, matters relating to their incarceration are under the control of the army." Fanni was enraged. "Does the British Army not respect the terms of its own Oath of Allegiance? These men have laid down their arms, and until the Orange Free State has been officially disbanded and created as a British territory, surely they are entitled to be tried by the appropriate Orange Free State judiciary body." The major had maintained his cool demeanor long enough. His chins quivered as he rose from his seat and directed his gaze at Fanni. "Don't bother me, woman. Don't you know I could have your husband and sons shot!"

Fanni had not expected this retort, looked to Baumann, who composed himself and spoke. "Major, I do not need to remind you of the consequences of executing civilians without due process. These men are accused of a crime which they deny. They have, until now, been denied access to legal representation, and it is my intention to ensure that this is remedied. Your threat would not only have serious repercussions among the civilian population in the Free State but could also land you in court-martial proceedings." Bennett-Hitchcock paused for a moment, then gathered himself. "Mr. Baumann, I am under orders to hold these men pending a trial in the near future. I am not an unreasonable man, and I respect the rule of law. I am prepared to make a concession because of the unusual circumstance of this case. As it is the weekend, I am not in a position to grant any access to the prisoners, but I will permit you to visit them for 30 minutes on Monday morning at 8 am. If this is not acceptable to you, I will refer the matter to a higher authority." Baumann glanced at Fanni, who gave a small nod of her head. "Your terms are accepted. I am assuming that Mrs. Weinberg will also be granted access to visit her family at the same time." The major shook his head. "I am afraid, sir, that my remit only permits visitation by legal counsel. If Mrs. Weinberg desires access, she will have to make an application through the regular channels." "And what might those channels be?" retorted Baumann. The major sighed, shrugged his shoulders, and replied. "She will have to make written application to the Provost Marshal of the prison, who happens to be me. If I am unable to determine the validity of her request, I shall refer it to my superior officer. That is all." He sat heavily, extending the fingers of his hands across his belly, and regarding the two petitioners with a contemptuous stare. Baumann struggled to control his anger. "We will comply with your request. Fanni, I will prepare the necessary document tomorrow once the Sabbath is concluded. We will reassemble on Monday morning."

Fanni returned to the hotel, a numb feeling extending throughout her body. There was a glimmer of hope, but her anxiety for her family gnawed at her constantly. Were they being adequately looked after? Would the British torture them to extract a confession? No, this was not their way. But there were no guarantees. She had heard rumors of the mistreatment of captives after various battles and had a waning trust in the British to respect the rules of war. She agonized throughout the night, sleep coming fitfully in the early hours on Sunday morning. When she finally awoke and passed the events of the previous day, she was suddenly struck by an idea which she believed would enable her to gain access to Edward and the boys.

Headquarters of the British Occupying Forces, Bloemfontein – Sunday, March 5th, 1900. – Roberts

General French arrived at Roberts' headquarters at 4.55 pm, a few minutes early for his summons to present himself at 5 pm. Roberts had established his headquarters in the house previously owned and occupied by Pres. Steyn, a building hopelessly vulgar both inside and out, filled with intolerable French statuary and rosebud -bedecked walls, everything from the Early Victorian period. Col. Chamberlain, Roberts' military secretary, met him and escorted him to Roberts.

Roberts looked up from his desk and nodded to the man who had entered the room. The office, unlike the rest of the house, was saved by its somberness. It appeared to have been used by President Steyn as a library. At any rate, it was stacked with books; large dusty volumes lay everywhere. It was a great bare room with a good-sized desk and tall windows looking out on rather a dreary garden.

Roberts pointed to a chair, and French sat.

"John, I wanted to speak to you about the upcoming case against the Weinberg family - I think you are familiar with the case." French nodded and replied. "I am aware of the case, and I also know one of the defendants, Jeannot. He and I had a drink together at his father's hotel. I met with him on the pretext of gaining insight into the life of the Boer commando in this war, but I had another motive as well. As you are aware, General, this war is far from over, and I anticipate that there will be more loss of life and property before a peace treaty finally puts a lid on things. One of our primary targets is the city of Pretoria, and it would be in our interests to move there with as little interference from the Boers as can be avoided." Roberts nodded and said, "Continue." "Well, you may not be aware of the fact that, prior to the war, Jeannot was living in Johannesburg and, I believe, traveled frequently between there and Bloemfontein during the year before the war. He is very familiar with the area and the terrain, and, I suspect, knows of a number of different routes between the two cities, and between Bloemfontein and Pretoria." Roberts sat up straight in his chair, now interested in what his colleague was saying. "So, I asked him whether he would be prepared to show me a back route between Bloemfontein and Pretoria, one that would keep us out of the attention of the Boer armies. And I offered him a sum of 10,000 pounds if he was prepared to assist me."

Roberts let out a breath. Ten thousand pounds was an awful lot of money; it must have seemed like a fortune to a young man of eighteen. "Well?" "The young scoundrel in the nicest possible way told me to go to hell!" Roberts smiled. "He told me that in spite of his Oath of Allegiance, he was still a citizen of the Orange Free State, and, since the Free State was still an ally of the Transvaal, my request was treasonous." Roberts nodded. "A bit of dramatic irony there, John, especially since the lad is now charged with treason against Her Majesty, and this is one of the factors the court will take into consideration when he is tried." "Agreed," said French, "but I cannot fault the boy for sticking to his guns and taking the moral high road. I would not have liked to have been put in that position, and I think he did what his conscience demanded." Roberts nodded and said, "I understand all that, but we are at war, man, and drastic measures are sometimes needed. You did the right thing, but it is a great pity we didn't find someone more pliable."

"What's to become of him?" asked French. Roberts closed his eyes for a moment, then looked at his colleague. "In isolation, this would be an open and shut case. The primary incident that led to his arrest was his supposed death threat to me made in a public place. A death threat against a senior British official is clearly an offense for which the death penalty would be appropriate. But things are not that simple. We have only just subdued the Boers in the Free State, and I can only imagine that there is a great deal of animosity towards us at present. I agree with you that the war is far from over. I think there is every chance we may see a resurgence of the Boer army in a different guise. I cannot see them simply rolling over and surrendering. And then there is the situation with the Transvaal, a tougher nut to crack than the Free State. We really do need to have an unfettered run at Pretoria without having to look behind us at what is going on in the Free State." Roberts paused as if marshaling his thoughts. "This lad is something of a local hero after Magersfontein. There were local newspaper articles about him and the other soldiers from Bloemfontein who fought there. To put him in front of a firing squad or, worse, to hang him, would not sit well with the locals. And the last thing we need with one eye on Pretoria is to have the other focused on civil disobedience in Bloemfontein. We have to find a way to punish him without opening a can of worms."

French sat back in his chair and reflected on what he had heard. Decisions like this were never easy, were the kind of decisions that required both strength and moral courage to address. At last, he spoke. "I think I may have a possible solution to this impasse. If we try him in a civil court and he is found guilty, he will hang. Clearly, not the outcome we are looking for. However, if we try him in a military tribunal on the grounds that he has broken his Oath of Allegiance and is therefore still a combatant, his actions would not be treasonous, but would simply be an aggressive act from one soldier against another. That being the case, we could pack him quietly off to a POW camp for the rest of the war, and this whole thing would die down." Roberts looked at French and slowly nodded his head. "I think that is a very elegant solution. I am in favor of it, and I believe the Provost Marshal will support it. And as far as the other members of the family are concerned, they can simply be released since none has broken their Oath of Allegiance - I think we would be unwise to try and bring an 'aiding and abetting' case against them since they were not active participants. How soon could we convene a military tribunal?" "By Wednesday, I believe. I will make the necessary preparations and alert the Provost Marshal."

Bloemfontein Jail - Monday 26th March, 1900 – Fanni

At 7.55 am, Fanni met Baumann at the entrance to the prison. She was carrying a bundle under her arm, wrapped in a kitchen towel. Baumann raised a questioning eyebrow, but Fanni just shook her head and smiled. "Let me have the first word," she murmured. They were shown into Bennett-Hitchcock's office at 8.15. The major was seated at his desk, writing in what looked like a logbook. He continued writing for a few minutes, then raised his eyes. "Well," he said.

Fanni spoke. "Major, I want to apologize for the harsh words that were spoken on Saturday. I am a wife and mother, and I am sure you understand the concern I feel for the safety of my family. I am also aware of the onerous and uncomfortable position you find yourself in. I do not envy you your situation, and I understand how difficult it must be when orders from above prevent you from doing the things your conscience dictates." Baumann looked quizzically at her, wondering even more now what was in the bundle she carried. The major was impassive. Fanni continued. "As you may be aware, we run the Royal Hotel not far from the prison. We frequently receive visits from your officers who eat in our dining room, and I have often heard compliments passed about the quality of our table, especially when compared with the rations provided by the army. I am sure you have similar thoughts, so I have asked our chef to prepare a chicken made according to our most popular recipe. I would like to offer this to you as a gesture of goodwill and a token of our appreciation for your kindness and consideration. It is not a bribe. I am just reaching out to you as a fellow human being caught in a situation not of our making."

There was a pause. Baumann felt his stomach churn, wondering how this would be received. The major thought for a moment then smiled. "Mrs. Weinberg, I want you to know that neither I nor the British Army are monsters. We are not all the ogres we have been portrayed in your press, nor are we seeking to make this war any more difficult than it already is. I appreciate your gesture, and I accept your gift. You can see ", he patted his belly "that I am fond of a good meal and, truth be told, there has not been any opportunity to enjoy one on combat duty. But this chicken will go a long way to remedying this situation." The tension drained from the room. Baumann let out a pent-up breath, and Fanni felt her knees regain some of their strength. "You are most welcome, Major, and please feel free to avail yourself of the services we offer at the hotel. You will always be welcome as our guest if you want to have a damn fine dinner."

The major smiled again. "Here is what I am prepared to offer. Mr. Baumann can visit with the men for 30 minutes. During that time, please feel free to return to the hotel and prepare a package of food for your men. We do our best to feed our prisoners a sustaining diet, but I am sure it does not compare with the good things prepared in your hotel's kitchen. If you report back to me at 9.30, I will permit you to give them your food and will allow you to visit with them for 30 minutes. Will this solution be acceptable to you and Mr. Baumann?" Fanni's shoulders relaxed, and Baumann assured him that these terms would be acceptable. The major nodded, indicated to Baumann to take a seat, and took his leave of Fanni.

Fanni hurried back to the hotel, relieved that the meeting had been so successful, and mindful of the consequences had it not. She now set about hustling the chef to prepare a hamper of provisions for Edward and the boys. By 9.15, a large parcel of chicken, boiled eggs, bread, cheese, and coffee had been assembled, together with some smaller items like chocolate and biltong. And of course a collection of tobacco products. At 9.30, she arrived back at the prison, accompanied by Simon carrying an array of packages. She was shown into a small office containing a table and five chairs. It was sparsely decorated, with a map of the Orange Free State being the only relief on otherwise empty walls. Simon was permitted to leave the packages in a corner and was then escorted out of the prison.

After 15 minutes, there was a knock on the door, which was opened by a corporal. He led Edward, Bernard, and Max into the room, and Fanni rushed to welcome them with hugs and tears. "But where is Jeannot?" she asked. "We have not seen him since we arrived here. My guess is he is being held separately as the main perpetrator," replied Edward. Fanni shrugged, clearly disappointed, and also fearful of what might have become of him. "Did you meet with Baumann?" she asked. "Yes?" said Edward "But Jeannot was not present. We do not know if he was allowed to speak to Jeannot after he met with us, but my sense is that they would not have denied representation to the most important suspect." He had barely finished speaking when the door opened again, and Jeannot was led into the room. The other four embraced him, relieved that he seemed to have suffered no more than they had. Fanni looked at the men in front of her. It was apparent that none of them had slept sufficiently, and that the confinement had raised their levels of anxiety about their future. All had an uncertain look in their eyes, the kind of look that suggests concern about how things might turn out. For Jeannot, it was the first time he had seen his father and brothers since they had been incarcerated, and he was relieved to see that they seemed to be in reasonable conditions.

Fanni was the first to speak. "Are they treating you well? Have any of you been beaten or tortured? Have you been getting enough to eat?" Her words poured out like one who has been anticipating the worst. Edward looked kindly at her. "As far as me and Bernard and Max are concerned, we have not been mistreated in any way. The cell is on the small side - 6 beds in the room, which we share with two other prisoners, the Olivier brothers who you will remember as the sons of Gerhard Olivier, who owns the hardware store near to the hotel. The beds are not that comfortable, but it is a prison after all. We have received three meals a day, although the portions are small, and are not nearly as tasty as our chef's, but we are not starving. All in all, we are being treated reasonably." He looked at Jeannot. "I have been treated in a similar way, although I am in solitary confinement, and the cell is a bit damp and smelly. Otherwise, nothing really to complain about." He wanted to say that it was certainly a step up from the uncomfortable nights he had spent out in the field at Magersfontein but kept this to himself.

Fanni was visibly relieved. "I know it is small comfort, but Chef has prepared a hamper of food for you, and the major has consented to me bringing it here for you." The men grinned - it was typical of Mama to be so concerned about whether they were getting enough to eat - she was, after all, a Jewish mother. "And what did Baumann say?" she inquired. Edward looked at Jeannot and asked, "Did they allow you to see Baumann?" Jeannot nodded. Edward continued. "Well, if what I tell to mother is different from what you experienced, please chime in. He told us that he had discussed the matter at length with the major and that we would all be tried together by a military tribunal on Wednesday. There will be no separate court proceedings for Jeannot - we will all stand trial together, but he felt that the sentencing would probably be different. Is this the same as he told you, Jeannot?" Jeannot nodded again. "The only problem is that he is not going to be allowed to represent us. It seems that a civilian lawyer has no legal standing in a military tribunal and that the British Army will appoint an officer to be our counsel at the trial. Not ideal, but probably all we could have expected under the circumstances. And, of course, it will be held *in camera*, with no attendance allowed from the public." Jeannot affirmed this with a bob of his head. "And did he say what the outcome might be?" she asked. "He does not know," said Edward. "He has no experience of military tribunals and is unfamiliar with their procedures. All he told us was not to panic and to tell the truth. We can only hope that the man they appoint to defend us is a reasonable fellow, and has not lost a brother or cousin in the war which would cloud his judgment. Otherwise, it is in God's hands." Fanni felt tears welling in her eyes, but she quickly blinked them away. "I know how stressful this is for all of us, but I can only hope that they will recognize that we are fundamentally good people and are driven by a love of country and family. You all know how much I love you and that I will leave no stone unturned to secure justice for you. I am your wife and mother, and I am here for you, now and always." The men nodded, and one by one embraced her and reassured her that they were fine and would hold their heads high. Fanni departed with mixed emotions, relief that her men were not being mistreated in prison, but with an unrelenting knot in her gut about the trial and its possible consequences.

Chapter 22 - The Trial

Bloemfontein Jail - Wednesday 28th March 1900 - Edward

The trial was held in a room in the prison not much larger than the one in which Fanni had met the men. It had a wooden floor and cream walls, both of which were showing their age and lack of maintenance. There were three wooden tables in the room in a triangular formation, the apex for the three presiding officers, the other two at the base, one for the prosecution and one for the defense. The chairs around the table were an odd assortment, evidently collected from various parts of the prison. There was a separate chair for the Sergeant at Arms.

The defending counsel was Lt. Francis Spenser Firth of the 2nd Battalion, East Kent Regiment. He was not totally unfamiliar with the law, having spent the year before the war as clerk to a barrister at Gray's Inn in London. This was, however, his first experience defending soldiers at a military tribunal. He had been allowed to spend two hours with the defendants the day before, leaving him less than 24 hours to prepare a defense. Not exactly how he would have wished it, but he was resigned to the fact that it was unlikely that anything he said would in any way alter the course of events. Nevertheless, he listened attentively to the four men, tried to understand their motivations, and assured them he would do everything in his power to offer a substantive defense. The defendants were not convinced.

The day before the trial, the former President of the Orange Free State, Pres. Steyn published a statement in the national newspapers addressed to the people of the Orange Free State. It was an impassioned appeal to their loyalty. 'Let us not be misled by this cunning ruse . . . The enemy now, by fair promises, seeks to divide us by offering a reward for disloyalty and cowardice. Could a greater insult be offered than to dissuade us from a sacred duty, thus betraying ourselves, betraying our people, betraying the blood that has already flowed for our land and nation, and betraying our children? . . . The man who has broken his solemn agreements with our people, will he now honor his deceitful promise?' The first promises had already been broken. There had been 'the shameful destruction of property at Jacobsdal and in Bloemfontein the arrest of citizens who had trusted his proclamation and laid down their arms.' The capital was in the enemy's hands, 'but the battle is not lost. On the contrary, it gives greater reason to fight harder . . . Take courage and be steadfast in your faith. The Lord God shall not suffer His purpose for our nation to be obstructed. Persevere in the struggle. The darkest hour is just before dawn.' Fanni, who had been allowed to visit the men the evening before the trial, smuggled the statement into the prison and passed it on to the men. It did far more to cheer them up than had their meeting with their army lawyer earlier in the day.

At 7.55, the Sergeant at Arms marched the defendants and their counsel into the room and sat them at the left-hand table. They were followed by the prosecutor, Capt. Robert Bellew of the 16th Queens' Lancers. At 8 am, the Sergeant at Arms called everyone to attention, and the three presiding officers entered the room. The senior presiding officer was Col. Chamberlain, Roberts' military secretary, accompanied by Lt.-Col. David Airlie of the 12th Prince of Wales Royal Lancers and Maj. Henry Montague Brown of the 1st Battalion, East Lancashire Regiment. Once they had taken their seats, the Sergeant at Arms stood and announced: "This military tribunal is now in session, Col. Chamberlain presiding." Bellew stood to read the charges, but Chamberlain waved him to sit down.

Chamberlain stood. "Jeannot Weinberg's accusation arises out of two separate instances that I shall delineate to the tribunal. First, that on March 13th, 1900, on seeing the Commander-in-Chief of the British Forces Lord Roberts riding his horse in the market square of Bloemfontein, the said Weinberg was overheard to say 'If he were out in the field, he'd not be sitting on that horse for long.' This statement was overheard and reported to the British authorities by a reliable source whose name cannot be revealed in this tribunal. Second, that on or about 14th March 1900, in the bar of the Royal Hotel, the said Weinberg displayed disloyalty to Her Majesty by refusing to assist Gen. John French in his quest for a shorter route to Pretoria. Both these actions together constitute the source of the accusation against Jeannot Weinberg. Mr. Jeannot Weinberg, please rise."

Jeannot stood slowly, his hands unclenched by his sides, his eyes firmly on Chamberlains'. "Do you, Jeannot Weinberg, admit to the correctness of the two incidents I have just related?" Jeannot replied in a calm voice. "Yes, I do, but I did......" Chamberlain cut him off. "Be seated, Mr. Weinberg."

Chamberlain continued. "Now that we have established that the facts are clear, we need to consider issues of legality and *locus standi in judicio*. This tribunal is here to determine the guilt or otherwise of four citizens of the Orange Free State who have taken the Oath of Allegiance to Her Majesty following the occupation of the Orange Free State by Her Majesty's armed forces last month. This is not a military tribunal in the conventional sense since one of the key legal issues to be resolved is whether the defendants were acting as civilians, in which case the charge would be treason, or whether they were acting as combatants, in which case the charges would relate to acts of military aggression. I am aware that when the defendants were arrested, they were told that the charge was treason against Jeannot Weinberg and aiding and abetting against the other three, but the nature of the charge is yet to be resolved by this tribunal.

Given that events have taken place in a very short period of time, we need to examine the nature of the surrounding circumstances.

All the defendants took the Oath of Allegiance less than a month ago, a month, I must confess, that has been fraught with uncertainty and confusion. No formal guidance has been given to the oath-takers as to the exact implications of the oath, or as to how Her Majesty expects her new citizens to react. Until such time as this has been clarified, and until a set of guiding principles has been laid out for the citizens of the now defeated Orange Free State as to how they should behave under British rule, I feel it would be harsh for the men to be tried for treason. Until it is made very clear to the population what the duties and responsibilities of that population might be, it is difficult to convict a man for something he perhaps did not regard as being treasonous."

Chamberlain paused, cleared his throat, and continued. "Let us turn to the other possibility - an act of military aggression against the British Army. The three brothers were all prior combatants, so this is moot when it comes to the applicability of military law and discipline to them. But Edward Weinberg was not, and never has been, a combatant. It would, therefore, be difficult to attempt to try him in a military court. So do we try the three brothers in a military court and the father in a civil court? I think not. My recommendation to this tribunal is that we dispense with the formality of these proceedings, and try to work out a solution that will result in all parties agreeing that justice has been done. Counsel for the prosecution, do you accept this proposal?" Bellew nodded. "We do, Colonel." "And for the defendants?" Firth looked at Edward, who nodded, too. "The defense agrees, Colonel."

"Then let me talk freely about the proposal discussed between the presiding members of this tribunal prior to entering this trial. This proposal has the support of Lord Roberts and his staff." Jeannot shifted in his seat, and his face became pale. He well knew that the most severe punishment would be reserved for him, was prepared to shoulder that responsibility, but feared for the sentences that might be handed to the others, especially his father.

Chamberlain resumed his speech. "In the case of Jeannot Weinberg. You have clearly broken your Oath of Allegiance and acted in a manner harmful to the forces to whom you have surrendered. To that end, I have no option to continue to regard you as a combatant and to recommend punishment according to the rules of war. The punishment we recommend is that you be taken from this place at the earliest possible convenience and remanded in a prisoner of war camp under the control of the British Army until hostilities shall have ceased, and peace shall have been declared between the warring nations." He looked at Jeannot, whose return stare was expressionless and unrevealing. But inwardly, his heart was pounding. POW camp! Can't be all that bad. Better at least than a firing squad or a hangman's noose.

"In the case of Bernard and Max Weinberg, the situation is simple in some respects, but more complex in terms of sentencing. You cannot be held responsible for the irresponsible acts of your elder brother, but as part of your Oath, you should have reported his activities to the proper authorities. If Jeannot Weinberg accepts his punishment of entering a POW camp, he will be taken from Bloemfontein and remanded in the POW holding camp at Greenpoint Track in Cape Town, pending his transfer to a permanent overseas camp. As he has shown himself to be prone to acts of indiscretion, we are concerned that, during the transportation to Cape Town, he may attempt to escape and rejoin the Boer forces. To encourage him not to do this, Bernard and Max Weinberg will be remanded in the Bloemfontein Jail as hostages until we receive a telegraph from Greenpoint Track that Jeannot Weinberg is safely in the custody of the commandant of that camp. On receipt of this telegraph, you will be released to your families. We do not expect that your incarceration should extend longer than a week to ten days."

"In the case of Edward Weinberg, this tribunal recommends that he be released immediately and that all charges against him shall be dropped. Counsel for the defense, you have ten minutes to confer with your clients before returning to the tribunal to relate to us the decision of the accused."

Outside the room, the four men hugged each other, and there were tears of relief in Edward's eyes. This was as good a result as they could have hoped for, and although it meant Jeannot would be sent to a POW camp, there would at least be no death penalty or civil imprisonment. The relief was palpable. Firth spoke. "So, I take it you are in agreement with the tribunal's proposal." Edward nodded. "Let's go back in there and get this settled."

Firth stood beside the accused once they had re-entered the room and taken their seats. "Colonel, I have consulted with my clients, and all four are happy to accept the tribunal's proposal." He sat and glanced at the four, who nodded their approval.

Chamberlain rose. "Jeannot Weinberg, you are now a prisoner of war of Her Majesty's armed forces and will be removed to the POW camp at Greenpoint Track in Cape Town. Bernard and Max Weinberg, you will be remanded in custody until word is received that your brother Jeannot Weinberg has been placed in the custody of the commandant of Greenpoint Track POW camp, at which stage you will be released for time served. Edward Weinberg, you are free to return home once this court has adjourned."

Bloemfontein Jail Cell no. 22 - April 5th, 1900 – Jeannot

Letter from Jeannot Weinberg to Fanni Weinberg April 5th 1900, Bloemfontein Jail

Dear Mother

You must indeed be pleased to have got Papa off as it would have been unjust for him to be sent to Cape Town. If Bernard and Max could get free, even better. They can do what they like with me. It does not matter whether I am sent to Cape Town or St. Helena, but I would prefer Europe. Here in jail is quite comfortable if only the bugs would not worry us so much. In a few weeks, there should be no more as we kill them by the dozen every evening. It is possible that we will soon be sent to Cape Town. I have a big container under my bed where I can store my clothes.

I would like you to send the piano from the dining room as I have much spare time, and if I do not become a good barman, I could develop to be a good Republican pianist. Please ask Papa to lock my bicycle away safely. Nothing special to report otherwise.

Geldenhuis is leaving today, as well as Julius Ortlepp. I wish Abe and Leopold would write. Although we have books, it is still monotonous. I now smoke cigars that Papa left behind.

The men Ellison and Wilson better prepare themselves for what is going to happen to them when I get out – I suggest embalming their skeletons in advance.

Greetings to Papa and the children.

Jeannot.

The saga of the combatant had ended; the saga of the prisoner was about to commence.

Part 5 – The Camps

Chapter 23 - The Train

Train to Cape Town - April 6th, 1900 - Jeannot

Early on the morning of Friday, April 6th, 1900, the door to Jeannot's cell opened to reveal two prison warders and a British Army lieutenant. The officer addressed him. "My name is Lt. Richards. I am to escort you to the train station where you will be placed on a train to Cape Town to be remanded in custody at the prisoner of war camp at Greenpoint Track. Gather your possessions and follow me." Jeannot did as he was asked, and followed the lieutenant to a small wagon with an iron cage on the back. Three fellow prisoners were already in the cage, and they shifted up to make room for Jeannot. A small crowd had gathered to watch the proceedings. Jeannot scanned the people to see if any of his family was among them. Unlikely, he thought, it is six-thirty in the morning.

He spoke to the lieutenant. "Sir, will our families be informed of the fact that we are being transported from Bloemfontein to Cape Town?" The officer nodded. "They will be told after the train has departed. We do not want the civilians creating any problems." With that, the horses began to move, and the wagon trundled slowly in the direction of the train station. A train stood at the platform, and Jeannot could see several carriages with iron bars on the windows. These, he surmised, were to house the prisoners. Once at the platform, the wagon was surrounded by armed guards who ordered the men out of the cage and onto the train. Each man was placed in a solitary compartment in the carriages, about eight-foot-long and five-foot-wide, with a bunk bed and bars on the window and door. There was a bucket in the corner for ablution. Jeannot was locked in one of the compartments - his few belongings had been removed for safekeeping. He was later told that men had ben allowed to keep their bibles, but Jeannot did not have one. He lay back on his bunk and waited for the train to depart.

The train ride to Cape Town was about a two-day trip, but given the fact that the country was on a war footing, it was estimated that the trip would take a bit longer. Jeannot was able to ascertain from one of the guards that the likely arrival in Cape Town would not be until Monday morning - this meant three days and three nights in transit in very cramped conditions. Jeannot's command of English enabled him to strike up conversations with the guards, who seemed bored and eager to have someone to talk to.

"Sir, when we stop at stations along the way, will we be allowed to stretch our legs?" he asked.

"I believe so." said one of the guards. His name was Pvt. Neville Paterson of the Welsh Guards. He was a shortish, wiry man with black hair, a black mustache, and a friendly face. He was secretly pleased to have pulled this duty. Although it was boring, it was nevertheless safe, and after surviving some of the battles in the western campaign, he was quite content to spend the rest of the war ferrying prisoners in comparative safety. "We will be stopping several times along the way, and I am sure the commanding officer will allow you to leave the train under armed escort."

"May we communicate with our fellow prisoners?"

"To the extent that you can talk to the men in the compartments on either side of you, I see no reason why not."

"How many prisoners are on this train?"

"Not sure, to tell you the truth. About a hundred or so, I would guess."

"And will we be fed on the trip?"

"Of course. I cannot guarantee the quality of the food, but there will be three meals a day."

"And when we arrive in towns, will the inhabitants be allowed to come and talk to us and perhaps give us things to eat?"

"In my experience, communication between prisoners and civilians has been prohibited. The folk just gather on the platforms and wave and shout encouragement, but no actual conversations are permitted. As for food and other items, they are given to us and distributed as we think fit. So, you men better behave or all the best *koeksisters* (Boer sweet cake) will be eaten by the guards!" He chuckled and patted his belly.

With that, there was a sharp blast on the whistle, and the train moved slowly out of the station. After a few minutes, there was a knock on the wall of his compartment.

"Jeannot, this is David Le Roux. What did the Englishman say?"
Jeannot related the contents of his conversation with Paterson, hoping to raise the spirits of his comrade.
"Doesn't sound so bad. We'll get through it. Thanks."

Later that afternoon, after a lunch of bread, some stew made with unidentifiable meat, and a mug of coffee, Paterson arrived at the door to Jeannot's cell. Since the door consisted only of iron bars, it was possible to converse without having to open it.

"Can I chat with you for a few moments?"
Jeannot looked around. "Sure. I'm not going anywhere!" Paterson smiled.
"I am curious, you see, to learn the perspective of the Boers on the British Army and its soldiers. I know we eventually were able to defeat you by weight of numbers and equipment, but I am interested to know what you fellows thought of us during the various battles you were involved in."

Jeannot looked at Paterson, trying to assess his motive. The man seemed genuine enough, did not appear to be trying to laud the British victory over him. He just appeared genuinely interested. He thought for a while before responding.

"I think there is no one answer to the question. I think you need to divide the army into three sections - the fighting troops, the officers, and the commanders. As far as the fighting troops are concerned, you can be proud of them. They are courageous, inventive, perseverant, and honorable. In short, they are a worthy foe, and we always had respect for the English fighting man. As regards the officers, this is a bit more difficult for me because your army has many more layers than ours does. We have commandants and veldkornets and not much more. You have lieutenants and captains and majors and colonels, and who knows what. So your chain of command is much longer than ours. And my sense is that the further you go up the chain of command, the less aware the officers are of what it is like at the firing line. And also, the longer the chain of command, the more likely it is that something will be misinterpreted." Paterson nodded his agreement.

"But I think the main problem was your commanders." Jeannot continued. "At least until Lord Roberts took over. It became clear to us that Gen. Methuen had only one strategy - a night march followed by an artillery barrage, then an infantry charge. Once we realized that he was not going to try anything different, we were ready for him. We were prepared to change our strategy to neutralize yours, as you saw at Magersfontein. You guys had no idea that we had put out trenches at the bottom of the hill - you just marched straight into our rifles! And you always attacked in close formation, making it almost impossible for us to miss. It was only when Roberts started making more sensible use of the terrain and our limited numbers that you were able to catch us out. Good example in the relief of Kimberley. He knew how many people we had, and he realized we could not defend every route to Kimberley, so he occupied the troops at Magersfontein with a feint attack, then sent French wide around our flank to Kimberley. We couldn't understand why you hadn't tried that a long time before."

Paterson shook his head. "We were often amazed at the way we were trying to fight a different kind of war using the strategies that were successful in Egypt and Abyssinia. This was a totally new type of warfare, and we simply refused to change. Far too many men were lost pursuing antiquated strategies."

Jeannot nodded. "And what did you think of our troops?" he asked. Paterson again shook his head. "Never seen anything like you lot. Well trained, incredibly accurate with your rifles, masters of disguise and camouflage, well-led - you guys were scary! We never knew where you were until we heard the lead whizzing around our ears, and then when we thought we had you cornered, poof, you disappeared into thin air. I have fought in a number of campaigns, and you were the toughest enemy I have ever faced. Or ever hope to face again. You know, we never even felt safe at a thousand yards because we knew you buggers could pick us off from that range. We got almost no rifle training. To us, the rifle was mainly a mechanism to house the bayonet for a traditional charge. Most of our fellows couldn't hit anything at more than a hundred yards. So what chance did we have against sharpshooters like you? We only won because we were able to bring 50,000 troops to the battle and swamp you with numbers."

Jeannot felt a sense of pride at this. "Yes, you are correct. For all the informality of our structure, on an individual basis, we were pretty effective, and we were fighting for our homeland, which gave us extra motivation."

The train wound its way through the Karoo, a dry, dusty region of half-desert and small thorn trees. The name 'Karoo' comes from an ancient San word meaning 'Land of Great Thirst.' This semi-arid region at the heart of South Africa covers an area the size of Germany. They passed the small towns of Springfontein, Colesberg, and Noupoort en route to De Aar, the first significant stopping place. When the train passed a station during the day, there were always groups of onlookers, some merely fascinated by the train itself, others offering wishes of hope and support for the prisoners. In De Aar, the train stopped, and the prisoners were allowed to disembark for thirty minutes under armed guards. They were surrounded by the local folk who had come to wish them well. Many brought food parcels which they gave to the guards on behalf of the prisoners. They were mostly of Afrikaner descent, but there was a scattering of English voices to be heard. The prisoners were allowed to talk to the visitors, and they were grateful to have this opportunity to feel at least a bit normal after the confines of the rail carriage. Even though it was April and technically Fall, the conditions in the Karoo were always hot, and the train itself had been uncomfortably warm.

When they departed De Aar, it was clear that David Le Roux was not a happy man. He could be heard muttering to himself, and occasionally swearing. Jeannot did not understand - they had received their food parcels (the guards for the most part behaving honorably), and conditions hadn't worsened since De Aar, so he inquired through the wall of the cell what the problem was.

"Man," said David "It's those Cape Afrikaners. We are all the same volk, all came originally from the same area in the Cape, but do you think those buggers offered their brothers and cousins in the North any support during this war? Nothing, not a commando, not money, not equipment, nothing. If they had rallied alongside us and opened a third front in the western Cape, you and I would not be sitting in the *verdomde* (damned) train! But no, they are a bunch of *verraiers* (traitors), English-lovers, too worried about maintaining their wealth by not offending the British than coming to help their own flesh and blood. Bastards! With their help and support, we could have sent the Redcheeks back to England licking their wounds!"

He was clearly upset. Jeannot had heard rumblings about the lack of support from the Cape Afrikaners, but he had never heard it as starkly expressed as David had just done. There were probably more Afrikaners of military age in the Cape than in the Transvaal and Free State together, and this would have been a tremendous asset to the outnumbered Boers of the north.

"Man, David, it is a shame that they didn't come to our aid, but we must remember that they didn't come on the Great Trek either. So, there must be a fundamental difference between them and the Boers who fought."

"Difference, *my gat* (my arse)!" said David. "We are all Afrikaners; we worship in the same way, we speak the same language, we all believe we have a covenant with God, in what way are we different? These people here are just too soft and self-centered to give up their lifestyle when their volk is threatened. It's a disgrace. And believe me, when this is all over, there will be ramifications. We Boers have long memories, and we will remember who came to our aid and who didn't. And you of all people should know that. You have been here less than ten years, you are a Jew, and yet you never hesitated to pick up your rifle and stand alongside us. We remember that sort of thing."

He went silent, and Jeannot left him to his thoughts.

The train continued its journey through the Karoo, past the towns of Merriman and Nelspoort, until it reached Beaufort West. This was the second time the prisoners were allowed to detrain. Beaufort West was in the heart of the Karoo and was widely known for being the center of the merino sheep farming in the area. The Karoo proved to be ideal terrain for raising sheep, and the citizens of Beaufort West had worked hard to make their town the center of this growing industry. Again, the townsfolk came to greet the train, and again food parcels were handed out for the prisoners. The train had now covered more than half of the distance to Cape Town. It was Sunday morning, and the prisoners were relieved that, in a day or so, they would be released from their cramped quarters and allowed to move about freely in the POW camp.

The Karoo sits atop of the South African high plateau that runs north from the Cape through the Transvaal and on to the sub-equatorial countries north of the Limpopo. About 150 miles after leaving Beaufort West, it passes the village of Matjiesfontein, and soon thereafter begins its descent of the Great Escarpment that divides the plateau from the lowlands of the western Cape. The first town at the bottom of the escarpment is Touws River, a beautiful village near the foothills of the Hex River Mountains. The landscape changes dramatically after the escarpment. The dusty, dry terrain changes to lush green meadows, rolling hills, and abundant natural vegetation. There are magnificent mountain ranges and verdant valleys, home to some of the finest vineyards and wineries in the world. To the young men of the Orange Free State, many of whom had never left their home town, this was a world of natural beauty they could not have imagined. Even David Le Roux was heard to mutter something about not wanting to give up a land like this to go and fight in the dry north.

There was a short stop at Touws River, a major rail hub for the traffic between the Cape and the hinterland, but the prisoners were not allowed to leave the train. It was approaching evening, and the sun could be seen setting behind an impressive range of mountains. The men knew that this would be their last night on the train, and this was a sense of relief. The next morning, the train pulled into Paarl, a magnificent town in the heart of the Cape wine country. Even from the train, the vineyards could be seen stretching as far as the eye could see, and the beautiful white gabled buildings in the Cape-Dutch style were very much in evidence. Again, the prisoners could not help but admire the beauty of the countryside, so different from what they had been used to.

The train arrived in Cape Town early afternoon, and the prisoners were taken from the station to the POW camp at Greenpoint Track in enclosed wagons with armed guards.

Chapter 24 Greenpoint Track

Greenpoint Track Prisoner of War Camp - April to October 1900 - Jeannot

Anyone who has visited Cape Town will tell you that it is one of the most beautiful cities in the world. Framed against the majestic Table Mountain, the city sprawls down to the sea and the harbor, interspersed with parks and beautiful residential areas. Sunrise and sunset are spectacular, with mountains and ocean combining to form a breathtaking spectacle. It is a place that, once seen, is never forgotten.

Green Point is a suburb at the most easterly part of Table Bay, the bay that houses the harbor. It was home to a large sports stadium that formed the backdrop to the large British POW camp named Green Point Track (then spelled Greenpoint) after the name of the stadium. It was not a permanent camp, but rather a staging post for temporarily housing prisoners of war before they were shipped off to St. Helena, Ceylon or Bermuda. The British authorities were very aware of the potential for escapees to rejoin the Boer forces still operating in the Free State and the Transvaal, so security at Green Point was tight. The fear of the men rejoining the Boer army was also the reason why the permanent POW camps were located in far-flung corners of the Empire.

Upon their arrival in the camp, the prisoners were photographed in groups of six for identification purposes. They then received camp equipment from the British authority, comprising: a suit, a vest, a pair of underpants, a pair of boots and a hat, as well as two blankets, a ground canvas, and a tin plate and mug.

In Green Point, the prisoners were housed in double-storied buildings, which had balconies running around them. Here they used to spend many hours of the day, for, not only could they see what was going on around the Camp, but also have a good view of the sea and passing ships. Each room held six men, and there was a sizeable mess-room downstairs in each building that held about ninety people. Each Boer officer had a room for himself. When, later on, the number of prisoners of war increased, tents had to be erected to accommodate them; but this could hardly be considered hardship in the climate which prevails at the Cape. The tents were put in lines of twenty each, and each score had a building attached for the men in that line to use as a dormitory if they chose. Jeannot and his contingent were housed in these tents. Excellent bathrooms and shower-baths were provided, together with a plentiful supply of water.

Letter from Jeannot Weinberg to his parents - Greenpoint Track - April 10th, 1900

Greenpoint Track
April 10th, 1900

Dear Parents

I am glad to be able to inform you that we arrived here on Monday afternoon.

This is a splendid place. It is a large Recreation Ground with a roomy pavilion, a cycle track, cricket pitch and football ground combined. There are bathrooms, and the water arrangement, on the whole, is very well laid out. Washing places and fireplaces have also been especially built. The air here is invigorating. The food is very good and plentiful. Meat, bread, potatoes, jam, and milk, etc. is the daily menu. Most of the Boers are getting very fat. In fact, I fancy this change will benefit me very much.

I have met Major Albrecht, Lt. van de Witz, van Heisteen, the Baumanns, Uys; all are looking well and healthy. They all send their regards.

There is only one thing that troubles me much, and that is the thought of having to pass Passover feast, which commences next Friday night without Matzos. If you would only speak to Maj. Poore about it, I am sure he will do something in the matter. You can even offer a security that I shall not run away and get me out on parole. This will suit me much better. Also mention to him that I have sworn and signed the declaration never to pick up arms against the British and have my permit still in my possession.

There is nothing of current importance that I can inform you except that all of us are still keeping good health. I have nothing else to think about but you and the children and my food. I pass most of my time reading and walking. Hoping you will try your best in the matter.

I remain with love to you all
Yours affectionately
Jeannot

Regards to Abe and Leopold

The feeding of the prisoners of war was on a substantial scale, and the daily rations per man consisted of $1^{1/4}$ lb. of bread, 1 lb. of fresh meat, 3 oz. of sugar, $1^{1/2}$ lb. of vegetables and 1/4 lb. of jam or fruit. Coffee, milk, and other items were also in like generous apportionments.

The prisoners were allowed to choose a corporal from their midst, and also to select a captain for each house. Over the whole Camp, there reigned a Boer Commandant, assisted by a Court of

"Heemraden," consisting of ex-landdrosts and lawyers appointed by the prisoners of war themselves. Any act of insubordination or inattention to the regulations, sanitary or otherwise, was brought before this court and the guilty party tried and sentenced. When the latter refused to abide by the judgment of the Boer court, he was brought before the Military Commandant, but for this, there was very seldom need.

The prisoners of war had permission to correspond with their friends and relatives and were allowed newspapers and books. Their letters, however, were rather too much censored, which fact constituted an annoyance which, with the exertion of a little tact, might easily have been avoided.

In the Camp, there was a shop where the Boers could buy anything that they required in reason at prices regulated by the Military Commandant. Beyond this, relatives and friends were allowed to send them fruit or anything else, with the exception of firearms. There were also coffee shops run by speculative young Boers. The prisoners used to meet there to drink coffee, eat pancakes, and talk to their heart's content. This particular spot was generally called Pan Koek Straat, and the wildest rumors concerning the war seemed to originate in it

At Green Point Camp, ample hospital accommodation was provided for the sick, and there was a medical staff thoroughly acquainted with the Dutch language and Boer habits. There was electric lighting in every ward, as well as all other comforts compatible with discipline.

Letter from Jeannot Weinberg to Edward Weinberg - Greenpoint Track -June 8th, 1900

Greenpoint Track

June 8th, 1900

Dear Father

Your last letter to land was dated June 1st and since then no news. How are you all getting on? I wrote to Mother at East London. I have received no reply from there either. I was very anxious to hear from you.

As far as I am concerned, I cannot complain. I enjoy excellent health and am growing fat. We have had terrible winds these past four days. Tents and everything else was lifted into the air. Any number of hats disappeared. We had very nice weather today. And this change is very welcome.

Do you get sufficient stock? How is Max getting on with his foot? I shall be glad to know Mother's address. Abe writes that Heepauw is in Siberia.

Have you heard from Asserokow already?

Guess who I have met here in the camp the other day? Can you remember the painter who had the wagon house in our yard at the shop in Phillipolis? His name is Rudgers. All the people thought he was dead long ago. He comes from Johannesburg.

The war is nearly over now, at least in the Free State. I wonder whether they let us go or keep us here till the end of the war. If so, we will have to wait another six weeks, I believe, if not more. I am expecting a box from Rauchfleisch soon. I have acquired an enormous appetite lately. You might be glad you do not have to feed me just now.

How are Albert and Molla? How I long to see them again.

Tomorrow it will be two months here at Greenpoint Camp. I hope this is my last month.

Have you got waiters and barmen already? How is Mr. Gerard? My best regards to him as well.

Yes, we have physical drill every second day. I don't mean the whole camp. Only the young respectable fellows, and this is the only work I have here.

Best love to Bernard and Max, Albert, and Molla and yourself.
Your dutiful son
Jeannot

The weather, which had been very good in the months of April and May, began to change as the Cape winter began. Cape Town has a Mediterranean climate - long, dry summers and mild, wet winters - and the Boers, accustomed to the dry conditions of the Free State and Transvaal, were not at home in the wet, windy conditions so typical of a Cape Town winter. Being at the southern tip of Africa, at the confluence of two major currents, the cold Benguela Current running down the west coast and the warm Mozambique Current running down the east side, it was not for nothing that the Cape had been known to ancient Portuguese mariners as "The Cape of Storms." The meeting of the two currents created a marine soup that swirled and eddied and threw off some of the most appalling weather known to man. And into this was thrust a group of upcountry men accustomed to heat, drought, and thunderstorms. The incessant rain and wind chilled the bones, and the men longed for the crisp, clear air of a highveld fall day.

Jeannot was not immune to the awful weather. Despite his upbringing in Europe, with its colder climate, he was ill-prepared for what he found in Cape Town that winter. He chafed under the restrictions the weather put on outdoor activities and soon grew tired of watching the rain drip from almost everywhere

Letter from Jeannot to his brother Bernard Weinberg - Greenpoint Track -July 18th, 1900

Green Point Track
July 18th, 1900

Dear Bernard

I received your letter the other day – many thanks. So, Mother and the children have left for East London. I wish I was there also. Who is looking after Albert and Molla? I suppose they are at liberty to do what they like just now! You ought to see that they do nothing of the sort.

How is Max getting on with his foot? Should an operation be necessary, the sooner it is done, the better because he must not delay his departure for the SAC. He has been idle long enough, and if he does not buck up just now, he will be in arrears of his last standard.

Business is still going well, so Father writes. I wish I could get out and let Father have a rest. I am sorry for poor Father – he must be overworking himself. Of course, you work hard, but that doesn't harm you because you are young.

I do not know that Bloemfontein is exactly a nice place to live in just at present. Still, I would rather be there than here. We have had some awful weather here lately. It rained for a whole week in succession. One had to remain in the tent for days at a stretch – it was simply miserable. The wind was also blowing, and the tent was nearly lifted into the air the other night. Today we had some passable weather. It did not rain much, but it was windy. Lloyd has not written, nor has he seen me yet. I had one letter from Abe in Phillipolis. They're all right down there.

In my opinion, the English are damned slow in finishing this struggle. I think they will buck up now as troops will be needed for these heathen Chinese. Isn't it horrible how these miserable curs have slaughtered the whites in Peking? I wish I was there to knock spots off them. There are any amount of men here who would volunteer to go to China to fight these fanatics.

Well, my best love to Father and the children

Your affectionate brother
Jeannot

How is it that you don't send me any more Bloemfontein Post?

(Author's Note: Jeannot was referring here to the Boxer Rebellion in China, which broke out in mid-1900.)

Ironically, it was the inclement weather that caused Jeannot's next flirtation with trouble. For months, the soil at Green Point Track had been rock hard, but with the winter rains came a softening in the surface dirt. An idea that had been germinating in his mind was now able to be nurtured and put into practice. He had noticed that one of the latrine blocks was located quite near to the wire fence, the distance being only about four feet. The latrine block was raised off the ground, leaving a crawl space between the floor of the building and the earth. Jeannot had long believed that it was feasible to dig a tunnel under the wire, starting from beneath the latrine block. However, in the pre-winter months, the soil had been too hard to dig into - especially since the escape would need to be executed in about three hours, coming after 'lights out' and giving the escapees enough time to get well clear of the camp before their escape was noticed. Jeannot figured that if a vertical hole was dug about three feet down, followed by a six-foot tunnel parallel to the ground, then another hole going up on the other side, he and several others could be out and long gone before the sun rose. He and his comrades were no strangers to digging - the creation of endless trenches on the battlefield had made them masters of the craft - so he figured it would take about ninety minutes to two hours to create the escape route. The problem was, of course, that they had no implements with which to dig.

He discussed the plan with his four closest comrades, Britz, Havenga, Reitz, and Swanepoel. All seemed to believe the plan had merit, and the next few days were spent seeking out improvised digging tools that could be used to create the tunnel. Swanepoel came up with a cricket bat, Britz and Reitz acquired some empty food cans, Havenga had a discarded Tommy helmet, and Jeannot found a metal tent spike that was lying near a deserted tent. These implements were hidden in the tent to ensure they were not discovered. The plan was to wait for a rainy night since the chance of being seen was reduced. They would leave the tent at 10.30 pm, one at a time as if going to the latrine. Once at the latrine building, they would go around to the back of the building and lay low until all had gathered. Then they would start to dig. The soil from the tunnel would be disposed of in the latrine, with the men passing it one to another using the implements they had collected. They believed that there would be no need to shore up the roof, since the ground was much like clay a few feet beneath the surface, and the tunnel was not planned to be particularly long.

The night of July 29th was a wild and rainy affair, with the wind whipping around the tents, making the conditions so miserable that it was unlikely that anyone would be wandering around. The four men sat in their tent, waiting for the siren that would indicate 'lights out.' It sounded at 10 pm, the usual time. They waited for half an hour, then quietly slipped out one at a time. After about 5 minutes, all four were gathered behind the latrine, shivering in the rain and wind. And they began to dig. The moistened soil made digging somewhat easier than digging trenches in the hard ground at Magersfontein, and after half an hour, the first vertical hole was completed. The men sat back and took a break, admiring their handiwork. Then they started on the horizontal portion. It was necessary to make the tunnel wide enough for a man to be able to crawl through using his elbows and knees without disturbing either the roof or walls of the tunnel. It was pitch dark, and down in the tunnel, there was no light at all. They maintained their direction with a rudimentary guiding string that was kept at 90 degrees to the vertical hole.

All of a sudden, the area was bathed in light, and there was a sound of rifles being cocked. The men froze. A crisp British voice pierced the silence.

"And what do we have here? What do you men think you are doing? On your feet, all of you. Backs to the wall!" Jeannot's heart sank. How had they known? Had someone betrayed them? It could not have been one of the escape group since they all stood to benefit from the escape. So, who then?

The officer continued. "Guards, handcuff the prisoners and take them to the guardhouse." There was a rustle of activity, and each of the escapees was pulled off the wall by a soldier and put in handcuffs. When all were secured, they were marched off in the direction of the guardhouse. The noise had woken some of the other prisoners who peered out of their tent, wondering what on earth was going on. At the guardhouse, the men were told to sit on the floor while their details were recorded. They were then herded into a cell and locked in. The officer told them that nothing would happen to them that night, but that they would stand trial for their attempted escape in the morning. The lights were turned off, and the men stared at each other in the darkened cell.

Britz was the first to speak. "What the hell? How the fuck did they get to know what we were up to? Did anyone spill the beans?" Everyone shook their heads - none had ratted on the others to the authorities. "Did anyone tell anyone else about it?" There came a low moan from Reitz. "Oh shit," he said. "I wrote a letter to my brother and mentioned that I would be seeing him soon as we were planning to escape from behind one of the latrines." Britz put his head in his hands. "You bloody idiot. Don't you know they censor all of our letters? You basically put them on the lookout for us - they were just waiting for us to show our hand." Reitz groaned. "*Bliksem* (damn), manne! I didn't think. I am so sorry. Now I've dropped you all in *diep kak* (deep shit)!" "Reitz, you are a *poopal* (arsehole)," said Havenga. "Who knows what kind of trouble we are in now." Now it was Reitz's turn to hold his head in his hands. "Sorry, boys, sorry. You are right. I am a prize *poopal*." The others nodded their agreement. Well, they were all in it now and would have to face the music in the morning.

The next day the men were taken before the Court of "Heemraden," a group of senior Boer officers whose task it was to adjudicate on cases like these. It so happened that the president of the court was Maj. Albrecht, who knew all the men well, having fought alongside them at Magersfontein and other battles.

"Boys, this is very disappointing. I know all of you well, and I know some of your fathers as well. And I am sure they would not be proud of you today. You are all brave soldiers, have served your country very well in battle, but now you feel it necessary to put the lives and treatment of your fellow soldiers in jeopardy." The accused looked at one another, somewhat bemused by the major's approach. He went on. "Are you being treated well in this camp?" The men nodded. "Are you getting enough food, is the medical attention good, are you being adequately housed, are your recreational facilities acceptable?" The men all nodded again. "Well, boys, the English have decided to treat us very well in this camp. The facilities are good, there is plenty of freedom within the camp, and they even give us the responsibility of controlling our own people. In other words, this is a pretty good deal, given the fact that we are prisoners of war. And now you rascals decide to go and try to spoil it for everyone by pissing off the English. If you have no concern for your own conditions, spare a thought for the rest of us who are living in better conditions than we could have expected for POWs. I know we all want our freedom back. Some of us want to return to the fight and defend our families. But we need to keep the peace here in the camp and, frankly, your little escapade is not helping in this regard. Do you have anything to say for yourselves?" Jeannot held up his hand. "Major, I want you to know that this was my idea, and that it was me who convinced the others to join me. So, when you hand down our sentence, please go easy on the others because it was really me who instigated the escape."

Albrecht looked closely at him and replied. "Jeannot, it is admirable of you to own up and to take responsibility. But it doesn't really matter whose idea it was. The fact of the matter is that you were all willing participants and took part of your own free will. Therefore, you will all receive the same punishment." Jeannot shrugged his shoulders and glanced at the other men. "Yes, Major. I understand, Major." "Right," said Albrecht. "Your punishment will be two weeks solitary confinement in the camp stockade on half rations. If any of you feel that this is unjust, you may appeal to the English commanding officer. That is the decision of this court." The men looked at each other and nodded. It was a harsh punishment, but nobody was about to throw themselves on the mercy of the English who might increase the sentence. So they all agreed to serve their time.

After the court had adjourned, Albrecht called Jeannot to one side and spoke to him. "Listen, man," he said. "I know as well as you that every person in a POW camp has a duty to try and escape. I do not fault you for trying. But we cannot let the English know this, or they will give us a much harder time going forward. We are doing very nicely here, and I want to keep it that way for as long as we are here. I know we will eventually be sent to St. Helena or Ceylon, where things will not be as comfortable as they are here, so I want our boys to be able to make the most of the good conditions we are enjoying here. Does that make sense?" Jeannot nodded his agreement. "So, part of me is proud of you for trying to escape, but the other part wants to protect our boys here. So off you go and serve your sentence, and we will talk again when you come out." Jeannot shook his hand and thanked him - Albrecht was a good man, a brave soldier, and a fair and upright gentleman who was respected by all who knew him.

Chapter 25 - Scorched Earth

Headquarters of the British Occupying Forces, Bloemfontein - June 25th, 1900 – Roberts

French stared out of the window, his mind in a state of confusion, his gut contorted with a nausea he had never before experienced. Roberts's words had left him speechless, incredulous, unable to formulate a rational response. He turned and looked at Kitchener. The man did not appear to be moved at all by what had just been said; a sang froid that chilled French to his core. He had served in this army for 30 years, but never before had he been called on to choose between his sense of duty and his own inner morality.

"Let me see if I totally understand what you are proposing, my lord. You are suggesting that, because the Boers have abandoned regular warfare and replaced it with a guerilla war, and because our army in its current format cannot counter the Boer guerilla tactics, and because it is the womenfolk who are enabling their men to continue the struggle...." French stopped, seemingly unable to verbalize the terrible thing he had just heard. He drew a breath, composed himself, and continued. "Because of these reasons, your suggestion is that we adopt a scorched earth policy, burn their farms, slaughter their livestock, set fire to their crops, and round up their women and children and place them in 'protective custody'?" Roberts looked at him quizzically, and before he could respond, Kitchener interjected. "I think that is exactly what his lordship means. And I support and endorse his views. The only way we can bring this scum to heel is to deal with them in a way that they understand." French was horrified. "You make them sound like savages with no sense of honor and no moral compass. This has not been my experience with them. They are honest men, deeply religious, proud of their lands, even prouder of their families. And you...." Roberts cut him off. "That is precisely why this is the only strategy that will make them come to heel. The Boer is prouder of nothing more than his farm and his family. Remove those, and we remove his will to fight. It is the only way. Kitchener and I have discussed this, and we can find no better solution."

French walked towards the middle of the room and looked directly at Kitchener. "General, have you considered the impact of what you are about to do on the future peace in this land?" His voice rose, along with his passion. "Do you honestly believe that these murderous actions on innocent women and children are going to win you the hearts and minds of these people once this war is over? Do you think acts of brutality such as these will produce a people willing to become a part of the British Empire? Mark my words, General. Apart from the fact that acts of this nature are in and of themselves inhumane, deplorable, and beyond my comprehension as an officer of the Empire and as a man, I believe you are sowing the seeds of resentment that will germinate and eventually be turned against us." He was furious now, and it showed in his face. "And what do you think our people at home will say about this? Do you think they will condone this sort of barbarism in the name of the Empire? Do you think it is worth shortening this war by a few months if it permanently tars the British with a legacy of crimes against humanity? I'll have none of this!" French picked up his hat and stick and marched out of the room.

Roberts looked at Kitchener. "He's right, you know, in everything he says, but the expediency of the situation and the amount this war is costing the taxpayer means that any way in which we can accelerate a negotiated peace will be well regarded in Whitehall." Kitchener nodded and replied, "There will always be fallout from this kind of thing. Happened in India many times. Today's news, tomorrow's fish and chips wrapper. I say we go ahead with it and damn the consequences. We simply cannot afford to have bleeding hearts like French obstructing our progress."

He continued. "Every bloody farm is to the Boers a supply depot and an intelligence agency. By interning them in the camps, we will cut off the guerrillas from this source of support. I am also counting on the strong sense of family among the Boers to come and join their women and children and leave their murderous ways. I also think it will keep the women safe from marauding blacks who may attack the farms when the men are not there. We will sweep the whole population into a couple of dozen camps, and that will be the end of it."

"Have you any idea how many people there are, and how you are going to administer these camps?" asked Roberts.
"No, and I don't care. It is our job to round them up. It is the civil government's job to run the camps and look after their internal administration and logistics. We are soldiers, not nursemaids." replied Kitchener.
"And who foots the bill?" asked Roberts.
"The civil government of the Orange Free State and Transvaal. After all, these are their people."

Roberts sighed inwardly. He had mixed feelings about being replaced as commander-in-chief of the British Forces in South Africa, but he was secretly relieved that this policy would not be carried out on his watch.

Chapter 26 - The Voyage

Transport Ranee Simonstown - August 1900 - Jeannot

Jeannot and the other potential escapees did not serve their full sentences. After four days, they were taken from the jail and told to pack their things to take ship to Ceylon. Clearly, the British did not want to have to deal with these potential troublemakers at Greenpoint Track and were happy to hand them over to their colleagues in Ceylon. Greenpoint Track was, in reality, a transit camp for POWs en route to other offshore prison camps, but it was likely that the men would not have been shipped off this soon had they not attempted the escape. They were packed into a barred wagon and began the short journey to Simonstown Harbor, from where they would begin their voyage to Ceylon.

The ship was the Transport Ranee, a Royal Navy vessel of 8,500 tons that had originally been used to transport the 2nd Dragoons and the Scots Greys from Greenock to Cape Town. Jeannot and his group were among the first to board, and they were told that it would be some time before the ship would sail for Ceylon since they were awaiting a group of 600 Boer prisoners who had fought under Prinsloo and surrendered with him. The men surmised that they had been sent to the ship early because the authorities at Greenpoint Track could not wait to be rid of them.

They were not wrong. No sooner had they set foot on the ship when they were brought in front of a Captain Hunter. He was to be one of the officers in charge of the prisoners on the voyage. "Ah," he said, "The tunnellers from Greenpoint Track. I was advised that you would be coming on board before the rest. We have a number of your sort already on the ship, those who felt it necessary not to avail themselves of the facilities offered by Her Majesty's armed forces at Greenpoint and Simonstown, but to try and tunnel to freedom of their own accord. You are known entities, and we shall be watching you very carefully. Particularly while we are still in port - know that any one of you who tries to escape from the ship will be shot on recapture without a trial. Once the ship has sailed, you can try to escape all you like. That is if you want to make a hearty meal for the sharks." The men looked at each other. Jeannot spoke - invariably, it was he who was the spokesman to the British, since his command of English was far superior to the rest. "Captain," he said, "we have no intention of causing any trouble. We understand your instructions, and you have our word that we will not try anything stupid. But we want your assurance that we will receive the same treatment as all the other prisoners on board, and will not be singled out for any especially harsh duties or reduced rations." Hunter drew himself up to his full height and scowled at Jeannot. "Young man, I do not think you are in any position to dictate terms to me, and your remarks are not appreciated. Nevertheless, in the spirit of fair play, I will assure you that if you play by the rules, there will be no differentiation between your treatment and those of the rest of the prisoners. Do I make myself clear?" "Yes, sir. Thank you, Sir." "And what is more," continued Hunter, "we are going to split up this little coven of escapees, to make sure you do not try to plot anything else. Report to the duty sergeant, and he will assign you to your sleeping positions - which I assure you will not be in close proximity to one another." The men nodded and were taken to a burly sergeant who directed them to their quarters after recording their particulars in a prisoners' log. The information that was recorded was quite detailed - it included prisoner number (which had been given at Greenpoint Track), surname, Christian names, nationality, age, home address, town or district, field cornetcy or commando, where captured, date of capture and date of receipt on board.

That evening, Jeannot wrote to his father.

Letter from Jeannot Weinberg to Edward Weinberg August 5th,

1900

Transport Ranee
Simonstown

August 5th, 1900

Dear Father

I daresay you have received my telegram stating my departure for Ceylon? I hope you will not worry on my account. I would have preferred to go home instead, but if matters have to turn this way, let us be happy and not fuss about it. Luvronia is also on board.

We had a rough time from Cape Town. This morning we got another 100 men from here, mostly Germans and Hollanders.
I have been sent here on account of suspicion being against me as regards a tunnel that was built at Greenpoint, which was unfortunately betrayed by one of our own men. I will tell you more about it should I live to see you again. It is not likely that I shall not.

We will probably leave tonight. It will take us three weeks before we reach Colombo. Don't you think that this trip will do me good? Besides, I will see a country which is worth seeing. I hope to buy you some good samples of real Ceylon tea.

I hope Mother will not be upset by this news. The voyage is perfectly safe. This steamer is a pretty big one – 6659 tons. I will write to you from Colombo next.

In the meanwhile, I wish you all goodbye and also that we may meet safe and sound by Christmas. My fondest love to Mother,

Bernard, Max, Molla, Albert and Bertha and the baby and yourself.

Yours obediently
Jeannot

Remember me to Mr. Gerard and all friends. Lloyd also."

Jeannot was wrong about the date of departure. The ship did not sail until August 14th, since the group of 600 did not arrive until August 10th. By this time, Jeannot had become familiar with the layout of the vessel and was able to help his fellow prisoners, who still seemed confused by the speed with which they had been whisked off the train that brought them to Simonstown and marched onto the Ranee.

The voyage - August - September 1900 - Gregory Heale

Letter from Gregory Heale to his wife Margaret Heale - September 9th, 1900

Colombo September
9th, 1900

My darling Margaret,

I trust this letter finds you and the children well. I apologize for not writing sooner, but as I explained in my letter in August, I have been on board ship for the past three weeks en route from Cape Town to Ceylon. We arrived in port yesterday, and I cannot believe the difference in the weather. Cape Town was cold and wet, Colombo is stifling and humid - almost too hot to bear. I am grateful I am only going to be here for a few days. I pity the poor lads who are going to be remaining here - theirs will not be a

happy lot.
But let me tell you all about the voyage. The ship was called the Ranee, and we had a 'cargo' of 600 Boer prisoners, some directly from the field, others from various POW camps in the Cape, primarily Greenpoint Track. Most of the men were just ordinary soldiers, but among the group we received from Greenpoint was a group known as 'tunnellers,' prisoners who had tried to escape by tunneling out of the camps. We needed to watch this group rather carefully while in port, to ensure they did not try anything silly. But once we were out to sea, it didn't really matter - there was no escaping in the middle of the ocean!

The ship is not uncomfortable - my quarters are small but comfortable, and my rank entitles me to my own cabin. The food is reasonable, and fortunately, the ship took on a good quantity of the really fine wines on offer at the Cape. This goes a long way toward making the journey more pleasant.

On the second morning, there was a kit inspection. It was remarkable the kind of things we found in these fellows' packs - a large number of articles captured from the British, among them soldiers' belts, great-coats, straps, " coats warm British," and two large mail bags labeled London to Pretoria. One man was in possession of a complete Field Artilleryman's kit. All of this 'treasure' was confiscated, much to the chagrin of the Boers! It is amazing the things a man will pick up on a battlefield, although one should not blame these poor fellows - they had little enough to begin with.

The daily routine is as follows:
Breakfast at 8 am
Orderly Room at 9.30 am
Parade at 10 am for the escort
Inspection of the troop and prisoners' decks by the Captain of the

ship and CO. at 11.30 am
Lunch at 12.30 pm
Guard-mounting at 4.30 pm.
Roll call for the prisoners at 5 pm
Dinner at 6.30 pm
Lights out at 9 pm

All quite leisurely, really. The officers seem to be a decent lot, especially the ship's captain, who regales us nightly with his tales (some imagined, I'll warrant) of his time at sea. The NCOs seem efficient and have retained reasonable control over the prisoners. Any offenders (and the offenses were relatively minor) were given deck and mess duty, which involved scrubbing the decks and the tables in the mess hall. A wonderful way of keeping the ship clean and shipshape!

Some of the prisoners arrived with serious wounds and illnesses. There is a hospital section, but I fear the care is not as good as it might have been had the men been in a land-based camp. Nevertheless, we have only had a few deaths on board, and these men have been ceremonially buried at sea. One of the older burghers acts as the 'predikant' or minister, and he seemed to be unaware of the regulation time the British Navy allocates to a burial at sea. After many rounds of prayers and hymns, he launched into lengthy sermons, some of which lasted nearly an hour! This nearly drove the captain to distraction, since the ship has to be stationary during a burial service, and the extended services were interfering with his schedule! All was well in the end, and we were able to make up the time lost.

Contrary to our expectations, not all the prisoners are Boers. There is a fair number of Germans, Hollanders, French, and several other races who came to fight with the Boers. What is interesting to me is the fact that there is no camaraderie whatsoever between the Boers and these foreigners - the Boers want nothing to do with them at all. This seems a little unfair to me since these men would have potentially given their lives in favor of the Boer cause, but they are not well regarded by the Boers who shun them at every opportunity. They bunk together, and there is little intermingling except at game times, which are quite frequent, and almost always consist of wrestling, boxing, and other sports that depend on physical prowess rather than ball skills. And the Boers do particularly well since they are a strong and sturdy lot, accustomed to manual labor on their farms.

I have had an opportunity to speak with some of the prisoners, although many of them don't speak particularly good English. I would hasten to add that my command of Afrikaans is even less that their command of English, so I cannot be critical! Overall they seem a thoroughly decent bunch, family men who sincerely believe in their rights to protect hearth and home. Difficult to argue with, really, especially since we all know the main reason we are in this war is to steal their goldfields. Some are really pious and spend considerable time on Sundays in prayer and services. They also hold shorter services three times a day on weekdays, and can seldom be seen without their bibles.

Many of the prisoners succumbed to seasickness in the early part of the voyage. These men, so hardy and hearty on land, were no match for the rough seas, and many a man was seen hanging over the rail returning his dinner to the fishes! After the first week, most were feeling better and had gained their sea legs.

The Boers have a great love for music and singing, and most nights there is community singing of Boer tunes that all sing lustily, The foreigners also participate in these activities. It is a joy to hear the songs of many lands being sung after the day's boredom. For boredom it is. There is little to do on board and almost no books or other forms of entertainment. The older ones sit and smoke and reminisce - the younger ones taunt each other and play practical jokes just to shut out the boredom.

When we crossed the equator, the ship's crew put on the usual festivities, which took the Boers completely by surprise. They were unfamiliar with the tradition, but joined into the spirit of the thing until a contretemps broke out between the Boers and the foreigners - who know what it was about - and we were forced to put an end to the festivities.

Everybody on board was very thankful when, on the 17th day after leaving Simonstown, we steamed into Colombo Harbor. The officers and men of the escort had nothing to complain of during the voyage in the way of accommodation, but the Boers were very crowded. It was almost impossible to thread one's way through them when they were all on deck, but after all, they could hardly expect to travel luxuriously.

So now I am in Colombo at the Officers' Mess of the local regiment, getting ready to return to the Cape when the Ranee next leaves. I imagine the voyage back will not be as eventful as the one I have just described since there will be no prisoners on board, and we will have to make do with our own company. I am not sure when the ship will be returning to the Cape, and I will try to write before I board.

I miss all of you terribly and wish I was home. Please hug Elizabeth and little William for me and tell them their Daddy loves them and that they are always in his thoughts as are you, my dear. I so look forward to the day that we will be reunited and can continue our life together.

I love you, and I send you my kisses and hugs.

Your faithful husband

Greg

The voyage - August - September 1900 - Jannie Retief

Letter from Jannie Retief to his wife Sanna Retief September 8th, 1900 (translated from the original in Afrikaans)

Colombo
September 11th on board Transport Ranee

My liewe Sanna

We have just arrived in Ceylon at a port called Colombo. I had never heard of the place before we got on the ship, but it is the port where the ship docked. From here, we will be taken to a permanent camp, although we do not know which one, since there are several camps in Ceylon.

After my capture at Winburg in July, four hundred of us were put on a train for Cape Town. We expected to be put in one of the holding camps at Greenpoint Track or Simonstown, and when the train stopped in Simonstown, we thought we were going to the camp there. But we were wrong. We were hurried aboard the ship Transport Ranee and told we were going straight to Ceylon. It seems that the ship was about to go there anyway and was not full, so they decided to send us along with the other 200 prisoners from the camps who were already on board. I think if there had only been the 400 of our group on the ship it would not have been too bad, but with 600 it was very crowded. The officers were put in second class cabins, four to a room, but they were not allowed to have any contact with the men. I am guessing the English did not want to encourage anyone to revolt. About 400 of the 600 were shut up in the forward part of the ship, but the remaining 200 were put in the back with the cows and sheep and chickens. Again I guess the English thought we Boers would be accustomed to sleeping with animals - I think most of them regard us as animals in any event. This part of the ship was never intended to hold men - the roof was very low, and it was almost impossible to walk without stooping. I feel blessed not to have been billeted in the rear part of the ship.

We are allowed to be on deck during the day, but at 8 pm we are herded down to our sleeping quarters. These are a mass of dirty, smelly hammocks, but there are not enough to go round, so those not lucky enough to have snagged a hammock must sleep on the floor. I was fortunate and took care to write my name very clearly on the hammock I was able to get for myself. The hold is very hot and stuffy, with only a few portholes high up that do little to circulate air and give almost no respite from the incessant heat. The heat generated by sharing quarters with 400 men is quite unbelievable, and the fact that our only way of washing us a quick dunk in a canvas bath once a day means that everyone is starting to smell quite ripe. It is one thing when you can smell others because you can always move away, but when you start to smell yourself, then you are really in trouble.

The food they give us is beyond disgusting. For breakfast, we get a sort of bitter-sour bread made from hops, with very weak black coffee and very little sugar. For dinner, there is weak vegetable soup (made from tinned vegetables), tinned salt beef, and cold, unpeeled potatoes, most of which are rotten. For supper, there is tea and the same kind of bread we get for breakfast. The plates are rusty soup bowls and pewter mugs, which definitely do not contribute to the taste of the food. We do get pudding on Sundays if it can be called such. It is half-raw dough with raisins in it. Doesn't sound like much, but the men certainly look forward to having something sweet.

The weather is much more pleasant than when we left Cape Town, which was cold and rainy. On the water, it was warm and sunny, and we were soon able to forget the miserable winter we left behind us. We often see shoals of fish and schools of porpoises, and these provide a break from the boredom of being on board this ship. I think boredom is the most difficult thing to handle. Yes, we play the occasional games on deck, and yes, we have long discussions, but the topics are always the same - should Cronje have surrendered at Paardeberg, how long will de Wet hold out for, what will become of Pres. Kruger, what will the country be like after the war. On and on and on until we get bored with being bored. The one thing that gives us some hope is the Boxer Rebellion in China. We speculate on whether the British will be forced to withdraw troops from South Africa. We also talk about what it will be like in Ceylon. None of us really knows anything about the place, other than the fact that it is famous for its tea. The British on the boat aren't any help - they don't seem to know too much about it either. So we carry on being bored and complain about the food and the accommodation until we get bored with that as well.

Besides the boredom, the mood of the men is unexpectedly positive. Once we had survived the period of seasickness (I suffered for three days), the men began to enjoy the warm weather and the sunshine. I think we are also relieved to know that we no longer have to be concerned that we might get shot this day or the next as we did when we were in combat. There is no honor in being a POW, but it doesn't hurt to know that you will be able to return home when the war ends. Unlike many of our colleagues who lie in shallow graves, never to see their families again. This is reassuring. Nobody knows how long the war will continue, but it cannot be too long since the British will just keep on pouring in troops until we are overrun. So who knows, maybe we will be home by Easter.

We eventually reached Colombo on September 9th, but I, for one, did not leave the boat until the 11th. We were housed in a temporary holding camp in Colombo awaiting transport to our final destination, and this is where I am writing this letter from. I have been told that I will be going to Diyatalawa Camp, which is in the interior of Ceylon - it is apparently the largest of the camps. It is about 125 miles from Colombo, and we will be transported by train, which should take about a day - the trains are rather slow here in Ceylon, it appears.

My dear, we are being called to assemble - I think we may be going to the train station. So I must sadly end this letter. I send you and the children all my love, and I will write to you as soon as I get to the camp.

I love you, and I miss you, and I pray that God will look after you and the children.
Your loving husband

Jannie

Colombo - September 12th, 1900 - Jeannot

Jeannot and his fellow tunnellers had kept their heads down during the voyage, trying to melt into the background and remain as inconspicuous as possible. Jeannot was fortunate to be in the front section of the ship, the part that did not contain the livestock, but the rest of his friends were in the back. Clearly Jeannot had been identified as the ringleader of the escape, and the British had been careful to keep him away from the rest. He did not know many people on the ship when he arrived on board. Still, by the time they arrived in Colombo, he had made a number of connections whom he was happy to consider friends. And friends would be needed in Diyatalawa, for that is where he was to be sent to sit out the rest of the war.

Chapter 27 - Diyatalawa 1

Ceylon - 1900 – Jeannot

At the heart of the Indian Ocean, Ceylon had been a trading hub even before Arab traders arrived in the 7th century AD with their new Islamic faith. Gems, cinnamon, ivory, and elephants were valued items of commerce. Early Muslim settlements took hold in Jaffna and Galle, but the arrival of a European power focused as much on domination as trade, forced many Muslims inland to flee persecution.

When the Portuguese arrived in 1505, Ceylon had three main kingdoms: the Tamil kingdom of Jaffna, and Sinhalese kingdoms in Kandy and Kotte (near Colombo). Lorenço de Almeida, the son of the Portuguese Viceroy of India, established friendly relations with the Kotte kingdom and gained a monopoly on the valuable spice trade. The Portuguese eventually gained control of the Kotte kingdom.

In 1602 the Dutch arrived, just as keen as the Portuguese on dominating the lucrative traffic in Indian Ocean spices. In exchange for Ceylonese autonomy, the Kandyan king gave the Dutch a monopoly on the spice trade.

The British initially viewed Ceylon in strategic terms and considered the eastern harbor of Trincomalee as a counter to French influence in India. After the French took over the Netherlands in 1794, the pragmatic Dutch ceded Ceylon to the British for 'protection' in 1796. The British moved quickly, making the island a colony in 1802 and finally taking over Kandy in 1815. Three years later, the first unified administration of the island by a European power was established. Diyatalawa is in the midland province of Uva, a large tea district about 150 miles from Colombo. Since it is in the highlands, about

4,500 feet above sea level, the temperature is somewhat cooler than Colombo, seldom going over 90 degrees Fahrenheit, but it is very humid, which no doubt contributes to the successful growing of tea.

Diyatalawa - September 1900 – Jeannot

The train trip from Colombo to Diyatalawa was relatively uneventful, although the men did notice a perceptible increase in humidity. Clearly, their sojourn in Ceylon was not going to be temperate. On arrival at the camp, the men were divided into two groups - those who hailed from the Transvaal, and those who were from the Free State. Jeannot, of course, joined the latter group. The camp was divided into two '*dorps*' or villages, one named Krugersdorp - after the president of the Transvaal - the other Steynsdrift - after Pres. Steyn of the Free State. The two villages were joined by a road, known ironically as Commissioner Street, one of the main streets in Johannesburg.

Accommodation was in corrugated iron huts, about 120 feet long by 20 feet wide, each housing 56 prisoners. They were divided into groups of 14, each under the control of a corporal, while a captain was placed over each hut. The huts were sparsely furnished, each prisoner having an iron bed with a coir mattress and a small locker to store possessions. There was a long table in each hut where the men could sit and talk or play chess or cards. Discipline was strict, with three hut inspections each day to ensure cleanliness and to prevent the spread of disease. The washrooms were barns built of clay with cement floors, with one washroom barn for every five regular huts.

In the early days, the food was not particularly good, especially when compared with what the prisoners had enjoyed in Cape Town. The meat was of poor quality, and the bread, made of bran, was often dry and tasteless. Things improved when civilian authorities intervened and increased the quality and quantity of the rations, but never again would they enjoy the excellent fare of Greenpoint Track or Simonstown. The kitchens were also of a poor standard, and the men found it difficult to prepare their food with the cooking equipment provided. Those, like Jeannot, who had gained weight in Greenpoint, soon returned to their leaner selves. Camp facilities were, on the whole, quite acceptable. There was a large recreation ground on which various games could be played, the most popular being rugby and cricket, and there was also a swimming pool that was used all year round, the weather being consistently hot and humid. But the main problem was boredom. For men accustomed to freedom and the boundless expanses of veld in South Africa, the camp was oppressive and restricting. There was only so much that a man could do to amuse himself during the hours of daylight, and it was inevitable that morale dropped as the boredom took hold. Conscious efforts were made to combat this by the senior prisoners organizing educational classes that the men could attend. These included language classes, reading, writing, and arithmetic - a number of the prisoners had been teachers before the war, and, since many of the men had received little formal education, this was an excellent way to combat boredom and give the men the fundamentals of schooling. Jeannot, who was proficient in languages, taught English to his fellow prisoners with good effect.

And there was no shortage of entrepreneurial enterprises. Jeannot described these in a letter to his father in September of 1900.

Letter from Jeannot to Edward Weinberg - Diyatalawa Camp - September 29th, 1900

Diyatalawa Camp
September 29th, 1900

Dear Father

This morning I received two letters that Mother wrote to me from East London. I am sending you my latest photo. It is taken by our camp artist and is not a very good one. I am anxious to hear from you all. Tomorrow the South African mail is expected here when I shall probably get news.

Life here is just as good and bad as Greenpoint. The heat is terrible during the day, and at night it freezes. Still, one can stand it. The only thing against my grain here is the meat we get. At Greenpoint, we received Australian frozen beef and mutton, and that was A1. But here we get beef only, and that is exclusively from Ceylon cattle. I have nothing against the animals, but their meat is awful. It has no taste and still worse luck; it is as tough as shoe leather. It is a miracle that I have been able to live on it these past few weeks, and if this continues, I shall be placed under the necessity of procuring a masticator for these India rubber steaks. I cannot understand why considering how near New Zealand is to this place, and we are not served with Australian mutton. Should the British Government do the aforementioned, it will, besides saving a couple of thousand teeth, earn the gratitude of the general public in this camp. This is the only complaint I have against this.

How are things generally in Bloemfontein just at present? Business ought to be going strong still. At least I trust it is.
The prisoners here in Ceylon have created quite a commotion among the local inhabitants who are daily expressing their grievances re the rising price of foodstuffs in general through the few rupees printed in Colombo. They not only blame the British Government but even shower insults by the bucketful on the poor helpless "Boere." The Irish Brigade is accused of being the cause of the considerable rise in the price of potatoes! And so

they go on. I, on the contrary, believe that since our advent on this soil, more than a dozen grumblers have reaped an unparalleled harvest for this island. But such is life.

I forgot to wish you a prosperous New Year. I did not fast this year because I did not know the date of the fast.

General Olivier and his three sons are expected here this afternoon.

It is strange that no letters have arrived for me. Perhaps it takes a long time to censor them all. I shall be glad should Bernard send me some papers occasionally. We are absolutely without news here.

Commandant Rouck, who stayed in our place during the war and that other German with him, are both here and send regards. Lt. Keuterwans that Hollander comes this afternoon.

You ought to see this camp. At every corner, one finds a stall where cigars, cigarettes, pipes, and matches are sold. There are two beer breweries here in camp. The Irish-Americans have one and the Germans the other. They make hop beer. It sells well. Of course, it is rubbish, but the Boers seem to like it nevertheless. These chaps are doing a roaring trade. There is a bakery here where fine cakes and pastries are baked. Leionis & Co. is an agency for illustrated postcards and decorators. Cigars are very cheap here. Just fancy 2 shillings a hundred! I will bring some with me when I return. They are inferior to the Mauillas, so it is said.

There are two pianos in the two different camps. There is any amount of talent among the foreigners. Several Hollanders and Germans are very good pianists, and one Spaniard is excellent with the violin. We get real classical music, and I am so fond of it.

Well, my best love to Mother and the Children. I will write again next mail.

Your loving son
Jeannot

Leionis wishes to be remembered to you. Also, Lombard of the artillery.

Diyatalawa Camp - October 1st, 1900 - Jeannot

Jeannot was sitting on his bed, rereading letters when a young man in a pair of ragged khaki shorts and no shirt entered the hut. "Where can I find Jeannot Weinberg?" he inquired. Jeannot stood up and beckoned the man to come over. The man extended his hand and said, "Pleased to meet you. My name is Louis Fouche from Pretoria. Are you the Jeannot Weinberg who was recently appointed captain of the Free State cricket team in Steynsdrift?" Jeannot shook his hand and replied in the affirmative. "Then," said Fouche, "I have a letter for you." He reached into the pocket of his shorts and handed Jeannot a folder piece of paper.

Hand Delivery:

The Captain, OFS Cricket Club

Dear Sir
The Transvaal Cricketers in the camp is happy to invite the team of the Orange Free State to play a match on the cricket field against the team of the Transvaal to the honor of both Presidents. This match will take place on this Saturday, October 6th, at 10 am. We have chosen this day because some of our players have been given leave on the Friday but will return on Saturday.

Respectfully yours
Russell Cleaver
Secretary

Jeannot read the letter, reread it and smiled. "So, you fellows want to get your arses kicked on the cricket field, do you?" Fouche grinned. "On the contrary, it is we who will be handing you your arses on a plate!" They laughed. "Go and tell Mr. Cleaver that the Orange Free State gladly accepts the challenge, and we look forward to showing you exactly how the game should be played!" Fouche gave a mock salute, turned on his heels, and left the hut.

This was a great opportunity. Jeannot had played cricket at the camp and had established himself as one of the better performers. He had been elected captain of the notional Free State team the week before, but it was more of a joke than anything. Who, after all, were they going to play? And who was the team? Now a worthy opponent had been found, and it was time to get a team together and get some serious practice in - after all, they had less than a week to get ready.

The day of October 6th was the usual hot, humid weather, but this did not deter most of the camp and many of the British guards and some of the local Ceylonese from turning up to watch the match. Equipment had been borrowed from the guards, the pitch had been set up, and the boundary was marked by empty vegetable cans that had been painted white. To ensure fair play and no prejudice, two of the guards, Corporal Emslie and Sergeant Franks, were appointed to be the umpires. The two sets of supporters occupied opposite sides of the fields, and friendly taunts and threats were hurled at one another. It was a great success. Even though the men were lacking in practice and playing in very unfamiliar conditions, the competition was fierce, and the two teams showed great skill and application. The Transvaal team eventually ended up as winners, but the camaraderie was excellent, and the men agreed that this should be followed by a rugby match

Diyatalawa Camp - 1900 – Jeannot

The activities in the camp did much to ease the boredom, but not the nagging anxiety about the passage of the war back home. News was filtering through of the commando raids that were being organized by the Boers who had refused the oath, and the early successes were encouraging but concerning. How long could this continue? What might the British do to retaliate? How would it affect the time before the prisoners were released?

One evening, a group of men was sitting at the table in Jeannot's hut smoking and talking when a man named Andries Fredericks let out a long, low groan. "Dammit, manne. How did we manage to throw this war away after all we did at Magersfontein and Ladysmith?" Eyes turned to stare at him. This had long been on the men's minds, but most were reluctant to raise the issue. Mental wounds are as dangerous as physical ones, and all the men carried these mental burdens. It was inevitable that a debate would eventually surface, filled with remorse and regret, and it seemed that this was the time.

Havenga broke the silence. "Andries," he said, "We all feel the way you do, man, but we need to look at the reality of the situation. South Africa is a small country, and to stand up to the might of the British Empire could really only have one result."
"Then why did we go to war in the first place, if it was a lost cause?" retorted Fredericks.

The men looked at one another. This was a question everyone had asked himself but had never wanted to admit it in public. There was a pause in the conversation, each man searching his own soul for a response.

Eventually, Britz spoke. "I wonder if it would be fair to say that the British would never have started the war if it wasn't for the Transvaal goldfields." Many men nodded their agreement. "So," said Fredericks, "you are telling me that it is the fault of the Transvaal that we are in this mess?"

This set up a to and fro of argument and counter-argument until an elderly Boer named Martinus Potgieter slammed his fist on the table and shouted, "Silence, manne. I know we are Freestaters, and I know it is easy to point fingers at the Transvaalers. After all, they were the ones who had something to gain from the war. But we need to think of a number of things. Firstly, we need to look at the reasons we went into the war. Sure, there was the question of the gold, but that was not the only thing in the mind of Oom Paul when he declared war. We trekked from the Cape in the 1830s to get rid of British rule and to live in freedom. It was God's will that some of us landed up in the Free State and others in the Transvaal, so it is not fair to blame the Transvaal. We all want freedom, and if we lose this war, we all know that we will return to the British yoke. None of us wants that, and that is what we are fighting to prevent. My beef is not against the Transvaalers; it is against the Cape Boers who did absolutely nothing to come to the aid of our volk in its hour of greatest need. We in the Free State knew all along we had little to gain materially from the war, but we signed a treaty with our brothers in the Transvaal, and when they were in need, we turned up to fight. So do not point fingers at our true brothers. Rather look to the *verraiers* (traitors)in the Cape who let their volk down."

Potgieter waited for the buzz of conversation to die down before continuing. "Secondly, let us consider the consequences of losing the war. Yes, I know we are still fighting with the commandos, but the reality is that the British will win out in the end. We all know that in the depths of our hearts. But when it is over, what will we do? How will we learn to live under British rule? What changes do we think will come, and how will we adapt to them? There are two paths, in my view. The first is to reject the British in every respect and to use every tactic to disrupt their ability to rule. This is the thinking of many of our leaders and is one of the reasons they are continuing the commando attacks. They understand the inevitable, but they are going to make it as difficult as they can for the British. This attitude will continue long after the war is over. If we cannot win the war, then lets at least win the peace. The opposite tactic is to try and work with the British to develop our country into something special, into a nation that is not isolated from the rest of the world, and that takes its rightful place on the world stage. The example of the Cape Boers is worth remembering. Yes, I know I cursed them for not supporting us and called them cowards and traitors, but the truth is they have done very well, have prospered under British rule. Perhaps the same will be true of us. Perhaps we, too, will benefit from their laws and institutions. Perhaps they will open opportunities to us we would never have enjoyed before."

The room again erupted into argument. There seemed to be no consensus on the best way to deal with the inevitable, and there were heated exchanges on both sides. Pride and nationalism ranged itself against compromise and collaboration until eventually Potgieter's voice boomed out. "Men, enough of this arguing and fighting. Let us all remember one thing, perhaps the most important thing of all. We are no longer citizens of the countries we originally came from, regardless of how long ago we came to this country. We are now and forever will be Men of Africa, Men of South Africa, whether we are Dutch, English, French, or German by ancestry. The past must be forgotten, and we need to go forward as South Africans, however that may look and however we may be ruled. We must stand tall together and face the new world in unity."

All heads nodded, and the room went quiet. Then a voice from the rear of the hut said: "What about the blacks?"

Later that day, Jeannot wrote to his father.

Letter from Jeannot to Edward Weinberg - Diyatalawa Camp - October 25th, 1900

Diyatalawa
October 25th, 1900

Dear Father

I received all your letters, except Mother's, which, if she wrote, I expect tomorrow morning. The draft arrived too, and I have had no bother with it. The Colonel simply credited me with GBP 10, and I draw GBP1or 2 from him at a time twice a week. GBP10 means 150 rupees in 'blikgeld' (tin money) as the Boers call it and will last me for a long time.

The photo is the best of the lot, and I am very pleased with it. You are all well taken, Bernard and Bertha less. Schlemiels will never make a good photo. They've always got to laugh or screw their faces into some 'mug' always comical. You look very well, and so does Mother. The baby, I suspect, has been crying, but Molla looks the most innocent and the sweetest of all. Max came out very well; only his collar is two sizes too large. Albert, although clad in a rather 'primitive' costume looks exactly like the little rogue he is.

On the whole, the photo is a very good one. I'll show it to Olivier as soon as I see him. I daresay you have received my photo.

I am passing my time pretty well lately. We have formed a cricket club, of which I am the captain. We played a match against the

Transvaal but were unlucky to lose the match by 17 runs. At present we are busy with a tennis club

When is this war going to end? It is sickening to hear the latest telegrams about the situation. There is no fighting going on, yet there is no sign of any negotiations or something indicating a speedy termination. You cannot imagine how most of us here feel. One day we hear this; the other day, we hear that. Yet neither has any significance.

Should the rumor that the refugees are allowed to return to the Transvaal be true, then we are doubtless not far distant from the day of our return home. But is it true? You wrote in your letter that by the time it reaches me, peace may be declared. I only mentioned this because one or two persons, and this afternoon dozens of people came to ask me for 'the good news.' This is a good sign that people are one and all craving to return home to recommence a peaceful life. There are only a few that would still maintain that the British have by no means won yet, although, however, they can't see their way clear to explain the possibility of our people winning. The chance of the latter is very small.

Heunis got a letter from his Father who said Heunis is to go back to Germany as soon as he can. He's sent an application to the Colonel to be released at Colombo and to be permitted to return to Germany without having to call on South Africa again.

This here is a wonderful country with a curious changing climate. One day it is cold, the other hot, the other raining, the other windy; the nights are all very cold.

Well, with many thanks for the draft, the letters and photo I remain with fondest love to Mother and the children and yourself.

Your dutiful son
Jeannot.

I have bought a few small elephants for the children (ebony).
Don't forget to send some newspapers.

Jeannot had purposely ensured that the letters he wrote home were not controversial or self-pitying. In the first place, he was aware of camp censorship, and he did not want to be earmarked as a troublemaker. But, more importantly, he understood that his letters were the only real news his family was receiving, and he did not want to alarm them in any way or make them worry about him more than they already were. So, wherever possible, he tried to remain positive and not give the family cause for concern. There would be plenty of time to fill in the details when the war ended.

Chapter 28 - Bloemfontein Camp I

Bloemfontein - October 25th, 1899 – Bertha

Elise did not return to Bloemfontein after the Michaelmas vacation. War had been declared on October 11th, and the family felt it was not appropriate to divide up the family in such troubled times. Erik decided to wait and see how the war might proceed, but when he learned that the Boers had laid siege to Kimberley on October 14th. Since Kimberley was only 100 miles from Bloemfontein, he was adamant that Elise would remain in Ladybrand.

Bertha was shattered. She loved Elise like a sister and missed her terribly. But she reasoned that it would not be a good thing to separate her from the family when everyone's future hung in the balance. Jeannot had already signed up and had recently ridden away with the Bloemfontein Commando. Bernard and Max were trying to persuade Papa and Mama to allow them to go too, so the war was taking its toll on the Weinberg family.

During the next year, Bertha and Elise wrote to each other every week, Bertha giving Elise news of what was happening at school and the hotel, and Elise describing life on the farm. Erik had joined up and gone to Natal to fight alongside General Botha. After the relief of Ladysmith, he returned to Schoonspruit for a short period and was then persuaded to join de Wet in his guerilla commando. He had not taken the Oath of Allegiance and felt free to continue the war in this manner. Elise and her family were, of course, very concerned about their father, and this became more evident the longer he was away. Bertha was able to share the news about Modder River and Magersfontein, the return of the boys to Bloemfontein, and the subsequent events that led to Jeannot being taken a prisoner of war.

Then the unthinkable happened.

Letter from Elise Schoeman to Bertha Weinberg December 9th, 1900

Bloemfontein Refugee Camp
December 9th, 1900

My dear sister Bertha

This is, without a doubt, the most painful letter I have ever written. You will notice from the address that I am back in Bloemfontein, although in very different circumstances from when I was last there. Let me tell you how I come to be here, and what has happened to me and the family.

As you know, after the defeat at Paardeberg, the burghers were ordered to sign an oath that they would not take up arms again against the British. My father was not at Paardeberg, but when he was later asked to sign the oath, he refused. The reason was he wanted to join the guerilla forces that Gen. de Wet was putting together, and to go on fighting for our freedom. He left home in June to go on commando with de Wet, and we have had no news from him since then. I do not know whether he is dead or alive, and we lived in fear of a rider arriving with news of his death.

So my mother and I were left to look after the farm and also to care for my little sister and brother. They were really too young to be of much help on the farm, but they did help wherever they could. I am a little older and was able to work with mother in the mielie fields. There has been no time for any school or studying, but I am hopeful that I will not have forgotten too much of what I learned in Bloemfontein when I was with you.

One day in November, riders did come, but they were not the kind we were hoping for, they were British soldiers, about fifteen of them with a sergeant and an officer. They burst into the kitchen when my mother was preparing our supper, and demanded to know where my father was. When mother told them she did not know, the sergeant punched her in the face, calling her a f.......g liar. Mother fell to the floor, but the sergeant picked her up and tied her to one of the kitchen chairs. He then started to ask her all sorts of questions about father - when did he leave, where did he go, who were his friends, which commando did he join, and so on? Every time mother said she did not know; he punched her in the face. By the time he was finished, she had two black eyes, a cut lip, and a massive bruise on her right cheek. The children had run to me and were sobbing in my apron. Then the sergeant called his corporal and said: "If she will not talk to me, maybe she will talk to you." The corporal gave a wicked grin - he had an evil, weasel face - untied mother and dragged her into the bedroom. There were sounds of clothes being torn, and then came a series of screams from mother, which broke our hearts. The children sobbed even harder, and the sergeant told me that if I did not shut them up, he would make all three of us go in and watch what was being done to mother.

After 20 minutes, they came back into the kitchen. Mother was black and blue, and her clothes were all torn - she could barely cover her nakedness. She was sobbing like I have never heard her sob before. The corporal said to the sergeant that she had told him nothing. At this stage, the officer stepped in and told the men they should switch to Plan B. We had no idea what this meant, but we were soon to find out. The soldiers tied us all up and sat us on the floor of the kitchen. They then proceeded to smash everything in the house - furniture, plates, cups, glasses, everything. They found our old family bible and tore it up, as well as all the little statues father had carved over all the years. Once they had finished destroying everything that we owned, they dragged us outside and forced us to watch as they set fire to the house. The house is made of wood, so it burned very quickly. Bertha, you cannot imagine the pain of watching the house you had lived in all your life going up in smoke in front of your eyes! It was heartbreaking to watch, and we all held each other and sobbed and sobbed. We knew how long it had taken father to build up our home to what it was, yet it took about an hour to destroy everything he had worked so hard to create.

But they were not finished, by a long way. Our small dog who had been out in the yard came running over to see what was going on. One of the soldiers picked up the poor creature and cut its throat in front of our eyes. The children screamed in protest, but they could do nothing - the poor thing just lay on the ground, blood pouring from its tiny throat. Then they went into the barn and brought out our milking cows and two horses, and shot them all on the spot. But still they were not done. They then lit torches and went out into the mielie fields and set fire to all the crops. The mielies were just approaching the ripening time, and they burned like matchsticks. Soon the whole farm was ablaze, with a huge column of smoke rising from the ruins of our crops.

This was the last straw for mother. She jumped to her feet, ran to the officer, and screamed at him. "Why us? Why us?" He pushed her away and shouted, "Now, you bastards will understand the consequences of your men not obeying the oath of allegiance." Then they loaded us into the back of wagons and took us from our home. I do not remember how long we traveled for, but we eventually arrived in Thaba Nchu around 7 pm. There were many other wagons like ours in Thaba Nchu, every one filled with Boer families, all looking anxious and bewildered. We were told to get out of the wagons and were led into an encampment where we were told we would be spending the night. They did not give us any food, but there was a water point in the encampment. None of us had been given any water since we left, and everyone was very thirsty. Mama helped us to find a place where we could cuddle up and sleep together. We had no beds or blankets, but fortunately, it was a warm night. We did not sleep very well, as you can imagine. They woke us at 6 am and gave us some very watery coffee and some rusks. These were a bit stale, but as we had not eaten since breakfast the previous day, we wolfed them down. At 7 am they put us back on the wagons, and we left Thaba Nchu - we were told we were going to Bloemfontein. My heart leapt because I thought I would have a chance to see you again, my dear sister. But sadly this was not to be. We arrived in the Bloemfontein area around lunchtime, but I soon realized that we were not heading for the town, but for a camp about two miles outside the town. When I saw the rows of tents, my heart sank. This was not the Bloemfontein I had grown to love - this was one of those camps that people talked about in soft and frightened tones.

We were offloaded and made to line up outside what looked like an office. Each family was called one at a time to go into the office, where they wrote down our names and ages and addresses and told us to go to another office to be allocated with our tent. Nobody told us anything about the camp and the regulations, and when Mama asked, she was told to be quiet and wait for instructions. We were allocated a tent together with a family called Minnaar from Winburg. There were four of us and five of them, making nine people in total. The tent was small and probably would have held five people comfortably, but we were going to have to make it work for nine of us. Mama and Mrs. Minnaar arranged how everyone should sleep. We had been given straw mattresses and two blankets each, but no other bedding. It was quite cramped, but we managed to find a spot for everyone. The four Minnaar children were slightly younger than the three of us - the youngest was only two - so the children did not take up too much space.

Bertha, all this happened three days ago, and this has been my first chance to write to you. Please try to help me - I don't know whether your father has any influence, but if he has, perhaps he can try to get us out. I am so miserable, and I miss you so much. I must go now since they are calling us for supper. Please write back to me.

With all my love
Your Sister
Elise

Bloemfontein - December 12th, 1900 – Bertha

Bertha was as shocked as she had ever been in her ten short years. She read and reread the letter, tears streaming down her face. Finally, she snatched up the letter and ran to the living room where her mother and father were relaxing after dinner. Fanni saw the distress on the girl's face.

"Bertha, what is it?" But Bertha could not talk, her body wracked with sobs. She handed the letter to her mother and ran to Spotty to hug him. Fanni read the letter slowly, the blood draining from her face. "Edward," she said, her voice trembling. "You'd better read this." Edward put down his newspaper and held out his hand for the letter. He read, and as he read, his face became solemn, and he shook his head frequently.

"Bertha, when did you receive this?" he asked.
"Today, Father. Just after supper."
"Have you spoken to anyone about it?"

"No, Father."
"Bertha, I want you to tell no-one about this letter, not the boys, not anyone in the hotel. Do you understand me?"
"Yes, Father."
"Bertha, I am going to do whatever I can to help Elise and her family. You must trust me on this. I am as sad and shocked as you are, and I cannot believe people could be so cruel. So I want you to leave it to me, and I will let you know when I have news. May I keep the letter for the time being?"
"Yes, Father. And, Father, I know Elise and her family will be so grateful if you can do anything to help them."
"Right," said Edward "Now go and take Spotty for a walk."

When she had left the room, Edward turned to Fanni. "I have heard rumors of this kind of thing, but when it is this close to you, it really strikes home. I was aware that the British were setting up refugee camps for people who had been displaced from their homes, but I did not realize that they were responsible for the displacement." Fanni nodded. "And the brutality! Rape, pillage, destruction of livestock and crops! Where will it end? Remember the words of Heine - 'Where they burn books, they will, in the end, burn people too.' This is an outrage, a crime perpetrated on the burghers and on humankind - it is despicable." "Is there anyone you can talk to?" inquired Fanni. "I am thinking," said Edward. "I did know a number of British officers who used to dine at the hotel, but they are no longer around. My guess is that I should try to get an audience with the mayor. Hopefully, he will have more information."

The next day, Edward went to the mayor's office and made an appointment to see him that afternoon. At 3 pm, he was ushered into Dr. Kellner's office.

"Mr. Weinberg. So good to see you. How can I be of help?"
Edward handed him the letter. "This is a letter my daughter Bertha received yesterday. It was written by Elise Schoeman, the young

girl from Ladybrand, who boarded with us at the hotel and attended Greenhill with Bertha. I would like you to read the letter before we speak." The mayor took the letter, put on his glasses, and began to read. He started to frown early on and shook his head on several occasions. When he had finished, he put the letter down, frowned, and looked at Edward.

"Well," he said. "This is very disquieting. I have been made aware that the British were resettling displaced persons in various camps. Still, I had no idea about the pain and suffering they were inflicting on the burghers, especially the women and children. It is shameful."

"I agree," said Edward. "How much do you know about the activities in the nearby camp that Elise is in?"

"Very little, I'm afraid. The British military is running the camp at present, and we civilians are not allowed to get involved."

"Are you able to get into the camp to inspect the conditions there?"

"No. Not at this stage. As I said, the military is playing it very close to the chest. But I will make inquiries about getting access."

"Good. I would also like to get visiting rights if possible. Also, if you could find out whether we can send food and medicine into the camp. I am sure these will be in short supply. You might also find out if they are accepting volunteers to assist with the refugees. I am sure that there will be plenty of locals willing to lend a hand."

"I am going to look into this right away, Mr. Weinberg." He handed the letter back and shook his head. "It was bad enough having to send our boys into battle; it's another thing to have our women and children brutalized and property destroyed. Leave this with me. I will get back to you."

The men shook hands, and Edward departed.

Back at the hotel, he told Fanni what had transpired. She was encouraged that the mayor was going to get involved, and she resolved to set up a women's group to rally round and support the camp inmates in whatever way they were allowed.

The next day, Bertha wrote back to Elise

Letter from Bertha Weinberg to Elise Schoeman - December 14th, 1900

Royal Hotel
December 14th, 1900

My dearest sister Elise

I was so shocked to receive your letter. I had no idea that this sort of thing was going on, and for you to be a victim is more than I can bear. Oh, you poor, poor thing. What a horrible experience! Any your poor Mama - what she has had to put up with. My heart is breaking for you, and I feel so helpless sitting here so close to you but unable to do anything.

I showed the letter to Father and Mama, and they were as horrified as I was. Father went to see the mayor and showed him the letter, and he has promised to look into the situation and try to do what he can to help. He is a good man, and I know he will do whatever he can to help.

I have been looking in the newspapers to see where there are other similar camps. And there are lots and lots. From Chrissiesmeer in the eastern Transvaal to Matjiesfontein in the southern Cape, and Vryburg, in the northern Cape to Pinetown in Natal. The paper says there are about 60 camps in total. Who could have believed that the British could do such a thing? They seem so civilized and well behaved. Obviously, they are not as nice as they look. How I wish I could come and visit you and get you away from that dreadful place. Father has asked the mayor to find out whether the people in Bloemfontein can send food and medicine, and come and visit. The mayor is going to find out. Mama is putting together a group of women volunteers to support all of you, and I will be helping her with that. Hopefully, we can bring you lots of things that will make life more bearable. It must be terrible not to have any news of your Father. I do hope he is well and safe. He is a strong man, and I am sure he will look after himself well. How are the young ones doing? In many respects, it must be a bit easier for them because they don't really understand what is going on, but for you and your Mama, it must be very frightening. Oh, I feel so useless not being able to help or do something. I do hope the mayor can sort something out so I will be able to come and see you.

Please write to me often, and I will write to you. I send you hugs and kisses, and to all your family as well.

I am your dear friend!
Lots of love
Bertha

Bertha decided to send a copy of Elise's letter to Jeannot in Ceylon, to let him and his fellow prisoners know what was going on back home. She felt sure that there would be outrage when the men learned of the treatment of their women and children, and she hoped they could bring some pressure to bear on the British where they were being held.

Elise and Bertha continued to exchange letters over the next few months. Conditions in the camp were deteriorating as more and more people were crowded in. Disease was becoming a real problem, and the lack of medical supplies reached critical proportions. Visits from civilians were not permitted before mid-1901, and as for food parcels sent to the camp, it was a matter of good fortune whether or not they ultimately made it to the inmates. In June 1901, Elise wrote another long letter to Bertha.

Letter from Elise Schoeman to Bertha Weinberg – June 28, 1901

Bloemfontein Refugee Camp
June 28th, 1901

My dearest sister Bertha

Thank you so much for your letter that I received last week. Hearing from you gives me such hope that there are still people who care.

I have terrible news to tell you. We lost little Marie yesterday from typhus. She has been losing weight for some months now, and three weeks ago, she developed a high fever with nausea and vomiting. We wanted to take her to the hospital, but, in the camp, the hospital is known 'The Tent of Death' because nobody who goes in there ever seems to come out. Mama and I nursed her day and night, trying to get her to eat some bread when it was available and some mielie porridge, but more often than not, she would vomit it back. She became very thin, and her fever would not go down. So eventually, Mama took her in her arms, and we went to see the nurse, Sister Kennedy, who is an angel. She examined Marie and confirmed that she had typhus, but she had no medicine to give her, not even something to stop the nausea and vomiting. Marie was wasting away before our eyes, and we could do nothing to heal her other than to pray. You may have seen the photograph in the newspaper of little Lizzie van Zyl who died last month. She died from illness and malnutrition and must have weighed less than fifty pounds when she died. I have never seen anything like it, Bertha. I could put my fingers around the top of her arms; she was so thin! We were so worried that the same was going to happen to Marie. We watch the two boys every day to see if they are showing the same signs as Marie, and, praise God, they seem to be healthy.

I have never known a death in my family other than my grandparents, but this is so different. This is my little sister. When I look at the authorities who run this camp, I wonder how they can sleep at night when they see how we are suffering. I am sure it is not all their fault. They are not being given enough food and medicine for us, and there is probably nothing they can do. But someone has to be responsible, and we can only hope that one day there will be justice. Sometimes we think that they are being cruel to us as payment for the attacks that our commandos are making on the British.

Conditions in the camp are getting worse and worse. Nobody has received any new clothes since we got here, and everyone is in rags. Our tents do not have any floors, so when it rains, the water comes in under the tent flaps, and everything gets soaked. When we arrived, it was summer, and we didn't really need the two blankets they gave us. But now that it is winter, we are freezing. They will not give us any more blankets, so we wear all our clothes in bed to stay warm, and we huddle up together to try to stay warm.

We have been issued ration cards, and we stand in line for food. We got meat (sometimes), sugar, mealie meal, condensed milk. The meat when we get it is of very poor quality, and it often so frozen that it does not even thaw out when we cook it. Frequently the mealie meal has weevils and other goggas ("insects") in it, which is disgusting. We carefully pick out the goggas before we make our porridge. There have also been rumors about people finding ground glass in the mealies. We have not experienced this, but if it is true, it is too horrible to think about.

We do not have a stove, so we use a paraffin tin outside the tent, with holes in the sides and irons to hold pots. There is no firewood, and all the women have to scavenge the veld for green bushes and mule dung to make fires. Water is brought from a river by cart, and every morning we stand in line to fill our buckets - we are always short of water.

But the biggest fear is disease. There is no proper hospital and not enough medicine. When Marie was in the hospital, I went to visit her, and I can see why people do not want to go there. Oh, the suffering of the inmates! The wards are dirty and untidy. It is very noisy as the staff stamp about in their boots. The patients are not separated by sex, age, or ailment, so an old woman with diarrhea can be lying next to a young boy with typhus - no wonder diseases are spreading so rapidly! The beds are full of goggas, and the inmates spend a lot of time trying to kill them and scratch the bite marks. But the most pitiful are the small children who never get enough food and cannot see their mothers but once a week and then only for 5 minutes. They are continually crying for more food, more blankets, and a kind word. It is quite pitiful to see it. But there is one good thing to report.

An angel has been visiting the camp. She is an English woman called Miss Emily Hobhouse, and she has come to see for herself how bad things are in our camp. People have often heard her arguing with the authorities about conditions - all the things we know about - food, medicine, water, blankets, the hospital - nothing escapes her gaze. We all pray to God that she will be heard by the people in power when she gets back to England. She has made one recommendation that the women are obeying. The water we get is from the Modder River and is not very good. Miss Hobhouse insists that everyone boil their water first before they drink it so that all the germs can be driven out. I wish we had known about this sooner because we have noticed that fewer people are getting diarrhea since we started boiling the water. She is wonderful, and I hope she will be able to do something to improve the conditions around here.

Please give my fondest wishes to your Father and Mother and the boys. And I hope things are not going too badly with Jeannot in Ceylon - you should know that there is a song we sing here in the camp in remembrance of our boys over there - it is called "Zij geniet die blouwe bergen op die skepe na Ceylon." — "They enjoy the blue mountains on the ships to Ceylon."

Your loving sister
Elise

Author's note: I have included this photo of Lizzie van Zyl to give readers an idea of the enormity of the cruelty in the camps.

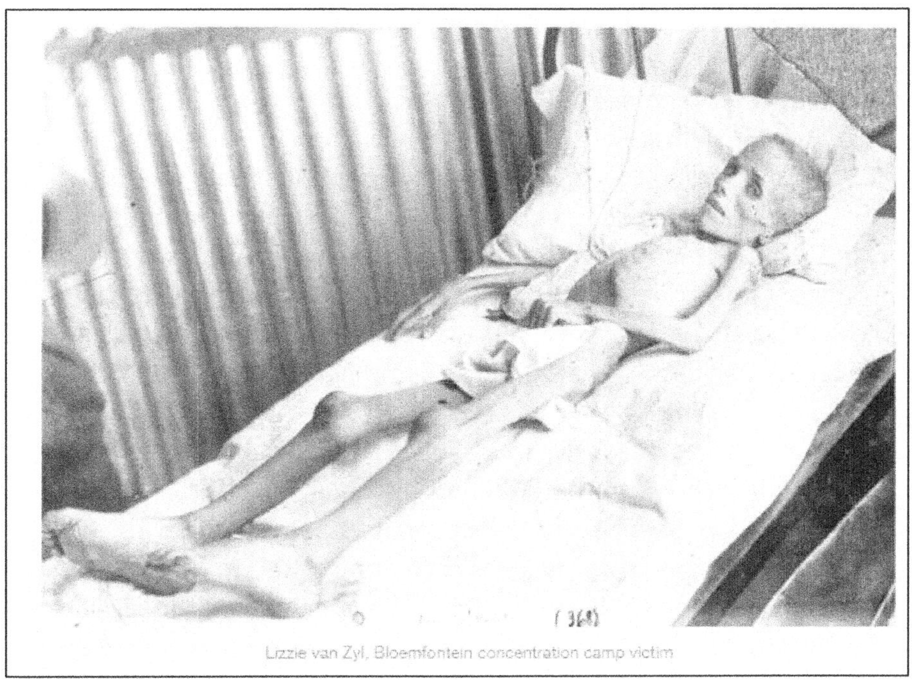

Lizzie van Zyl, Bloemfontein concentration camp victim

Bertha was horrified at the contents of the letter, especially the death of Marie. For if Marie could die, so could Elise, and her Mama and brothers. It was all too much for a young girl to bear. She went sobbing to her parents, gave them the letter, and ran to her mother for comfort, sobbing all the time. Edward read the letter with a stern expression, shaking his head in disbelief. "It is getting worse and worse." he remarked to Fanni. "The little girl Marie has died from typhus, and it seems any illness that occurs becomes rampant. I know of the good works of Miss Hobhouse that Elise refers to. I can only hope more can be done for these poor wretches." Fanni was too overcome to speak, but she managed to say that she hoped the food parcels that they had sent were getting through, although she doubted it.

That night, Bertha copied the letter carefully and sent it to Jeannot.

Chapter 29 - Diyatalawa 2

Diyatalawa - November 1900 - Jeannot

He read and reread the letter Bertha had sent, first with a sense of disbelief, then dismay, then downright anger. He had heard rumors of the mistreatment of civilian prisoners, but this was as close to home as if a member of his own family was suffering the indignity and cruelty of the camps. He put the letter in his locker, lit a cigar, and began to walk alone around the camp perimeter.

It was difficult to reconcile in his mind the chasm between the British fighting man on the field and his behavior off it. In battle, the British had been a worthy adversary, conversant with and observant of the rules of war, brave yet merciful, tough yet fair, aggressive yet not ruthless. But the behavior towards the civilian population, specifically targeting women and children, seemed incongruous. Could these possibly be the same people whom he had met on the battlefield, who showed appreciation for the Boers taking water to the wounded, who saluted them when released at Magersfontein? How could these same people commit such atrocious acts off the field of battle against unarmed non-combatants? And what of the willful and unrelenting destruction of property? This was not looting, which would have been bad enough. This was punitive, aimed at crippling the nation and condemning it to a future of hardship and need. This could not be how things were supposed to work - to be brave and honest on the field, yet cowardly and pitiless off it.

Jeannot was learning the lesson of war. Not warfare, but war. He well understood the rules of warfare, but war is a different matter. The battlefield is only a part of the overall picture, a picture that has to be viewed in the context of power and money. Wars are not fought for the benefit of the soldier or the general; they are fought for the politicians and the financiers. To understand the anomaly Jeannot was wrestling with, he would need to understand this distinction. And the plight of the Boer women and children in the camps was the first lesson in this education of disillusionment. Little did he know his own world was about to be turned upside down.

Letter from Jeannot to Edward Weinberg - Diyatalawa Camp - November 27th, 1900

Diyatalawa Camp
November 27th, 1900

Dear Father

This mail has not brought me any letters from you. This is the first time since I am here that I am without letters whatever. Next mail will probably bring me some.

I am quite well and pass my time in some way or another. I feel very sad, sometimes. It will be a great relief to set foot on South African soil again. But when will that be? It does not seem that the war will terminate soon. On the contrary, the Boers are at present, taking advantage of the British, and a few engagements decided in their favor encourages them very much. I have given up hope for a win for the Boers, yet it is rather amusing or rather sad to hear of the wanton destruction of so much property and of the many insignificant skirmishes which still take place so frequently.

I am sure you know that Bertha has written to me about Elise and what has been going on with the camps and the plundering. It is shameful, and I cannot believe that these are the same brave men we met on the battlefield. How can they do things like this to innocent women and children? Mark my word, there is going to be a big backlash. Lots of prisoners here have received similar information, and the mood is very bad. I suspect a group will get together to send a complaint to the authorities before long.

Oom Paul is in Europe, presumably begging intervention. I am sure he is, or if he is not yet, he will be the subject of ridicule for the versatile caricaturists on the Continent. Which of the powers is going to risk a European war for the sake of the two petty Republics? There are undoubtedly thousands of sympathizers ready to receive Oom Paul and help our people in some way or other, but still, they cannot pull them from out of the fire. Our people have lost, and miracles are things of the past. The Lord above does not seem to heed the prayers of these people, and many of them are beginning to doubt there really is a God in Heaven, but they never think that they are losing because the Lord is punishing them for their sins.

We shall not return to South Africa before next year. The names of the foreigners have been taken down. They put me down as Russian – I wonder where they got this information. There is some talk that all foreigners will be sent home to Germany, Holland, etc. That'll be a fine joke if they send me to Russia. Do you think I should go? I don't, and if the above rumor is true, by God I'll tell them the truth and that I am an OFS burgher and if they want to send me to Russia which is only my birthplace, I'll ask them to be so kind as to send me back again to Africa.

I am sending you a Christmas card. We cannot look forward to a very pleasant Christmas down here.

I hope Mother is well and also the children. Business is, in all probability, still going strong. You cannot imagine how I feel when I come to think of how useful I could have been to you during the time you were so busy. One and a half years have already been wasted through this horrible war and who knows how long it will still last. You know, old Boning was perfectly right – he said that this war would last 18 months and he was right.

Well, with fondest love to Mother, the children, and yourself.

I remain
Your dutiful son
Jeannot

At the time of writing this letter, the fate of the 'foreigners' was not yet known. By the time he wrote his last letter from Diyatalawa, it was clear he was being sent to a new camp......Ragama.

Letter from Jeannot to Fanni Weinberg - Diyatalawa Camp - December 31st, 1900

Diyatalawa Camp
December 31st, 1900

Dear Mother
I believe it is some time since my last letter, and I beg of you to forgive me for what seems like neglect on my part. I wrote to Bernard and Father, and therefore you have not been without news from me. To write a letter is a very difficult job here because there is nothing to write about. News is scarce, and that which is not scarce is not news at all. My health is excellent, although I cannot say I have put on much fat here.

All the foreigners have been ordered to have their luggage ready by Tuesday morning, and the men here expect to leave for Ragama (a new camp not far from Colombo) on Friday, 4th prox.

I don't know how it was managed, but my name importantly figures among the 'Russians.' I made my application to remain here, but it has not met with any success. I will know tomorrow for sure if I am going or not. I would not mind to go if some of my friends came with, but they are all Afrikaners. The Germans and Hollanders I met here are, with few exceptions, a most disreputable lot. They are without exaggeration the 'scum of the scum,' and it is my unfortunate lot to have to mix with them now that I have avoided them since our arrival here. The couple of Frenchmen who are here present a great contrast to the rest. There are some with very little education, but they know at least how to behave themselves, and the better ones are real gentlemen. If I have to go to Ragama, I shall try my best to keep with them.

There must have been great excitement in Bloemfontein lately on account of the Boers crossing into the Colony. This latest move of the Boers may develop into a serious 'business.' I only wish the war would near its end and that we might return to our homes.
Have we had any more news about Elise and the camps? It is a tragedy what is happening, and I hope the British know how much this has angered the Boers. I fear for their safety once these men are released.

The mail came in the other day. I got some papers up to November 21, which Bernard sent me but strange to say no letters have yet been delivered to me. I noticed that Father's advertisement has been withdrawn from The Post since the 24th. I hope he has received his license.

Jan 3rd. My application failed, and I have to go. The Colonel told me he could not exclude my name from the list. We are leaving for Ragama on Monday the 9th. The boat with the Boer prisoners should have arrived at Colombo today. The Governor is expected here on a tour of inspection. The people make such a noise that one can scarcely write. We passed the New Year without any extra celebration or ceremony. It was a miserable day. In the evening, the Uitlanders kicked up a frightful row in their hut, probably a protest against being transferred to Ragama. Well, I cannot be a part of that - if they want to send me to Ragama, well and good. One camp is as bad as another when you are a prisoner, and I long for the day I can return to the Free State and to Bloemfontein.

Well, with fondest love to Father, the children, and yourself.

I remain
Your loving son
Jeannot

Diyatalawa – 1901 – Jeannot

As he mentioned in his letter to his Father, Jeannot's letter from Bertha regarding the camps was not unique. Many other prisoners had received similar news. It became clear that the camps were not isolated examples, that they were widespread, and impacted all areas in the two Boer republics. The effect on the men at Diyatalawa was significant. Not all shared Jeannot's quandary about the difference between behavior on and off the field, but all were gripped with the anger and hatred the news engendered. And then there was the sense of hopelessness. Here they were, thousands of miles from home, incarcerated in a strange country, cut off from their loved ones and without the means to right this egregious wrong. Hopelessness led to frustration, frustration to suppressed fury, suppressed fury to the need to do something positive to make their anger understood. And so it was that a committee was set up under the aegis of the officers in the camp to assemble all the information available from the letters, and to craft these into a dossier of evidence that would form the basis of a means to express their disgust and dismay.

By July, the committee felt it had assembled sufficient evidence to draft a letter of protest to St. John Broderick, Secretary of State for War in the British Government. Although Jeannot had left Diyatalawa for Ragama some six months previously, news of the letter filtered through to Ragama, and it was wholeheartedly supported.

Diyatalawa Camp - Letter from Boer Officers to British Secretary of State for War - July 25th, 1901

Diyatalawa Camp, 25 July 1901

To the Right Honorable St. John Broderick

Right Honorable Sir

We, the undersigned officers of the burgher forces of the Orange Free State and the South African Republic, at present prisoners-of-war at Diyatalawa, Ceylon, wish to bring the following to your notice.

A number of facts, having reference to the treatment of our relatives, being non-combatants, whom your military forces have been lately busy in collecting and removing to certain camps in the two aforementioned states, as well as in The Cape Colony and Natal, and whom they are perhaps still collecting. Declarations have been made by men in this camp, which they are prepared to swear to, regarding the ill-treatment to which they and their families have been subjected. The facts, as appearing from a large number of letters received in this camp from friends and relatives in South Africa, of which letters translated extracts are hereunto annexed, are as follows:

Women and children, as well as old men unfit for military service, and old women in the Free State and the South African Republic, have been removed from their dwellings where they have been left by us, and where they were living comparatively at their ease, and could have gone on living, provided their private property had not been taken from them in disregard of the laws observed by civilized nations in warfare

In some cases, very insufficient provision was made, and in some cases, none whatever, for the removal of these women and children to the camps, and consequently those poor victims had to suffer great privations

In some cases, large numbers of women and children arrived at camps, where no provision at all had been made for their reception. In other cases, women with large families remained for days exposed to the inclement weather of the South African winter

By order of your military authorities, clothes and bedding found in dwellings from which women and children had just been removed, or which they were on the point of leaving, have been maliciously destroyed, and as in the camps such articles were not provided, or in only insufficient quantities, our women and children were compelled, in several cases, to go barefooted and, in some cases, completely naked.

On account of the privations and exposure suffered, hundreds and again hundreds have succumbed to the first attack of disease, which was reigning so generally in the camps, which latter were, even in the most favorable circumstances, unfit for such large numbers of persons, principally on account of want of sufficient water and fuel.

The declarations referred to heretofore need not be enumerated; they speak for themselves and are found in the annexure to this letter [not included here]

We are sorry to state that the information which we have received, after same has undergone strong censorship, and which we have the honor now to submit to you, as well as the declarations of men within our midst, have considerable increased the existing race hatred. We cannot believe that it could possibly be your intention to completely exterminate our race, and therefore we wish, in the interests of future relationships between the Africanders and the British in South Africa, to protest most solemnly against the transgressions of the rules of warfare between civilized nations and to request that you observe these. In the matter of the women and children in the camps, we scarcely know what to suggest. As they have been deprived of all their earthly possessions, and in most cases, even their habitations have been destroyed, we cannot ask you to let them go back to what was once their homes. What we demand, however, considering that, according to letters received here, whole families have died out, is that the worst camps be immediately removed to clean and more suitable places; that better food, more clothes, and other necessary articles be provided, and that, in general, the circumstances be made more bearable for these poor unfortunates in the camps.

Lastly, we cannot but assure Your Honor, that the tortures to which those beloved by us have been subjected to in South Africa, have only strengthened us in the determination not to take any oath of allegiance to the throne of Great Britain, as long as a single commando of our compatriots is still in the field, neither will we recommend any of our men to take such an oath.

We have the honor to remain
Honorable Sir

[a list of signatures of senior officers in Diyatalawa Camp]

The letter came at an opportune time. Voices were beginning to be raised in the British parliament, and Emily Hobhouse was completing her tour of several of the camps. There was no evidence that the petition directly impacted the conditions in the camps. However, it is likely that the fact that criticism was being received from several quarters eventually encouraged the British Government to take action.

On 14 June, speaking at a dinner party of the National Reform Union in England, Sir Henry Campbell-Bannerman, leader of the Liberal opposition, observed that the war in South Africa was being carried on by methods of barbarism.

On 17 June, MP David Lloyd-George in England condemned the concentration camps and the horrors inflicted on women and children in the camps in South Africa. He warned, "A barrier of dead children's bodies will rise between the British and Boer races in South Africa."

On 18 June, Emily Hobhouse's report on concentration camps appeared under the title, "To the S.A. Distress Fund, Report of a visit to the camps of women and children in the Cape and Orange River Colonies." Summarizing the reasons for the high fatality rate, she wrote, "Numbers crowded into small tents: some sick, some dying, occasionally a dead one among them; scanty rations dealt out raw; lack of fuel to cook them; lack of water for drinking, for cooking, for washing; lack of soap, brushes and other instruments of personal cleanliness; lack of bedding or beds to keep the body off the bare earth; lack of clothing for warmth and in many cases for decency ..." She concluded that the whole system was cruel and should be abolished.

On 26 June, Lord Kitchener sent a telegram to Milner: "I fear there is little doubt the war will now go on for considerable time unless stronger measures are taken ... Under the circumstances, I strongly urge sending away wives and families and settling them somewhere else. Some such unexpected measure on our part is, in my opinion, essential to bring the war to a rapid end."

On 16 July, The British Colonial Office announced the appointment of a Ladies Commission (known as the Fawcett Commission) to investigate the concentration camps in South Africa. The commission, whose members were reputed to be impartial, is made up as follows: Chairlady Mrs. Millicent G. Fawcett, who had recently criticized Emily Hobhouse in the Westminster Gazette; Dr. Jane Waterson, daughter of a British general, who had recently written against "the hysterical whining going on in England" while "we feed and pamper people who had not even the grace to say thank you for the care bestowed on them"; Lady Anne Knox, wife of Gen. Knox, who was presently serving in South Africa; Nursing sister Katherine Brereton, who had served in a Yeomanry Hospital in South Africa; Miss Lucy Deane, a government factory inspector on child welfare; Dr the Hon Ella Scarlett, a medical doctor. [*Author's note: hardly an impartial commission*!]

While it is probable that the British government expected the Fawcett Commission to produce a report that could be used to fend off criticism, in the end, it confirmed everything that Emily Hobhouse had said. Indeed, if anything, the Commission's recommendations went even further. The Commission insisted that rations should be increased and that additional nurses be sent out immediately, and included a long list of other practical measures designed to improve conditions in the camp. Millicent

Fawcett was quite blunt in expressing her opinion that much of the catastrophe was owed to a simple failure to observe elementary rules of hygiene.

In November 1901, the Colonial Secretary Joseph Chamberlain ordered Alfred Milner to ensure that "all possible steps are being taken to reduce the rate of mortality." The civil authority took over the running of the camps from Kitchener and the British command. By February 1902, the annual death-rate in the concentration camps for white inmates dropped to 6.9 percent and eventually to 2 percent. However, by then, the damage had been done. A report after the war concluded that 27,927 Boers (of whom 24,074 [50 percent of the Boer child population] were children under 16) had died of starvation, disease, and exposure in the concentration camps. In all, about one in four (25 percent) of the Boer inmates, mostly children, died.

Gen. French had been correct in his belief that the camps would be remembered long after peace was made, and would influence the relationship between British and Boers for a long time. The resentment the camps caused was not something the Boers could quickly forget, nor was it something they wanted to forget. It was a rare brand of cruelty that seemed to permeate how Britain dealt with its colonials who rebelled. The example of India was a case in point, where the British had used extreme measures during the Indian Rebellion of 1857. South Africa, too, seethed under the yoke, and this was a feeling that would plague Anglo-Afrikaner relations well into the future.

Chapter 30 – Ragama

Letter from Jeannot Weinberg to Edward Weinberg - Ragama Camp -February 3rd, 1901

Ragama Camp
February 3rd, 1901

Dear Father

I have not had any letters since one date, September 12, 1900. I expect some next week as the mail has already arrived. I am anxiously waiting for the result of your settlement with Bernard. I don't know why, but I have a presentiment that Bernard has not turned up. I trust, however, that my suspicion is unfounded. I sincerely hope that you are all in the best of health as I am just now.

This place is very hot. During the day, the heat is very great, but the mornings and evenings are very nice and cool. Van de Wits is here and wants to be remembered to you. Heunis is still doing well and greets you well. Life is as bad here as anywhere else. I suppose when one is a prisoner in a palace or in a common house, it makes no difference. Oh, how happy I will be the day I get my freedom back again. Truly one does not conceive what freedom means until one becomes a prisoner like we all here are. Just fancy another couple of months, and I will be a year in captivity. Oh, it is terrible to think of it. A whole year of one's life wasted, which is only very short. Life would not be so bad to me under the conditions if only I knew that you are all well. But as it is, I am always in uncertainty and anxiety.

I thought the other day that it would be better if Mother and the younger children were away from Bloemfontein. Somewhere at

East London or so because I am rather uncertain about the fate of the town. Foodstuffs will become very scarce soon and certainly very expensive, and, in their case, it is always better to be out of the place unless already provided for any contingency. This war will not end soon, oh us! I don't think so anymore. There is no hope for settlement between the Boers and the British any more. The Boers do not trust them anymore, and they are not to blame. We will certainly remain here for months and months to come.

All the prisoners who are still in Africa will soon be shipped to India or Australia. The reason for this measure is obvious. I wish they would send the foreign prisoners of war to Europe. I would prefer to work for my living in Europe to this miserable life.

I have finished my shorthand studies and am practicing rapidity now. I am improving my French and German also, in fact. My German is awful. But we will see in a few months. Thus you will see that I am not exactly wasting my time here.

I hope you have received my letters with the request for money. If you cannot send the money, though, you might ask Abe to send me some. He seems to be flush with money, according to his letters. I had a letter from Barendz; lately, He says he is going to Bloemfontein to visit you. I don't think Bloemfontein is the ideal place for a holiday just now; thus, Barendz poor chap won't enjoy himself very much I am afraid. Passover is near and no matzos. I am becoming a regular heathen, all this because of the British.

My love and kisses to Mother, Bertha, Molla, and the children, with beloved faith from your son.

Jeannot

Bloemfontein - January, 1901 – Edward

Edward was a man in a quandary. He was loyal to the cause of the Boer Republics but secretly wished that the war would have ended after the surrender of Pretoria. This would have meant the return of Jeannot from POW camp, and the resumption of a normal, peaceful life. This was not, however, how things played out. The refusal of many Boers to honor the oath and the subsequent guerilla warfare had caused the war to drag on indefinitely. It was impossible to predict when the British would find a way to bring the Boers to heel. Already they had tried the scorched earth policy and the cruel concentration camp system, but neither seemed to have dampened the resolve of the Boers. It was only a matter of time before new, and more drastic measures were introduced by Kitchener. And this is what concerned him.

Bloemfontein had been relatively calm and uneventful the previous six months. The hotel was doing well, and the children resumed their schooling and helped Edward with tasks around the hotel. But Edward was continually plagued by the possibility that, when Kitchener finally tired of chasing the elusive Boers around the veld, he would seek some vengeance against the townsfolk. And this would spell trouble for the burghers of Bloemfontein and Pretoria in particular, these two towns being the capitals of their territories. Edward was further concerned that there might be reprisals against the Jews. Nothing had been done to date, but who knew with Kitchener? There seemed to be no end to his brutality.

After wrestling with the issue for several months, and after lengthy discussions with Fanni, a decision was finally reached to leave the country, at least until peace was declared and things returned completely to normal. They mulled over the most appropriate places to go: Germany, Belgium, England. Eventually, the decision was made to seek refuge in England. Even though it may have seemed unusual to move into the bosom of the enemy, there were practical considerations that made it the most suitable choice. English had become the children's first language. While the older ones still spoke some German and French, the younger ones spoke only English and Afrikaans, the latter being useless outside of South Africa. Considerations of schooling and assimilation were foremost in their minds, and eventually, it was with great reluctance that the family made preparations to leave Bloemfontein and take ship to England. Edward decided not to close the hotel. He had sufficient confidence in van der Horst to look after the management of everyday matters; Chef was more than capable of running the kitchen and the bar, and, once a rooms manageress had been found to take over Fanni's chores, Edward felt comfortable that the hotel would continue to be run competently in his absence.

So it was that in January 1901, the Weinberg family headed for Cape Town to take ship to England. They booked a one-way passage, not knowing how long the war might continue. It was a hard decision, but one that Edward and Fanni believed to be the most advantageous to the family.

Letter from Jeannot Weinberg to Edward Weinberg - Ragama Camp -March 13th, 1901

Ragama Camp
March 13th, 1901

Dear Father

This is my second letter to you, which I am writing since receipt of your cablegram. I had a note from Henry Orkin, and he says that he cannot understand how it is that I am not writing to you often enough. This seems rather strange to me because I can assure you that I have never missed a mail. The letters must be lying somewhere in South Africa. I hope to get news from you by the beginning of next month.

On what boat did you come over? How did the children like the trip, and did they suffer much from seasickness? I trust not. How is the climate in England just at present? It must be cold there. According to the French papers to hand, the winter seems to be very severe in France. Have you made up your mind already about your ultimate residence? What has been done with Spotty? Did you take him with, or is he with Bernard? Poor little thing.

It is very hot here. You cannot imagine what it is like. We are situated near the equator. There this heat is only natural. I have lost my appetite. It is so hot that I cannot eat. I am not the only one who suffers from this heat. Leirio and many others, usually healthy chaps, look bad and thin. Up to the present time, there have been only 11 patients in the hospital. But I am positive there will be many more there before long.

The Hollanders are continually sending us 'Liebesgaben.' The other day we had 50 cigars each and then again 15 each, and White Jacket, etc. Truly they are the only people who have shown signs of sympathy with the wretched prisoners of war. The Germans brag a lot and do little. The French ditto. Whenever the Germans sent something, it is expressly for Germans. I always profit by the distribution, but still, I do not think that nice. The Germans are very cross with their Kaiser. Really, they don't know how to defend him anymore. There is no excuse for his recent self-advertisement.

I am very glad that you are out of South Africa. The worst has only started now. Oom Paul knew what he announced when he said he would 'stagger humanity.' In fact, he has. The situation in South Africa is a puzzle. If the Colonials have not risen, then there is not much chance for the Boers. But if they did or will rise, then the game is up for the British. The latter has again suffered two defeats lately. Col. Pilcher on the one side and Smith Dorrien on the other have not had it all their own way. Trains have been wrecked all over our country, guns and horses captured, and the general outlook is very bad for the British. Why will they not try and come to a sort of settlement? At this rate, the war will last for years – although Kitchener has things under his control.

The foreign powers ought to come together and pass a law that prisoners of war should not be kept longer than one year in captivity. Really this would be fair and nothing more. Because it seems we shall not return to the OFS so very soon although rumors are rife and reports that an armistice has been suggested and that peace negotiations are on. I am long enough from home now, and it seems to me we will not get away very soon.

When you write, please mention all about the conditions of the agreement with Bernard and about Bernard's business. Where is it situated? What did you do with the furniture and the pony and the cows and calves, etc.? Bernard sent me a postcard dated December 27th, but he does not mention anything else besides that you were leaving for Cape Town.

What about my release? I cannot understand your mention in your cablegram re the above. I have made up my mind to stick here for another year and, therefore, you will understand the idea of regaining my liberty before that time is not altogether unpleasant to me. May it but turn out into a fact! I shall be glad to know to which address I have to write in future. I had a letter from Berwitz. He seems to have had a fine time at Gerson's. He did not fight and has not lost anything by it.

Best love to Mother, Bertha, Max, Molla, Albert, and Louis. They must all write if well. Kind regards also to Mrs. Assersohn and family. Leionio and de Witz wish to be remembered to you too. Graf Rothkirch! Do you know him? He is also in our camp.

Well, accept my fond love and wishes for a pleasant sojourn.
Your loving son
Jeannot.

Ps. Max must not forget to send me all sorts of papers

You will be able to meet Graf Sternberg and Dr. Proksch and Lachmann in Germany.

Onboard ship - Cape Town to London - February 1901 - Edward

The fact that Edward had decided to remove his family from South Africa until the end of hostilities had an unexpected benefit for Jeannot. It resulted in his early release from POW camp. On the ship to Europe, Edward chanced to meet a delegation from the Cape who were en route to discuss South African affairs with the Colonial Secretary, Joseph Chamberlain. These men included a Maj. Richard Lewis, who had been a member of Lord Roberts' staff in Cape Town. Lewis and Edward spent many hours on board discussing the war and its possible aftermath. The topic of Jeannot arose during one of their earlier conversations.

"Edward, you told me you have eight children, but I seem to have only been introduced to seven. Who is the eight child?
"Hardly a child, Richard, he is twenty going on twenty-one and is in a POW camp in Ceylon. Ragama, to be exact."
"Was he a combatant?"
"Most decidedly. He fought at Modder River, Magersfontein, and Paardekraal. He managed to slip away before Cronje's surrender."
"So how does he now come to be a POW?"

Edward told him the story of the circumstances surrounding Jeannot's arrest and sentencing. Lewis raised his eyebrows when the incident with French was discussed, as he was well known to Lewis, and he made a mental note to talk to the General when he next saw him. Edward also told him of the unfair treatment he had received, being classified as Russian and moved to a camp for Uitlanders.

"But," asked Lewis, "did he take the Oath of Allegiance?"
"Indeed, he did," replied Edward. "But that did not mean he was treated as a non-combatant. Rather the court figured that his actions violated the Oath and that he should be regarded again as a combatant. Good thing, really. He could have been hanged for treason if they had tried him as a civilian."
"Not so," retorted Lewis. "If someone were to take the Oath, then he cannot be tried for seditious acts committed prior to the Oath. The Oath, like baptism, washes away past sins."
"Well, the events that led to his arrest all occurred before he took the Oath," replied Edward.
"Then they had no right to court-martial him or take him POW. There has been a miscarriage of justice here."
"And what can we do about it?" inquired Edward.
"As soon as we land, I shall take the matter up with the authorities and make sure that this wrong is rectified."
"That would be most helpful. I am in your debt," said Edward.
"On the contrary, Edward, it is we who are in his debt. He has been incorrectly incarcerated, and we must do whatever we can to get it put right. Where will you be staying in London so I can get hold of you?"

The men exchanged addresses, and nothing more was said about it for the rest of the voyage.

The family settled into rooms in Finsbury Square in London and began to become familiar with the city and its charm and beauty. A month went by since they landed in England, and no word had been heard from Maj. Lewis. Then, early in April, a telegram arrived for Edward. It was from Richard Lewis.

"Confirm release Jeannot Weinberg from Ragama Camp effective March 25th, 1901. Send money for transportation to Postmaster, Central Post Office, 10 McCallum Rd, Colombo."

Jeannot was to be set free! For the Weinbergs the war was over!

Chapter 31 - Bloemfontein Camp II

Bloemfontein Camp - April 1901 – Elise

The war may have been over for the Weinbergs, but not for Elise and her family. Still held in captivity, in pitiful circumstances, Elise watched the daily deterioration of her mother and brothers. She felt herself to be strong but knew this could not last. And then there was the cough that had started insidiously in March and was now becoming more serious as the days progressed.

One thing that encouraged the prisoners was the presence of Emily Hobhouse. She was always to be seen inspecting conditions, talking to prisoners, arguing with the authorities, and generally making herself the hero of the prisoners and the scourge of the authorities. Then, in January 1901, she published her famous report on the camps that was sent to the government in England.

Excerpt from "Report on the Bloemfontein Concentration Camp" - January 26th, 1901 - Emily Hobhouse

Author's note: This report was prepared by Emily Hobhouse to highlight to the British Government the mistreatment of prisoners in the Bloemfontein Camp. It is reproduced here to provide readers with insight into camp conditions, as seen by one of the most important philanthropists to champion the cause of the Boer women and children.

"The camp was situated in a plain, 2 miles from the town of Bloemfontein. It was occupied by about 2,000 people, including 900 children. The camp consisted of tents, together with three corrugated iron hospitals and live rows of corrugated iron huts in which about 100 families were accommodated. During the day, there was terrible heat and a plague of flies in the tents. In each tent, there lived on average six persons, in some cases, even up to 9 or 10, which meant that the tents were greatly overfilled. When it rained at night, the water streamed into the tents. There were only a few mattresses so that most people had to sleep on the ground. I demanded straw and hay from the military so that the camp's inhabitants could at least make their own mattresses. The hospitals had 16 beds each, together with three tents, and were always full. The daily food rations consisted of half a pound of meat, including bones and fat, two ounces of coffee, half a pound of coarse flour, 1 1/2 of a tin of condensed milk, and half an ounce of salt. Earlier, there had sometimes been potatoes, one per person. There was no soap. There were 50 cows in the camp, which for lack of fodder yielded only four buckets of milk, which were urgently needed for the many children in the camp. Up to my arrival, the drinking water taken from the river had not been boiled, so that many people were sick of typhoid. On this, I commented to the commandant: "We have much typhoid and are dreading an outbreak, so I am directing my energies to getting the water of the Modder River boiled. As well swallow typhoid germs whole as drink water - so say, doctors." Not everybody was able to cook, let alone to boil the water since there was not enough fuel for all. There were also no vessels in which to keep the water once boiled. I, therefore, proposed that at least one bucket or can should be distributed to each tent, and instructions be issued to boil all drinking water. I also proposed acquiring a railway train boiler to boil the water for everybody. As a result of my initiative, cooking stoves and water containers were provided. Because of the numerous cases of typhoid, an epidemic was feared. I previously wrote of Bloemfontein that they had already had 70 cases of typhoid, as well as a measles epidemic, pneumonia, and tonsillitis, together with other diseases. On this, the hospital was expanded in stages. There was only one nurse in the camp, who had worked there from its inception. As well as her normal duties, she had to train two Boer girls to help her in the future. I can report that: "The nurse, underfed and overworked, just sinking on to her bed, hardly able to hold herself up, after coping with some thirty typhoid and other patients, with only the untrained help of two Boer girls - cooking as well as nursing lo do herself." Not only the nurse was undernourished: the children in the camp were particularly affected. I wrote in my report that it was the children that were hardest hit by the cruelty of the camp system: I call this camp system a wholesale cruelty. It can never be wiped out of the memories of the people. It presses hardest on the children. They droop in the terrible heat, and with the insufficient, unsuitable food; whatever you do, whatever the authorities do, and they are, I believe, doing their best with very limited means, it is all only a miserable patch upon a great ill."

As a result of this report, changes started to be made in the camps. But these changes did not come in time for Elise.

Letter to Bertha Weinberg from Jane Smith-Behm - Bloemfontein Camp - May 1901

Bloemfontein Camp
May 11th, 1901

Dear Bertha

My name is Jane Smith, and I am a nurse at the hospital at the Bloemfontein Camp. One of my patients, Elise Schoeman, talked incessantly of you, how wonderful you and your family had been to her, and how much she loved you.

My dear Bertha, I'm afraid I have some bad news for you. Elise was brought into hospital last week with pneumonia, and while we did our best to cure her with the resources made available to us, we were unable to save her. She went to her Maker yesterday at three in the afternoon.

I went through her things and found the letters you had written to her. How beautifully you write, and how much you did to raise her spirits. It was from these letters that I found your address, and decided to write to you with the unhappy news.

Elise is now in a better place. I have been a nurse for many years now, and I have never felt as helpless and powerless as I have done here in Bloemfontein. There is no humanity here, no sanctity, no kindness. We have no medicines to give to the patients, and we must stand by helplessly watching them die when they are looking to us for help. My heart has been broken many times since my stay here, and I am sure Elise's death will not be the last time. It is all so sad how wretched the people are here. Not enough food, medicine, clothing, not enough shelter from the heat and the cold, not enough of everything. Oh, Bertha, I am so pleased you were not subjected to any of this. From your letters, you seem to be a kind and sympathetic person, and I'm sure your heart must be breaking as well when you think about how cruelly your friend was treated. Know that she loved you and had q very special place in her heart for you.

Please write back to me. I would so love to hear from you.

Your friend
Nurse Jane Smith-Behm

The letter was delivered to the hotel long after the family had left for Europe, so it was six months before Bertha eventually received it. The time did nothing to soften the blow. How could it? Some sorrows will never quite heal.

Chapter 32 - Release from Ragama

March 28th, 1901- Ragama Camp – Jeannot

The day was like any other - hot, humid, unpleasantly muggy. Prisoners went about their daily routines with little enthusiasm, sticky from the sweat that poured from every pore of their bodies. Only one man seemed oblivious of the torments of the climate, a man for whom the window of freedom was about to open.

The previous day, Jeannot had been summoned to the office of the Commandant, Captain Ingram. He was ushered into a small room with a table and four chairs and told to wait. After a half-hour, the Commandant entered the room. Jeannot stood.

"Sit, young man." said the Commandant, taking a seat at the table. "Well, Weinberg, how long have you been with us here at Ragama?"
"Since January this year, sir."
"So less than three months?"
"Yes, sir."
"Not like Diyatalawa, no?"
"No, sir. But not too bad."
"Young man, I have some interesting news for you. Yesterday I received a cable from British Army headquarters in London - from the Department of Personnel to be exact. It seems you have friends in high places, Weinberg."

Jeannot looked bemused - he was unaware of any such connections.

"Well, someone interceded on your behalf with the authorities in London, claiming you have been falsely accused of treason since you had taken the Oath of Allegiance."

Jeannot nodded. "And it seems that, on reflection, the powers that be agreed. So, my instructions are to release you immediately to the civilian authorities in Colombo, pending the arrival of funds with which to buy passage home."

Jeannot could not believe what he was hearing. Who had interceded on his behalf? How had they got to hear of his story? What was he to do now?

"It appears," continued the Commandant, "that your family has moved to London and that you are to join them there. A wire will be arriving for you from your Father explaining what steps to take, and where to meet them."

Jeannot looked incredulous. Had his father managed to do what he had promised and secure his release? His head was in a whirl.
"The wire is being sent to Government House in Colombo. You are to pack up your things tonight and report there tomorrow. Are you all right? You look a bit pale."
"I am fine, sir. Just a bit shocked. This has all happened so quickly. I don't know what to think."
"I am sure it is both a shock and a relief. You have been incarcerated for a long time, and you will need to take time to assimilate in a non-prison environment. Keep your wits about you and behave like the gentleman that you are, and all will be well. Now off with you and get prepared for tomorrow."

Jeannot walked slowly back to his hut, the conversation turning over in his mind. He had not yet grasped the fact that he was a free man, that he had come through the war physically unharmed, and was now about to retake his place in society. This was all too much for him to process - he went and sat quietly under a tree, and let his thoughts wash over him. He awoke about an hour later and wanted to pinch himself to make sure what he had heard this afternoon was true. No doubt it was since it had been told to him by the senior officer in the camp. So, he went to his hut to break the news to his fellow prisoners. Not all the prisoners were overjoyed at the news. It is hard on a man when a colleague receives something you know you cannot share, and many of the men were unhappy that 'strings had been pulled.' But in general, there was an atmosphere of happiness for Jeannot. He had been a popular figure in the camps, and most of the men wished him well. The next morning, he stood ready with his few possessions, waiting for a vehicle to drive him to town. He had been provided with new clothes and a little cash to see him on his way. As he stood and waited for the transport, he reflected on his time in Ceylon. Life had been reasonably good to him, although he had grown thin, and he had begun to suffer from pains in the joints of his legs that made walking difficult. Still, he thought, at least I still have my legs unlike some of those poor fellows on both sides crippled by their wounds. The rest of his body was quite healthy, and he was grateful that his diet would change to one restoring some of the meat on his bones that had been lost as a result of camp food. But it was the mental anguish that would be a more lasting legacy, both of the war and the camps.

Within a few days, I shall take leave of Ceylon. My exile, with all its tortures and sorrowful memories, will belong in the past, and I shall return to my country. Whatever may happen, it will remain mine - the just inheritance from my father - and the fact that today we have lost the right to govern ourselves does not make the blood-soaked fields of the country I call home one iota less dear to me. I knew what true faith was in the hours of danger.

Chapter 33 - Jeannot Reflects

The journey from Colombo to London was not without difficulty. Jeannot took ship from Colombo to Alexandria, then a further ship from Alexandria to Southampton. The leg from Colombo to Alexandria was without incident, but the second leg proved a disaster. The ship was blown off course by a storm in the Mediterranean, and it limped into Civitavecchia, the port of Rome, with no possibility of continuing the voyage. This left Jeannot in the position of being stranded in Rome without any means of getting to London, and without too much in the way of money. Not enough, he soon discovered, to buy passage from Italy to England. He telegraphed Edward, but the family was traveling, and the message was not received.

Jeannot, despite his age, had been in difficult situations before. He didn't panic, preferring to trust his instinct and resolve. But, as it turned out, neither was required - it was fate that came to his rescue. He was on his way to the British Embassy in Rome to explain his predicament when he overheard two men on the street ahead of him speaking a language he recognized - Dutch! He immediately approached the men, and discovered to his delight that they were part of a South African delegation to Italy! When he had related his story to them, they took him under their aegis, made sure he was housed and fed, and organized passage for him to England by a combination of a train ride to Paris, followed by a ferry from France to England. They also arranged for notice of his journey to be sent to Edward, so that the family could meet Jeannot when the ferry docked in Dover.

The protracted nature of the journey provided Jeannot with an opportunity to reflect on the events of the past two decades, and the part he had played in these events.

His past

There could have been few young men of his age that had experienced so much in such a short space of time. He had lived in five countries (Latvia, Russia, Belgium, South Africa, and Ceylon), in nine cities and towns (Riga, Moscow, Brussels, Port Elizabeth, Phillipolis, Bloemfontein, Johannesburg, Cape Town, and Diyatalawa/Ragama), spoke five languages (English, Afrikaans, German, Russian and French), fought in two wars (the Swaziland Rebellion and the Second Anglo-Boer War) and spent time in three prisoner of war camps (Greenpoint Track, Diyatalawa, and Ragama). And all before the age of 21! On reflection, he concluded that his existence had been too frenetic and unsettled, and he longed for a time of peace and stability when he could live a normal, settled life, acquire a profession and enjoy the bounties of his family and land. Although he had spent several periods of unencumbered time in the POW camps, these were wasted times, good for philosophical reflection, but not helpful in preparing him for the life to come. True, he made some great friends, bonds that would last for a long time, but the camps were transitory; the war would end and so would they. Now was the time to consolidate his life and look forward.

His family

Jeannot knew he had been blessed with a family of great love and courage. Never afraid to face the unexpected, never afraid to admit defeat, and move on to something new, never constrained by the events going on around it, always tightly knit and supportive of every member. Jeannot understood that his father was a dreamer, a person who was prepared to experiment with the unknown and find a new dimension within which to operate, always harboring the belief that everything he did was for the benefit of his family. He provided his children with an example in life that stressed the taking of calculated risks while emphasizing the attributes of honor, justice, and charity. Fanni was the bedrock of the family. It was based on her sense and sensibility that the family grew into a close-knit unit, always supportive and loyal, and it was her calmness that provided a sounding board for Edward when the dreamer was at his most creative. She was the quintessential Jewish mother, deeply concerned about hearth and home, but always ready to take on the challenges life threw at her.

His siblings were Jeannot's treasures. He was intensely proud of Bernard and Max for selflessly following him to war, even though he felt that neither of them should really have gone - they were too young and inexperienced. But they acquitted themselves well, and he applauded this. The younger boys had been a source of continuous pleasure and entertainment. They were an irrepressible group, always up to something, always full of mischief, always stretching the envelope. But it was Bertha who held a special place in his heart. As the only girl, she was continually put upon by the boys, who found great sport in teasing and ribbing her. But she was a young lady with a big heart and a kind and selfless disposition, and Jeannot had long seen it as his role to be her protector and champion. He was devastated by her experience with Elise, wished that he could have been there to comfort her in her time of trial, and deeply moved by the love and loyalty she had shown to a poor and mistreated friend.

He knew how much he had owed in the past to his family. He resolved to ensure that he fulfilled the promise he had made to Edward on the ship to South Africa - ever to be mindful of the importance of family, and to ensure its continued existence and prosperity.

The country

It was clear to him that South Africa would be the place in which he would live his life. He had enjoyed the times he had spent in the various other countries, but none other had struck the chord in him that South Africa had. Here was a land of vast landscapes and big sky, of multifaceted population groups, opportunity and adventure, and, above all, of heart and strength. He knew and understood the difficulties that lay ahead, not just between the various white groups and their black counterparts. Still, the divisions that existed within each, that threatened disunity in the land. But it was a challenge he accepted and accepted with pride and pleasure. How good it would be to make a contribution to the future of this land, to make an impact on its development, and be a part of its growth to respect among the nations.

The war

He reflected on time spent on the battlefield. He thought of the times of fear, the times of exhilaration, the times of despair and despondency. No man can predict how another will behave in times of extreme crisis, who will stand firm, who will cut and run. When all is considered, you count only on yourself; any help from your colleagues is a bonus you would like to count on, but with them, there are no guarantees. The fortunate soldier will have steadfast colleagues and good leaders, providing the best chance of staying alive. Jeannot was grateful that he had both, and that together they had acquitted themselves with honor and courage.
Julius Caesar says of war, "It is easier to find men who will volunteer to die than to find those who are willing to endure pain with patience." But should a young man be made to make such a decision? Can one of tender years be expected to weigh the import of his own mortality against that of the common weal? It is said that it is the old who lead us to war, only for the young to die. But did we, he thought, ever think about danger and dying? Even in the heat of battle, with lead in the air about us? No, he reflected. It was the anticipation that was the hardest part, the fear, not of the enemy, but the unknown. Will I live to see another sunrise? Will I see my family again? Will I become a cripple? These were the

hardest times, the times when the deepest recesses of the soul were dredged for residual courage. Battle was easy. There was no time to think or be afraid. But the waiting, the waiting.......

His colleagues

But it was his colleagues he would remember the most. The manne. The lads. The boys. The group of such diverse individuals from whom such a close-knit team was created. The endless nights around the campfire, drinking coffee and talking of the days before the war. And what they would do when the war was over. The times of hardship, always easier to recall than those of joy. The funny times always made funnier by time. The sad times, always lessened by time. The bond of men thrown together in trying circumstances, developing a strength of association, a circle of support, and courage. How well he remembered them - Britz, who had shouted "Hands up" to the Redcheeks; Havenga, who had taken water to the wounded; Veldkornet Raaff, who had always made sure that his boys were well looked after; David Le Roux, who overcame his disappointment in the Cape Afrikaners and became a true friend in the camp; Reitz, the idiot who innocently betrayed their escape from Greenpoint Track; Martinus Potgieter, the greybeard who gave us true perspective about the war. And so many others, almost too many to remember, but men who would live on in his heart would never be forgotten. Men like him—just ordinary men.

The last word

And so we leave Jeannot with his thoughts as he travels across Europe to reunite with his family. Few men have, as he did, so completely "filled the unforgiving minute with sixty seconds worth of distance run." And, in this way, and in this time, "Your grandfather became a man, my son."

Appendix

Author's Reflections

Jeannot, my grandfather, died in 1961 when I was nine years old. Although I remember him vividly, I was too young to discuss the reasons behind his participation in the Boer War. So, I can only conjecture on what his views would have been of South Africa as a republic under the control of the National Party. For it was under this regime that apartheid was formalized into the repressive regime that occurred under Afrikaner hegemony. Jeannot was a follower of Jan Smuts, who had led South Africa in a situation of de facto apartheid, rather than the de jure system introduced mainly after the NP took power in 1948. To attempt an understanding of his views, we must examine the causes of the Anglo-Boer War, and the different approaches of the two sides in the conflict.

In their excellent paper, published by the Center for Research on Inequality, Human Security, and Ethnicity (CHRISE), Graham K. Brown and Frances Stewart postulate the following reasons why wars occur.

1. "Wars by proxy." During the Cold War, the East and the West supported the different sides in some locally fought conflicts with funds, arms, and "advisers" in order to capture a particular country for their own side. Examples are the wars in Central America, Vietnam, Mozambique, and Afghanistan. Some of these wars ended with the Cold War, but others gained a life of their own (e.g., Afghanistan). New forms of proxy conflicts are associated with the war against terrorism, such as the current US military-supported counterinsurgency operations in the secessionist Muslim south of the Philippines and support for the suppression of the Taliban in Pakistan.

2. Military "interventions" in domestic conflict by outside powers, generally motivated by political or economic objectives of the

intervening country. Since the end of the Cold War, particularly, this type of conflict has predominantly been associated with the West. Examples are Kosovo, the 2001 invasion of Afghanistan, and the wars in Iraq. But other examples do not involve the West, such as Vietnam's invasion of Cambodia.

3. Revolutionary or ideological wars that aim to overturn the established order. Examples are the wars waged by the Khmer Rouge in Cambodia, the Colombian conflict (especially in its early stages), the Shining Path in Peru, and the Maoists in Nepal. Rebellions aimed at installing democracy in repressive regimes (as in Syria) or at imposing a particular ideology (e.g., to institute sharia law, as in Mali) are also examples.

4. Wars fought for regional independence or autonomy, such as the wars in Eritrea (Ethiopia), Biafra (Nigeria), Sri Lanka (the Tamils), Chechnya (Russia), southern Sudan, Kosovo, Spain (the Basques), and the southern Philippines (Muslim separatists).

5. Wars fought to gain (or retain) political supremacy by particular groups representing specific cultures (ethnicities or religion). These include the conflicts in Rwanda, Burundi, Northern Ireland, and Uganda. Such wars may be fought primarily by individual groups or by coalitions of groups, as occurred, for example, in the conflicts in the Democratic Republic of the Congo (DRC) and Sierra Leone.

The first and third examples do not have any real application in the case of the Boer War, but the second, fourth, and fifth certainly do. Britain's participation in the Boer War was primarily an example of the second cause, motivated by political or economic objectives. The economic objectives are very clear - Britain was desirous of ensuring that the goldfields of the Transvaal should become a part of the British Empire, to reserve the economic benefits for the Empire. Politically, the desire to expand the influence of British rule to all parts of the globe, as envisioned by men like Rhodes and Milner, was the second underlying reason behind Britain's participation. As far as the Boers were concerned, examples four and five are relevant, but both were not necessarily espoused by all who participated. In the case of the true Boers who were the children of the Great Trek, both four and five applied equally. Autonomy from Britain, and the desire not to be ruled by a foreign power, were high on the agenda, as was the desire to preserve their specific culture - the concept of the sanctity of the 'Volk.' These men did not want the traditional values that had hallmarked the rise of the Afrikaner people to be diluted by foreign powers. These values included the unquestioned supremacy of the white man and the separation of the races into distinguishable pockets of race and ethnicity.

Then there was the group who espoused the fifth example, but not necessarily the fourth, and this is where I perceive Jeannot's intention can be deduced. As an immigrant into South Africa who adopted the Orange Free State as his new home country, Jeannot would have fought to protect the territorial integrity of his new homeland, and would not have wanted it to fall into the hands of another country. I would submit that many would have fought to preserve territorial integrity, without the accompanying protection of culture and way of life. So my theory is that he would not have fought to secure white supremacy and the subjugation of non-white South Africans, but rather to protect the borders of his adopted country. I cannot believe that he would ever have supported the subsequent policies of the National Party that sought to make South Africa the nation of the Afrikaner. I believe that his views would have been more 'African' than Afrikaner; in other words, Africa for the Africans, irrespective of race, creed, culture, or origin. I have long wrestled with the fact that I, as a political liberal, could have an ancestor who fought for what would eventually become a repressive regime in which the Afrikaner sought to mold a society in compliance with a policy of white supremacy. It is for this reason that I can continue to be proud of Jeannot for what he did - protect his country of adoption from an invading force, rather than to preserve an ideology that I believe he would have found to be pernicious. In many ways, his attitude would have been similar to the non-Nazis who fought for the protection of Germany, but not for the Nazi ideology that underpinned it.

I cannot be sure of this, but my knowledge of him as a man leads me to believe that he was a patriot but not a nationalist. As such, he would have been motivated by a desire to protect his homeland, rather than the ideology that would use that protection to perpetuate a way of life that I am sure he would have found abhorrent. For this reason, I am proud to have been able to record his exploits, secure in the belief that his participation in the war was a matter of territorial preservation rather than cultural protection.

The Boer War and The Hague Convention of 1899

The activities that relate to combatants and non-combatants during the Anglo-Boer War must be examined in the light of The Hague Convention of 1899. The preamble to this convention is worth noting.

"Considering that, while seeking means to preserve peace and prevent armed conflicts among nations, it is likewise necessary to have regard to cases where an appeal to arms may be caused by events which their solicitude could not avert;
Animated by the desire to serve, even in this extreme hypothesis, the interests of humanity and the ever-increasing requirements of civilization;
Thinking it important, with this object, to revise the laws and general customs of war, either with the view of defining them more precisely or of laying down certain limits for the purpose of modifying their severity as far as possible; "

The Hague Convention, officially **"Regulations concerning the Laws and Customs of War on Land. The Hague, 29 July 1899"** was attended by Great Britain, but not by the two Boer Republics. The Boer Republics were not invited to attend, and the British Government made it clear that it would not attend the Convention if the republics were there. Nevertheless, although the Boer Republics were not signatories, some believed that, since non-signatories could accept the terms of the Convention by simply informing the Netherlands Government, this was a minor omission. So both the British and the Boers should, in the view of most commentators, have considered themselves bound by the terms and spirit of the Convention.

The following are pertinent extracts from the Convention as they relate to the events of the Boer War. It is fair to say that, in most cases, the British adhered to the convention in matters of combatants and prisoners of war. Still, their conduct in respect of the civilian population shows a flagrant disregard for the provisions of the convention.

"SECTION M.---ON MILITARY AUTHORITY OVER HOSTILE TERRITORY

ARTICLE 43 The authority of the legitimate power having actually passed into the hands of the occupant, the latter shall take all steps in his power to re-establish and insure, as far as possible, public order and safety, while respecting, unless absolutely prevented, the laws in force in the country. *[The concentration camps could hardly be said to have 'insured.... public order and safety.]*

ARTICLE 45 Any pressure on the population of occupied territory to take the oath to the hostile Power is prohibited. [*The Oath of Allegiance described in the book is a clear disregard of this article.]*

ARTICLE 46 Family honors and rights, individual lives, and private property, as well as religious convictions and liberty, must be respected. Private property cannot be confiscated. [*Both the scorched earth policy and the concentration camps were clear contraventions of this article.]*

ARTICLE 47 Pillage is formally prohibited. [*Likewise, the pillage that took place during the scorched earth policy was a contravention of the convention.]*

ARTICLE 50 No general penalty, pecuniary or otherwise, can be inflicted on the population on account of the acts of individuals for which it cannot be regarded as collectively responsible. [*This is perhaps the most damning article in its contravention. It is clear that the scorched earth policy and the concentration camps were retribution for the 'acts of individuals,' in this case, the Boer guerillas. Holding the women and children 'collectively responsible' for the acts of the guerillas was clearly forbidden by the convention.]"*

It should be clear to even the most parochial reader that Roberts and Kitchener acted in direct contravention of the Hague Convention in the sections detailed above. In modern times, these would be considered war crimes, and those responsible would be tried by an international tribunal in the way that Radovan Karadžić was tried for crimes during the Balkan Wars in the 1990s. Suffice it to say that neither Roberts nor Kitchener was ever held to account for the atrocities they instigated and carried out during the Boer War. Instead, history, at least British history, has deified them for their strategic abilities in bringing the Boer War to a conclusion satisfactory to the British Empire.

History, as we know, is written by the victors, while the tales of the losers tend to be relegated to the apocrypha of mainstream reporting.

References

- Pakenham, Thomas (1979) *The Boer War*: Avon Books
- Van Heyningen, Elizabeth (2013) *Concentration Camps of the Boer War*: Creda Communications
- Reitz, Deneys (1929) *Commando - A Boer Journal of the Boer War*: CruGuru
- Rosenthal, Eric (1970) *Gold, Gold, Gold*: The MacMillan Company
- Le Roux, Etienne (1983) *Magersfontein O Magersfontein*: Hutchinson
- Rompel, Frederick (1903) *Heroes of the Boer War:* The Nederland Publishing Company
- Sternberg, Count (1901) *My Experiences of the Boer War:* Longmans, Green and Company
- Hillegas, Howard (1900) *The Boers in War:* D. Appleton & Company
- Gale & Polden (1910) *A Handbook of the Boer War:* Butler and Tanner
- Conan Doyle, Arthur (1900) *The Great Boer War*: Smith, Elder & Co
- Brink J. N. (1904) *Recollections of a Boer Prisoner of War in Ceylon:* Jac. Dusseau & Co.
- MacKenzie, John: *Britishbattles.com*
- Theheritageportal.co.za
- Angloboerwar.com
- Samilitaryhistory.org
- Wikipedia.com
- The Anglo-Boer War Museum, Bloemfontein

Made in the USA
Monee, IL
16 February 2022